The Red Hand

By

Michael Stephen Daigle

Copyright © 2019 by Michael Stephen Daigle
ISBN: 978-1-944653-19-4
Publisher: Imzadi Publishing LLC
www.imzadipublishing.com

Cover Art designed for Imzadi Publishing by Anita Dugan-Moore of Cyber-Bytz, www.cyber-bytz.com.

If you would like permission to use material from this book for any reason other than for review purposes, please contact the publisher at: imzadipublishing@outlook.com.

ACKNOWLEDGMENTS

For Terry, Max, Emily, Elana, and Aedan.

A special thanks to dear friend Virginia Justard, without whom Frank Nagler would not exist.

A special thanks to the team at Imzadi Publishing, whose small size does not represent the work and support they offer: Janice Grove, Anita Dugan-Moore and Kathleen Tate.

Special thanks also to dear friends and fellow writers, Diane Havens, Devorah Fox and Alice Marks, whose work and support are inspiring.

Thanks also to the gang at the Phillipsburg, N.J. Library Writer's Group, whose comments have been deeply valuable.

Last, a thanks to the readers of the Frank Nagler series. Your encouragement and support make this work possible and rewarding.

AUTHOR'S NOTE

The Red Hand takes place about twenty years before *"The Swamps of Jersey"*, the first *Frank Nagler Mystery*.

Readers had asked about Nagler's backstory, about his wife Martha, and the troublesome Charlie Adams, who is a presence in the series.

This story attempts to answer those reader concerns, an expression I hope, of their support in Frank Nagler and Ironton, N.J.

TABLE OF CONTENTS

PART ONE

The long dry season

Of course they were red, the handprints. The color of blood, red; the color of life, dripping between the hollow cracks of the siding. Leaking, crimson, chosen carefully. I'm here, the killer said, bragging. Try to find me.

— Jimmy Dawson —

CHAPTER ONE

Someone is experimenting in death

The first mark had appeared after the third death: A red handprint dripping paint slapped on a wall of the busted-up hotel where cab driver Felice Sanchez had been found dead. Underneath, "HAND OF DEATH" splotched in an awkward scrawl.

Is that a joke? Detective Frank Nagler thought when he saw the mark for the first time. Pretty crude, but you might be in a hurry to leave your calling card after you killed a woman. But he wondered: Where were the marks left after the deaths of Nancy Harmon and Jamie Wilson, the deaths that were now believed to be the first in this cycle?

Police Chief Robert Mallory had ordered the markings scrubbed from the wall, after the police work had been completed: Photos, samples, measurements, interviews; the victim's family, don't you know. Then he changed his mind: Who would know to place that mark at that exact spot? That made it a statement, a claim of ownership. Instead, the chief ordered the buildings with the marks to be included in daily foot patrols. "They'll fade in time," he had said. "The public will stop paying attention." Was that a taunt, a challenge to the killer? Nagler wondered, the chief in fact saying, "We know you've been here. We will get you."

Of course, the public did not forget, but turned two of the marks — at the hotel and the old train station — into instant shrines with bundles of flowers, photos of missing friends and family, and hand-made posters.

For Nagler, staring at the red mark on the hotel had been the door that had cracked open, exposing a dark and sinister place, but the call that a body had been found near the downtown train station was the moment that his new job became real.

He'd been a detective for a month following another round of police department layoffs. He had investigated a burglary or two, probed a potential arson that destroyed an empty house, broken up a few husband-wife fights, but he felt he was running just to keep up, slogging through the everyday stuff of what he didn't know, what he couldn't imagine, one hand outstretched to feel the fog.

3

And now, ready or not, he was learning the awful lessons of murder firsthand.

"Where is she?" he asked a patrolman standing sentry at the dark edge of the train station.

"Half-way down," the patrolman replied, his voice a drip in a tin can echo. He tipped his head to the left. "It's bad, Detective. Just sayin'."

"Thanks," Nagler replied, trying to sound confident. How bad?

Dispatch had said she was carried or dragged to the train station.

Nagler winced.

And then, if there wasn't enough for Nagler to absorb, Medical Examiner Walter Mulligan forcefully said this: "Someone is experimenting in death," while leaning over the body of the latest victim.

That's when Nagler felt the ground shift and a tiny hollow spot opened in his heart. We're supposed to be dispassionate, professional, he reminded himself. Try as he might, that hole never closed.

He ran a shaky hand through his sweat-soaked hair and squinted into a golden haze of a rooftop spotlight across the railroad tracks from where the body was found, and then nodded to Mulligan, trying to appear that he knew what that meant. My first murder case, and it's an experiment in death. Oh, man.

It wasn't the statement alone that startled Nagler. It was the chilling tone, an end-of-the-world whisper, a voice inside a dark cave. And the certainty. How does he know that?

Three women, murdered, apparently weeks, possibly months, apart, killed in different ways, in different parts of the city; different jobs, lives disconnected from each other.

And now a fourth.

THE IRONTON RIPPER, an out-of-town newspaper headline had screamed when the third death had been announced.

Nagler absorbed the scene: Dim lights from the train station platform, silhouetted cops, shadows shifting, lighted then gone; faint grinding of late night city noise, bugs buzzing, heat as thick as syrup.

And she lay dead, slashed, exposed, dragged, discarded.

Crap, Nagler thought, shaking off the pity, seeking resolve. Where is this going?

Any doubt Nagler had about what was ahead dissolved when he looked into Mulligan's face. He was wearing that face, the one experienced officers had warned about, a mix of resignation about the need for his services and a dark anger, a stay-out-of-my-way face.

"This death is related to the others," Mulligan pronounced after he pulled Nagler aside. "Examine her body closely."

"So that's the experiment?" Nagler asked, nodding at the detail that according to the reports he had read, had been present previously. "That makes him a serial killer?" he asked, barely aware of what that term meant.

"A technical term for academics," Mulligan said, as he shook his head in disgust, and then smiled, trying to encourage the new detective. "We have four deaths, Frank. Just follow the evidence. Don't worry about the meaning yet." He reached for Nagler's arm. "But this is a detail you should keep to yourself. Knowing it, and the time to release it, could be critical to catching our killer."

Nagler nodded and turned to speak with the first patrolman on the scene.

"Who found her?" Nagler asked.

The patrolman pointed to a man clinging to the side of a patrol car. "Our drunken friend."

Oh, great. Nagler approached the drunk. The man shifted, then leaned, then tipped back, arms folded, head nodding.

"Hey, thanks for calling us," Nagler said.

The man squeezed his face into a grimace and through squinting eyes, looked up at Nagler. "I didn't call. Just yelled. Your guy was driving past the train station and stopped. Hurray for me." He tipped his head to the right and closed his eyes. "I'm tired, man."

"Okay, where were you headed?" Nagler asked, admiring the man's existential gallantry.

"An old shed, down in the rail yard. Got a…got a sleeping bag there."

Nagler smiled. "Bet you do. Know what? We'll put you up for the night."

"Naa, that's okay. Someone will steal my bag, and my, um, stuff, if I don't… Maybe I can get a drink?" He leaned forward and nearly toppled.

"Ahh, no." Nagler pushed him upright.

The man wiped his nose on his filthy jacket sleeve and shook his head again. "Too bad."

"Yeah." Softly. "Yeah." Firmly: "Look at me."

"What?

"Look at me. Got a couple questions. Did you touch her?"

"Who? Nooooo. Never. She's dead, man. She was bleedin' and all. No. Shit, I didn't touch her." Shrugged. "Okay, kicked her shoe to see if she was, maybe… naw… dead." He jabbed out his right foot and nearly fell.

Nagler shook his head. "Maybe…if she had some money on her?"

The man shrugged then wiped his nose. "Maybe."

"Did you see anyone with her?"

The man closed his face as if the question was too hard.

He was fading, Nagler knew. Last chance. "Hey, buddy. Was anybody with her?"

The drunk grabbed a handful of his hair and yanked on it. Irritated. "I'm thinkin'." He glanced up at Nagler and then off to the left.

"A guy. Ran off that way." He waved in all directions. "'Hey,' I yelled. 'You left your friend.' Then I looked at her and she was pretty dead."

"Big guy? Fat? Short? Skinny?"

"Shit, man, I don't know. Little dude. Seemed so…" Voice fading. "Little dude…I…guess. But he was far away."

****

Nagler hunched along the dark street and parking lot following the blood trail back to the Chinese restaurant on Warren, apparently the original crime scene. A crime tech photographed the blood drops, exploding light into the darkness. "Lotta blood," the tech said. "Man."

Why carry her to the train yard?

At the restaurant, a shapeless pool of blood filled the sidewalk a few feet from the door to the China Song restaurant, and a smeared trail of blood leaked off toward Blackwell and the train station for a few yards and then stopped at a point the assailant must have picked her up. A blotch of blood was centered on the side window of the corner phone booth, as if the assailant had staggered for a moment under Chen's weight.

Pretty strong for a little guy, if our drunk friend was right, Nagler thought. But the victim was a small woman, so I guess anything is possible. It reminded Nagler of one of those nature specials where a

6

lion kills a zebra and carries it off to be devoured later. A hunt, a kill. A trophy. Of course. That's what Mulligan meant.

The restaurant lights were still on and Nagler saw the face of a man peeking around a red pillar inside the second, inner door. A grocery bag of packaged food had been spilled on the sidewalk, and a purse leaned against the curb.

A bloody spot dotted the brick wall. A second medical officer took samples.

"Related?" Nagler asked.

"Seems so, from what the dishwasher told us," Patrol Sergeant Bob Hanrahan said. He had run from the City Hall police station a half-block away and secured the scene. "She apparently stepped out of the restaurant, carrying that shopping bag. The attacker rammed her into the wall. She was probably stunned by the blow to her head, staggered and then was stabbed."

Hanrahan nodded to Nagler. "It's your scene now."

Nagler examined the oversized purse and found a locked blue canvas overnight deposit bag containing what felt like two or three inches of bills. "Probably not a robbery." He found a wallet with a driver's license.

Joan Chen, thirty-one. Weston Street, Ironton.

Nagler felt his head spin, exploding with details almost faster than he could examine them.

"You alright, Frank?" Hanrahan asked.

"It's like I just took the plastic wrapper off my 'Crime 101' manual and the killer is on to volume two." He screwed up his face and glanced at Hanrahan and then at the ground. "I want to do this right."

Hanrahan grabbed Nagler's shoulder. "Slow it all down. We know some stuff. It'll come."

Nagler nodded.

Hanrahan said, as he shrugged toward the restaurant door, "That guy's the dishwasher, said he stays after closing to clean the place for the next day. She's the manager and was going to the bank to make a deposit. He was locking the doors when someone came out of the street, slammed her into the wall, and stabbed her. He said he ran back into the main part of the restaurant to grab the pistol they keep behind the bar, and when he came back, she was gone, as was the assailant. He said the attacker had his head covered, wore dark clothes, but the attack was fast."

"Did he say anything about the attacker's size?" Nagler asked. "Our witness at the train station, as drunk as he is, said it could be a small person."

Hanrahan shook his head. "He said it happened really fast."

"Any other witnesses?" Nagler asked. "Customers?"

"No. Place closed at nine-thirty, two hours ago. Dishwasher said Chen's habit was to eat a light supper, close out the daily receipts and hit the bank on her way home."

"Weston's on the other side of town. She must have a car parked somewhere," Nagler said as he scanned the street. "Bet she left at about the same time each night. Someone who knows that pattern..." He sighed. "This could be the first one of these that makes sense. She married?"

****

These, Nagler thought bitterly. How much more impersonal can I make murder?

He sat in the far table at Barry's diner the next morning and watched the morning crowd lean into their coffee and eggs, the hum of chatter swirling with the dense, sticky air. He had read the files on the other three deaths after his wife Martha had fallen asleep. He had brushed a stray hair from her cheek as she slept, and then shook away the worry.

He sipped his coffee. These deaths. Four dead women. Strangers? We're supposed to look for connections, patterns.

One is random, or an accident.

Two makes you wonder.

Three becomes heavy.

Four brings fear.

He mulled the details: Jamie Wilson, thirty-two, a secretary; Nancy Harmon, thirty-seven, a doctor; Felice Sanchez, thirty-five, a cab driver; and now Joan Chen, thirty-one, a restaurant manager.

The records showed all the women seemed to be approximately the same height—five-foot-four or five. Harmon and Wilson had been reduced to skeletons when they had been discovered, subject to predation and the unseasonable heat. Both Sanchez and Chen weighed between one-hundred-ten and one-hundred-twenty pounds. So, small, he thought. Smallish. He closed his eyes, trying to capture an image that might offer some comparison. No. He smiled. He had conjured the image of his wife Martha lying naked on their bed. Martha was five-six, and he never asked her weight.

He mulled that detail. Smallish. Could be overpowered with enough force and surprise by an equally small person.

How?

We have no clue about why.

Jamie Wilson had been found in the Old Iron Bog, and Nancy Harmon in an empty warehouse near her medical office. Felice Sanchez was found in the abandoned Wilson Hotel on North Sussex.

All three had been killed days or weeks before their bodies had been discovered.

And now Joyce Chen, attacked in the open at her restaurant, on a public street, and with a witness, then dragged to the train yard and discovered on the same night. That one was brazen. Why now, and why change the pattern? Getting bolder? Or a different killer?

Nancy Harmon had been declared missing after a colleague and several patients who found the office locked at the time of their appointment called the department, the report said. At first, her death had been considered a suicide.

Jamie Wilson's family had called after she missed a weekend family reunion. The cab company called the department after they found Felice Sanchez's cab on a back alley off Richman Avenue with the keys in the ignition.

To the public they were all random, isolated deaths.

And that's what they had remained. Nagler stopped reading and wondered how much the changes in the department had affected the investigation. Names on the reports were those of officers who had retired when the department downsized; each previous case had been assigned to a different officer.

He circled the officers' names on the various reports. He'd have to chase them down.

What tied them all together was the detail of their deaths the department would not reveal, something that was collectively decided only the killer would know. When do we use that? Nagler wondered.

They had discovered Joan Chen's white, late model Dodge in the ramshackle central parking lot along the river, the site of the old iron mill that had dominated the city for a hundred and fifty years. When it was torn down, the site became a shopping center with a drive-in movie theater, and when that was torn down it became a parking lot, trash trapped in a bent chain-link fence, potholes and crushed concrete steps, a symbol of Ironton's economic demise.

The parking lot was across Warren Street from the restaurant, so it made sense her car was there, probably in the same spot she used every working day. Her car had not been touched, nor had her home, half of a duplex in a neighborhood that was a buffer between the old workers ghetto where Nagler grew up and the nicer neighborhood where Nagler and his wife Martha now lived. Chen lived alone, her neighbors said.

Nagler stirred the cold coffee and stared at the newspaper headline. "DEATH TOLL MOUNTS!!"

"Ironton police are at a loss to explain the recent deaths of four city women. The latest victim, Joan Chen, was found in the Ironton train station after she had been brutally attacked at her place of employment, the China Song restaurant, less than a block from the police station. Police had no comment on how Chen was taken to the station, or why.

Marion Demint, the owner of the Ironton Laundry around the corner from the murder scene, said she was scared.

"Why can't the police find this person? I don't feel safe."

"And the red handprints!" said commuter Ron Allen. "What's with the red handprints? It's a gang sign, I'll bet. City's going to hell."

Nagler dropped the paper on the table and nodded to Barry for a refill.

Hysteria much? he thought.

Who wrote the story?

Jimmy Dawson. Wasn't he in sports? What's he doing writing crime stories?

"Tough stuff, hey, Frankie?" Barry asked.

Barry's was the survivor in downtown Ironton, an eatery that had weathered all the ups and downs. It hadn't always been called Barry's, but no one, not even the current owner, whose name was Barry, knew when it got that name or who named it.

"Yeah, it is," Nagler replied. "I wish we knew more."

Barry leaned over. "Me, too. I see customers with guns under their jackets, talking about where they can buy more guns. I don't like it. Something's gonna happen."

He turned then stopped.

"Hey, Frank. If I find a red handprint on my front window does that means I'm next?"

Nagler smiled and shook his head.

"No, Barry, no one is coming after you for Tony's lunch special."

"Hey, Frank," Tony the cook yelled back. "I heard that."

But Nagler asked himself: What came first, the deaths or the handprints? Where they a warning or a sign of some declaration of victory?

CHAPTER TWO

What do I know?

Mulligan had determined that Joan Chen died from a severe loss of blood after being slashed with a thin-bladed knife. The assailant had, as the dishwasher described, rammed her into the wall, cracking her skull, and then slashed her left to right across the neck and chest, then again right to left across her chest, the cuts forming an "X." It appeared that she fell at the spot of the attack and was dragged along the sidewalk for ten to twelve feet before her killer picked her up and carried her to the train station and then dumped her.

Was that slashing pattern a symbol, or just the result of the killer swinging away, trying to inflict damage? Somewhere there's gotta be a bundle of bloody clothes, Nagler thought, but a search of the immediate six-block area had not produced it.

The death seemed pretty personal, Nagler thought.

Who comes charging out of a dark street and stabs another person to death unless you know something about the victim. Can't be that random, can it?

But what do I know?

Steps, he thought. All the advice from the experienced officers rattled through his head.

None of it made sense.

It did not appear that any of the women knew one another. It seemed possible that the others had eaten a meal at the China Song, a popular downtown spot, but none had used Felice Sanchez's cab, and Dr. Nancy Harmon had not treated any of the other women as a patient. Jamie Wilson, the first victim, was a secretary to a bank executive. She had no contact with customers and made no bank deposits.

Had she been at her desk when Joan Chen was killed Jamie Wilson would have had a perfect view of the crime from her second story office window.

These are the things we're supposed to look for, Nagler thought as he gazed over the moonlit, glistening green-gray sheen of the Old Iron Bog.

Connections, similarities, patterns. Big dotted lines on a graph that start at the corners and somehow slide to the middle of the page, crossing all the other lines until there is one central dot where they all cross, and we stand smiling at the dot, applauding our ingenuity because that is where the pieces of all these lives intersect with the slimy trail of the killer.

But all they had so far was four photographs of the victims, their faces blurry in the enlargements, pinned across the top of an otherwise blank office wall, their names, approximate dates of death, ages, addresses, locations of their discovery listed line by line, information both important and meaningless, Nagler decided.

Jamie Wilson was single, a party-girl, her friends said, an idea confirmed somewhat when several bartenders nodded and smiled when shown her photo.

"She'd come in with the same general group a couple nights," Art, the bartender at Mario's, had said. "Friendly. Seemed more like friends, rather than couples."

Nancy Harmon got her degree from the state medical school and after five years at a Newark hospital, set up a practice here. She worked with the non-profits to provide care to low-income families. Not married, family scattered around the state. Her main practice, which seemed to be doing well, was centered on women's health.

Felice Sanchez was known for her kindness, the cab company said. Always popular with seniors who needed a run to the grocery store. Worked hard.

Did she answer a call at the Wilson Hotel?

"No, never," Cal Dougherty, her boss said. "That place was on our list of no-goes, as in never take a call from that place, or drop anyone there. Besides, it's been empty, for what, twenty years? Why ain't they tore it down? Only ones who go there are junkies and whores."

And yet, Nagler thought, there she was. The place was a leftover from the booming canal and railroads days. There had been a handful of railroad hotels, then, he knew. Back when Ironton was the central depot, not just a stop on the east-west line. Rowdy, noisy places, life spilling out the doors and windows, roaring down the dark streets, grabbing the city by its collar, the smell of cheap booze, spilled beer and the scent of a woman floating along, enticing the timid, no, demanding attention, because the alternative was silence.

Just like now, Nagler thought when he had earlier examined the hotel wreck. He picked at the warped plywood nailed over broken windows, kicked at soggy doors, repelled by the layers of odors, mixed to be undefinable. Silence, then death.

So, Felice Sanchez had to be hauled into the hotel. They found her cab a couple blocks away.

Then Joan Chen. Assaulted at her workplace; someone told Nagler that the dishwasher had scrubbed the sidewalk with bleach every day since.

****

A new red handprint, this time without the slogan, was found slapped on the side of the empty train depot near City Hall. It was sloppy, where all the others had been precise. Uneven daubs of red paint on the wall suggested the painter had perhaps been interrupted during his task; blotches of red paint led away from the side of the building to nearby Sussex Street.

It had appeared four days after Joan Chen was killed. What, Nagler thought, forgot you were supposed to leave your mark? Seems a little sloppy.

But then, he thought, we don't know for certain when the first three victims were killed, so we don't really know how soon after their deaths the red marks appeared. Investigators had still not found red handprints that they associated with the Harmon and Wilson deaths, so maybe this one was a make-up: A sign in a random, public place. When he ran that thought past Mulligan, the medical examiner, the doctor said, "Slow it down, Frank. Examine what the evidence tells you. Draw only those conclusions based on facts. All others will lead you into trouble."

Nagler re-examined the red mark on the train station. Maybe this one is not the killer, Nagler thought. Sort of careless. The murders had generated a lot of talk around Ironton, as expected. But no clues. The victims seemed like regular, hard-working, normal people. It seemed to him that even normal people piss someone off, can create enemies, foster jealousies.

But they had found none.

Can a killer pick four random people out of thousands?

Maybe that was the point, Nagler thought.

He stared at the new red hand and screwed up his face. No one said it would be easy.

The rail line had been built years ago by the railroad that served two long-closed iron mines and needed a connection to the mills, and the depot had served as a freight house. Plywood sagged in the windows holes. Is there symbolism in marking that location? Other than the fact that hundreds of people walked past it daily on their way to the train station, would see the mark and feel a shiver of fear down their spines.

The location was just confusing, Nagler thought. The old train depot was a long block from where Joan Chen had been stabbed, and five blocks from the modern train station, where her body had been discovered. But the China Song restaurant was in the middle of a busy street, and its wide, tall windows gave a clear view of the entire street. The train station was active at nearly all hours.

To be sure, the old depot was opened up and searched, and no victim was found.

Nagler shook his head as he pinned the new photo, ID'd with a location and date, alongside the others on the incident wall.

Made no sense. He studied the pattern to see if they might like connect-the-dots be forming a letter or a number, but they seemed to be random, and the wall was covered with a spaghetti string of red lines.

Maybe these are places that mean something to the killer, Nagler thought. Places that say something about his life. Maybe the victims were just in the wrong place.

Then: Who is he mad at?

****

Nagler had shaken away that thought and drove to the Old Iron Bog. Besides having become one large, messy crime scene, there was a quiet there Nagler found calming, as if all the trouble hidden beneath the dark water had meaning; he had stood on the crumbling bog trail after Martha as a teenager faced cancer treatment the first time, screaming as a bright half-moon had flashed from behind shifting clouds, briefly lighting the scattered, twisted trees and rock piles, casting his pain into the broken landscape.

The old bog was sizzling with sound — insects, peepers, bullfrogs, the harsh cry of night birds, a rattle of sunburnt dry weeds in a slight wind slithering beneath the faint grumble of traffic. The bog smell had been intensified by a few months of hotter than normal weather and the lack of rain. The sun had squeezed out of the mud the greasy mix of rotten plants, moldy, sweating trash, motor oil that had leaked from dismembered, rusted cars parts, and the musk of dead animals, and then compacted it, so that when a visitor stepped down the six-foot incline from Mount Pleasant Avenue to the main path into the swamp, the smell hung there like water thick and brown as blood.

It wasn't that bad when we were kids, Nagler thought, me and Del Williams jigging for frogs, and then me and Martha Shannon in the back seat of that old Dodge, naked and sweating with the windows closed because the mosquitos were so thick.

He smiled at the memory. "Officially," as they reported to their parents, they were at the movies or the library or something at the high school, not at the bog, in the dusty back seat of an old car, experimenting, testing, tasting. At least her dress never got dirty; her parents had to know.

The mud along the trails squeezed out like nearly-dried cement and clung to Nagler's shoe treads which left behind well-defined footprints. He kicked out his right foot unsuccessfully trying to dislodge the mud.

So why didn't we find any footprints when we found Jamie Wilson? Nagler asked himself as he flashed the ground with his light. Does that make it winter? The cold weather had come late then had been hard for three weeks but warmed up so quickly, starting in early March when the spring rains failed. He shook his head. That made sense and no sense. If they had been killed during the cold spell, the whole time line was off, he thought.

Is this one cunning killer, or are we missing everything? There had been so few clues. Or maybe, he thought, recalling Mulligan's words, this was an experiment with death.

They had found Jamie Wilson's ten-year-old VW angled on Mount Pleasant with the doors open. A shoe had been found near a drag line that appeared to start near her car, but the road side dust held no clear shoeprints, just evidence of a shuffling line of travel. Mulligan estimated her weight at about one-hundred-twenty pounds. Was the killer her size? It might seem that a larger man could have carried her, or did he drag his feet, purposely leaving an indistinct trail? Who drove the car? Was she forced to drive it herself, hugging the wheel in terror, snuffling, coughing, begging? The steering wheel only revealed her prints, and there was no blood inside the VW.

The driver's seat seemed shifted to a position suitably comfortable for a person of Jamie Wilson's height.

She was discovered fifty feet in on the main path, tossed into the tall grass. Why didn't we see her? he wondered.

The hot weather that blew in with early spring, and the generally corrosive nature of the bog had worked on her body, Nagler knew. The bones were scattered, a few missing, as if her body had been savaged by animals. That was why he wondered about Mulligan's exacting declaration. How do we know that the one identifiable common element at the crime scenes had been done by the killer, and not, as could be the case with Jamie Wilson, by a fox?

Mulligan said it seemed possible that Wilson had been strangled with the scarf found around her neck. Nagler sighed: Everything about her death was just awful.

They hadn't found Dr. Harmon's car. That would make sense: Killed for her car. But that wouldn't explain the brutality, Nagler thought. We need the pieces to fit together for us, but the way we put them together was probably not the way a serial killer did. He sighed into the darkness. I'm lost.

The bog covered a thousand acres. Old timers told Nagler about how they would dump steaming truckloads of iron waste into the black water or pour drums of shimmering purple-red chemicals into the deep weeds.

He pulled himself up the slope and back to the road. A single dim streetlight marked the intersection maybe a quarter-mile away. Few houses had ever been built here, mostly on Hancock to the west. The rest was dirty, dark, and hollow, like the bog itself, Nagler imagined, a hole carved by an ancient glacier, endlessly deep, perfect for death.

For one moment the air was silent, the creatures, the distant traffic rumbling, even his breathing, stilled. Did something move in that shadow? A spidery chill ran up his back and he shook his shoulders to release it.

Nagler stood near where the VW had been found and waved his flashlight over the dust and brown grass. We've been here before, but…. The beam bounced off the stiff, waving grass, picking up the glint of an occasional shard of broken glass, a tin can, a coin or two. He kicked at the gravel with the toe of his shoe, flipped over flat rocks, raked his fingers through clumps of dry grass. One time, he thought, one time, I will come here and I won't be too late.

Then his last kick uncovered more than roadside junk. A bracelet with three diamonds, and what could be small rubies and emeralds. He gathered it in his handkerchief and flipped it around in the palm of his hand while he illuminated it. This is really worth hard cash, if those stones are real, he thought. A gift for a special occasion? Is that an initial? An inscription?

Why here?

****

Nagler thumped into the dark house, banging his knee into the heavy, ancient front door that was always jammed. No amount of sanding would offset the leaning of the door frame as the old house settled. It was well after midnight, and Martha's parents would have gone to bed hours ago.

He had dragged his damp, muddy shoes three or four times on the stairs' concrete edges and wiped the smooth soles on the mat again and again but failed to remove the sticky swamp mud; the greasy odor of plant rot, motor oil and the ancient decay of the Old Iron Bog's secrets, remained in his clothes like the guilt of a forgotten anniversary.

Finally, he just took off his shoes and socks and left them on the porch.

It had taken Nagler months to adjust to living on the second floor of Martha's childhood home, even though he had been a guest there more times than he could count since he and Martha had paired up; one day in the third grade they walked home from school together and had been walking together ever since.

The house had been built by her grandparents at the turn of the century in one of the last hurrahs of the dying iron business that had built Ironton, New Jersey. It had been erected in the northern hills, on crests that overlooked the dusty industrial valley; the bright elaborate homes of the business class made darker the shadows of the adjacent worker's ghetto, where Nagler grew up.

It was the house where the young lovers rolled laughing on the flouncy, dusty bedspreads of the four-poster bed her grandmother had

19

left behind and where on more than one quiet summer afternoon they filled the empty house with the cries and moans of youthful passion.

It was also the house where he found her sitting in a dark corner of the bedroom pulling at her long red hair and crying at nineteen as the first rounds of chemotherapy showed its effects; they celebrated the remission at twenty-one by lying quietly on the four-poster bed, her head resting on his chest, a knowledge, a fear, set in their eyes.

****

Barefoot on the cool tile of the kitchen floor, Nagler peeled off his jacket and draped it over a chair; he brushed a trace of bog dust from the left sleeve.

It had been Martha's idea that he needed new, grown-up clothes for his new job. He would have been happy just to wear his comfortable brown jacket, even if the elbows were shiny, but she insisted. At least he had his old, worn-in shoes.

She had dragged him to Benny's Menswear where for an hour she had him model suits and jackets and pants, smiling at his reluctant effort as the selected and rejected clothing piled up on a display case and nearby chair.

"I'll not have my detective go to work on his first day looking like Willie Loman," she whispered in the store while she draped one more new tie around his neck.

"You worried?" She had asked on his first day

He kissed her hair. "Jitters. But it's cop work, right? I think I'm more concerned about the potential for turmoil after the latest round of lay-offs. A lot of popular guys, senior guys, are gone. People got passed over and you know how that goes. And I'm a young guy, twenty-four, with only a couple years on the force, just out of the academy. Gonna get my share of grief, I suspect."

Martha had hugged him tighter and then buried her head into his chest.

"The forces of evil are many, my love. Battle well," she laughed.

"Where did you get that?" he had asked with a surprised, wrinkled smile.

"Macbeth, Hamlet, Dylan Thomas, I don't know." Her smile faded to worry. "You do a lot of reading when you're in a hospital bed trying not to die."

He kissed her hair. Oh, Martha. No. "But all that reading is about dying. 'Don't go gently…'"

She held his face in both hands. "It felt like practicing, Frank," she said, her voice dry and hollow. "Back then, I couldn't tell you how real it was."

She lifted her head from his chest, slivers of tears caught in her eyes. "No more," she said as she wiped her eyes and turned her smiling face upward. "I've already worn black for another reason. I'm not ready to do it again. Just make sure you come home," she had whispered.

****

Standing alone in the silent, dim kitchen, Nagler recalled that first-day scene.

Just come home.

A demand, a wish, a prayer. What he had said when he was in the hospital gray-faced and sleepless as Martha fought for her life. Please, come home. What the empty-eyed families of the dead women had said tearfully as they handed him a photograph, an address book or some personal item they believed would help their family member return.

Just bring her home, they would whisper. No matter what you find. Bring her home to us.

This is where she belongs.

There was hole in the heart that needed patching, a space, a vacuum that needed air, a chasm filled with pain. The hollowness of loss. Families with an empty chair, a smile not returned, a phone call flipping to the recording machine again and again, a place in an album awaiting a photo.

Just come home.

He reached into the left pocket and extracted his handkerchief that held the bracelet. It seemed to be an older style, maybe a family heirloom. Why hadn't we seen it when we canvassed that road before?

But he had found the bracelet more than a hundred yards from where Jamie Wilson's car had been discovered. Too many possibilities, he thought. We missed it, or a thief dropped it, or it fell off the arm of a woman… But no one goes to the old bog for romance now.

Then the awful thought…maybe the one true thought: The killer has another unknown victim, stole the bracelet as a trophy, and placed it along

Mount Pleasant after we searched the bog. Maybe he is watching us.

"Frank?"

Martha slipped into the light of the kitchen from the bedroom, her voice dark with sleep.

"If you've been with her again, I'm going to be royally mad, you know there, buddy," she whispered into his chest before she reached up and kissed him.

He held her tight. "All four," he said. "Again."

"Tell them you're mine."

"Yeah," he sighed and kissed the top of her head.

She leaned back and pushed herself away from him and reached for a glass on the counter and the filled it with water. "A lot of late nights," she whispered as she stared past the reflected light into the darkness. "So little time."

He reached his arms around her shoulders and kissed her neck, pressing his lips on her skin for a long moment; he left a quick kiss and then pulled back.

"I wish they weren't so long. But so much is piling up, I need some time alone at the end of the day to sort it out. I don't want to bring it home to you."

"I know," she said as she guided his hand under her shirt and placed it on her left breast and then reached up to kiss him.

"Oh, Frank." A comic, swooning voice.

"Oh, Martha."

Then they laughed.

"You can stop now," she said, smiling.

"Stop what?"

"Playing with my tit." She pulled his hand out from under her shirt and turned toward the window. "There was a commotion across the street earlier tonight. Trash cans, banging, I don't know. Seemed like it was coming from that empty lot, the one with the junk that we complain about all the time." She playfully punched him in the ribs. "Who could I call about that? Hmmm. Maybe a cop I know?"

"What time?"

"About ten. I was reading. I heard my dad open the front door and yell out, 'Hello?'"

"I'll look at it in the morning."

Martha leaned over the sink and gazed out the window into darkness. "We should install another light, maybe on the side porch."

That was odd, he thought. "You afraid?"

She turned away from the window.

"No, but with all that's going on, the dead women and all... This neighborhood's not as full as it used to be, empty homes." She shook off the gloom. "Maybe just animals or a homeless person."

Martha started back to the bedroom and noticed the jewelry.

"A bracelet?" Mocking. "A bracelet, mister?"

"I found it along Mount Pleasant by the bog," he said.

"Ooh," she said, pulling back from the table. "That is creepy, Frank. Cree-py."

He winced. "I know. Should have taken it to the department, but there is no one there but a dispatcher. Do it in the morning. I have no idea if it means anything."

Martha wrinkled her nose and waved a hand over the bracelet. "Still, ick. Cover it up. It might belong to a dead woman. Frank!"

CHAPTER THREE

There is quiet

Nagler slipped behind the wheel of the 1979 gray Impala he'd been assigned and listened as the suspension groaned when he sat. He glanced at the speedometer: 115,312 miles. Hard miles of slamming and grinding on Ironton's pitted, pot-holed streets; a mile of downtown had been finally repaved after century-old trolley tracks resurfaced and the mayor's new white Caddy bottomed out making a left turn.

He had walked along the empty lot across the street from where the noise had come, but it didn't seem any more disturbed than usual. Probably animals. He glanced back at the house's roofline. Maybe Martha's right, he thought. A spotlight high on that roofline might cast enough light over here to discourage human activity.

He had rolled down the two front windows to vent the heat trapped in the car and felt his shirt shrink to his skin. The day's heat had already set in, even before the sunlight dusted the hilltops east of Ironton; he knew the new blue light wool-blend jacket would be draped over the passenger's side seat, his sleeves would be rolled to his elbows, and the tie wrenched to one side. Nagler had listened as a radio weatherman happily babbled on about Bermuda Highs, the jet stream this, the jet stream that, all of which was unusual for the Northeast in mid-May. "It's like August," the weatherman exclaimed, with too much cheer.

****

Mulligan had quickly examined the bracelet and found some initials and what appeared to be a jeweler's mark on the inside. The diamonds were real, as were three small rubies and the two small emeralds. "I'd say this was a gift to mark a significant event, a birthday or anniversary," he said. "It is not a style that fits with what we know of any of our victims, unless it was given to them, perhaps, as a keepsake."

"Does that mean…"

"Another victim?" Mulligan asked. "Perhaps a theft." He rubbed his forehead. "What a sad state of affairs that a mere theft would be an

25

improvement. Here, I've photographed the piece. The jeweler's mark seems to be "IR," so perhaps Manny could shed some light on its owner. I'll examine it closer for any other material."

Manny Calabrese had run Ironton Jewelers for maybe twenty years, taking over from his father, Big Manny. His grandfather had started the businesses at the turn of the century, crafting fine jewelry and selling it to the iron masters. It had seemed to Nagler that while the bosses protested loudly about the flood of immigrants in the city, they never minded paying them starvation wages to work their mines and mills or buying for wives and lovers well-crafted baubles from Rocky Calabrese with whom they negotiated the price in a garble of English and Italian.

Manny had made a special silver broach for Martha when she went into remission.

"Franky," Manny Calabrese yelled over the clattering shuffle in the store when Nagler pushed the door open. "Give me a minute."

If Manny called you by your name and added a "y," you were in tight. Since he couldn't add a "y" to Martha, Manny called her Marta. "Marta, Marta, Marta."

He waved Nagler to a corner of the glass counter and draped a telephone receiver over his shoulder and the chord across his chest.

"Whatcha need, Franky? Something for that sweet Marta?"

"Soon, Manny. Her birthday is coming up in August. I'm thinking maybe a necklace with a thing…a hanging thing."

"Pendent? Maybe her birthstone. Good."

"Yeah." Nagler blushed. "A pendent. But I came for this, Manny. I found it up by the bog. It seems to have your mark." He handed the jeweler the set of photos.

It only took a second.

"That I made for Marion Feldman. By the bog, you said. What's it doing there? Marion's old. She don't get out much and if she did, she wouldn't be screwing around the bog."

"Remember when you made it?"

"Ah, Franky, I remember all the pieces, especially the good ones. Walter, that's Marion's husband, hell of a salesman, wanted something special for their fiftieth wedding anniversary, maybe ten, eleven years ago, eighty-one, eighty-two. Know what? Rocky made their wedding ring. That was a beautiful piece. Hang on, got a picture."

It was a beautiful piece, Nagler thought. Gold ring, not too thick, almost delicate, with a centered ruby and tiny diamonds set as a circle.

Manny frowned as he handed back the bracelet photos. "Nothing happened to her, you think?"

Nagler shrugged. "Don't know. Have an address?"

****

The Baker Hills section of Ironton was developed by one of the city's rich bankers more than a century ago as a swanky neighborhood for the business owners and top managers of the city's iron industry. The soft, green-lined roads featured fancy homes with turrets and wrap-around porches, landscaped, fenced yards, some with small gazebos, and a few with wrought-iron gates across their stone driveways. The neighborhood was on the west side of the city, set on rising hills planted with fragrant flowering trees and an entangled wall of tall Norway maples that had grown to block the view across the river of the black, belching mills and the workers ghetto where soot rained down like Hell's mist.

Nagler as a kid had wondered as he delivered newspapers to the homes protected by those tall maples why the rich folks didn't want to see how they made their money.

Nothing bad ever happened in the Baker Hills.

That's what Nagler was led to believe. As proof, he had always looked at the names of the streets there: Harvard, Princeton, Columbia, Yale, the Ivy leagues, as if living on streets with such names raised the aspirations of their children.

In truth, he had grown up believing — rather, having to believe — that nothing bad ever happened in Ironton, his hometown, at least nothing that could not be overcome. It's what you do in a poor town, he learned. Have hope; everything else is darkness. The floods, the factory closings, the homeless living under the bridge, the permanent bend of his father's back after work, then the thousand-yard stare when the mills closed. Somehow, Ironton survived, got up from the knock-down and trudged on, the limp a little more pronounced, the tear stains a little deeper on the dirty faces of hungry kids. He grew up believing that things would always be better. Martha Shannon, his true love since the third grade, was proof enough of that: She hadn't lived in the workers' ghetto; she had led him out of it.

He had grown up on Fourth Street, a block over from Third, and two blocks from Sixth. They weren't street names, just lines on a map — Street One, Street Two, Street Three; nothing poetic or inspirational, mere designations created because some city engineer had needed a way to make sense of the tangled mass of winding alleys, trails, and odd-sized lots that covered the east side of Ironton's hills; nothing more. What lived beyond the engineer's solution were the informal names of alleys that reflected the immigrants, the Germans, Italians, Irish, Poles — the whatevers — who, despite hard lives, filled the tiny homes with generations, spilled over the hillsides brawling and battling with life, dancing, joyously laughing and singing, trying to stand, then to be knocked down again, wishing the rays of sunlight were not so gray, and that the air didn't taste like ash.

Nagler slipped the Impala off the state highway into Baker Hills and left the bright clutter of commerce behind; like a gate, silence descended and deepened as he drove beneath the smothering tunnel of shaded streets where the morning sunlight had yet to fully penetrate; a sterile silence, sound absorbed by sentinel homes, by the dense leafy overhang, more a setting, a stage, than a place.

Nagler maneuvered the clanking car cautiously over the scattered speed humps, as if unneeded speed would disturb the unnerving peace. There is quiet, he thought as he had searched for the turn to West Harvard and the Feldman home. There is quiet with movement and light. Then there is too quiet; this.

****

The Feldman's home was at the dead end of West Harvard; a narrow dirt path ran along the far edge of the property into a stand of trees, separating the yard from the brush-strewn rubble of a cliff that rose to the west. The adjacent house was built at the far opposite side of its lot, leaving an open lawn between it and the Feldman home, which felt disconnected from the rest of the street, even though the homes were maybe forty feet apart.

Nagler greeted Patrolman Tom Jenkins in front of the house.

"What's up?"

"I heard the call when I was on the state highway, a couple blocks away…" Jenkins replied.

"What call?" Nagler asked.

"About the tall grass and the newspapers? Neighbor called it in."

"What the hell is going on, Tom?" Nagler asked. "I was coming here because a bracelet belonging to a woman who is supposed to live here was found out at the Old Iron Bog. You know, where one of our victims, Jamie Wilson, had been dumped, and you're here because the lawn ain't been cut?"

Nagler surveyed the yard. The grass hadn't been cut in a couple weeks, he guessed. But it was the newspapers, maybe ten or twelve, that riveted his attention.

"What's with the papers?" he asked Jenkins.

"A bracelet?" Jenkins asked as he squinted in confusion. "You think…?

"Don't know what to think, Tom. You talk to anyone?"

"Yeah, the lady next door, a Mrs. Thomas, she called it in. She said she returned from Florida a couple days ago and saw the Feldman's grass was tall," Jenkins said. "She said Mrs. Feldman, um," he glanced at his notebook, "Marion Feldman lives alone and apparently hired a company to mow the lawn. When she inspected the grass, Mrs. Thomas said she saw newspapers all over the lot and sidewalk and called us."

"Feldman? That's the name the jeweler gave me. Did you look around?" Nagler asked.

"Just walked up the side path a little. There's a shed and garage out back," Jenkins said. "Both locked," he shrugged, "There's a car in the garage."

"Um, okay. Is Mrs. Thomas still home?"

"Yeah. What do you want me to do?"

"Walk out back, you know, just to see."

Nagler rapped on the Thomas's front door and glanced up and down the street as he waited. I remember this street. Delivered papers to this house, Number 10, 12, the blue house on the corner. They had a dog, a snarling Shepherd or something. Never let me in the yard. So, I threw the paper from the street to the porch and sometimes the dog retrieved it and chewed it to pieces. A couple of cute girls lived at the other corner. Funny.

He turned back as the door opened.

"Hi, I'm Detective Nagler…"

"Of course, you are," Mrs. Thomas said after she opened the door. "Our favorite news boy, Frankie, all grown up to be a policeman."

Nagler felt his face flush.

"Yes, ma'am. Thank you." Mrs. Adele Thomas. Same woman. Brassy blonde. Tight, white shorts, bikini top and gauzy cover, clothes meant for a younger woman. Sometimes she had answered the door in just a bathrobe. Always inviting me in to wait while she got her change to pay for the paper. Lousy tipper.

"So, you called us about Mrs. Feldman?"

"Yes! Her lawn is always so neat. They come weekly, you know. I love how she has made them trim the grass along the sidewalks," Mrs. Thomas pointed to the long sidewalk that divided their lawns from the street; shaggy grass drooped over the edge on the Thomas portion.

"Do you remember when you saw her last?"

"Care to come in, Frank? Can I call you Frank, or Detective?"

"Frank is fine, ma'am. But I can't come in."

"Well, a month at least. I've been in Florida, at my sister's. Just got back. I'm not sure when I saw her before that. Marion rarely left the house or the yard after she had injured her hip in a fall, maybe two years ago now. I felt bad for her since her husband died a few years back. Such a nice man, loved her deeply. They traveled, you know. He had been a salesman for a chemical company, and the traveling bug never died, even after he retired. I was envious. Paris, Brazil, the Far East…"

"Yes, ma'am. Do you remember who was on that lawn crew, or a company name, maybe on the side of a truck?"

She rolled her eyes up and over and then centered them on Nagler. "No, not really. Mostly teenagers, with one older boy, maybe twenty, twenty-one, as supervisor; good looking boy. There was one very small boy. I thought he might be too young to work, but he might have been a brother of one of the older boys."

Nagler pulled out a business card. "If you think of anything else, call me, please. And thanks for your time."

"Oh, certainly, Frank. And good luck. And, oh, how is Martha?"

Nagler glanced at the floor. "We're married." He smiled and nodded.

Mrs. Thomas leaned forward and placed a sloppy kiss on his cheek. "Good for you. Little Franks?"

"Not yet. I'll pass along your greeting."

As he walked away: I almost said, "We're practicing." How weird would that have been?

****

Jenkins greeted Nagler at the head of the dirt lane.

"Back door's open," Jenkins said.

"Look in?" Nagler asked.

"Just stuck my head in. Yelled once." Jenkins shrugged. "No reply."

"Yeah," Nagler replied. "Okay. I noticed some neighbors are stirring. Ask them if they saw anyone around the house." Jenkins turned to cross the street. "Oh, yeah, ask them if they know the name of the lawn company that did yard work here."

Nagler stepped to the back door, open a few inches. The window shades were drawn, even on the door itself. Were they always like that? Couldn't see who was at the door unless it was opened. He leaned back and glanced at the windows on that side of the house: All the shades were drawn.

The door opened on a coat room, probably an old mud room, with seven pegs along the right wall. Six were empty. A blue knitted sweater sagged from the remaining hook. The inner door was partly open and gave Nagler a view into the kitchen, where a tall Hoosier cabinet lined the wall. Martha's mother had such a cabinet and on hers the wide, flat shelf was covered with a gingham cloth, and a cookie jar, and a set of spice jars nestled under glass doors. Cook books leaned into the corners and a towel often rested in the middle of the shelf, tossed casually.

This shelf was empty, dusty, and a streak of fingers left a trail that led to what appeared to be a palm print.

Nagler elbowed open the door.

"Hello? Anyone here? Ironton Police. Hello?"

Just an echo.

The air in the room had the thickness of sunlight through dust, but there was no taste or sharp odor, only the dense smell of an old, dark closet. It should be hotter in here, Nagler thought. Maybe that door was open for quite a while. Why didn't any one notice?

Judging from the outside of the house and the neighborhood, he expected the kitchen to be well appointed.

It was nearly empty.

A bargain basement kitchen table rested in the middle, edged by two cheaply painted chairs. An empty plastic napkin holder was toppled in the center of the table. A small, aged refrigerator with a big latch handle filled a corner. He pulled the door open and saw a few plastic containers of cooked food, a pint of milk, and some stale lettuce. The greasy odor of food gone bad leaked from the refrigerator.

The house was so silent even the air felt heavy.

Nagler sighed. What a sad place. Dark and empty. The room looked like the family had moved out, leaving behind the things they didn't want. Nagler knew the feeling; one hurried move, the truck rumbling in the driveway, overflowing cargo roped to the frame.

Two clean plates, a tea cup and saucer, and a saucepan rested in the dishrack next to the sink, dusted with a fine gray film; a white towel with a faded, brown stain was draped over the front the front of the sink. The cabinets were nearly empty, except for a box of elbow macaroni, three cans of soup, a jar of spaghetti sauce, and a box of tea.

Nagler closed the last cabinet door and glanced around the room, shaking his head? This was the woman who traveled? he asked himself. Where were the photos, the kitsch from foreign places? There was nothing on the walls but a few nails centering broken plaster, chipped paint, and filigrees of dusty webs. How lonely was Marion Feldman?

But more important: Where was Marion Feldman? What room am I going to step into to find her dead on the floor, he wondered, resigned. Call it in? Not yet.

"Hello," Nagler called out again, louder. "It's the Ironton Police. The door was open. Hello? I'm Detective Nagler. Anyone here? Mrs. Feldman?"

Like calling into a dark cave, his voice bounced off the bare, solid walls.

No reply. He stood, listening, head tipped, as still as he could. Nothing; just the settling of the old house slipping through the weighted silence, the creaking complaints of time. Not even a ticking clock.

The living room carpet was worn to the point that the tough strings that once framed the wool laid exposed. What was that in the middle of the rug? Nagler fumbled at the archway for a light switch and the bare center light cast its harsh glare. If the kitchen had been still, empty of life, the living room provided evidence of movement — is that a possible sign of struggle, or just the stumbles of an older woman with a bad hip unable to keep her balance? A table lamp was tipped onto the floor against a far wall, its shade crumpled. The thin carved wooden arm of a chair had been shattered, a few magazines were spread across the floor. Someone could have fallen, Nagler thought, tripped on the worn carpet edge, or unbalanced in the throes of a possible heart attack. But, if so, where was the body?

The heavy damask couch was at angles to the room. He lifted one end; it was not meant to be moved. He called out again: "Hello!"

Then, oddly, Nagler thought, silverware. Three knives, a couple spoons and a fork or two, scattered around the carpet.

And that spot, irregular, and after a closer examination, containing strands of gray hair. He kneeled and touched an edge of the stain, which was hard and dry.

Enough.

Nagler stood and reached for his radio.

"Yeah, Mattie, need back-up at West Harvard. The medical examiner, too."

Outside, Nagler had Jenkins to begin a slow searching walk down the dirt lane.

"She's not in the house," Nagler said as he scratched his neck. "Maybe the woods."

"So, she's dead?" Jenkins asked.

"Until we find her, she's not, but..." Nagler shrugged.

Four patrol cars and Dr. Walter Mulligan's black van rolled to a stop in front of the house.

"Where's the victim, Frank?" Mulligan asked.

"We're looking," Nagler said," a statement that even puzzled himself. "Apparently Marion Feldman. Manny said it was her bracelet that I had found at the bog. But I got here, and Officer Jenkins is responding to a call about the grass and newspapers. A neighbor said she lived alone, and maybe had a hard time getting around after she broke her hip a couple of years ago. I don't know why we didn't find her."

When Mulligan sighed, Nagler took him into the house and displayed the rooms.

"There was no one here," he said, his voice a defensive shrug. "The rooms were empty and dusty. The bedroom seemed unused, a second room has just a dresser and the bathroom is, well, a bathroom. There's five or six boxes stacked in front of the stairs leading to the second floor, but they are covered in dust and don't appear to have been moved in a while. It seems almost like she lived in the kitchen and the living room. I found a blanket stuffed under the couch. Then there's the silverware, and the spot on the rug. We're searching the property. Sorry, doc."

"Not to worry, Frank. Let me begin. It could appear that some violence took place in this room, or perhaps a fall. But you said she had a bad hip? Maybe this disorder is the result of her inability to maintain her balance and the spot on the floor the result of a fall. But as you said, where is the body? A suggestion? Search all the yards. Perhaps she did fall, and stunned but mobile, wandered out, trying to reach a neighbor. Let's also have an officer reach out to the hospital."

"Think we have another victim?" Nagler asked.

Mulligan just exhaled.

****

Dusk brought flashlights. Nightfall, spotlights.

A roadblock at the state highway screened residents of the six-block neighborhood as police from surrounding towns, county search teams and state police joined the effort to locate Marion Feldman. The prospect of another death in the series brought additional help.

Ironton General Hospital had no record of any older woman fitting Marion Feldman's description being admitted or treated in the emergency unit; the administrator, familiar with the Feldmans, said he would reach out to her family doctor.

Families watched from porches; then pairs, then just fathers. Lights in homes were one-by-one extinguished, leaving a dim canyon of porch lights narrowing to a red-and-blue emergency flasher pulsing atop a patrol car at the end of the street.

With darkness, silence, save for the faint shuffling of boots through brush or an occasional shout.

Working west-to-east from the end of West Harvard, then yard-by-yard, shed-by-shed, and block-by-block leaders pronounced the area searched. Scattered mounds of loose earth were probed to reveal nothing. The shallow stands of trees and the deep yards settled back to darkness, the searchers and their bouncing lights withdrawn.

What remained was the river.

In the gray-yellow dawn of the next day, Nagler watched from Waterworks Park as three boats held searchers who prodded the mossy banks to give up their secrets. Poles extended then withdrawn, lights slivered through shifting tall green weeds, revealing blackness behind.

"Think she's in the river?" Nagler asked search team leader Sergeant Ray Martinez.

"Not here so far," he said, and scratched his chin. "Light's getting better. In full daylight we'll go upstream, but there's no clean access to the river until you get to Wharton. It's all scrub brush and trees, no paths or roads. If she's there…" and his voice tailed off and he cast a side glance at Nagler. Martinez clenched his jaw. "Best bet is she's downstream, if she went in. But the water's so damn shallow." Shook his head. "Then there's why." He glanced at Nagler. With a hollow voice: "Or how."

Nagler wearily nodded. He'd been at the scene all night and placed one hurried call to Martha around midnight; he listened as the sleepy worry filled her voice.

****

Nagler could hear a high-pitched commanding voice from the street.

"Did you photograph those boxes? Good. How about the stairs?"

Nagler pushed his way into the kitchen.

"Hey, be careful," the voice ordered. "Don't touch anything." Then: "Who are you?"

Who are you? Nagler asked himself. And who left you in charge?

Nagler extended his hand. "I'm Nagler, Detective Frank Nagler."

"Right, the new guy. I'm Foley, Senior Detective Chris Foley. The chief assigned me to the case this morning. Four dead. Now maybe five. It's more than a priority now. It's a necessity that we solve this. Where have you been?"

Weighed down by fatigue, Nagler was not about to get into a jurisdictional pissing match. "Sure. That's good. We searched the house yesterday morning, and the yard, and found nothing. I was down at the river. Ray Martinez…"

"You mean Sergeant Martinez."

Nagler shook his head. "Right. Sergeant Martinez. That's gonna be hard. I've known Ray — the sergeant — since grade school. Anyway, they'll expand the river search in full daylight."

Foley turned to face the middle of the kitchen. He was short and thin with dark, burning eyes. Ambitious eyes, Nagler's father would say. That's what he had called the eyes of the plant supers who would stalk the production line looking for workers to fire even while the work piled up, knowing what came next was a cash reward for workforce reduction.

Foley stood with his hands on his hips. His paisley tie had been wrenched to one side and the sleeves of his powder blue sports coat were pushed to his elbows.

"Hey," he yelled. "Where's the evidence van? We need to move these boxes to the station."

Foley turning back to Nagler.

"Why wait?"

Nagler closed his eyes and yawned.

"Nighttime. And it's a dangerous stretch of the river, especially as low as it is." His gravelly, worn voice took on the weight of authority. "The canal had crossed there, and parts of the old gates are buried in the mud. Even in slow water, the currents can be swift and unpredictable. Better to be safe than sorry."

Foley squinted at Nagler and then scratched his forehead. He hurriedly scanned the kitchen counters. "Yeah, okay. Good. I didn't know that."

"I grew up here," Nagler said softly, trying to end the conversation so he could go home, get some sleep and avoid the distaste for Foley that was rising in his throat.

"Well, that would be helpful." Foley tried to smile, but only got as far a grimace.

"I thought so."

Nagler turned to the door.

"Why are you moving the boxes?" he asked. "We don't know that she is dead. Could be missing."

Foley placed his hands on his hips and shook his head.

"First big case, right? Trust me. She'll be dead. We'll find her bones somewhere."

****

At his desk the next afternoon, Nagler gazed at the color photo of Marion Feldman. It was in one of the boxes that had been blocking the stairs. It was a professionally shot photo and was matched in a folding display with a photo of her husband Walter. Probably their fiftieth anniversary, Nagler thought.

She had white hair, styled for the photo, round glasses, bright eyes and a wide, knowing smile. Boy, does that say "Grammy."

The earrings and necklace she wore seemed matched, distinctive, Nagler thought. He searched for the photo of the bracelet he found at the Old Iron Bog. The jewelry was of a similar style. Maybe Rocky or Big Manny Calabrese at Ironton Jewelers made it as well. In the photo, the jewelry seemed yellowish, maybe gold, but the color tones were slightly off, so it was hard to say. Manny would know.

He taped the photo to a copy of a press release that was going to be issued and ran off a few dozen copies. Then he took the photo and attached it to a formal missing persons announcement that would be faxed to police departments, copied that, and placed it into the machine for distribution, and pushed the start button.

Detective Foley thought it was presumptive to release a missing-persons report, which Nagler thought was odd since he had all but declared her dead. But the chief said in this case with an older woman, a possible injury, and no local family, it seemed to be the reasonable thing to do. Nagler had agreed, citing the comments by the neighbor Adele Thomas, who in a subsequent discussion that first day, showed a keen knowledge of West Harvard Street's coming and goings. Besides, Nagler had said, according to Mrs. Thomas, Marion Feldman might have been missing a month or more.

The machine hummed and rattled as the announcement was drawn through the copier, held in the hopper and then dropped as the machine beeped its completion of the task.

He thumped into his chair, leaned over his desk, and scratched his forehead.

Is this number five?

CHAPTER FOUR

Marion Feldman was not there

The phone call from Marion Feldman's granddaughter had cleaned up one mystery: Why the house seemed deserted.

She was preparing to move Marion Feldman to a nursing home, explained Kathy

Dennison, of Columbus, Ohio. Most of the furniture had been sold or donated, and the remainders were items like the kitchen table and couch that were needed until her grandmother moved. There had been a snag in the nursing home paperwork, she said. She was only supposed to be there about another week.

Police Chief Robert Mallory had ordered the boxes returned to the Feldman home unopened.

"But it's evidence," Chris Foley had protested.

"Evidence of what?" the chief replied. "She's missing, Detective. Not dead. Unless you know something you are withholding."

Nagler recalled how Foley's face smoldered when the chief gave the order to return the boxes to the Feldman home.

"Not till we have permission," the chief had said. "Find a family member."

Nagler had discovered Dennison's name and phone number written on the calendar in the kitchen but had taken several days to finally speak with her. The month displayed was April, except it was now May. A date — April 10 — was circled, with a notation: "DOC." He made a note.

She hadn't known her grandmother was missing. Nagler listened to her gasping breath and muffled sobs through the phone. He hadn't thought that she didn't know. Why didn't I think of that? Who'd want to get this phone call?

"I had placed the boxes there to keep her from trying to climb the stairs to sleep in her bedroom on the second floor." Dennison stumbled through the explanation, her voice harsh, catching. "That was how she fell and broke her hip. She and Walter had slept in the bedroom for more than fifty years, and after he died, she would crawl up the stairs, pulling her arthritic knee up stair by stair with both hands to spend the night there, you know, to be with him. They loved each other so much, Detective, Marion and Walter. She fell on the stairs when she lost her balance lifting her bad leg. Once she was out of the hospital, I set her up on the first floor and began to make plans to move her out and sell the house. There was a nurse the first year, but she fell more than two years ago. She had seemed fine. It was just taking longer than I thought." Then her voice cracked. "Is there any news?"

"Um, well, we don't know…"

"Sir, she was seventy-eight and could barely walk." A short laugh. Then a wet whisper, "Guess I'll really be selling the house. It seemed so far off. Know any local real estate agents? And get rid of the car."

Nagler heard the phone line hum. "I'm sorry, Miss. We must list her as missing. Did she drive? Why did she still have a car? May I ask? Are they any closer family members than yourself, or any others?"

An earful of breath. "No, officer. Marion and Walter had three children. She used to drive… I just never got rid…." Sighed. "One son, Walter Junior, died in the Army in an accident, years ago. Their eldest daughter Madison contracted cancer and died twenty years ago. And my parents — my mother Nancy, their youngest daughter, and my father Jack Dennison — died in a plane crash in Bolivia five years ago. I'm the last family member. I've been traveling back and forth from Columbus to Ironton."

Wow, he thought. "I'm sorry."

"Thank you. If something changes, I'll expect your call. Oh, God," her voice broke and Nagler could hear her deeply inhale before, she spoke again. "I'll be up to Ironton as soon as possible. I guess I'll need to go through the house."

"Yes," Nagler said softly. "And perhaps go through the boxes to, you know… With your permission…we would like to examine the contents, for" — clues, he almost said, — "contacts like yourself."

"Yes, of course. Thank you, officer."

"Yes, thank you. Oh, there was a note on the calendar, DOC, maybe a doctor's appointment? Does that ring a bell?"

She coughed. "Um, maybe her therapist, for her leg? I don't really know. Dr. Melman was the family doctor. Perhaps him."

"Okay." Silence. "Any idea why the calendar showed April, not May?"

A question too far; she wept into the phone. "Is it possible she's been missing since April, officer? Oh, God. Marion. Just bring her home, please, Detective Nagler. Please bring her home."

Nagler hung up the phone, his hand lingering on the receiver for a moment.

The boxes had held little but photo albums and a few family announcements: Births, anniversaries, deaths. Life squeezed down to a few simple dates. Maybe the granddaughter would see something else, something to explain… Nagler thought.

But Mrs. Taylor, the neighbor, had been right: The Feldmans did travel. National parks, oceans, lakes and cabins, foreign cities, odd spots along any of the nation's interstate highways, a great American life, apparently filled with joy, excitement, and love.

Something to be envied, Nagler thought.

And now just a bunch of stuff in dust covered boxes. Nagler stared at the contents and lifted an item or two before dropping it in back in the box. Here you are, he thought. And yet you're not here.

Interviews with Feldman's neighbors, mostly younger families, generated little information. No one, it seemed, paid much attention to the old lady at the end of the street.

They did know the landscaper, though. Green's Lawn Service.

"We started cutting the Feldman's lawn in 1969," owner Dan Green told Nagler. "They lived there maybe sixty years?" He waved one hand. "Something like that. Walter and I were golfing buddies, and I bought out the company that was servicing their lawn. We'd pick a hole and if I beat his score on that hole, he'd have to buy lunch for my crew. If he beat me, I cut his lawn for free one week." He forced a smile for a second then pursed his lips and shrugged. "I think…think we about broke even." He blinked away tears.

"Did any of your crew notice anything odd at the house over the past few weeks?" Nagler asked.

"Bobby, the lead man, did mention the papers, so I called the Register to ask them about it." He shook his head. "I can't remember if they got back to me."

"The lawn hadn't been cut in a while," Nagler said.

"Yeah, the granddaughter from Ohio stopped the weekly service because Marion was moving out. We had arranged to cut the grass a couple times while it was being sold, you know, just to keep the place better looking for a buyer. The last cut" — he pulled out a thick, brown ledger — "was three weeks before you guys showed up. Before that? First cut was late March, even though it's been dry. Appearance, don't you know." His voice faltered. "Trimmed the sidewalks."

Nagler scratched his head. No lawn service for three weeks, and there were nine papers in the yard, the oldest one dated fifteen days before we got to the house, and the newest one, four days before.

That almost made no sense, Nagler thought. There weren't enough papers in the yard to match the three weeks when the lawn was not cut. What does that mean?

"Thanks. You'll make your crew available to us?"

"Yeah, sure. End of the day tomorrow okay?"

****

Nagler stared at the Feldman house from across the street. He leaned on the warm hood of the Impala, arms crossed, head tilted to the left, his face screwed into a puzzle. Sunlight filtered through leaves dappled the windows of the upper story, light on water dancing, shape shifting. Nagler wanted to see a face, a smiling child, a flash of a yellow headed girl, and a yell to Mom about her brother pulling her hair; wanted to peel the Feldmans from the Kodak shots so they sat in the parlor and pointed and laughed at the places they traveled, told the stories again, and smiled.

There would no longer be any Feldmans smiling in that home, he knew.

He had followed up Dan Green's mention of the Register, which had stopped delivery of the newspaper a couple months ago. So, who tossed the papers in the yard? Maybe that explained the out-of-sequence dates.

Teams had searched the entire neighborhood two more times, both in daylight, and then went through the empty house again. The river was poked and screened; officers in wetsuits crawled through the thick shoreline grasses.

But Marion Feldman was not there.

Nagler instructed Ray Martinez — Sergeant Martinez; how many times am I gonna hear about that from the Foley guy — to start searching two of Ironton's larger and more notorious wet spots — the Old Iron Bog, where Jamie Wilson had been found, and Smelly Flats.

The ancient bog — Ice Age ancient — was a known dumping spot for stolen cars, appliances, assorted junk, and back in the iron days, all the material that could not be used or was badly made, the waste. In the Twenties, town legends said, the Mob sank cases of booze into the black muck to hide them from the feds, and then had hauled the booty out and sold it. Legends also said a few Mob associates had been sunk into the middle of the bog as payback when the deals went bad.

Smelly Flats was a broad slow-moving whirlpool formed when the fast-flowing river emptied from its narrow chute into a flat plain and slammed to a halt. The slow circular swirl carried enough soil so that each spring a thick crop of water weeds sprouted only to die in the late summer when the river's flow dropped to a trickle. The scent of the rotting weeds rose like a wall. Dead animals caught in the current had been sometimes found when the weeds died, and once in the Fifties, the body of a teenaged boy who had been raped and killed by his stepfather was found in Smelly Flats after a summer-long search.

The thought of finding Marion Feldman in either of those spots sickened Nagler. Not there.

And yet her bracelet had been found on the road near the bog. I don't even know what that means. One more impossible thing.

The house had given up few clues.

The majority of fingerprints on surfaces had been Feldman's, even the finger smears and palm print in the dust on the kitchen cabinet. The rest were not identified or were the granddaughter's.

But the spot on the carpet had proved to be blood, Feldman's, as was the gray hair.

But the medical examiner could not conclude how it got there.

While Nagler stared at the house, a kid scrambled down the slope at the end of West Harvard. He was nimble enough, Nagler thought, swinging from the trunks of small, bending trees, jumping from rock to rock, hitting a slide made of sand and riding on his ass to the bottom.

"You do that a lot?" Nagler asked when he crossed the Feldman lawn.

The kid stopped short and dusted his pants, surprised at the sight of Nagler. He looked like he was ten, skinny and short, but his face seemed older.

"All of us do," the kid said. "It's a shortcut from Saint Mary's to downtown. The highway don't have no sidewalks once you get past the hospital."

Before Nagler could ask the kid's name or if he knew Marion Feldman, the car's radio barked to life.

"It's Nagler."

It was dispatcher Mattie Washington.

"Have another situation, Frank. Another old lady. Up on Pennington, near the high school. Her son is there. ID'd her as Edie Smith."

By the time Nagler turned back to the kid, he was a block away, running.

Is this six? Nagler asked himself as he slipped into the car and started the engine.

At the end of West Harvard, where it intersected with Princeton, Nagler thought he'd see the kid, but he was gone. Man, he's fast.

CHAPTER FIVE

Why would someone take that?

Pennington Street was in a well-kept neighborhood on the north side of Ironton. Most of the homes had been built after World War II and many had been bought by veterans. The street was about eight blocks from Elm Street, where Martha Shannon grew up, and where she and Nagler now lived.

With flashing lights and a squawk or two of his horn Nagler had elbowed the Impala through the gathering on-lookers to park behind the medical examiner's van.

The only home on the street that had not been built after the war was Edie Smith's. Built by her banker grandfather, and the first house in the neighborhood, it occupied the two corner lots at a bend in the street. The home was three stories tall, set on an elevated platform that was reached via a wide bi-level concrete stairway; it dominated the neighborhood. The old banker had its name — The Homestead — carved into a granite arch above the main porch entrance.

"Came from money," a neighbor at the curb whispered assuredly to Nagler when he was asked about the house before unloading a mouthful of tobacco juice into the beer can he was holding. "Nice lady, though."

Observant fella, Nagler thought; "came from money" seemed a little obvious. "When did you last see her?" Nagler asked. "Why are you worried about her money?"

The man grinned and shrugged. "'Cause there seemed to be a lot of it. Wouldn't you?" He waved the beer car around. "Know what? Really didn't pay her no mind. A few weeks back, maybe not. You know I work. She was in and out. We didn't actually exchange Christmas cards, there, officer."

Nagler found Dr. Mulligan, the medical examiner, at his van. He appeared to be leaving.

"Am I that late?" Nagler asked. "I just got the call."

Mulligan frowned. "There is no victim, Frank. Again. But unlike the Feldman home, there was no overturned lamps, furniture or any sign of a struggle or accident. There was however a rotting caldron of soup on the stove. The house reeks. The mailman called when the odor had become so strong he could smell it outside the porch. He told the dispatcher he thought it smelled like a rotting corpse. What I don't understand is why the postman, contrarily, was still delivering the mail if he suspected the occupant did not appear to be home. Why didn't he report that suspicion? The house was closed up, and in this unseasonable heat.... See what you can ascertain, Frank. Your partner Foley is making a mess of this, it seems. He wants to see what is not there."

"Does it mean there is no victim?"

"Not at all, Frank. We, at this point, do not know. So, we look. We haven't found Mrs. Feldman yet, have we? I understand this is the home of another older woman. It could mean anything. Call me."

As Mulligan opened the rear of his van, Nagler spotted police photographer Robbie Karpinski assigned to the scene.

"Robbie. Shoot the crowd."

"What?"

"The crowd. Shoot the crowd. Makes sense. Don't you do that at fire scenes? Why not here?"

The photographer nodded. "Yeah. Got it. Catching on, there, Frank."

Nagler patted the man's back. "Right. I wish."

Nagler arrived at the front of the house in time to hear Chris Foley say, "I don't believe that you are telling us everything, Mr. Smith. I could ask you to come to our headquarters."

"What would you like me to say?" Mr. Smith yelled back, leaning forcefully over the shorter Foley. "I told you my mother was here approximately four weeks ago, and that she leaves the house, the state and even the country without consulting me. I live in Manhattan. She is a grown woman of independent means and does not have to consult with me. Should she at her age? Perhaps, yes. But she doesn't. It has been her habit, annoying as it is, for all my adult life. It has been her way. If you'll excuse me, I need to hire a locksmith to repair the front door, since you chose not to wait for me to arrive with a key."

"Couldn't wait," Foley spat. "Someone could have been in trouble..."

"I was five minutes away, Detective."

Foley and Smith stared at each other in a steaming silence.

Nagler nodded to Foley as if to say, "Walk away for a minute. Let me try."

Foley glared at Nagler, then at Smith, and finally stepped back.

"Mr. Smith. I'm Detective Frank Nagler. I understand your concern."

Smith scowled, waved his hands and then clenched his fists. "I…"

"Look," Nagler said firmly. "This is the second call we have received in the past three weeks about an older woman missing from her home. I know you understand your mother's habits, but I was told there was a pot of soup on the stove that had been there so long it rotted. That has to be troubling, correct? Would your mother leave a pot of soup on the stove and then go on an extended trip? How old is your mother?"

Smith sighed the bluster away. "Probably not, detective. Of course. But, she'd been known… She's seventy-two. In good health."

"There is always a 'but,' sir." Nagler said. "Why the soup?"

"She was a very generous woman, officer. She volunteered all over. She probably made that soup for the food bank."

"Thanks, Mr. Smith. That's good. The food bank. Something we can follow up on. I'm just trying to slow you down here. Your mind is running at a million miles an hour. You're trying to think of everything she could have done and everywhere she might have gone. Take a breath or two."

Smith wiped his face with a large white handkerchief that he had taken from an inside jacket pocket. He folded it in half, and then in half again before replacing it. He glanced up at the house and then into the street before taking a deep breath.

"So," Nagler said. "The soup. That would be recent. Is there any chance that she would have made the soup and someone else was supposed it to take to the food bank? Someone else who might have a house key? Is there one hidden on the property?"

"That's possible," Smith huffed. "You know, Detective" — Smith was at the end of his patience — "I don't know my mother's friends, or her social calendar. As I said, she was an independent woman and had a lot of money. She outlived three husbands, had invested well, and despite my advice, seem hell-bent on spending as much of it as she could before she died."

Nagler smiled. "That's good. I'm going to ask you to walk through the house with an officer, just to see if anything might be missing. It could be important. Okay?" Nagler nodded toward a patrol officer. "Would you please accompany — I'm sorry, what is your name?"

"Gregory. Gregory Smith."

"And what do you for a living?"

Smith furrowed his eyebrows and shook his head. "I'm a banker," he said with some irritation. "Corporate banking. Executive vice president. We're worldwide." He retracted a gold business card holder and passed a card to Nagler.

That wasn't so hard, Nagler thought.

"How is it that you happen to be here, in Ironton?" Nagler asked.

"I was in town for a development meeting when I got a call about an alarm at my mother's house," Smith said.

"Alarm?"

"Burglar alarm," Smith said with force. "Turned out to be you cops breaking in the front door."

Nagler shrugged. "From what I understand so far there was some emergency call, and the smell…"

Smith closed his eyes and shook his head once. "Fine."

"Do you know the name of the alarm company?"

"No. I don't, Detective," Smith yelled. "If you don't mind."

Nagler took a step back. "Okay. Thanks." He nodded to a nearby patrolman, who stepped toward the house with Gregory Smith.

Foley, who had been standing off to the side, turned back to face Nagler.

"Don't ever…"

"I can see why you were yelling at him," Nagler said lightly. "Do you suspect him of something?"

"Look, Detective Nagler…"

Nagler's face hardened and his voice took on a deep authority. "No, Detective Foley. I don't know what kind of a bug you've got up your ass, but we have to work together on this, right? I don't really care about how much of a senior detective you are."

Foley squinted at the ground and then up at Nagler. "Okay. You know I heard about you from some of the department guys who were let go. Said you were a hard-ass. Not a game player."

"What kind of game are we playing here, Detective Foley?"

Foley turned and walked into the street. "You'll figure it out," he said over his shoulder. He stood in the street and his shoulders rose and fell as he took several deep breaths.

Nagler closed his eyes and settled into a calmness. What have I got myself into? First big case and I'm fighting with cops over it?

"Officer," Gregory Smith yelled as he lumbered down the steep front stairs.

Before he could speak Nagler asked, "Is there a back way into the house? These stairs seem quite steep for an older person to use daily. A back door that leads to more level ground?"

"Yes, of course. There is a back porch that leads to the yard. The driveway and garage are accessed by that side street."

Nagler followed Smith's pointing finger to a narrow lane beyond a stone pillar that marked the boundary of Edie Smith's property. Came from money, he thought. No joke.

"Was that back door locked, Mr. Smith?"

"I would guess so…" Smith shrugged.

"Her car?"

"Doesn't own one. Stopped driving years ago."

Foley jumped in. "Was anything missing in the house?"

Gregory Smith shook his head. "Nothing of value," he said.

"But something was missing?" Foley asked.

"A doll. A handmade cloth doll that students at the community center gave her a few years ago. She supported the center financially and volunteered there a few days a month."

"Why did you notice that it was missing?" Nagler asked.

Smith waved his hands and shook his head. "It was on the mantle, always. Why would someone take that?"

"If she was traveling, would she take it with her?" Nagler asked.

Smith shook his head vigorously and turned to stare back at the house. "No, officer. She barely took it down to dust it." His eyes narrowed and his face sagged. "Now I am worried."

****

A further search of Edie Smith's home found jewelry in place, even a hundred-and-ten dollars in small bills on a bedroom table, and no disruption of the home at all. Didn't seem that the home had been robbed. The mantle where the doll had been placed was examined for prints, but none other than Edie Smith's were found.

Nagler stared at the kitchen.

Why here?

It seemed to be the center of, whatever it was. At a second review, it seemed to be messier and dirtier than the rest of the house. Like someone had not completely cleaned up after making homemade soup, Nagler thought; when his mother had made soup bits of chopped vegetables, potatoes, and other ingredients were found in the sink and on counters until the soup had started cooking. Maybe that was just Edie Smith's life: Soup for the poor. And driving her son crazy by leaving without a message; not a power struggle I'd want to referee, he thought.

A random note: was that soup fully cooked?

Did someone drag you out of your house while you were cooking? he wondered. Did you wander off and forget you were making the soup?

And then turn off the gas?

He sighed. Another old lady.

The sourness that had been grinding in his stomach for couple of days rose up and twisted his face. They just don't wander off, do they?

Samples were taken of dried liquids on the counter near the stove and a smear of something dried on the light switch. "Is that blood?" Nagler asked the crime tech. The guy shrugged and took a sample.

Nico Gonzalez, the manager of the soup kitchen, later confirmed that Edie Smith prepared a big pot of soup twice a month. It was usually cooked, but not always, he said. "We can cook it here, and sometimes Miss Edie was in a hurry." Volunteers would pick it up, Gonzalez said. They used a spare key stashed in the garage, entered the home and took the soup. Later, they would return the clean pot the same way.

Gonzalez said he had been waiting for her call about the soup.

"But, Miss Edie, sometimes, she forget to call," he said.

Which left them with nothing. Maybe, she is traveling the world, Nagler thought sourly.

"Hey, Frank. We found these."

It was Lieutenant Dan Nelson. He had led the team that had searched the hilly neighborhood where Smith's home was located.

"Newspapers?"

"Yeah, newspapers. Eight of them."

Nelson dumped the soggy papers on Nagler's desk. "Eight," Nelson said, and then shrugged. "I got no idea."

Nagler nodded his head. "I do. Edie Smith's son said she didn't subscribe to newspaper home delivery because she took off unannounced so often. I'll bet when I look at them, the dates are out of order, just as they were at Marion Feldman's home."

He slipped the elastic off one of the papers and rolled it flat.

"Look. Last December."

A second paper was dated February, and the third, March.

"Was someone posing as a newspaper delivery kid to stalk those two houses?"

Nelson nodded. "So…"

"We go back and see if any of the neighbors found random papers on their lawns, or if any unknown person tried to sell them a subscription. I'll call the Register and see if they received any complaints."

Nelson nodded and then left.

Son of a bitch.

Newspapers, he thought. Actually, not a bad cover if you're trying to find out who lives in what house, or what time people leave for work, if you're planning a heist, or worse. The Register was a local paper, then there was a big daily from Newark, a couple weeklies. There's the morning delivery, the collections, sales drives from time to time with kids knocking on doors and leaving door hangers. I hated sales drives. No, cost too much. What a rag… It's like electric or gas meter readers — someone in a green jacket with a patch and ball cap with a company name, and no one would question their presence.

But what do we have here? Two empty homes belonging to older women. The homes are more than a mile apart. A woman with a bad hip who didn't leave her home, and a woman who always left her home. Who would know that?

Nagler folded flat the December newspaper on his desk. The headline was about a snowstorm. Someone was stalking that place. Why there? He made a note to ask Joan Chen's neighbors about possible solicitations. Issue a citywide warning? Oh, then we'd have every utility company and delivery business in town yelling at us. Could tip off any suspects. Wait.

Edie Smith could show up tomorrow complaining that we kicked in her front door while she was in London, like her son expected, doll or no missing doll, he laughed.

But Marion Feldman? Nagler had a bad feeling, and it centered on that spot on the carpet and the strand of hair. "Oh, crap," he said. It's eight o'clock I need to get home to Martha. Haven't talked to her since this morning.

He started to collect the papers into a single pile. Could have been a fall. "I just think we would have found her," he muttered under his breath.

Her granddaughter was expected to arrive in Ironton in two days. Nagler circled the date on his desk calendar and wrote, "Feldman."

As he reached to extinguish the desk light, he heard Chris Foley yell, "Detective Nagler. Glad you're still here."

Makes one of us, Nagler thought.

Foley pushed the papers aside sat on the edge of Nagler's desk.

"Hey, look. I didn't mean to be pissy the other night. We have to work together on this. But that Gregory Smith just ticked me off. What a jerk. Did you see him with that handkerchief? Folding it ever so carefully. Man, I thought he was going to pull out a spritzer of perfume and spray it and then wave that snotrag in our faces like Louis the Fourteenth. Who does he think he is? You and me, we're just working guys, and I don't think rich guys like Gregory Smith appreciate that."

Nagler leaned back in his chair. "Okay. So..." Why does this visit seem forced, planned, part of a game?

Foley nodded. "Anyway, I got a call from him later. A little apologetic, which I appreciated. He said his mother had seven kids. Remember how he said she outlived three husbands? She had kids with each of them, gave them all trust funds as babies and they apparently live all over the country in the height of style."

"Was she in touch with any of them?"

"Gregory Smith said he has reached out to them — and his secretary will provide addresses for them all — but there is a chance she was last seen by one of them at a Florida vacation home."

Foley shook his head. "Imagine what it's like to be so rich," he mused. "We should look at the guy's bank, you know, to see if the institution is in trouble, and maybe look at the others kids' finances to see if any of them are in a bind, know what I mean?"

"But no one on the neighborhood said they had seen anyone around the house, especially the adult children," Nagler said. "Not even the woman who lived two houses down and told us she once cleaned the home, when the kids lived there. She'd know them, don't you think?"

"I guess we'll see."

Nagler pushed the chair back and stood.

"Thanks for telling me, Chris. I've got to meet my wife, so I have to leave. But all that doesn't explain the soup or the apparent mess in the kitchen. We don't know what we have in either house, although I suspect Marion Feldman is more than just missing, but where would she be?"

"Think you're right. I get the feeling that we're going to find old Mrs. Feldman's bones in the woods somewhere."

What the hell? That was the second time he had said that. Nagler fake-coughed to avoid forming an answer.

Foley pushed himself away from the corner of the desk and tipped his head to examine the papers.

"Newspapers," Nagler said, as he collected them into a single pile. "From Edie Smith's house. The search team found them, and she didn't subscribe to a newspaper."

Foley wrinkled his brow and reached for the top paper. "Interesting."

"Hey, Chris. I have to go. Wife's waiting." Nagler stopped talking, trying to disguise the irritation. What is it about this guy?

"Yeah, okay. Sure."

Nagler picked up the receiver to the desk phone and dialed a few numbers to pretend to make a call. He nodded to Foley, "See ya," and then waited as the detective walked slowly away. He then collected the papers and dropped them into the deep bottom drawer of his desk.

****

A plain cloth doll missing. A fancy bracelet found. A bunch of newspapers and red marks on walls. Totems, symbols, fetishes, things. He takes things and leaves others, Nagler mused: What did he take from Dr. Nancy Harmon, Jamie Wilson, and Felice Sanchez? What did he leave?

CHAPTER SIX

Why can't we find you?

The neighborhoods where Edie Smith and Marion Feldman lived had been searched again. Neighbors questioned, garages, sheds, and woods searched. The homes had been combed again for details, strands of information, dusted and scoured again for clues.

The test on the red stain on the light fixture at the Smith house showed it was tomato sauce, not blood. Nagler examined the photo of the switch. The sauce was deposited in an upward smear, like it was on a knuckle. I don't know what that means.

A patrol car had been rolling along Pennington Avenue near Edie Smith's house off and on since she'd disappeared. Her bank accounts had not been touched, and her passport had not been used. The announcement of her absence had been broadcast and posted. Her son had hired a security company to babysit the house, and one-by-one police had contacted her other six children, who like Gregory Smith, had little on-going contact with their mother. That's some family, Nagler thought.

Marion Feldman's home had finally been cleared for sale, her granddaughter tearfully handing the keys to a real estate agent. Nagler spent part of a day watching as the movers and house cleaners removed the last of Marion Feldman's possessions from the house and garage. If the house had been stripped by the granddaughter of most of its goods, the garage was a time capsule of Walter Feldman's life. Toolchests, lined neatly with sets of screw drivers, wrenches, hammers, bottles of screws, and loose nails stored in a wooden frame where they could be screwed into the cap for storage. Ten-year-old calendars printed by Craftsman tools, soda companies, car makers, faded red circles marking dates. Two bags of golf clubs leaned against the wall, and Nagler recalled the choking retelling of Walter Feldman's golf games with Dan Green the landscaper.

Rakes of various sized and purposes were gathered with hoes, shovels and other lawn equipment. "How come there is no wheelbarrow?" one of the movers asked absently. "With all this other stuff…"

Nagler registered the comment but was focused on the car.

He halted the removal of the ten-year-old Chrysler for one last inspection, but only found a yellowing receipt from Ironton Florists for a dozen roses under the front passenger's seat. He laughed softly. What love.

The thick dust on the Chrysler had only been disturbed by the tow-truck operator: Two glove prints on the trunk were placed there when he leaned over to connect the chain, smears at the driver's door when the key was inserted in the lock and the handle turned to open the door.

If someone killed these two older women, what was their motive? Nagler wondered. Why are you keeping it a secret?

Did Edie Smith die because she wouldn't give up an old, hand-made cloth doll, the only item her family said was missing? Doubt it.

And Marion Feldman. Her home had been nearly emptied in anticipation of her upcoming move to a nursing home. What did she die defending, if that was her fate?

"And why can't we find you?" Nagler yelled one late night at her empty house.

****

Medical Examiner Dr. Walter Mulligan peered over the tops of his glasses at Detectives Foley and Nagler.

"I'm not ready to declare either woman dead — we simply don't have enough evidence to conclude that — but after consultation with the crime scene officers and a couple experts, I believe we can say that the ruckus at the Feldman home was not the result of her taking a fall and reaching out for support. There is greater evidence of an attack."

"What do you have?" Foley asked.

Mulligan examined the photos on his desk and selected the one of the dusty palm prints on the Hoosier cabinet.

"While we initially thought that this print was a sign that Mrs. Feldman reached for the cabinet while she was falling, a closer examination discovered a partial fingernail trapped under the shelf, suggesting that she had grabbed the cabinet to resist being apparently forced into the living room," Mulligan said.

He picked up and displayed a second photo of the partial fingernail wedged under the shelf.

"The nail had some blood, and we determined that it was Mrs. Feldman's," Mulligan said firmly. "As to what happened next, all I can say is that the hair on the rug was hers and had been violently pulled from her head."

"Like she was dragged?" Nagler asked, somewhat horrified.

"Possibly," Mulligan said. "Perhaps while standing, though. You saw the room, Frank. A couple broken pieces of furniture, but not a lot general disruption."

Nagler's face closed into a sour squint. He reached out a hand and formed a fist. "Like she was dragged by her hair and tossed," he said, as he threw his arm across his body and at the peak of the shift, unclenched the fist. "Then maybe she hit the chair and that's what broke the arm."

Mulligan nodded. "Reasonable."

"But awful, Jesus. Okay? So, who are we looking for?"

"Perhaps this might help," Mulligan said, as he handed Nagler a folder on his desk. "It's newspaper clippings from about seventy years ago about the curious case of Phillip O'Hanlon, a collier. It appears he was Ironton's last serial killer."

Foley: "Collier?"

"He delivered coal," Nagler said, slightly rolling his eyes at Mulligan's archaic description. "My parents' house had a coal chute. Guys would come a couple times a month. Open the chute and slide a few wheelbarrows of coal into the coal bin in the cellar. Pretty common in Ironton at the time. The old iron mills ran on coal."

"Exactly," Mulligan said. "O'Hanlon was a mill worker who stoked the furnaces, and on the side, sold coal to homes, some, perhaps all of which he stole from his employer. He killed four people on his route. But he was remarkably average looking, kept to himself, and until he began to brag about killing women, no one really paid any attention to him. There is a newspaper story from the time with surprising details on his activity, an apparent confession. Because he was never in court. The story suggested he was drunkenly bragging about his exploits in a downtown bar one night and someone wrote it all down. The story has no byline. They found O'Hanlon in the canal."

"Why would that be of interest?" Foley asked, his faced screwed into a disapproving grimace.

Mulligan rubbed his hands together. "Because I believe that our killer is, like Phillip O'Hanlon, someone lost in the crowd. He was someone so average looking it was easy to overlook him. It seems from these stories that he was aware of how he was perceived and resented it. His acts of murder were his expression of that rage. O'Hanlon delivered coal on a regular route and his customers knew him, and never gave him a second thought. Because he was so common, no one suspected him of anything. I'd wager that until he got drunk and talked, no one would have connected him to the brutal killings he committed. I suspect he wanted to tell someone. That is some secret."

"How does that relate to our situation?" Foley asked.

"Because of the red hands," Nagler said. "I get it. He's looking for attention."

"That's right, Frank," Mulligan said. "When police returned and examined the deaths in the O'Hanlon case, they found he had left markers, in his case, his initials "OH" carved into doorframes. No one had thought anything of it." Mulligan nodded. "You're catching on, Frank. Good. We will need our best effort to capture this criminal."

Foley, stone faced, nodded. "We still need to prove it. How do you plan to do that, Detective?"

He left before Nagler could answer.

****

The next morning, Mayor Howard Newton announced a ten-thousand-dollar reward for information that led to the arrest of the killer. He had failed to tell the police chief in advance that the reward offer was forthcoming, so the department was caught without a tip line system.

Once in place, the calls received numbered in the hundreds per hour. Nagler chuckled as he had read the summary: Lots of killer cousins out there.

When Nagler got back to his desk, there were a dozen messages related to the reward announcement.

Most just left a number. One stuck out and had a note from the officer who took the call. "Sounds legit, Frank," the note said.

The message said the killer was named Charlie Adams.

Nagler had listened to the call. The background was noisy — traffic, passing voices. Probably a payphone, he thought. The voice was soft, muffled, as if spoken through fist or a cloth. "It's Charlie Adams."

It was not a name they had come across on their lists of sex offenders, violent criminals, wife beaters, armed robbers and other criminals.

Nagler wrote the name in two-inch letters with a black pen on a white sheet of typing paper and taped to the wall with the other photos, maps and case information. Right in the middle, above all the rest of the papers there.

Charlie Adams.

He stared at the name. Who the hell is that?

****

The next afternoon, Chris Foley quick-stepped into the office and found Nagler at his desk, leaning back, his fingers linked behind his head.

On the desk was a stack of crowd shots taken at the initial Edie Smith visit. On top was a somewhat blurry side shot of the kid Nagler had seen at the Marion Feldman house, the kid who tumbled down the slope and ran off when Nagler had answered the call from dispatch. Nagler had just placed the photo back on the desk and was thinking about how to find him when Foley arrived.

Foley paused at the edge of Nagler's desk and turned to the wall, his face pale and pinched.

He nodded at the wall. "Who's that?" he asked in a dry, thin voice.

"Who?" Nagler replied.

"On the wall. Charlie Adams."

Nagler spun his chair around. "A name we got from the mayor's hotline. The only name, in fact. Know the name?"

Foley seemed to be in shock; slowly recovering, he said, "No." A pause. A wistful, "Interesting. It was a call in? They aren't often known to be reliable."

He turned away from the wall.

Nagler thought Foley's tone was odd but shrugged. "True. People are turning in a lot of brothers-in-law. Still. It is a name."

"Anyway," Foley coughed out, "I think we found someone."

Nagler rocked back to a full sitting position.

"What? Who?"

"Patrol picked him up earlier this morning. He was trying to get into the garage at the Smith house. Claimed he had been sleeping there for weeks. He's downstairs in the holding cell. Slept it off."

Foley glanced at the photo on the top of the pile. "May I?"

Nagler nodded. "Know him?"

"Who is he?" Foley asked and examined the photo again.

"Some kid I saw outside the Feldman's home. He came running down that little hill at the end of West Harvard. And this was taken at the Smith house." Nagler took back the photo and placed them all in a folder and closed it. "Why would the same kid be at both places?"

Slight head shake, almost uncertain. "Naw." Non-committal.

"Sure?"

Foley tipped his head to the right then shrugged. Then shook his head vigorously.

"Thought for a moment we might have talked to him last year about a series of petty thefts on the east side. Mom-and-pops were hit. Sodas, candy, a little cash.

Turned out it was a neighborhood bunch of kids."

"Gang related?"

"Thought so at first, but it was just kids stealing stuff for kicks. Why would you think some kid did it?"

Nagler rubbed his hands together and cracked his knuckles. "Did what? Who's our guy downstairs?"

"Seems to be a regular," Foley said. "Patrol knew him."

"That's Danny Wilson," Nagler said, disappointed. "Hey, Danny." He shook the metal caged door to the holding cell to wake up the sleeping man. "Starting early this year, or what?" Nagler tuned to Foley. "Danny has a habit of breaking into houses in the fall. Gets six months at the county lock-up and basically free housing and meals for the winter. Why'd they bring him in?"

"He was breaking into the Smith garage," Foley said.

"I wasn't breakin' in. Fuckin' door was unlocked. Been like that for a long time." Wilson rolled off the cot and tumbled to the floor. He leaned back against the cot's frame, tipped his head, half smiled, and said, "Hey, Frank."

"Christ, Danny. Got kicked out of the shelter again?"

Wilson coughed loudly and gagged before vomiting up a green liquid, the odor of which pushed Nagler and Foley away from the cell.

"Sorry, man," Wilson said looking at his shirt and pants. "There's someone in that house, Frank," he said, his voice suddenly clear. "For a week or so."

"Nonsense. Patrols drive by and there's the private cops hired by the son out front," Foley said.

"I seed 'em. They're sitting in that car playin' with themselves or something. They never get out and they never check the back. In the woods, there's a path that leads to the homeless camp in that hollow behind the high school. The lady that lives in that house used to leave food in the garage for us. Where'd she go, anyway?" He kneeled on the floor. "Man, I'm gonna be sick…"

Foley covered his mouth and gagged while Nagler turned away, shut his eyes, and covered his mouth.

"Crap." The sour aroma filled the closed space. "Better get Ralph down here with a bucket of soap and bleach," Nagler said, as he pushed open the side door and stepped into the parking lot.

Outside, the air was Ironton fresh, which meant it smelled like gasoline. But it was better that the air inside that room.

Nagler scratched the back of his neck and took a deep breath.

"How long have you been in Ironton, Chris?" he asked.

"Three years. Why?"

"'Cause there's a lot of guys like Danny Wilson in this town. Drunks, addicts, down on their luck. They get hauled in for minor offences every few months. We need to sort them out from the actual potential killers."

Foley turned and leaned over the fence along the wall of the old millrace. Below, the dark, starved river rattled past the clustered rocks.

"I'm just thinking we can't rule anyone out," Foley muttered. "You don't know the heart of everyone, what they hide."

Nagler coughed out the last of Danny Wilson's green vomit scent. What the hell was that? "We need to move beyond these guys," he said forcefully. "We could arrest all of them and we won't find our killer of four women. Even on the days he's sober, Danny Wilson couldn't hold two thoughts in his head at the same time. The only thing he's killing is his liver. If we're going to seriously look at guys like him, we'd have to look at that kid who keeps showing up. I think we need to talk to him because he does keep showing up. But he's our killer? Doubt it. But he might know something."

Foley stared into the bright distance.

"Why'd that name, Charlie Adams, shake you up?" Nagler asked.

Foley's face settled into a defensive, authoritarian mask.

"Shaken up? No, Detective. I was just surprised that the hot line had produced a name so quickly." Foley stared at the ground while he answered.

Voice was too weak, Nagler thought.

"Look, I know we don't have a lot of evidence. We need to focus on what little we have tells us," he said. "Say we sit down tomorrow and you can lay out your thoughts, give us some direction. We haven't really done that yet."

Foley stepped back from the fence and over his shoulder while walking away said, "Two p.m."

Nagler watched as Foley slipped around the corner and wondered: How much am I supposed to push? I haven't got a clue about what I'm doing, but it doesn't seem that anyone else does, either. Is that how investigations go? If so, how do we catch anyone?

****

Nagler walked. Shook out the official chatter, the empty theories, the "we need to find an answer" talk. Walked into the solace of the humming Ironton streets.

An answer to what? People can leave, even an old lady with a bad hip. There's too little here, he thought. Too much space to fill, so we fill it with what we don't know; we guess.

The meeting with Foley produced some information. Nancy Harmon's sister from New York had called the department in January when a fellow doctor had called her to inquire about the locked office. The postal service reported the mail had piled up in her post office box, and a number of patients reported to the front desk their concerns about her absence.

An officer was assigned, the door was rattled, neighboring homes and businesses were questioned, the mail was retrieved. And none of that information made its way to us, Nagler thought. Why? Maybe the officer who knocked on the door was let go in the job cuts, he thought. Did his job, filed a report, now stuck in a cubbyhole somewhere, and he's gone.

Foley also had said the cab company had called in February to report Felice Sanchez missing when she didn't come back to the garage at the end of her shift; her empty cab was discovered two days later, and she was found dead in the Wilson Hotel two days after that.

Jamie Wilson's boss had called police the day after she went out for a late lunch and never came back, Foley reported.

All these pieces had never been connected because there was no reason to connect them. Three deaths about six months apart. They all seemed to be singular, random events: People die, get killed. Sometimes no one is caught.

Yet, Mulligan had said all the deaths were connected.

Why are we holding on to that key evidence?

And a second, unsettling thought: Why did Foley keep all this to himself?

Nagler walked then paused at the train station site where Joan Chen was found.

"Could we have stopped the killer and saved you?" he asked himself softly.

Then another disturbing notion: Who gains by your death?

Nagler had collected the lists, the timelines, the reports and absorbed the theories and understood that these deaths would not be solved inside the four walls of the police station.

But Mulligan's charge remained: An experiment in death. An experiment. Chemicals dumped into a glass vial, bubbling away, releasing a gas; a test. Can I get away with one? How about two. Then three. Testing methods, weapons. If I make it look random, will it take longer for them to catch on? What should I leave to tell them who I am? Because the scientist does want recognition, after all. A little at a time.

So Nagler walked.

Martha's worried face hovered as he had lain on the bed; her soft hand brushed his brow and cheek. "So much to worry about," she had said. "Give that worry to me." No, he had thought. Can't give it to you. And then she had kissed him, warm lips lingering, and in that instant, took it.

Walked. In the heated, dusky hours of midweek. Ironton streets bustling, shouting, sweaty dancing.

Past the shuttered factories, windows wired, glass broken, spider webs of debris.

He walked seeking ghosts, clues, understanding.

Are you hiding in these shadows, your face a smear on the light, an echoed voice? Are you following, spying, choosing, jumping?

I know these streets, grew up on them, chased friends down narrow alleys; waited as unsmiling mill workers trudged limping, smear-faced, back from the dark, factory hollows; listened as the wind slammed through broken windows, through thin coats, under collars.

I know how misery turns the smiles on kids' faces. Know how the darkness can descend, stealing hope.

But I don't know you. Don't know you.

Yet, Nagler thought.

Walked. Asked. Who knows; who among us knows? Knows why. Someone does.

Past the dark coolness of bars, doors open, the blast of cold from air conditioners pushing against the sidewalk heat, dry and burning, leaking jukebox sounds, the clinking glasses of afternoon loneliness.

Past the grumbling train station, soot covered seats, paint chipped, broken slats, an old lady clutching two shopping bags. An eastbound train grinds in, a whoosh of open doors, feet flat on metal stairs, slapping broken concrete, riders step from shade to glare and shield their eyes with a folded newspaper. A horn blast, squeaking metal wheels, then rolling, ground shaking, then silence.

Past the dry river bed, leaning wearily on the hot metal Sussex Street railing, head down, squinting against the watery glare cast from the last pools hidden in dry rocks and sand. Water so low from lack of rain, the banks had hardened, browned and cracked. He thought of Marion Feldman. We would have found you by now.

Walked, called out, voice raw. Demanded; waited.

Past the stoops, the blocks of neighborhood stoops; old men with straw hats and beer in brown bags, women in long, colored loose skirts yanked thigh high and waist-tied blouses yelling at kids with soccer balls to watch for cars; grandmas and diapered babies rocking in a corner of shade, sweat on soft cheeks, the sighs of innocence.

Nagler walked. Are you all safe in your friendly groups? Will your laughter protect you?

Peered into alleys seeking a shadow, down sunbaked streets, looking for a face, squinted into flashing sunlight shining off shifting windshields; into the wreckage of industries past, arched hollows in brick walls, birds flapping in gritty shade, plywood slathered doorways, dripping, softened to paper.

Are you hidden in the darkness, or standing in plain sight?

Walked; stared, seeking the soul of the city, ear tipped for a voice; questioned, waiting for a whisper. Lives on hold. A table seat empty, a question hanging, unanswered; space left where someone should be.

When do I begin to figure all this out? When do I begin to feel I'm not running behind anymore? When does this make sense?

He leaned over the railing of the Sussex Street bridge and let his mind drift like the river of dark water that floated without logic around the rocks on the banks, that curled and spiraled, and with each pass, ground away one more infinitesimal layer of stone, making sand, the tiny destruction of something solid.

He knew he needed to push the confusion aside, to ask again: What do we know?

This: Six women gone.

Not gone.

Gone could be voluntary.

They were taken.

PART TWO

How the storm builds

It is more than just a cloud that settled over this city. It is a cancer, a disease that we suck in with each breath. It flows through our lungs, stops behind our eyes so they darken with suspicion; then it settles in our veins, in our blood, replacing love with pain, leaving us with only the darkness.

— Jimmy Dawson —

CHAPTER SEVEN

Cast them out from our sight

When Nagler arrived, the end of Grant Street was awash with red and blue flashing lights and filled with huddled, shrouded clusters of neighbors either staring blankly at the ambulance that blocked the street or pointing toward some upper floor of a nearby house.

He pushed wordlessly through the grumbling crowd, looking for Officer Dedman, who was first to arrive to the reports of gunfire, and found him blocking the enraged advance of an older man waving his cap toward the ambulance, where some kid was having his arm treated. "Calm down."

"I'm gonna jus' talk to him," the man yelled. "Talk to him. Ask why he was lookin' in my windows."

"You'll do no such thing," Dedman said. "You already took a shot at him."

"What's this?" Nagler asked Dedman.

"This is Mr. Ortiz," Dedman sighed. "In the ambulance is Joshua Martin, who it seems was shot with this." He held up a pistol. "Ortiz claimed Martin was trying to break into his house, while Martin claimed he was walking down the street trying to juggle a couple of books and a couple loose cans of beer when he dropped one of the cans, which popped, after which Ortiz opened his front door and fired a couple of times, striking Martin once in the arm. Winged him."

Dedman nodded toward the house. "The beer cans are on the sidewalk, and the books are in the flowers."

"What you expect," Ortiz spit out. "Strangers on the loose. All these dead women. Could be my wife. Could be my daughters. We all waitin'. Standin' by the door with guns. What you doin' about that, huh, Mr. Officer. "What you doin' 'bout that?"

Trying, Nagler thought. We're trying.

****

The next day, Mayor Howard Newton declared a citywide nighttime curfew.

He removed his trademark white Panama hat and waved it to make every point.

"We can't have average citizens playing vigilante," Newton bellowed from the steps of City Hall. "Let the police do their job. Report suspicious activity, but do not, I repeat, do not act on your own. We don't need any more shootings."

Nagler watched the mayor from the edge of the crowd and thought that yelling at the residents was not the way to gain their support. The chatter was like leaves in the fall: Blowing wildly, swirling in harsh winds that drew curses from neighbors. It filled the dense air at Barry's. I heard of a guy on West Blackwell; my neighbor put up spotlights and double locks, bought a gun, carries a knife now, pepper spray, kids being walked to school and home again; cops on street corners, stores and parks empty at night; a lid descended, screwed tight.

"I will post police officers on every street corner," the mayor yelled out. "I'll request the National Guard. But we will have peace in this city."

It was odd, Nagler thought, that the mayor did not pledge to his voters that the murders would be solved, the criminal brought to justice, and that their lives would return to normal. Maybe I don't understand the language of politics.

Posters and flyers with photographs and phone numbers and the blaring question "HAVE YOU SEEN HER??" had been nailed to light posts and taped to the dark widows of closed businesses, a gallery of pain; a fist tightening, a hollow cry. The women on the posters were not the women we were investigating, Nagler thought as he examined two flyers glued to a telephone pole. They were younger, kids really. He didn't recognize the names or phone numbers. He closed his eyes to block the thought of more bodies, bodies discovered one by one in the dark, empty places of the city. More crying mothers, angry fathers seeking revenge. He had used his pocket knife to remove the two flyers and folded them into a jacket pocket.

As he listened to the mayor railing against the world and the inability of his police department to solve a simple crime, he pulled out the flyers and glanced at them. He screwed up his face. The paper seemed wrong, like school art paper. The photos seemed wrong, yearbook pictures, and the block printing seemed childlike. He shook his head and put the photos back in a pocket.

Still, the department had assigned an officer to chase down the women in the photographs. Maybe one of the flyers would produce a lead.

But, Nagler thought, there was a something wrong there. Dozens of Ironton women did not just go missing at the same time.

The police chief had held two press conferences in an effort to calm rising fears. Extra patrols. State police working with Ironton Police. A special phone line for emergency calls and another for tips.

The preachers and the doom-sayers were out. Soapbox criers calling for the end of the world. Black-cloaked and wailing like the Puritans at the Salem Witch Trials. Stone them, hang them, oh, this unholy place where the demon walks among us.

Nagler heard them, gathered at the train station and the China Song restaurant with their sign-waving, murmuring followers, Oh, yes. Dear Lord. Condemn the wicked. A shout! Cast them out from our sight. Send them back to their own kind. Make an example of them and lead us to the salvation.

The city air, heated to a flash point by the long dry spell, was singed with talk, fevered with anguish and fear and damnation. No wonder the old men sit behind the closed doors with loaded guns, Nagler thought. That scene the other night on Grant Street was just the beginning, he knew.

Once, as he watched a rapturous gathering outside Saint Francis Catholic Church, Sister Katherine, the old nun who had run the Catholic grade school, sidled up to him and said, "Ah, they would do better to be in church on Sunday, dear boy. They would be surprised though that God would seek redemption and forgiveness in their hearts, not revenge."

Nagler had laughed. Sister Katherine was the most un-religious of any of the nuns he had known, skeptical of doctrine, yet in her work on the poor side of town, she practiced the most basic tenets of her faith; the important part of "God's work" in her life, she told him more than once, was not about preaching, but about offering hope. Saving souls came after a warm blanket and a meal, she would say.

As he watched the mayor, Nagler wondered what was in the heart of Howard Newton.

Newton was a hustler. A small-time produce merchant, he had maneuvered his way into political power and two terms as mayor. Somewhere he picked up the white Panama, which made him look suspiciously like Boss Hogg, the crooked sheriff from that hillbilly television show. Nagler had wondered if he understood that, but then decided with Newton it didn't matter.

Standing with Newton was the police chief and Senior Detective Chris Foley, newly appointed head of the serial killer investigation.

Nagler had been told that morning that he was now working under Foley, who had not issued new directives, but instead offered a pep talk; viewed on the City Hall steps, Nagler thought, Foley was a little too grabby, vigorous handshakes and a fist grabbing an elbow, a too-broad smile and a suit that seemed a little bit over polished, a little too fancy for a cop.

"We'll see," Nagler had said to himself.

He turned away from the crowd and headed for Richman Avenue to poke around an empty warehouse where callers had said they had seen strangers breaking in.

"Hey, Nagler."

He turned to find reporter Jimmy Dawson crossing Sussex Street.

"So, what do you think?" Dawson asked, squinting.

"About what?"

"Foley and the whole serial killer plan. Weren't you the lead on that?"

"Unofficially. We're just getting organized," Nagler replied "Lot of guys in new positions, including me." He looked back at the mayor. "Probably too many. Look, I'm not commenting for your story, Dawson," Nagler said, turning away.

"Not looking for one," Dawson said as he glanced back to City Hall to see the mayor's hat slip inside the front door. "I'm new to this beat. So, I'm looking for friends."

"Sources?"

"I got sources. Need people I can trust. Look, the more I get involved with the department, the more I can see that there's a lot of stuff going on — power games, favors being done, some ranking officers taking order from outsiders."

"So, there's a lot of back-slapping. Since when is that different?" Nagler said.

"Because it's more than that," Dawson said. "Maybe as a new detective you don't want to see it. I'm outside looking in…"

"You think I'm a dishonest cop?" Nagler's voice flared. "You need to be careful, buddy."

Dawson held up a hand. "Hey, hey. No. Not at all. But I can see it. Remember that case a few months back about the busted parking meters?"

"Vaguely," Nagler said squinting to recall.

"That's what they wanted," Dawson said. "For everyone to vaguely recall it. It got buried, because someone was skimming funds. Those meters weren't broken, they were rigged."

"Why didn't you write about it?"

"I was still in sports. Adam Kalinsky was assigned the story, and then it disappeared."

Nagler nodded. "I remember him. A big deal hotshot. Right?"

"Was," Dawson said, screwing up his face. "Left all of a sudden. I got his beat and his notebooks."

"Sick?"

"Booze, maybe drugs. Either way…"

Nagler scratched his neck and let out a long breath.

"Hey look, Dawson…"

"Jimmy. Call me Jimmy."

"Okay. I gotta run. Checking on an empty warehouse. Maybe our killer is there." He shook his head, chuckled, then coughed, a catch in his throat, as the disappointment of being downgraded on the case finally surfaced. "Why are you telling me all this?"

"'Cause Foley is Newton's inside man." Dawson squinted up at Nagler. "Read it in the notebooks. Don't trust him."

Nagler's face hardened; then he stared into the distance. Softly: "I became a police officer because I watched the mill wear down my father until he was just a nub of a man, back bent, knees broken, earning, but not earning enough to keep the winter cold out all the time. It killed him. The job, impossibly hard, the mill owners, greedy to a fault, careless men using up their workers a dozen at a time, until there was no need for them. I try to stand up for them, guys like my father. If you're looking for someone to play that inside game, look elsewhere."

How noble, Dawson thought. He pursed his lips, nodded once, and turned away then back. "You don't have to play it, Frank. Just know that it's being played. Know the rules, because one day when you think you're free and clear, it'll be waiting for you in the alley. Just sayin'."

Nagler watched as Dawson turned and with one hand raised, skipped through the traffic on Sussex before entering City Hall. He felt a distance descend like a haze.

****

"Peterso... Manu... Ironton."

Letters lost, not even the ghostly outline stuck to the thick, gray-green glass of the front door. Nagler knew the place, Peterson Manufacturing Inc. They had made denim work clothes, heavy stuff for mine and factory workers; his father's Peterson coat had hung on a peg in the kitchen the day he went to the hospital for the last time.

A battered sign advertised the place for sale; wind had torn away the last three digits of the company's telephone number at the flapping end of the sign.

Nagler shuffled along the block-long brick structure, pausing now and again to peer into the lighted windows of the opposing homes to gauge how anyone there might have seen someone on the street. He rattled a metal door at a loading dock in the middle of the building, but it did not budge. Where did they see our strangers?

At the end of the building, a rusted chain-link fence had been rolled back to create an opening to what probably used to be the main loading area, now cluttered with broken wooden pallets and the wreck of an old trailer. The river, shallow from the dry months, whispered over exposed rocks beyond the leaning fence.

The whole place was too quiet, Nagler thought. Where are the kids playing in the street, the cars, trucks slamming loads at the junk yard next door? Our parents couldn't keep us out of a place like this, he chuckled.

Have we scared them so much no one will even venture out during the daytime?

A metal door leaned open at the far corner of the building. The doorknob was broken, the lock hollowed out, and the dust was smeared along the outside edge, brushed away by many recent hands.

Inside, a gray film of sunlight brushed past the dirty glass to filter to the cluttered floor. A trail of footsteps had kicked aside the dust layers on the wooden floor. Could be anyone.

Metal stairs to the wrecked upper floors swayed with a ghostly creak when he pushed on them, so Nagler chose not to climb up. Whoa. He flinched as pair of pigeons dropped in flight from the dark rafters.

Looks like a homeless hovel, he decided. Wood scraps arranged to make small covering sheds, old rags, blankets piled around the edges, torn plastic sheeting draped over the tops to keep out the dripping water; here and there the burned scars of small fires, ripped sweaters, empty food cans, cracked pints of Canadian, forties of Miller Highlife.

He found an old broom handle and poked at the loose piles of stuff, chasing out an occasional rat.

He frowned. He knew the old stoveworks complex on the west side was a winter home for a homeless community, so why not here?

Maybe that's who the neighbors saw.

A black plastic bag drew his attention. It was dusty, but too clean to have been in that building for long. He dragged it out of the corner and while rolling it over with the broom handle, caught one corner on a nail head, causing a tear.

He leaned over and stuck a finger into the hole, and then grabbed the edges with both hands, widened the hole, and pulled out a garment.

It was a skirt; wool blend, it seemed.

He partly pulled out another piece and saw it was a blouse.

Jesus.

Nagler stood up and quickly scanned the dark corner of the mill. There were no other plastic bags.

Wish I brought my car, I could call this is in, he thought.

Instead he gathered up the bag and covered the hole he had made as well as he could.

He scanned the space before him, squinting into the fading light.

What are we going to find here?

He had turned to walk out of the mill, when the rear door opened.

"Hey!" Nagler yelled, and then began to run.

It was that kid. The one sliding down the cliff at the Feldman home, and in the crowd at Edie Smith's.

"Hey, wait," Nagler yelled.

The kid paused, and then grinning, jumped off the platform and disappeared.

As he ran to the door, the bag slipping in his arms, Nagler glanced out the factory windows on Richman Avenue to see if the kid ran past.

Shit. Probably went over that back fence into the junk yard.

Nagler ran to the gate, struggling with the torn plastic bag, and yelled at a worker, "See a kid come through here?"

The worker, baffled, yelled back, "No."

Nagler walked a few blocks till he got to the Salem Street Bridge and, leaning on the railing, glanced back toward the Peterson mill. He scratched his head and spit into the dark water below. He glanced at the torn, black bag.

"Who the hell are you?"

****

Foley barged into the Mulligan's office while an officer carefully removed the garments from the bag and spread them across a couple tables.

"What's this," Foley said as he reached of the black bag. "Why didn't you call me, Detective?"

"Don't touch it," Mulligan demanded. "Possibly evidence."

Foley paused, hand still suspended above the bag, then stepped back. "From where?"

"The Peterson mill," Nagler said. "Neighbors had reported strangers there, remember?" He paused. "You sent me."

"Okay, right."

"You alright, Detective Foley?" Mulligan asked. "You seem out of sorts."

Foley stared at the clothing then shook his head. "Just busy." Then to Mulligan. "The guy just left it?"

"We don't know what this is yet,' Mulligan said. "It could be a bag of clothes stolen from wash lines. Frank said there seemed to be evidence of people living in the mill."

"We need to get—"

"Already did," Nagler said, trying to disguise the irritation he felt. "And I asked Sergeant Hanrahan to assign a rolling patrol to the neighborhood because that kid was there. And I asked Sal, I mean Sergeant LaStrada, to send a unit to photograph and document the building contents."

Foley squinted. "What kid?"

Nagler pulled from his jacket a copy of the photo and handed to Foley. "This kid. I showed you his picture before. He was there, trying to enter the place as I was leaving. He ran off. He's been at two of the homes where missing women lived, at a shuttered factory, to the point apparently of bothering neighbors, who have been asked by the city to call in suspicious persons, and if our drunk witness to the Chen murder scene was right, the kid fits the description of someone leaving there in a hurry." Nagler hoped that his comment did not sound as sarcastic as it did in his head. "Maybe we'd like to speak with him. Didn't you say you thought you knew him?"

Foley handed back the photo. "Might have been wrong. There's a lot of kids out there like him. Post it on the wall. We'll see." He handed Nagler several sheets of paper. "Here's a list of known sex offenders. Need to check on their whereabouts."

"None of victims have been sexually assaulted, that we know of, right, Doc?" Nagler said. Mulligan did not respond. "I know that we can't tell that about the woman found at the bog, but Garcia and Chen were not. So…?"

"Experts say that some serial killers are sexually driven, and it manifests itself in violence," Foley said.

Manifests, Chris?

"But they also say that it can be about power," Nagler said, then smiled. "I did some reading after Dr. Mulligan brought up the topic."

"What's more powerful than rape?" Foley asked with an edge. "Are we going to have a problem here, Detective?"

Nagler pretended to read the papers, just so he didn't have to answer Foley.

"No problem, Detective," Nagler said after a moment.

"Gentlemen," Mulligan interrupted. "This is not the time for debate. Could we please focus?"

"Sorry, Doc, "Nagler said.

"Report your findings to me, Detective," Foley said. "Doctor." He nodded to Mulligan.

Nagler watched Foley spin on his heels and march stiffly away.

****

The black bag contained six pieces of women's clothing: The skirt that Nagler first saw, two blouses of different styles and sizes, a light jacket, two pairs of pants, one dressy and one casual, and a bra.

"Looks like a granny bra," Nagler said, trying not to smile. The cups seemed excessively large and reminded him of the end of his mother's life, when it seemed the only thing that had not shrunken on her was her bosom, which she covered with a kitchen apron.

"Detective!" Mulligan scolded lightly.

"Sorry." Nagler turned to hide his smile. "Those clothes are not from a single woman, are they?"

Mulligan flipped the pages of a chart he was holding.

"And I'm not sure they fit our victims," he said. "Joan Chen is too small for any of these items to fit her, and she was clothed when we found her. Miss Garcia was a slightly larger woman and might have worn casual pants to her job as a cab driver, but these pants seem too large."

He put down the chart. "This could just be a bag of clothes, perhaps stolen. You indicated the building could house homeless, so, perhaps..."

"Maybe. But why steal a bra?" Nagler asked. "That's odd." He rubbed his neck. "Know what? I'll ask the families to look at photos of the clothes. Maybe they'll remember something."

****

Retired Detective Bill Lawrence wiped the bar when Frank Nagler sat and greeted him. Lawrence had been pushed out of the department in the latest budget purge and turned his part-time bar tending job at Dominic's into a full-time spot.

"Actually, didn't mind, Frank," Lawrence said. "The place had gone to hell. No resources, old cars, bad radios. So many cuts over the years, left too many of the wrong people in the wrong spots, know what I mean? With bad feet and all," his face shrugged, lips pursed, nose wrinkled, "Time to go."

Nagler nodded. "But aren't you on your feet all the time behind the bar?"

Lawrence laughed. "Ain't the same. Better shoes and rubber mats. I've actually lost weight. Besides I don't work the busy night shifts. A little running at lunch, but a lot of time watching reruns on the TV."

"Department's not any better now," Nagler said. "Made a lot of cuts, but there's no money to make things better. So, we slog on." A pause. "Mind if I ask you about Jamie Wilson?"

Lawrence's face soured; he motioned for Nagler to take a seat at the far end of the bar. "Wondering when someone would ask," he said.

"Yeah. I'll bet," Nagler said. "Sorry it took so long."

Lawrence laughed softly. "You're working with Foley, right? Not a surprise. The man's a phony, Frank. Be careful. There's no one he won't try to screw."

Nagler stared at the table and made no reply. "Jamie Wilson."

Lawrence squinted to jog his memory. He had a face that had seen to many late, dark nights, too many stinking alleys, heard too many lies that stuck to his skin like August sweat. The squint pulled the lines around his eyes into focus and his mouth to a tight line.

Nagler perused Lawrence's face. When you've seen as much as he had, he guessed, a confusion settles in your eyes because after all that time, you understand there are no answers, just fewer questions.

"Yeah, so she's in the Old Iron Bog," Lawrence began. "Dumped in the weeds. Just bones." His voice softened, wandering. "Had a scarf wrapped around her throat, clothes had been ripped away. Couldn't tell if it was the killer or animals. Her car was on the road, Mount Pleasant, door open, but that you know."

"How come no one had reported the car to us?" Nagler asked.

"It's the bog. Nobody goes there. End of winter, no young lovers, know what I mean?" A hollow laugh.

"But she was found by a guy dumping car parts. Right?"

"But farther down, toward Hancock. There's a flat spot. He pulled back on the road, saw the VW. He told me he thought about towing it away, using it for parts."

Nagler nodded, "Really?" He tipped a shoulder. "Man. Then what?"

Lawrence let out a long breath. "Then not much, Frank. You saw the reports. We talked to her friends, family, boss, the bartenders. There was one guy, an ex, nasty split, but he was out of town. Her car showed nothing. Figured it was a rape then a murder." He stared past Nagler to the wall covered with sports memorabilia.

"One death in a city of thousands. Wanted it to be more, Frankie. But couldn't get there. Felt bad for her family."

Nagler nodded. "We had a name called into the hot line. Charlie Adams. Ring a bell?"

Lawrence wiped his mouth. "Yeah. Some kid punk asshole on the east side. Small-time shit."

"Why would his name come up on a murder hot line?" Nagler asked.
"Don't know. Maybe there's more than one."

****

Sunlight drained away from Ironton's streets; shadows rose from silent, steaming sidewalks.

Nagler stared at the red print and the slogan HAND OF DEATH that had been painted on the side of the old train station.

Mayor Newton had ordered them removed, but the police chief overruled the order declaring they were evidence in the crime investigation; to reinforce that declaration, he ordered foot patrols to pass by the sites during all shifts.

Nagler had a thought that not just the placement of the markings, but how they were placed, might help identify…what do we call him? he asked himself, staring at the creepy, dripping handprint. We don't know that the killer placed the handprints, but we can assume that. Makes sense, but there's no real proof.

As he had examined the photos of the marking, Nagler decided they did not give a full representation of the scenes.

Standing close to the wall of the train station, he reached up with his right hand that was holding a pencil and scratched a line at the top of his reach. He took one step to his right and with his left hand, repeated the action.

He was about to measure the height of the pencil marks, when Chris Foley bolted from the main door of City Hall and, without looking, ran across Sussex Street into the alley adjacent to the drug store.

Where's that boy going?

Nagler pocketed the pencil and tape measure and slipped over to Richman Avenue. Behind the drug store was an alley that led to a dark pathway along the river; Nagler knew he could view that path from the overgrowth and building gaps along Richman which traced the river from the opposite bank. And if Foley wasn't on that path, Nagler could cross to Bergen and then down to Blackwell.

Even in the fading light, Foley was east to spot. His pale blue sports coat flashed when he stepped from dark to light as he passed through the dappled tree cover along the river. He had stopped running, but skipped a few steps, and then walked briskly till he reached the fenced parking lot that once been the site of a nightclub that had burned down decades ago; a mob arson, the story said.

Then he stopped and pulled out a handkerchief and wiped his forehead and neck. Nagler watched as Foley shook out the handkerchief, folded it in half and then in half again before dabbing his upper lip and slipping it into an inside jacket pocket.

Nagler, in the shadow of a vacant house across the lot, nearly laughed, but coughed it back. And Foley thought Gregory Smith with his elaborate hanky waving was a dandy. Oh, man.

Foley jerked his head around, and said, "What the hell are you doing?"

Shit! Caught, Nagler thought.

But then Foley said, "You can't let anyone see you."

Nagler heard a voice reply, but not the words.

Foley: "Good. Just be careful. You getting caught is not going to help us."

The other person stayed in the shadows while they talked, the conversation lost in a sudden burst of traffic along Richman.

Then they parted. Nagler waited till he saw Foley turn to Blackwell and then west, then he stepped from behind the house, across a lot to Salem, and searched for someone who might seem to be in a hurry.

The street was empty. Nagler strolled along Salem toward Blackwell, peering around the corners of shops and bars, into the alleys between houses and saw no one.

****

POLICE PROGRESS IN DEATHS.

The headline screamed out in double-sized black print wherever Nagler looked as he scanned Barry's lunch crowd. Damn Dawson again.

I understand the need to keep the public calm, but to outright lie? Nagler thought. What will we tell them in two months when we don't know any more than we know now and still haven't made an arrest?

"Good news?" Barry asked as he refilled Nagler coffee cup.

"It's good news that no one else has died," Nagler replied. "But..." He slumped back into the seat. "I don't know. We're working."

Foley had at least backed off playing boss. Maybe he had exhausted all of his grand schemes, or the case seemed as baffling as it had been all along. Need to find out who he was meeting with, Nagler thought.

Either way, after detectives had sought the locations of sex offenders, drug users, dealers, car thieves, bookies, or anyone one else with a police record, Foley admitted it was back to examining what they knew: Four women were taken off the streets of Ironton and killed, and two older women were missing from their homes.

The diner's front door banged open and Nagler glanced up to see Jimmy Dawson squinting around the room and then with a quick smile, moved toward Nagler's table in the rear.

No, no, Nagler thought sourly, but then offered a stiff nod as Dawson motioned to the empty seat. "Thanks," Dawson said.

Nagler held up the front page declaring progress in the case.

"Did you have even the slightest doubt?" he asked.

Dawson smiled briefly and sighed.

"You know the old expression about keeping your enemies close…"

"Who's the enemy?"

"Foley. He's one of the most ambitious knob polishers I've come across," Dawson said. "And I'm from a business where grandstanding is like breathing."

He nodded to Barry for a cup of coffee.

"Look. I know Foley is lying about stuff. He hints about information he might have, people I should speak with who might have something of interest." Barry brought the coffee and Dawson said, "Thanks. I knew guys like that in sports. Players trying to get a coach they didn't like in trouble. Bitching about playing time, their pay, the locker room… whatever."

Nagler leaned back and absorbed Dawson's description of Foley. Maybe I could get along with this guy, he thought.

"But this story is mostly a lie," Nagler said, pointing to the paper. "Look, I know Foley. He wants to be standing next to the mayor when we name the killer, well, when we, us working cops, find the killer, and the mayor takes credit for it. And you'll put that photo on page one. Between you and me, we really know nothing about this case, just that four women are dead, and two others are missing. Don't you worry that your paper would help create a false sense of security or turn this horrible set of events into happy news?"

Dawson leaned into to his cup of coffee and sighed.

The Red Hand

"People believe what they want to believe. Look at that big bank fraud story out of Washington, savings and loans? Look at the spin put on that one. I'm more concerned that the big guys will try to manipulate the facts to keep the populace fat and happy, and I have a publisher who will hitch his sail to that breeze as long as it suits him."

He placed his elbows on the table and leaned close to Nagler.

"It's like this: Tell a lie the same way long enough people believe it. Need a killer? Find one. Blame him. Bury his past, but he hasn't got much of one to begin with. He's a nobody, no one would miss him. He can't explain where he was on March thirteenth at ten in the evening, because he probably wasn't anywhere. No one saw him. No one will defend him. Get him a public defender who wouldn't know court procedure if it was tattooed on his arm, present a lot of circumstantial evidence and ya got a conviction. The city takes a deep breath and the mayor gets re-elected."

Nagler smiled. "So, between you and me, what do you think about this case?"

Dawson glanced around the diner to see if anyone was paying attention then grinned. "I think you're all fucked."

Nagler swallowed a chuckle. "I might agree, but why?"

"Besides the fact that you have virtually no evidence? Two empty houses, three women left dead in odd places, and even with the killing of the restaurant manager, the ME didn't find what he would usually expect to find at a crime scene. He told you that, right? So, you're all guessing."

"What, this is the smartest killer in the history of the world and we'll never catch him?"

"Not at all." Dawson leaned in. "I'm an outsider to this but here's how I see it. The guy was operating in the shadows before, but after Joyce Chen's death, the spotlight was brighter." He waved his hands. "And it is. You've got cops on street corners at night, patrolling in cars." Dawson nodded at Nagler. "And you, you're running all over the place tracking down tips, kicking in doors of empty buildings…"

"I don't kick them in," Nagler laughed.

"Whatever. The next time he kills, you guys will almost expect it. But you won't catch him then. But he's gonna make a mistake. Then he'll kill again just to show off. Then it will be a race to catch him before he does it again."

83

Nagler covered his mouth with both hands and exhaled.

"If I didn't know better, your description could be taken as a game plan for a serial killer," he said.

"Oh, please," Dawson, said. "I got it out of a text book." He laughed softly and shook his head. "You'll get him."

They exchanged a hard glance and then looked away.

"Foley's gonna be the problem, you know," Dawson said. "He sees this case as his path to chief, and maybe mayor, when Newton retires."

"Yeah, I know…Not much to do about that."

"Except be the guy who catches the killer." Dawson raised an eyebrow and tipped his head.

"We all want that." Nagler replied, dismissing the notion.

"Oh, I know. But, hey, you'll get him."

Nagler let a silence fall between them. Maybe this is how the game is played. He reached inside his jacket pocket. "Wanna help, you know, you and your awakened cynic?"

Dawson screwed up his face. "What."

"Help me find this kid," Nagler said as she slipped Dawson a copy of the photo of the unknown boy.

"Who is he?"

"Don't know, but he's been near three investigative scenes and he ran out of that warehouse I told you I was looking into. Might be nothing, but then…"

"Okay, a test. Interesting."

"Maybe," Nagler said. "Or maybe I need help finding the kid. Just don't put the picture in the paper. There is no prize."

Dawson nodded and grinned. "Yeah, okay. I get it. What's in it for me?"

"Questions to ask."

Dawson smiled. "Got it." Then he left.

A step, Nagler thought, smiling. One step; one he never thought he'd take.

CHAPTER EIGHT

Romeo

The river flowed like sluggish gold, dripped in the setting sunlight below the bluff; to the east the water darkened to orange, then purple, and then the shoreline slipped to darkness.

The park above was silent, save for the separate calls of a pair of jays that rattled the treed edges. The day's heat hovered.

Nagler absorbed the park's shaded silence with a deep breath as he shed the clattering investigation; soaked it in to purge from his head the clamor of the past ten days; welcomed the semi-darkness to cover scenes of flashing lights, the pale face of the latest victim; drew in the drifting aroma of the wild roses that draped the wooden fence along the bluff.

Martha, laughing, had run ahead of him into the park, a favorite place. There were spots in the dark corners of bushes and behind the mossy boulders that they had claimed, socks and panties left behind, forgotten in haste, mud on teenaged shoulders and knees explained to parents through finger covered mouths.

Martha picked a spent rose from a bush as Frank arrived at her side and pulled off the remaining petals one by one. Teasing: "He loves me." She smiled and wiggled her eyebrows. "He loves me not." She shook her head. "Oh, you fool. He loves me…smart man…uh-oh, you're in trouble, Frank. There's only one more petal and it's a 'loves me not.' What are you gonna do about that, huh, buddy?"

Nagler snatched the flower from her hand and tossed it over the bank. "Guess we'll never know," he said as he kissed her neck.

"Oh!" She leaned over the fence and with comic drama reached for the falling flower. "Ah, me. Lost." She faced her husband. "What if that had been me, falling into the darkness?"

Nagler touched her face and then ran a finger across her lips. "I would have caught you."

Her eyes grew dark, half closed. "There will be a time when you won't be able to, you know."

He stared at his wife, at her lower lip gripped between her teeth, the darkness around her eyes, and decided the whole thing this time was an act. She had done it when she first got sick years ago; it was how as kids they held off the horrible alternative.

"Bet your ass I would," he said in his best wise-guy voice as he leaned into her and pinched her ass.

"Oh, good." She laughed, pushed him off and turned to face the river and pulled her hair to one side. "Zipper," she whispered.

****

Martha shivered when she rolled her bare back on the wet, cool lawn; her hair stuck to her shoulders and legs, and strands were glued to her sweaty breasts.

"How many times have we been here?" she asked, smiling, an arm draped across her head.

"Enough times so we should remember to bring a blanket," he laughed.

"Do you remember the first time we came here?" Martha asked as she picked another rose, this one freshly petaled, and inhaled its soft scent. Then she offered it to him, and he buried his nose in the flower before kissing her hand.

"It was seventh grade, after you played Juliet, opposite, what was his name?"

"Bennie Garza," she smiled. "Bennie, Bennie, where for art thou, Bennie? He was always trying to tongue me when we kissed. But I had braces, and he'd jam his tongue against them. I almost laughed in the death scene."

She threw an arm across her breasts. "I pointed at you in the front row when I said, 'Where for art thou, Romeo.'"

"I remember. I felt there wasn't anyone else in that auditorium but you and me."

He leaned over to kiss her but stopped and pulled down her lower lip. "Nope. No braces."

She smiled and bit his finger. "And then you were mad at me the entire time we were here because you had just wanted to make out in the bushes and all I had wanted to do was recite Shakespeare, I loved the language so much," she laughed, then rolled sideways to kiss him. "I was still high from the performance. Even with Bennie Garza as Romeo, it was such fun."

She held up the rose.

"What is this rose, dear one, what are its charms…"

"Oh, here we go."

Martha just smiled, and then comically cleared her throat.

"Does it not blush, as do I, at the mention of your name, at the touch of your hand?" She brushed the flower across his cheek and he smiled deeply at her performance. "Does it not pulse with life when brushed with pollen, drink in the dew?" She pulled off a petal. "And is it not so frail?" She pulled off another petal and let it drop gently from her fingers to Nagler's chest. Her voice softened and trembled. "Its time is so brief, its beauty so rare." She jerked off the remaining petals, leaving a bald stalk. Her voice harsh and firm. "It is time that I want, time with you, sweet rose, before the petals fade; time I do not have. Time no one can give me."

She threw the rose stalk away and rolled into Nagler's arms, closed her eyes and signed deeply.

"How was that?" she whispered. "I liked acting a lot. I wish I hadn't gotten sick when I did. I would have loved the chance to act in college."

Nagler lay down on his back beside her. That had been the shock and the great test, he knew. Leukemia at nineteen. And two years of treatment, then two more of recovering her strength and watching her parents' worried faces sag, the voices crack, the distant stares.

"I would have been a better Juliet in college, you know, in case you were wondering," Martha said to the sky after she had rolled onto her back. "By then it was more than words. I knew about the loss, the pain, facing death and had already experienced the great love" —she touched his face— "and felt the poetry flow through me, the words of a soul's awakening coursing in my blood, bursting through the brain's barrier, throwing open the world." A soft, teasing laugh.

She rolled to her side and faced Nagler, gently touching his face with a single finger and kissing his eyes, cheeks, and mouth.

"That's what that…that damned disease nearly took from me, Frank," her voice now hard. "That chance. You were my Romeo, dear Frank. And for a moment I thought I would lose you."

"No." Words were trapped in his throat, unable to move. "Never," he coughed. "Maybe that chance comes again."

She kissed him, holding his damp face in both hands.

"Could be," she said, her voice distant. "I had already lived that death scene. Had already known the poison in my veins, felt the dragging pain of disease and how it felt to fade away. I knew how it felt to have limbs stiffen, breath slow, colors fade, to see a descending haze and have no way to cry out. To see the hovering outline of a dark companion." She covered her mouth with her hands and stared at the ground, eyes moist. "I knew the loss," her voice soft and shallow. "It would have been easy to act it out on a stage, when I had already lived it. To die and then recover. The hope of finding my love at my side. The tears on my face at that moment would have been real." She paused and caught a breath. "Then my eyes opened, and it was Bennie Garza. Oh, why Lord?"

Nagler rose to an elbow, alarmed. "Hey," he pulled her close. "That's past, right?"

She touched his face. "They think so, the doctors. There has been no sign of it returning." She sat up and faced him. "But is it called remission, not a cure, for a reason."

"Are you not telling me something, Martha. Is it back? I know you told me not to ask, but if…"

"No, Frank. No, no." She shrugged. "But still they test." A fading voice.

She stood up abruptly to end the questioning. "Got a shirt there, buddy? You've got a naked woman covered in grass clippings here. What would my mother say?"

As they left the park, his pager sounded with a short message: "New victim."

Martha had been unusually quiet on the drive home from the park. She had placed an arm against the window frame and with eyes closed, laid down her head. When he asked, she said she was just tired; a long day. He thought she seemed pale when he laid her on the bed and kissed her before leaving for the crime scene.

Maybe we shouldn't have…

She seemed drained; he watched for a moment as she drifted deeply into sleep. Not again. Please. Not again.

CHAPTER NINE

How many phone booths are there in this town?

By the time Nagler had arrived Foley was pacing at the eastern end of the rail yard, where the yellow tape marked off the trail to Smelly Flats.

"Where have you been?" Foley demanded.

"Just got the page," Nagler said. "When did we get the call?"

"Within the hour." A scolding voice.

Nagler stared at the man, dressed in a blue suit not for a walk down a narrow, muddy trail, but for a dinner date, and held back an answer to that question, but asked, "What are you doing in the parking lot if the body is in the Flats? And why did it take so long to page me?"

Foley glared then stared at the ground. "I can't deal with that smell. It gets to me."

Jesus.

"Gets to everybody. Who's down there?"

"Dr. Mulligan and Sergeant Sal LaStrada, and, you know, others." He exhaled. "I don't know why it took so long to page you. It is working properly?"

"It worked, didn't it," Nagler growled. "Hey, I got it," he said, and pushed past Foley, lifted the yellow tape and stepped into the dark trail, while thinking, what's wrong with this?

Nagler thought of telling Foley to canvas the train station passengers and train crews, but then thought I don't need a fight about who is in charge.

He knew what he was walking into: The Smelly Flats in full rotting aromatic glory. He could never figure out why the thick smell of the rotten vegetation and stagnant water never penetrated outside the area of the pool that gave the piece of the river its name. As he walked closer, whiffs of the odor had leaked into the air; at the last turn, he reached for his handkerchief. The river had shrunk inside its shallow channel, leaving layers of slimy mud; it should be full this time of year, Nagler thought, eight feet wide and churning over piles of stones and broken

89

tree limbs that added to the danger of visiting the Flats at night. The smell, usually held in check until late summer, had bloomed early.

Beams from flashlights bounced across the dark landscape.

Mulligan was bent over the body of a woman lying face down on the muddy bank. He adjusted his footing as he slipped on the thick, slippery muck.

LaStrada, head of the crime scene unit, nodded a welcome and stepped over to greet Nagler.

"ID?" Nagler asked.

"Tamika Austin," LaStrada said. "Found a purse. Two hundred in cash, a fold or two of probably coke. That was her drug of choice, right?"

"I know her," Nagler said. "Busted her a few times at two in the morning for giving head at the train station for twenty bucks a pop. Think it's a john?"

LaStrada shrugged. "Hard to say. But for all the years she's been out there, who's knows? Don't recall her reporting any trouble."

"Possible cause?"

"Maybe head meets rock."

"Ugly."

"Indeed," Mulligan said as he rose from the dead woman. "Her head did strike a rock — there are blood stains — but because that rock is still in the ground, I cannot say whether it was an accident — a trip and fall; it is uneven ground — or perhaps she was pushed. Or even if it is the actual cause of death."

Nagler asked the question that had been hanging in the air. "Is this the work of our guy?"

LaStrada, resigned, shrugged his right shoulder toward the body, while Mulligan said, "Look at what we have, Detective."

Nagler glanced at the body and sighed. The same physical evidence they had found on the other victims. "Damn it. I wish some of this would begin to make sense," he said, before he grabbed a tree for support after he kicked at and missed a loose stone.

"I need better light to fully examine her," Mulligan said with irritation. "Sergeant, where is the fire truck that was supposed to illuminate the scene from the bridge? I can't really see a thing. The flashlights are inadequate. There are possible scratches on her neck, and a bruise on her right shoulder. And there is some evidence of a white powder in her nostrils."

"Time of death?"

"Impossible to pinpoint without a better examination, but I'd say at least twenty-four hours. Her lower torso was in the river, which altered her body temperature."

LaStrada pointed at the ground. "The mud near the water is too soft to hold a footprint, and where the body was left, it's too hard to accept an impression."

Nagler scratched his head as he watched officers stumble along the dark, steep gully. "Twenty-four hours, and someone just called it in an hour ago?"

"Seems so," LaStrada said. "It is odd, but given her line of work…"

Nagler fumed, still mentally engaged with Foley. "So maybe she came down here to get high, or higher, and fell on the rocks?" he said, incredulous. He closed up his face and shook his head. "No. Who the hell would be down here? Someone sharing her dope? A customer? That's not right." He rubbed the back of his neck. "We know a lot about this place, Sal. Hookers don't come down here. Too far, too wet. Too many other places for a quick trick. She wouldn't be working the train station at rush hour anyway. I don't know."

LaStrada waved a hand. "What are you working on?"

Nagler scanned the darkening scene and frowned. "Something that makes sense. Nobody comes down here just to hang out. Kids don't come down here to drink beer and screw, and this is not a common shortcut. So, who found her? Who called it in? And who called it in a day after she died? Did the caller specifically ID this place? Who would know she was here?" He closed his eyes in thought. "Had to be the killer." Then softly, "Had to be. Claiming credit." He turned and looked back up the narrow trail toward the train yard. I got paged at six p.m. or so," Nagler said, and pulled out the pager to confirm. "Yeah, here, six-thirty. So maybe the call came from the train station during the hour before that, during part of rush-hour." Then he shook his head.

LaStrada shrugged. "Potentially a lot of witnesses. Maybe someone listened in?"

"Or potentially a lot of people too busy going home to notice," Nagler replied. "It makes sense that someone coming off this trail, possibly sweaty, muddy, might be noticed. Maybe someone in the railyard saw something. They almost had to come that way. The railyard has that, what, a ten-foot wall, and a wobbly fence above that. Not an easy way out." He blew up his cheeks and let out the long breath. "We need to listen to a lot of phone calls. Crap, how many phone booths are there in this town?" he muttered.

"Man, I don't know," LaStrada said. "I'll lock the site down and post officers at the train station and the roadway above. I'll order up the big lights and get a crew in here to scour the riverbanks."

****

Apparently, Mayor Howard Newton didn't remove either his white Panama hat or dark shades even while he was sitting inside behind his desk.

Nagler, sitting head down while he, Foley and the police chief were getting yelled at, found the hat distracting. Hard to take a scolding from Boss Hogg.

"What is the problem here, gentlemen?" the Mayor yelled, elbows on his desk. "I've given you more resources, stretched the city budget, and still no killer. You've got to get this cleaned up. I have investors interested in some of the old mills, and their interest will fade if this killing spree does not end. Got it?"

"We've never seen anything like this before, Mr. Mayor," Chief Mallory said.

"Well, I've never been mayor before, and I'm figuring it out," Newton said.

Foley stood up. "I think what the chief means, if I may speak…" He glanced down at the chief, who nodded. "In such past cases a lone killer follows a pattern of methods and behaviors. We have not yet been able to establish his pattern. We have ideas, but nothing solid."

"You want a pattern? He's killing woman. That's a pattern." The mayor sat so forcefully his hat slipped forward on his face. "What I gotta do, bring in some fancy head shrinkers? Get outta here!" He waved his hand for the police officers to leave."

"No, wait. Chief, what's this I hear about drug gangs?"

"There are always drug gangs, Mr. Mayor," the chief said, his voice a weary shrug.

"I want them gone," the mayor yelled. "We can't move that real estate on the east side with hoodlums selling drugs, on top of all these dead women. Jesus Christ."

Later, Nagler and Foley stood with the chief in front of their incident board that now included a photo of Tamika Austin.

"She was a hooker?" the chief asked.

"She was a drug addict," Nagler said. "Had been since high school. She attended the county college off and on, worked a number of jobs and did tricks when the money got tight." He expelled a long breath. "I knew her brother. She was a smart kid but went off the rails after he was killed in a car crash a few years ago."

"Okay," the chief replied, and waved his hand at the board. "Does that fit our pattern? A doctor, a secretary, restaurant manager, two old ladies, and now, a hooker."

Foley broke in. "We don't know that these are all connected. We shouldn't…"

"Mulligan thinks so," Nagler interrupted. "Said as much the night Joan Chen was killed. Called it 'an experiment in death.' He told you that, right?"

Foley glared at Nagler and turned away then back. "The good doctor thinks every death is connected, a cosmic conspiracy to keep him away from his chess game."

The chief, and then Nagler chuckled. That was funny, Nagler thought, especially coming from Foley.

"What's common about these women?" the chief asked. Gotta be something. Best we can tell they were alone when they were killed, or in the case of the old ladies, lived alone. Is that their vulnerability? Frank, start at the beginning. Look at each of these women like we know nothing. Their homes, neighborhoods, family, friends, place of worship, businesses, hobbies, I don't know, what they ate for breakfast. Somewhere they crossed paths with their killer before he killed them. Had to."

The chief tapped the board a few times then hit it loudly with an open palm.

"Chris, start canvassing police departments, state police. See if they have anything like this in their records."

"Shouldn't I be out on the street?" Foley asked.

"From what I heard, you and the street don't get along so well," the chief said before he walked away. "Let's go," he said over his shoulder. And what's with those red handprints? Any connection or a sick joke? Find out."

Foley glared at the chief's retreating back. "Where'd that come from? You say anything?"

"About what," Nagler asked. "Smelly Flats?"

"Yeah."

"Damn it, Chris, I wouldn't go there unless I had to, that smell. Don't worry about it. Chief's feeling heat from the mayor, that's all. Let me ask you, Chris. If you couldn't tolerate the scene because of the smell, why didn't you follow up at the train station or train yard?"

"I wasn't feeling well. I threw up after you left. I went home." Foley's face remained solid and dark. "Let me know if you find anything."

Can't you lie better? Nagler asked himself as Foley strolled away. It wasn't the smell, or the messy path. You didn't come to the Joan Chen scene either. What is your game?

Ask about the kid? No. Save it till you need it.

****

The photos finally arrived.

Nagler had asked Sal LaStrada's unit to photograph the homes, neighborhoods and workplaces of each of the victims, even those of Marion Feldman and Edie Smith, the missing older women.

Nancy Harmon's medical office had yet to be cleared out, even though Nagler had been told her private patients had found new doctors and the low-income health center where she volunteered shifted her patients to other volunteers. Harmon owned the small building where she practiced, but the real estate company had not fielded any bids. Held up in probate court, Nagler had been told.

Joan Chen's duplex was being emptied by her family, and Felice Sanchez's place of employment, her favorite parking spots used between calls, and the old Wilson hotel had been photographed. And Jamie Wilson's apartment had been rented.

All of that seemed normal, Nagler thought. What am I missing?

As he tacked the photos to the incident wall under each victim's name, he noticed that three of the locations were adjacent to empty, slightly overgrown lots, or in the case of Harmon's office and the cab company garage, across the street from empty buildings, all potential vantage points for a stalker.

He glanced again at the address for the cab company. It was a block and half away from the Peterson mill where they had found the bag of clothes.

He pulled out an Ironton city map and marked the location of each spot that had been photographed. Only Marion Feldman's home was outside of the ten-to-twelve-block rectangle that the connected marks produced. Maybe, he thought, that is progress. Then he laughed bitterly. We don't even know who we are looking for. We don't have a description, a fingerprint, a witness. The victims seemed to be loners, or at least single women — none were married — scattered friends and distant families. Does that make them easier targets? He examined the map. But maybe this is the hunting ground.

His phone rang. It was Mulligan.

On his way to the medical examiner's office Nagler recalled the night Martha told him that there has been a disturbance across the street from their home. The noise had come from an empty lot, overgrown with small trees and brush, just like those pinned on the incident wall. He shook away the thought that the coincidence might have more meaning.

****

Mulligan and Sal LaStrada stood over a metal examination table that did not hold Tamika Austin's remains, but two forks and a steak knife.

"Oh, shit," Nagler said.

"Yes," Mulligan said. "It matches the silverware found at the Feldman home."

Nagler steadied himself against the table. "That means…?

"I'm afraid so. Besides the physical evidence we have, this could confirm that Miss Austin is a victim of our killer," Mulligan said softly. "And the silverware contributed to her death. When we examined her here, we found repeated stab wounds in her abdomen. Since there were no tears in her clothing, and only spots of dried blood in her inner shirt, it may be possible that she was partly dressed when killed, and then was redressed, or the killer raised her clothing to stab her. This a new development, a new intricacy."

Nagler stared at the silverware.

"So, what was the cause of death?"

"She bled to death, but it wasn't as simple as that. Her head struck the rock at the riverside, which stunned her, and she was stabbed. That means…."

"That means this might have been an ambush attack, like with Joan Chen. Does that establish a pattern?" Nagler asked.

Mulligan smiled to LaStrada. "He's catching on." Then to Nagler: "Let's be sure. Examine two actions: How did she strike her head in a rock embedded in the riverbank, and how was she stabbed?"

Nagler frowned.

"Don't be discouraged, Detective," Mulligan said. "We have to be precise. I'd suggest re-examining the scenes of the three earliest deaths, Dr. Harmon, and Misses Wilson and Sanchez."

LaStrada said. "We know that the white power in her nose was cocaine. We also know she was homeless, living on the streets and sleeping in abandoned buildings. You know where the homeless bathe in the summer?"

"Smelly Flats."

"Yup."

Nagler scratched his head. "So, she was down there taking a bath? How did he know?"

"What are you thinking, Frank?" LaStrada asked. "I'm thinking he followed her."

"Just random, then," Nagler said. "What if she was living in the Peterson mill and that bag of clothes we found was hers? Don't we have patrol going by there?"

"Yeah, but the homeless who might have been there have scattered. And the owner put on a new door and lock," LaStrada said.

"Looks like I need to visit the stoveworks," Nagler said.

LaStrada glanced at Mulligan: "More homeless people."

Before Nagler and LaStrada left, Mulligan said they have more tests to run and would get toxicology results in due time. "The state police lab has fast-tracked our request. And gentlemen, this evidence, like all distinctive evidence, must remain private."

Both Nagler and LaStrada nodded. When, Nagler wondered, do we inform the public that our killer cut the hands off his victims?

In the hallway, Nagler stopped LaStrada.

"What do you know about Foley?"

LaStrada grinned slightly. "He's a bit of a showboat for my taste. Why?"

"He was not at the Joan Chen scene, was in the parking lot with Tamika Austin, and he's not here now. Seems strange, no? Especially for the mayor's team leader?"

"What are you saying?"

"Not sure. Just wondering."

"Let's focus on our killer. The rest will take care of itself. You can be a hero later on."

"What?" Nagler yelled as LaStrada walked away. Then he shivered. The voice of that reporter Jimmy Dawson filled his head: Inside guys, inside games. Is LaStrada straight up?

CHAPTER TEN

Boilermaker

Jimmy Dawson hunched in the back, far corner table at Mario's.

The place was empty except for a couple of beer drinkers at the bar staring like zombies at the TV replay of a Yankees game; music tinkled in the air, leaking from hidden speakers.

Given the reputation of the person who had asked to meet with him, Dawson thought the red velvet bar with polyester seats might not have been the best spot.

He wanted a boilermaker to knock down the jitter; he sighed and ordered a Coke.

Ironton seemed like it was going to snap.

It wasn't just the murders. They were happening at an almost casual pace. The city recoiled in horror when police announced each new one, just as it had with the last murder, the one when the victim was found in Smelly Flats. A loud scream of horror, then back to life as usual, an accepting civic shrug which said that's how life is, brutal and deadly, but it's someone else's problem.

It was something subterranean, continents grinding, an oozing, deadly pressure seeking release; no one would want to be there when it popped.

It was like the heat had sucked out all the wrong that had once cooled and coalesced in the hidden corners of the city and spread it around; the wrong that rose up on a bad Saturday night when the dice rolled sideways, when the beer tasted a little sour, when the glint in an eye across the room was a threat, and when a wink to the wrong woman led to bodies on the floor; when a teenaged girl in a dark room said no and got smacked then pinned crying; when knives were sharp and swift; the wrong that had kids robbing the little corner stores, the moms-and-pops and the bodegas, fights at the high school over girls and cars; gay kids being bushwhacked, back alley turf wars between the upturned leather collar crowd and the headband, unlaced Jordans gangs.

There was nothing to hide in, no gray fog of forgiveness, no cooling mist that hung on dry faces, just the shadeless heat, laser beams bouncing off hot glass, the needle-eye reflection, a city blinded, sweating, dulled and beaten to indifference.

And Dawson was its witness staring unblinking into the fury. On the sidewalk with blood leaking into dry sand, at the bar with the shattered front door, a face missing teeth like a broken beer bottle; asking why there were red hands painted on walls, why there were dead women, and why no one could find the killer.

He wanted — needed — that shot of whiskey. But it would smudge all those images with their garish colors, the kaleidoscopic, dripping wash of Ironton's streets, dull the chemical taste of destruction. He drained the Coke, and apologetically ordered another. The caffeine sugar rush would have to suffice.

The bar door opened and the sunlight glowed around the tall man, who slowly scanned the room, and nodded when he spotted Dawson.

He stopped at the bar and Dawson heard him say, "Seltzer."

When the drink arrived, he picked it up and sipped off the top, and then sidled past a few scattered chairs and tables and sat down.

"Mister Dawson."

"Call me Jimmy."

"Bartholomew Harrington." He paused. "Bart."

Dawson knew him by reputation as the sharp-elbowed, world-stage Ironton lawyer with a soft spot for the little guy. He had been before more state courts, including the Supreme Court, than anyone had a right to expect. He won his cases with ironclad knowledge of the law and a flamboyance that at times wore down his legal opponents.

The seltzer surprised Dawson.

Harrington's side reputation was that he hadn't met a drink he couldn't name.

"Surprised you, didn't it?" Harrington asked, and nodded at the glass. "The soda water."

"I'd heard." Dawson shrugged.

"An act, Mister Dawson, sorry, Jimmy. "I'm as sober as…um, no, since I know those gentlemen, more sober than a judge." He grinned, absorbed in his own cleverness. "I return home to read Shakespeare and law journals, watch soap operas, and water my flowers. I have the loveliest orchids." Harrington chuckled. "I sometimes appear in court with my tie askew, jacket sleeves pushed to my elbows, and scuffed shoes. You'd be surprised how disarming that appearance is to my friends in the other chair."

All well and good, Dawson thought.

"Why are we here?" he asked. "Not, I presume, to discuss your winning ways in court."

"Do you know what is going on in this city, Jimmy? Well, besides the obvious?"

"People are dying. And it's hot as hell. What more do you need?"

Harrington pursed his lips and waved a hand.

"They are being sold down the river, block by block, empty building by empty building," he said, squinting and leaning over the table.

"By whom?"

Harrington laughed, throwing his head back. "Whom? Good one. I thought for an old sports hack you'd ask, 'Whatcha mean, buddy?'"

Dawson leaned in as well and scowled. Sourly, and suddenly, out of patience: "I'm not stupid, Harrington. What's on your mind?"

"The mayor, mostly. Howard Newton, the vegetable seller. Has everybody fooled, or he thinks he does. That Coupe de Ville. On a" —he wagged his hooked fingers in the air— "'loan' from a car dealer, mostly likely a payoff. The white Panama, a South American gangster hat, the dark glasses. The man of mystery. Ha! As much an act as my disheveled court attire. And the cigars, the Cubans. Do you know why he smokes Cuban cigars, Jimmy?"

Dawson, once a cigarette smoker, had turned to an occasional cigar for comfort. He'd never had a Cuban.

"Because they're illegal," Harrington said. "Ill-legal. Unlawful. Against the law. Banned, and not just in Boston...."

So full of himself, Dawson thought, shaking his head.

"Makes him look like a big shot, waving that six-inch Cuban in the air. He should care about them because they are finely crafted by traditionalists from tobacco grown and dried with exquisite care and smoke with sweet, almost orgasmic pleasure." Harrington bit his lower lip and chuckled. "I enjoyed some when I worked as a law student on a land-use case in Havana. Oh, so secret, the case. But the cigars, heavenly." He scowled. "Howie Newton likes Cuban cigars because he can buy them off a truck in Newark, stashed under a load of bananas or romaine lettuce. If he was a cigarette smoker, his Winstons would not have a tax stamp."

Dawson looked this watch and scratched his head. He didn't know whether to believe Harrington or not. Very entertaining, but so far, pointless. Dawson knew Newton was shady. He wore that same scent given off by coaches who were skirting the rules, hiding a nineteen-year-old, six-eight ringer behind a phony birth certificate and an aunt who suddenly moved into the district. Being the big guy, out front and cheering, smiling and winking at the same time. Play the kid for a year, get him to a college, get some tickets to the NCAAs, or maybe a little bonus, and a tryout for that one good guard.

He had seen it, Jimmy Dawson had. The games, the crooks, the messed-up lives. "That's a big charge, Harrington."

Harrington downed his seltzer.

"Someone in the local government is using City Hall departments to launder money to buy Ironton buildings for themselves with city funds. I have come across some disturbing paperwork that I am still examining. The books, as is the phrase, are being cooked."

Harrington rubbed his neck and placed his elbows on the table. "Once this gets embedded, it will be worth millions, and the city might never know what hit it."

Dawson screwed up his face.

"Okay, got an example?"

"The hosiery mill." Harrington tapped the table with his index finger. "You know how to read legal ads, Jimmy?"

"Yeah. Sure."

"Good. Watch for foreclosures, tax sales, and special planning board meetings. It's all out in the open, but you have to know how to read the tea leaves, so to speak. They are moving quickly on that one." He paused and leaned over the table. "And then look at past city budgets. This is a long-term scheme that began with systemic disinvestment in the city's streets, sewers and water lines. Drives down the value of those old industrial properties and makes them easier to steal. Someone says. 'eh, get rid of it of it,' and it happens."

Okay, Dawson thought. "Why now?"

"The murders provide cover."

Dawson felt his face flush. "No," he protested. Then: "Really? That's damn cynical, isn't it?"

Harrington smiled a crooked, knowing smile.

"Despite your protest, you don't sound surprised, Jimmy. It's more than cynical, it's brilliant. Stolen in the light of day. And no one saw it because they were distracted."

He stood.

"I must go."

"Wait a minute. How do you know this? Sounds like you're saying the police have a suspect, but are, what, playing out the string, so they can steal millions while more people die?" Dawson asked. "How are you going prove it?

"Jimmy, I've defended guilty people all my life. I've learned from the best. They can be remarkably clever when they need to be. But they always leave a trail. I'll be in touch." He turned toward the door then paused. "They are also setting up a fall guy, in case it goes south." He left, a tall shadow in the dark room, then a shadowy form in the sunlight as the door opened.

Dawson sat in the cool dark of the bar and wiped his face with both hands. What to believe. He reached for his Coke, now all gray-brown ice water. He nodded to the bartender. Money and murder, he thought. Lifelong companions.

"Boilermaker."

CHAPTER ELEVEN

Take the game to them

Nagler stepped carefully over the pile of rusted sheet metal and broken lumber that jammed the opening into the largest building at the stoveworks complex. Pigeons flew in the rafters and the echo of dripping water cut through the silence.

The factory had been one of the Ironton's largest employers, making cast iron cooking stoves for kitchens, small versions for camps, and during wartimes, even backpack sized heaters for soldiers.

And now it was one of the city's biggest wrecks. The mill owners walked away and left the buildings that soon fell to ruin and a city that collapsed into an aching silence.

In a distant cavernous room, a bottle skittered across a cement floor, rolled a couple of times and smacked the wall with a glittering echo of broken glass.

Indistinct sounds crept from the dark hollow and became laughter, solidified into voices, grumbles, curses. Sit your ass down, man! Keep passin', keep passin'. Yo fifty cents ain't worth more than mine. Where that bitch go? I need some. You ain't getting' some with my kids here. Oh, woman, ain't I your daddy? Hey, you two, settle up somewhere else. Nobody else need to know your shit.

Nagler leaned through a hole that had been bashed through a wall, flashed his light on the greasy puddle on the other side, and stepped over it. A flickering light filtered around another wall and he followed it to the voices.

Sulfurous smoke rose from a fire; bodies like unformed hulks shifted in and out of the shaky light.

"Need a word with you guys," Nagler announced as he stepped into the edge of the light.

"Who the fuck are you?"

"Bet he's a cop. Damn it!"

Bodies scrambled into the darkness. Three men walked with menace toward Nagler. "You need to just go, man."

"Ease up, brother. I know this man. That's you, ain't it, Frank."

"Yeah, Del. I need the help of you and your friends," Nagler said softly. "Just a couple questions."

He hadn't seen his best high school friend Delvin Williams in a couple of years. Nagler knew he had gone in and out of the army, then fallen on hard times, but in his search, Nagler always found himself a block away, six months late; something.

Del lumbered over and threw his arms around Nagler. "I'm here buddy. Whatever you need."

Nagler closed his eyes and held his breath with fat cheeks as the odors rising from Del's body and clothes enveloped him. Whoa, man.

Still, he embraced his friend, and silently suffered his condition.

"So, then, what you need, Frank?" Del waved to the homeless collection. "Hey, get yo asses over here. Help my friend."

After they circled, Nagler pulled out a photo of Tamika Austin.

"Anyone know her?" he asked. "Yeah, and I am a cop."

"Ain't gonna bust her, are you?"

Nagler shook his head.

"I'm sorry if you know her. She's dead. Been killed. We're trying to find out where's she been, who she knows, to try to find out who killed her."

A woman in the back said, "Yeah, she's been here off an' on. She'd crash, she'd come here. We take care of her."

"Who killed her?" A voice from the darkness. "Wasn't that freak who dumpin' women in the bog, is it? That's sick, man. Sick."

Nagler stared at the dark, sullen faces, and decided they needed to know. It could save their lives.

"Could be," he said. "We don't know who it is, but it could be. When was the last time any of you saw Tamika?"

Shuffling of turning heads. "Couple weeks," the same woman said. "Had just gone back to working downtown. Paid me the twenty she owed me from long back. I told her, Girl, you need to stop that shit, but she just smiled. She was usin' again. Saw the jitter in her eyes. Told her she needed to go away, get outta this damn town. But she just smiled. Poor lost kid."

No one else spoke, and the crowd filtered back toward the fire.

"Hey, thanks," Nagler called after them. "You be safe. Watch out for each other. I know you don't like cops, but Del and I go way back. You get arrested, you're on your own. But if you need something else, find me. I'm Detective Frank Nagler."

As the group thinned, Nagler pulled Del aside.

"What happened this time, Del?"

Del shook his head and stared at the ground.

"Lost a job, a couple jobs. Pissed it all away." He shrugged. "One day, Frank, one day, I'll get it right."

"You know I'll help you."

Del smiled crookedly. "Some days I know that. Some days I don't."

There's an edge, Nagler knew. Junkies and drunks stand on it all the time. Any step they take could send them down the cliff, or up it. He had seen Del Williams on that cliff more times than he could count or want to remember. He had no lecture for his old friend, just a sadness in his heart.

He pulled out the photo of the kid, just for the heck of it.

"Seen this kid, Del? He come around here?"

Del held up the photo to catch some of the firelight. Then Nagler shined his flashlight on it.

"Yeah, we know him," Del said. "Chased him outta here bunch of times. He tries to sell us stuff, like we got money," he laughed harshly. "Sometimes he comes in late at night trying to steal stuff. A few weeks back. But one of the big guys who ain't here no more caught him and woulda killed him, if we hadn't stopped him. Don't need that shit on us here. They kinda leave us alone."

Damn it, Nagler thought. "How long ago. What kind of stuff?"

"He ain't been here in, I don't know, what month is it? Maybe four, five weeks?"

"Okay," Nagler said. "What kind of stuff was he trying to sell?"

"Sometimes clothes, but last time he had a real fancy bracelet, diamonds and all. Trying to give it away. I mean, his stuff is stolen, but no one here wanted that bracelet. We'd end up at the county if we tried to fence that piece."

A silence fell between the old friends.

Marion Feldman's bracelet. Did the kid throw it out at the Old Iron Bog after he couldn't sell it or give it away? Did he steal it from the Feldman's home? Damn it. Gotta find him.

Del reached out for Nagler's elbow. "So how you doin', Frank? Them killings has got us all riled up. Could be any of us. Or some wanna-be hero cop will blame us. How you doin' with all that?"

Nagler stared onto the watery eyes of his friend. "Getting there. It'll come. Not much help, getting some interference. But, you, man, you gotta get out of here, Del," he said softly. "I can help you."

"I try, Frank. I surely do. They need me." He waved his arm toward his huddled, dark crowd. "I try. But then I fall. But, know what, Frank? When I fall, I bounce. Sometimes it's not all the way, up, but one day I'll bounce, land on my own two feet and won't fall again."

"Hope you do, man." Nagler's voice was wet and soft.

"Hey, Frank, was thinkin' about this a recent day. You remember how we ran that alley-oop in high school?" Del asked. "Nobody could stop that play." Del laughed a couple of times. "Hee, hee. Remember that?"

What? Nagler thought, then he chuckled. "No one could stop it because you could out-jump everyone in the county. No one could stop you."

"Yeah, that was probably true." Del nodded, the memory full in his mind: He soaring above the heads of all the other players, hands outstretched, the ball floating, then the jam, and he landing on the floor grinning. "I could jump and run, but that play worked because of you, my friend. Remember what you did to set up that pass?"

Nagler waved his hand and grinned. "What did I do, besides making sure that ball stayed in the gym?"

"Faked 'em out, man." Del acted out the play, shuffling side to side, looking into the darkness, then flicking his right hand towards Nagler as if it held a basketball. "You'd dribble to the left a little then back to the right, all the while lookin' at the guy in the right frontcourt and the defense would follow your eyes. Then practically without a peek, you'd flick that ball to the left toward the basket 'bout rim high, and what you know, there I was." Del laughed deeply, a laugh that had not been heard, Nagler guessed, in a long time. "We was somethin', Frank. Just somethin'. That play worked because you took the game to them. They didn't know what hit 'em. Faked 'em out and took the damn game to them. Sometimes that's what you gotta do — take the game to them."

CHAPTER TWELVE

Our killer has been too quiet

That damn kid. A damned distraction, Nagler thought. I need to be looking for a killer, and I'm spending all this time looking for some punk kid.

Nagler leaned in the shade of an ancient maple and scanned the Feldman house and the end of West Harvard. The home had not been sold. The lawn had been recently mowed, and the doors to the house and garage had new locks.

Nagler stopped dead in his tracks when he discovered four newspapers on the front steps. He peeled off the rubber bands and examined the dates. Three were from April, and the fourth was early May, after the house and the neighborhood had been searched. What the hell?

Neighbor Adele Thomas, who had initially called the police about the height of the Feldman's lawn, was not sure the kid in the photo was the same one she thought she saw with the landscaping crew. "Sometimes I didn't wear my glasses," she told Nagler. "So, while I can say there was smaller boy, I didn't really see what he looked like."

"Did anyone try to sell you a newspaper subscription recently?" Nagler asked.

"Oh, no," she said.

"Did you see anyone looking around the Feldman's house?"

Her face wrinkled, and she covered her mouth with one hand. "A car with a young couple drove by, maybe two weeks ago. They seemed to be looking at the property. Oh, and a single man got out of his car and walked the lot several days ago."

"But no one selling newspapers?"

"Is there something wrong now? Did Marion not move to the nursing home?"

****

Dan Green, the owner of the landscaping company, said sometimes one of the kids would bring along a younger brother because

109

there was no babysitter, but the little kids weren't supposed to do any work. "Did they?" Nagler asked. Green smiled. "They probably did some raking."

Nagler walked along the base of the cliff at the end of West Harvard and tried to recall the path the kid took the first time he was sighted near the Feldman home. At the top, there seemed to be a series of fences, probably yard boundaries for the homes there. But there were gaps, and it was probably through one of those gaps that the kid started down the hill. Why was he up there? And why was he jumping down that hill to run past the Feldman home.

He was checking to see if anyone was there. Had to be. And when he saw me, he ran off.

"Our little thief was coming back for seconds," Nagler said aloud.

He had spoken with Marion Feldman's granddaughter about the bracelet, but she said she didn't have an inventory of her grandmother's possessions, although she said she recalled one perhaps like it being worn at a family event four or five years ago, maybe a birthday.

"By then I had moved to Columbus, Detective," she said.

"Do you know if she locked the house?"

"No, but probably not. She lived in that neighborhood for so long it must have felt safe to her. Even with her bad hip, when we talked she would tell me she would take short walks until she got to the point over the last year that she couldn't. It was therapy. Her doctor didn't want her to just sit around. That's when we decided it was time to sell and move her to a nursing home."

The newspapers, Nagler thought as he circled the Feldman home again. A phony reason to be here, casing the neighborhood. If he's trying to steal stuff from the homeless in the stoveworks, then why not here? He walked the length of West Harvard to the intersection with Princeton and back. At the edge of a small stand of trees, he found a stack of dirty newspapers, a stash. The plastic bag that had once covered them had blown off.

"That's why he was at the Smith house. That's why he was here." Nagler said aloud to himself. "Intelligence gathering." Foley had said the kid was part of a theft gang on the east side. So why not graduate to homes, especially empty ones?

He scanned the cliff again. It was a solid natural boundary, but there was evidence at the bottom of a lot of manmade disruption. Piles of sand, dirt and rock, all sprouting weeds, had been dumped along the base in a ragged line, and tangles of dead trees and brush lined an old path. Construction debris, Nagler thought, dumped when they were building these homes.

He stepped carefully around piles of rock and tree stumps up the narrow trail for a few yards until he was blocked by a pile of brush. Was that pile there before, the first night of the search?

Nagler sighed. I said I'd walk those paths, but not in a new suit and dress shoes, I'm not.

As he climbed back into his car, he wondered: How did the kid know about the Smith event? He was there before I was.

He shook his head, weighed down by this thought: Home burglaries and thefts involving youth. How much paperwork is that?

Was Marion Feldman out walking when he stole the bracelet. Or was she sleeping? Did she wake up? The thought a dart of troubled light in his reeling mind.

****

The neighborhood hummed with window fans and a few air conditioners. The cool scented air of May had never arrived; June instead brought parched lawns, aching for rain, brown before their time. The city imposed water restrictions.

Nagler sat in the hot Impala at the end of his driveway and listened as the engine grumbled to a stop and then filled the air with the pings and clicks of cooling metal, that sound then overwhelmed by the buzzing of a million unseen insects driven into a copulating frenzy by the unseasonable heat.

The city awoke each new morning expecting the newspaper headline to scream out ANOTHER DEAD WOMAN. COPS BEFUDDLED.

Instead, the day's news was the heat. Sidewalks broiling, heat waves rising like sin from soul-melting concrete. Tempers flaring, fights spilling out onto sidewalks. Fire hydrants flooding the streets with dark puddles and splashing feet; the soft jazz of stoops on hot nights, transistor radios and wine in brown bags, tossing empty beer cans toward the open trash can, only to miss and smile as the tin rattled along the curb. Passion in alleys, sweating lust and a woman's soft cry and her man's grunting thrusts; a city on fire, dry caverns baking under heat no one could explain, a smolder waiting a spark, an instant of fear that becomes conflagration.

It's coming, Nagler knew as he stepped into his dark house. It's going to ignite at some unexplained moment for no reason, and we'll all burn.

Our killer has been too quiet, he thought as he walked toward the house. Two weeks since the last death and still no answers. Aren't they supposed to brag about all the killing? Isn't that the thrill?

****

Nagler arrived at the fight scene the next afternoon to see a raging man with a baseball bat drive the barrel into the shoulder of one the officers sending him in pain to the sidewalk, take a swing at another officer before a third officer from behind encircled the man's arm with the bat and his neck and subdued him.

"Hey, stop!" Nagler yelled too late as the first officer rose from the ground and punched the bat-swinger three times in the face. Nagler pushed that officer back, and with the help of an EMT and LaStrada, both of whom had just arrived, they handcuffed the swinger and tended to his bleeding face.

"What the hell was that about?" LaStrada demanded. "What'd this guy do?"

The officer with the injured shoulder pressed an icepack to his arm and said, "We got a call about a disturbance at Angelo's, something about the killer drinking at the bar."

"This guy?" Nagler asked, before catching LaStrada's eye.

"Yeah," the officer continued. "A couple of pool players started raggin' on him because of his name, and then a brief scuffle broke out. The bartender asked this guy to leave, and he did, but not before picking up the bat from behind the front door and waving it at the pool players."

"Why are you guys here?" LaStrada asked.

"We got a call about the killer with a baseball bat," the third officer said. "Figured…"

"This is a mess," Nagler said to LaStrada. "Even if he is the killer, he just got beat up by a cop."

"Yeah," LaStrada said. "Fuck it. Hey officer, why did the pool players think his guy was the killer?"

"They said his name was Charlie Adams, the same one that was called in," the officer said over his shoulder as they assisted the injured, hand-cuffed suspect into the ambulance.

"That was never released to the public," LaStrada said to Nagler. "Who were those pool players?

****

A staggered breeze could not shift the molasses air as the heat settled. The open windows filled with the rattling death songs of insects, born for a moment of breeding, then crushed to the welcoming soil.

Frank Nagler had left the office that afternoon in disgust. Walked away, done with the Chris Foleys and Charlie Adams of the world, done with the web of chatter that had engulfed the investigation and the city; every step was across a sticky strand that grabbed at his heels, the city ground to a dark and silent stop.

He and Martha had spent the afternoon out of the city at the lake, where white sails captured the sunlight and plumes of spray behind water skiers rainbowed the water; then dinner lakeside as the sun settled behind the green, soon darkened hills.

The effect of the treatment was evident. She was paler and at times lethargic. She had trimmed her hair.

Later, she had settled into their bed under a thin sheet, hugging him.

"Do you remember the first time we kissed?" she asked with a grin.

He laughed and kissed her forehead. "We were like seven."

"Right, Einstein. Outside the school after Miss Kalan had basically yelled at me for not paying attention because I was drawing doodles of your name on the math test."

"She was angry, wasn't she? You were her best student." He stared at the ceiling and recalled that day. "But there you were, crying in the playground."

"And you came over, called her a silly old bat, and kissed me." Martha pushed up to an elbow and touched his face. "Right there. Put your finger on my chin, lifted my face and kissed me. Damn it, Frank. We were seven. I was floating. And you were so embarrassed. You never let me tell you how long I had been thinking about that. My mother would have killed me. Kissing a boy? She would have sent me to Sister Katherine in a minute. And you, you barely let me thank you. You stood there as stiff as a board when I hugged you. Silly boy."

113

"I didn't want you to be hurt, especially over something so silly as a math test." He shook his head. "It just came to me. And as soon as I did it, I wondered if I was wrong."

"Not wrong, Frank. Perfect." She brushed a finger across his worried eyes.

Then Martha smiled and giggled.

"The first time we Frenched I thought you were going to fall over," she said.

"Yeah. Oh, I know," he said. "We had been kissing every day we were together, Little pecks, baby smooches. I had just really loved walking home with you and holding your hand. Then, what we were thirteen, and you stuck your tongue in my mouth. Man. Knocked me over."

"You got the hang of it pretty quickly," she laughed and rolled back to her pillow. "Then we spent the next five years lusting after each other. I couldn't wait to kiss you. And then I couldn't wait for you to touch me and kiss my skin."

"Then we stopped for six months, some stupid fight." He leaned back and closed his eyes against that refreshed, broken-hearted-teenage pain. "I stood outside this house staring at the light in your window. You wouldn't take my calls. I remember standing in the doorway of that old shed across the street, trying to stay out of the rain. I would get home after midnight and my mother would just kiss my forehead silently because she saw how it all hurt."

Martha ran a finger down his jawline and turned his head to hers.

"And then the teenager stuff stopped. We grew up right then," she said. "You were across the street on a night like this, hot, miserably sticky, and I walked over, and we just fell back into each other's arms. That was the sweetest kiss, like the first one ever. None of the others, and nothing else mattered. It wasn't lust although I was aching for you. It was just you and me, bodies pressed together, lips soft and lightly brushing each other's mouth. A little peck, then a long, electric kiss I didn't want to end."

He touched her face. "I was trying to figure out how much you had been hurt, so much that you wouldn't even talk to me." He kissed her forehead. "Trying to figure out what I'd done, because I'd had to have done something."

She kissed his palm, and then licked it, smiling.

"Sometime distance is just distance, nothing really, a gap, that makes a wall." She looked up and smiled softly. "We had to push through it."

She sat on his lap and took his face in her hands. He tried to speak. "Hush," she said. Then she kissed him for just a second or two, then again. Their lips not parting but resting together. Then deeply; she drew a breath from him. Then she smiled.

"That's what it was like, Frank. Just like that." Her voice was wet. "Everyone since. At the hospital at nineteen, then home in Granny's old room. Giving you what I could, taking what I wanted." She kissed him again, and he relaxed into her embrace. "That's what they will be like until I can no longer give you any."

She curled in and soon fell asleep; he stared at the ceiling, eyes wet, trying to contain the pain he could feel growing in that dark corner of his heart.

He woke early and slipped from the bed. Martha smiled and mumbled, "Go get 'em, Frank," before falling deeply again asleep.

CHAPTER THIRTEEN

Leonard

Nagler slammed the office door open, startling Chris Foley at his desk.

"Don't you knock, Detective?" Foley asked.

"We got a big leak in this department, Chris," Nagler said, ignoring the question. "How did those punk pool players know about Charlie Adams, the one name on our hotline tape unless someone inside the department told them?"

Foley just tipped his head. "I've already addressed it, Detective. Division heads were told to speak to all officers in their units." He stared at Nagler with shaded eyes. "Anything else?"

Too cool, Nagler thought.

Try this: "We need to talk to that kid," Nagler said, tossing out a challenge. "And you know who he is. Why hasn't he been in here yet? I heard that you and he met in the old nightclub parking lot a few days ago. Why were you there?"

Foley leaned back in the chair and arched his fingers in front of his face. Then he shook his head.

"Hey, look. He's nobody, a, um, you know, a street punk." Foley's voice faltered, even as he glared back at Nagler.

Nagler stood leaning over the desk, waiting for Foley's next half-truth.

"Come on! What is it with this kid? You paying him for something?"

Foley stood and placed his hands on the desk and leaned toward Nagler.

"I don't like your implication, Detective. I could…"

Nagler ignored the threat, and leaned in. "Then why isn't he in here?"

Foley stood upright. Sweat had broken out on his upper lip. He glanced down.

"He's my eyes on the street. The deal we made after we caught him breaking into stores on the east side."

Nagler leaned back and shook his head. "Right. Eyes on the street. So what valuable information has he brought you? Like who is poking around in the old Peterson factory? Why was he there? Are you keeping eyes on him?"

Foley picked up a stack of papers and shuffled them together and the tapped them on the desk.

"What do you mean? What are you suggesting? That I have him spying on you?" His voice, never full or commanding, weakened.

"Well do you?" Nagler laughed. "We all have eyes on the street, Chris, guys we know who know stuff. But this kid was trying to sell Marion Feldman's bracelet to the homeless guys at the stoveworks. And weren't you a little curious that Mulligan identified silverware from the Feldman's house at the Tamika Austin crime scene?"

"You don't know that, about the bracelet." Defensively: "How do you know that?"

Nagler recognized the shift and honed in.

"I asked them, Chris. Come on." He waved an arm toward the door. "We'll ask them again."

"What are you suggesting?" Foley asked, as he sat down. "Are you saying he might be the killer? You saw him. He's not that big a kid."

Nagler leaned on the desk, holding his advantage.

"I'm just wondering if he is using the information you pass along to him, even accidentally, to follow us around and break into the homes we are investigating."

He glanced out Foley's office window into the burning glare. The fire was suddenly gone; Martha soft eyes filled his vision. He hadn't shaved; he had stared at his face in the bathroom mirror for twenty minutes, Martha's soft breathing from the next room in his ears. He had watched his face settle into a darkening gloom.

"I just think…I just think that it's a possibility," Nagler said slowly and sighed. "Didn't Danny Wilson say that someone was inside the Edie Smith house? And why did we get a photo of him in the street crowd on that first night." Nagler turned toward the door; his voice softened. "How did he even know to be there? I think I'll go ask someone else."

As Nagler stepped into the doorway, Foley said, "Okay. Look, I'll bring him in so we can talk to him. Let him tell us where he got that bracelet."

Nagler glared back, and then sighed and ran his hand through his hair and across his jaw. "You just need to keep an eye on him."

Nagler nodded and stepped into the hallway from Foley's office. A small smile, tongue in cheek.

****

In the parking lot, Nagler exhaled deeply and clenched his fists to calm the jitters. He had planned to be as confrontational with Foley as possible without crossing a department line. It seemed to work, he thought, but I wonder what the pushback would be.

"I really can't do that again," he whispered. "But it did feel good," he said loudly.

It wasn't just the sounds of Martha's voice in his head, but Foley. How do I separate all this? Martha. Foley. Dead women. The kid. All running in his head, crashing. Just stop.

I don't know. I want to be sitting with Martha, telling her that it would be all right. I don't want to be out here chasing some stupid teenage sneak thief or a mystery killer. I need to separate the two. Martha will be okay. Martha will be okay. He glanced at his watch; she would see the doctor in three hours.

Nagler leaned over the railing of the old mill race and watched the dry river leak past the exposed rocks. He couldn't recall the river running so low.

It's like us on this case, he thought, focusing. Dry as a bone. Everything laying out there obvious, like a trick painting. All we need is to hold it at the right angle, turn it by degrees until the lines and circles match and the face of the smiling cat emerges.

He tried to organize the jumble of information in his head.

They had released their bat-swinging Charlie Adams. He had filled the lock-up like a storm cloud, flashing and glaring at any officer who walked by, rattling the steel door and yelling, "Let me out. I don't know nothing about no women or painting red hands on buildings. I ain't no freak. Let me out or I'll break down this door."

And he could have, Nagler decided, when he unlocked the cage, and watched Charlie Adams shoulder his way out, muttering, "Fucking cops."

He was just a guy with the wrong name, Nagler thought. He was a dock worker, in the bar at the end of a ten-day shift.

But the question remained: How did the pool players know about

Charlie Adams, and know to bring it up just when that big guy walked into the bar? That just didn't seem like an accident.

So, we ask, and ask, and ask, Nagler thought.

There wasn't a lot to go on — witnesses, evidence — for the first three deaths. They occurred before we even recognized there was a pattern, he thought, before Mulligan declared they were all related.

But Joan Chen and Tamika Austin were active, and with fresh details. Crime scenes, potential weapons, and in Chen's case, a witness.

What didn't we ask?

The missing women, Edie Smith and Marion Feldman, were, well, missing. So, they stayed separate. I need someone to walk that old trail off West Harvard. But who? He laughed. Suddenly I don't trust anyone. Damn it, Dawson. That little bug in his ear; everyone's a spy.

The long blast of a train whistle split the dull rumble of downtown. Drawn by the sound, Nagler pushed off the railing and walked toward the train station.

The pay phone was broken, the receiver ripped out. So much for the theory that the killer called us about Tamika Adams from here.

Nagler strolled around the busy station, flowing with the rush-hour crowd jumping from the open train doors, leaning with brief cases and pocketbooks, jackets draped over arms, men's collars open and ties wrenched to one side; women in summer dresses. The crowd parted at the stairs and merged into one mass at the sidewalk, then surged to the street, where they bunched again like lemmings at the light; then singly, in pairs, they broke off to fill the spaces between cars or marching like a phalanx down the sidewalks.

No one looked up, Nagler noticed. No one looked at the pay phone, or even with whom they were walking. Tamika Austin's killer could have walked through there unnoticed.

He crossed the street and leaned on a mailbox and just examined the scene as several trains in both directions stopped at the station. All the movement. So easy to hide. He eyed a train heading east, picking up speed, screeching into the turn out of town to Denville. The dark spot in the tree line just to the left of the tracks was the pathway to Smelly Flats.

He shook his head with a sour look on his face. Damn it, I have to go back down there, he thought and pushed off the mailbox.

A voice behind him: "So, your killer is a rail commuter?"

It was Jimmy Dawson.

"As good a bet as any, right now," Nagler replied as he turned to greet the reporter. "Why not? The FBI sent us a report that said serial killers are masters at blending in, staying unnoticed. So, maybe our guy takes the train in from Newark or Manhattan each day. Comes to his job, makes sandwiches, fixes toilets, designs machinery, whatever. Goes out for lunch, buries his head in your newspaper at a diner, watches a ball game at a bar leaning over his pastrami and Swiss and a beer, sits in the park. And watches. Blends in. Just…watches. Maybe he's that guy always in the last counter seat at Barry's, the one with the Mets hat and the permanent scowl."

"That's creepy," Dawson said. "But do you really believe that?"

Nagler smirked. "Don't believe it but have to think it. What I really think? He's ours. We made him, carved him out of the empty mills, cold-water flats, trashy dark alleys, battered wives, hungry kids. A creature of ourselves."

"Thought you were going to give me something, you know. Tips?"

A slight smile crossed Nagler's face and he nodded his head.

"Remember that kid, the kid in the photo?"

"Yeah." Dawson screwed up his face. "Was looking for something else."

"The kid keeps showing up at our crimes scenes. And I can't find him, and I don't know why. I've showed the picture around a little, but no bites."

Dawson said, "Me too. A couple schools, a couple of social workers I trust. Nothing."

"Can you run it in the paper, maybe as a police item? Looking for a suspect in a break-in, police said." Then he smiled.

"Is that even remotely true?"

"If you say it was a West Harvard Avenue address, it is."

A train whistle split the air, and Nagler witnessed another load of passengers march through the station like robots

Dawson asked, "What are you going to get from that?"

"People talking," Nagler replied. "Maybe. What's been missing in this case has been tips, whispers." He shook his head. "All there has been is leaks from the PD to you. Yeah, so, thanks."

Dawson rolled his eyes. "It's how this job works. Dribs and drabs."

"Who's the leaker?"

Dawson stared at Nagler, and then sighed. "Some kid dispatcher. Foley has promised him something, probably a shot at patrol." Then he laughed. "You amaze me. Don't you hear any of the department bullshit? Are you that...I don't know is it either aloof or obtuse?"

Nagler's face hardened. "I hear it, but I've got stuff outside of work, family stuff." He glanced sideways at Dawson. "My wife is sick."

"Jesus, I feel like a fool. Sorry, Frank."

"Don't. Not a lot of people know. I don't talk about it. But, thanks," Nagler said softly. "So, I focus on the case." He tapped the mailbox four times, stopped, then tapped it three more times, harder each time. "In the back of my mind, you know, what I'm waiting for something big here, a real break. But at the same time, with everyone in the city on edge and packing, I'm waiting for someone innocent to be in the wrong place at the wrong time." He stared at Dawson. "And we'll have a victim of a different sort."

Dawson held his head with both hands. "I'm surprised that hasn't happened already."

"Me, too."

Dawson nodded a couple times and thought, might as well. "There is something else, you know."

"What's that?"

"Someone is apparently ripping off city hall. Real estate, phony accounts, phony buyers."

Nagler exhaled deeply. "Jesus. You working on that?"

"Just heard," Dawson shrugged a shoulder. "Starting. I'll let you know. Sounds really bad. I'd keep an eye out, if I were you."

"Why?"

"Something like this creates victims, even innocent victims." Dawson's memory rattled with Harrington's warning about a fall guy. Am I looking at him?

Nagler pushed off the postal box and eyed Dawson coldly. "Who's running the show?"

Dawson squinted into the setting sun and scratched his right ear. "Newton, I've heard. The mayor. With helpers." He felt lighter, saying that.

"Well, shit." Nagler chuckled softly. "It's almost funny, Jimmy.

There's nothing in Ironton to steal, and they're gonna steal it anyway." Nagler squinted at the ground, then closed one eye and smiled. "Keep that dispatcher talking?"

Dawson grinned and shook his head and said, "Yeah…" but Nagler lifted his head, looked into the distance past the train station, and told Dawson to remain quiet.

"Hear that?" He held up one hand.

Then faintly, a voice distinct from the hum the train crowd. "Help me! Please. Help me. Stop it!"

"Sounds like it's near St. Luke's," Nagler said as he stepped off then ran toward St. Luke's Methodist Church, adjacent to the train complex.

"Hey!" Nagler yelled as he saw three kids grabbing or punching a man prone on the sidewalk. He sidestepped and jumped between cars lined up to pick up train passengers, smacking the hood of one Dodge whose driver wouldn't slow down.

"Let's go," one of the kids yelled and two of them turned and ran. One stood slowly and turned to face Nagler.

It was the kid. He turned to the charging officer, slipped his hands into his jeans pockets and smiled before running off.

You little asshole, Nagler thought. But now I know what you look like: Five-four or five, skinny, a hundred pounds, little more, dirty blond hair and missing a front tooth. The kid was standing in a shadow, so half his face was lighted, and half was dark; better than nothing, Nagler thought, and turned to aid the beaten man.

Nagler called dispatch and described three kids running from St. Luke's maybe east on Blackwell or up Bergen, heading for the alleys. Blue shirt, red shirt, a brown jacket or something, one in a ball cap, fourteen or so.

He leaned over the man on the ground and saw that he was just a boy himself.

"They're gone," Nagler said. "Can you sit up?" And he reached over to touch the boy's arm.

"No more. Stop!" the boy cried out as he swung his arm widely in the air.

"Wait," Nagler said as he ducked the swinging arm. "Wait. It's okay. I'm a cop."

The boy pushed himself up and the crawled backward to lean on the base of the church wall. He kicked out his feet and swung his arms aimlessly. "Go away. Go away!" Then he covered his face with his hands and wept.

Nagler knelt down and gently pulled the boy's hands away from his scratched face. He was blind. "No," the boy cried.

"My name is Frank, Frank Nagler. I'm a detective." He placed the boy's hands in his lap. "I need to look at your face, the cuts, okay?" He paused. "You can't see me, can you?"

"No," the boy said, and relaxed against the wall and let Nagler brush the hair away from his forehead. The cuts were minor, but he could see a bruise starting to rise next to his left eye. "My ribs hurt."

"Okay," Nagler said and reached for his radio to call for medical help.

"I don't need an ambulance, Detective," the boy said. "I've had worse beatings. I learned how to cover up."

"How did you know I was calling in?"

"I could hear you reach for the radio," the boy said. "I hear very well. I can identity those boys, if you need me to." The kid wiped his forehead with the sleeve of his shirt.

"Really?"

"I know their voices and the pace of their steps. We are, shall we say, familiar with one another."

Nagler nodded. "How many times?"

"Four, no five. This makes five. They steal the change in my box. I sell pencils to the train riders."

Nagler wrinkled his face and stared at the station. Damn. "How old are you, son?"

The boy reached around on the ground, searching with splayed fingers for the metal box that rested just out of reach; Nagler leaned over and handed it to him. A few coins sparkled on the ground.

"What's your name?"

"Leonard."

"How long…"

A hard voice. "Since I was eight. I was in a home for poor kids. They misdiagnosed an illness and I went blind."

"How old…where do you live?"

Leonard smiled. "I'm sixteen. I used to live at the School for the

Blind, but it was shut down by the state three years ago. They lost track of me, and I ended up on the street. So, here I am. I get by."

No, Nagler thought. "No, you don't. You get beat up by gangs of kids, and you probably haven't eaten a good meal in days. Am I right?"

Leonard stared at the ground and then covered his face.

Nagler picked up his radio.

"Dispatch. Hey, Mattie, it's Nagler. Please call social services for me. Got a customer. Young man needs a bed and a meal tonight."

Dawson arrived.

"Run that picture, Jimmy."

CHAPTER FOURTEEN

A day behind

She had been beaten and stabbed.

In daylight.

In the parking lot across from City Hall.

And no one saw anything.

Nagler scanned the three buildings south of the parking lot.

"Lotta windows in those apartments," he nodded to Sergeant LaStrada. "Think anyone saw anything?"

"Nothing they'll tell us," LaStrada replied before nodding toward City Hall. "Don't look now."

Charging across the lot with one hand clamping his white Panama to his head was Mayor Howard Newton and behind him was Chris Foley.

"What the hell are you people doing?" the Mayor bellowed. "I thought I told you to find this guy and now we have another body?"

Foley quickstepped to get between Newton and Nagler and LaStrada.

"Let them do their job, Mr. Mayor," Foley said. "We are making progress."

"Hey Sergeant, LaStrada," a patrolman near the damaged chain-link fence that separated the parking lot from the river called out. "Got a purse."

"See Mr. Mayor," Foley said. "A purse. That's good." He steered Newton away from the scene. "I'll report to you later."

"Progress, gentlemen," the Mayor demanded walking away. "I want progress."

Foley returned to Nagler. "And you're worried about talking to some street punk. Did you release that photo?" He shook his head. "Dangerous," he said before stalking off to speak with Mulligan. "What do we know…"

The parking lot was about a quarter-mile long, part of the former Union Iron Mill site between the river and old canal path. Besides the frontage on Warren Street, the lot had a half-dozen entry points, Nagler knew. It was a busy lot, mainly for employees of the downtown shops and offices. It would fill up daily between seven and nine each morning.

And no one saw anything.

The purse held a driver's license: Deborah Jones, 23. Rockaway Avenue.

Nagler approached Mulligan after Foley returned to City Hall.

"What?"

"Miss Jones was struck with a round hard object, two blows to the head, then stabbed twice," Mulligan said flatly. Always emotionless, Nagler thought; suppose he has to be. "It appears she was first struck in the lower back, spun around, punched in the face a couple of times, fell, and then struck on the head. Then stabbed." He motioned to a nearby EMT. "Please shield the body."

"Another ambush attack," Nagler said. Just like that kid Leonard. "We know Joan Chen was killed in a similar style attack. What are the odds that some of the other woman were also ambushed? Could we prove it?"

Mulligan paused in his examination of Deborah Jones. "It could make sense for Miss Sanchez, the cab driver, and perhaps even Miss Austin, found in Smelly Flats. For Dr. Harmon, found in the warehouse, and Miss Wilson found in the bog, it is a plausible theory but there is much less evidence."

"Do we know when Miss Jones died?"

"About nine-thirty."

"Jesus, doctor. At that time this place would have had hundreds of people heading to work."

"People don't get involved, Frank," Mulligan said. "They see what might be a disagreement between a boyfriend and girlfriend, or husband and wife, and they turn away. When they look back, the couple is gone. So, they conclude it was nothing,"

"Which is why we don't know anything about any of our other deaths," Nagler said. He replayed his visit to the train station and how no one interacted at all, focused instead on themselves. So, we'll find out where she worked, check her address, ask if she had any enemies, argued with anyone recently, broke up with a lover or spouse…

"Agreed," Mulligan said as he stepped away and supervised the placement of Deborah Jones, 23, into his van.

LaStrada, near a wall at the south end of the lot, called to Nagler.

Tucked under a pile of brush and trash was a three-foot pipe with two leaf-covered splotches of that seemed to be blood on one end.

"Sounds like what Mulligan described," LaStrada said. "Tried to hide it. Odd, though. Never left a weapon before. No knife, but it's something."

Nagler squinted into the sunlight, scanning the crowd that had gathered, but was held back at some distance because of the size of lot. "That's a taunt, isn't it? Here's a clue, assholes," Nagler muttered. "He's here. I know it."

LaStrada agreed and quickly scanned the lot and the gathered on-lookers.

"He's probably been watching all of them, every time we come out," Nagler said. "So why are they getting more public?"

LaStrada smiled. "A shrink might say he's trying to get noticed. Dropping bodies in remote places didn't get the response he'd hoped for. Killing someone across from City Hall becomes a statement of control. But, know what, Frank? Screw the shrink talk. The cop in me says this is just him standing in the crowd giving us the finger."

"Some guy saying, 'Can't catch me.'"

LaStrada nodded. "Yeah. I wonder where we'll find the red hand." LaStrada smirked, but his eyes were hard. "Dead woman, red handprint."

"Why does it feel like we're a step, a day behind, Sal?" Nagler asked.

"Because it always feels like that, Frank," LaStrada replied. "Until the day we're not."

Nagler nodded. "Just keep digging, huh?"

"That's all you can do. Say, who is this kid you're chasing?"

Nagler scratched his neck. "Not really sure, but he keeps showing up at crime scenes. He was at the Edie Smith house almost before we were. It's like he knows something, but for the life of me I can't figure out what."

"I've known some ambulance chasers, Frank. They seem to have a nose for it."

Nagler watched as LaStrada returned to the search of the parking lot perimeter. Beyond them, he saw Dawson waving an arm to get Nagler's attention. Later.

He ordered Robbie Karpinski, the department photographer, to shoot the crowd. We're gonna have to make our own luck, he thought.

CHAPTER FIFTEEN

My own damn street

"There he is! Get him."

Nagler, walking on the north side of Blackwell, heard the cry and turned in its direction. A crowd half a block away across the street parted as a wild-eyed man stumbled furiously along the sidewalk, slipping to all fours, then pushing himself off his hands to run again.

"Back-up. Blackwell and Salem." Nagler yelled into his radio and ran toward the fleeing man.

"Stop him!" A voice from a group or five or six men jamming through the walkers. "Grab him!"

Confused women and men flattened themselves against storefronts or stepped between parked cars to clear the sidewalk. A teenager grabbed for the runner and held his left arm for a second, but the man spun away.

Nagler blocked the sidewalk and the man slowed but tried to elude him.

"Stop!" Nagler yelled. "I'm a cop. Stop!"

"Gotta go, man. I didn't do nothing."

The man tried to run around Nagler, who spun him to the wall. "Why are you running? Why are they chasing you?"

Before he could answer, two patrol cars pulled up and officers placed themselves between Nagler and the rushing group. Five men pushed against the police officers, who stood their ground as the energy of the rush petered out.

A sixth member of the group ran into the street and circled around the police cars and before anyone could stop him, launched a running punch into the side of the head of the man they had been chasing. The man let out a scream as his head cracked against the concrete wall. Nagler and one of the officers grabbed the puncher and wrestled him to a sitting position against the wall.

"Cuff him," Nagler ordered. "Call rescue."

The other officer stood in the center of the sidewalks with his arms outspread.

131

"You gotta let us have him, officer," one man shouted. "He looks like the killer." A chorus of agreement. They pushed against the officers, now supported by Nagler. A hand from the group reached out toward Nagler's face, but he jerked back in time. The hand instead grabbed his tie and tugged the knot to a tiny ball.

"Let go!" Nagler yelled as he grabbed the man's wrist to pull away his tie.

Two more patrol cars; four more officers jumped out and surrounded the crowd; Nagler freed his tie.

The man who threw the punch collapsed wearily against the wall. The runner held an ice pack to his swollen jaw.

Now outnumbered, the crowd which had been chasing the runner slumped to a soft circle. Nagler took several deep breaths. He was surprised in this heat the chase had gone on as long as it had; the chasers were red-faced, open mouthed and leaning hands on others' shoulders to recover.

Nagler stepped over to the encircled men.

Slowly: "What the fuck are you doing?"

Breath recovered, the men also rediscovered their anger.

"We're doing your job, officer," said the man who had strangled Nagler's tie. "All these women dead, and you're do nothin'."

"Why were you chasing this guy? Nagler asked.

"Where's that flyer? Because of this," the tie strangler said. "That's the guy," and he pointed at the runner.

"Where the hell did you get this?" Nagler asked, taking the paper from the man. "We didn't issue this. What the hell?"

"It said Ironton Police on the bottom," the man said. "You said there was a suspect, so we chased him. Caught him. Doin' your job."

Nagler glanced at the poster. It did indeed say "Ironton PD" on the bottom. But it was more in quality like those missing women posters that had briefly been stapled to light posts a few weeks before. It hardly looked official, but to a riled up, over heated crowd anything was possible.

Nagler shook his head.

"This is not an official document," he told the men. "Doesn't look anything like him." He shook the flier in the faces of the crowd. "This is not a wanted poster and Ironton is not the goddamn Old West." Then it boiled out — the frustration, anger, disappointment and fear — "What the fuck is the matter with you people? This is just some guy, just like you. And this" — he shook the flyer at them — "hardly looks real. In fact, it looks like some high school art project. If you were in your right minds, you'd know that."

"If you'd catch the killer, maybe we'd be in our right minds, officer," the man yelled back. "What about our daughters, our wives? What are you doing to protect them?"

"We're trying to catch the bastard," Nagler glared back. He waved then paper again. "And this…this is…bullshit." Then: A distraction, he thought. This is not an accident. Crap.

He waved at the gathering. "Just go on home, huh? This poster is not real, and this guy is not the killer. The men glared back. "Just go home, kiss your wives and daughters." Nagler grabbed the arm of the man who had strangled his tie. "You owe me a new tie."

An EMT treated the runner's scrapes as his pursuers turned away.

"Crazy, huh, Detective," one of the patrol officers said.

After the crowd dispersed, and the police officers returned to their patrols Nagler stared at the flyer he had taken from the chasers. This one was more sophisticated than the previous "missing women" flyers. Using the department's name and number was clever and provoking.

The sweat dripped from his brow as he stared into the burning sun, sitting on the western rooftops yellow and as big as all the questions in the world.

Posters, handprints and slogans. Maybe the guy is trying to tell us who he is, Nagler thought.

****

She had taken again to scarves.

He hesitated when he entered the house and saw Martha, held her tightly when her smiling face collapsed into a lip-biting frown and she stared at the floor with wet eyes.

"I have to go into the hospital for a couple days," Martha said to his shoulder, her voice airless. "They want to do more testing and probably start a new treatment."

He squeezed his eyes closed and tipped his head to one side. "I don't…" he sighed. "I don't want to have to do this again. I don't want you to have to do this again."

"Don't have a choice, buddy. It will be okay, Frank," she said, staring out the window with troubled eyes.

It won't be okay, he knew, but he said, "Sure," and kissed her hair. "I'll go with you."

"Not yet," she whispered. "Not yet." She stared into his eyes. "I'm coming back."

Later, they sat on the porch late into the night letting the heat of the house subside.

"Where did that boy go?" she asked.

Nagler placed the beer bottle on the steps. "The blind kid?"

"Yes. Leonard, you said."

"Social services picked him up. They are searching for a place for him that would let him take classes, get him some physical therapy, just a safer place." He kissed her forehead. "How'd he survive out there? And how come we never saw him before?" He shook his head. "Man. Seems he was abandoned. Tough kid."

Martha settled into his side. "Let him stay here."

"What?" Then he laughed. "Martha…"

"We have the room, Frank. Downstairs, those two empty rooms in the back that my parents have used for storage. And I'll be home. He'll be better here, around people in a home, not an institution. It'll be good for him. I already spoke to my mother. She's excited. It would be like having another child."

He hugged her shoulders. "Saving the world."

"Need to save something," she whispered.

He finished the beer.

"Was thinking there has to be dozens of kids like him out there, homeless, probably desperate," he said. "Where do they go every day?"

Martha leaned back against the porch post. "I see them at the park. Hanging together, sharing smokes, maybe sandwiches or a drink. One of them will break away and panhandle, get rejected, and after a second or two yells at the person who just rejected them. Then they come back to group. Where do they live, Frank?"

He rubbed her leg that she had draped over his thigh.

"Stoveworks, in the summer in the woods beyond the high school, empty buildings, maybe in this dry spell, the Old Iron Bog. There's some sort of outcroppings, like islands, but they'd have to live with the bugs." He wrinkled his nose and shrugged. "Still, we've found remnants of tents and rough shelters. They sneak into the community center for lunch but split before anyone can ask them questions."

"Feral kids."

"I wonder sometimes why I didn't end up like them," he said. "The workers ghetto was no place for kids."

"You're not them, Frank. Not like them at all. I know the ghetto. It was a hard place. I walked through there looking for you sometimes."

He spun his head. "You never…"

"Why would I tell you?" Martha asked. "You would have run away." She reached her arms around his neck and kissed his cheek. "I needed to be sneakier than that. I saw his boy with the dirty pants and the blue sweater, and he was smarter and more gentle than anyone. But I knew that he was ashamed of where he had come from," she deepened her voice in an exaggerated growl, "the poor side of town, the wrong side of the tracks." She smiled and stared into the darkness. "But for me there was no wrong side of the tracks, there was just you."

His hands were shaking, and tears filled his eyes. "I would have been there still if not for you."

She smiled and ran a hand through his hair. "What else was I supposed to do there, Romeo? I saw you and nothing else mattered." He held her face and kissed her deeply. "That's okay," she said, winking. "I know you felt the same way. You could say it, but you're the strong, silent type. The words are in there somewhere. They'll come out." She laughed. "One of these days. But not tonight. I'm going to bed."

The door shut softly behind him and Frank Nagler stared at the ground with a helpless look on his face. What would I have done without her?

He looked up sharply as something he could not see crashed through the brush on the black vacant lot across the street. A second of silence, then shuffling, tripping, dragging, and the sounds of branches being pushed aside and brushing the old shed.

Too large for an animal, Nagler thought. But who…?

He didn't have a flashlight on the porch and his service weapon was locked up inside the house. Damn. What was that? He stared into the dark lot for a while, but there was no more sound. Need to install that spotlight. I'll check that shed in the morning, he thought as he turned to enter the house. Kids? Homeless?

Martha slept soundly while he brooded. He recalled that she had told him a few weeks ago that she and her father had heard someone or something across the street. Is someone living in that old shed now? His mind blanked out as he tried to sleep. Those kids, the ones who beat up Leonard. What turned them into street thugs? They weren't more than fifteen. Sure, things in Ironton were bad, but have we fallen to the point where kids have to turn to crime to survive? When the iron business crashed, that was bad. No work anywhere. Guys I knew… He dozed then started awake. And the killer. Those ambush attacks, so angry. Is that what we have become? So angry. Did we make you? I could have been… He is one of us.

In the morning, Nagler paused at the side of the Impala and softly cursed, "Son of a bitch."

Across the street, painted on the side of the old rotten shed, was a red hand and the phrase HAND OF DEATH.

****

While he waited for more investigators, Nagler angrily snapped a few Polaroids of the red hand and slogan. That had been last night's noises. How long had they been watching our house? Fuck this. Now you've made it personal.

He felt a shiver run up his back, not for himself, but for Martha. This was a threat. His eyes wrinkled to worry. How can I protect her?

A trail of fast food wrappers, bottles and cans circled the broken shed. It was the last structure standing on that lot. The home had collapsed decades ago and now rested as a haphazard pile of rotted timbers and bricks inside a stone foundation. Some cardboard had been jammed into the shed's one side window and nails had been forced into the door hinges. Lotta work, he thought.

The debris was a mix of old and new. Some of the paper bags had been stepped on and chewed by animals while a few of the bottles contained a few drops of liquid. Who's out here and why hasn't anyone seen them? Why haven't I seen them?

The door had been set at angles, the bottom grabbing the frame; it took both hands to yank it open.

"More junk," he said as his eyes adjusted to the interior darkness.

Except for the one piece that wasn't junk.

"Holy shit, Frank," LaStrada growled as Nagler led him to the shed. "It means…"

"It means," Nagler "That whoever broke into Edie Smith's house was here, across the street from my house. Now, I'd like to think that is as just a coincidence, but I know it's not." Nagler's face closed to a hard, narrow-eyed stare. "He's watching. Just like killing Debbie Jones in the parking lot across from City Hall. No one is safe."

After photographer Robbie Karpinski photographed the inside and outside of the shed, Nagler placed the small doll into a plastic evidence bag. It matched the photo that was hanging on the case board at police headquarters.

"But why you?" LaStrada asked.

Nagler gazed up at his house and paused for a moment when he saw Martha step away from a window. No, he thought. Never. "Don't know, Sal. Part of the puzzle."

LaStrada coughed out some dust he had inhaled inside the shed.

"He's been here a while, Frank. We found some waste buckets." LaStrada let that thought settle.

"I'm gonna have Hanrahan put this area on the patrol list," Nagler said. "My own damn street." My own damn street.

He punched the side of the shed.

****

Foley had been unimpressed that an item belonging to one of the missing women had been discovered across from Nagler's home. And less impressed about the discovery of the red hand and slogan.

"Could be neighborhood punks," Foley said, the disinterested calmness of his voice grating on Nagler's raw nerves.

He exploded. "Punks? No. It's the fucking killer." He leaned over Foley's desk. "Let me repeat that. It's the fucking killer. Stalking my house. Leaving his mark."

Foley leaned back in his chair, eyes withdrawn.

"Do not threaten me, Detective."

Nagler swept a pile of papers off the desk to the floor.

"I don't believe you," he yelled into Foley's placid face. Then he back off and took several deep breaths. "I will defend my wife, Chris. Depend on it."

Foley silence ground Nagler's nerves.

He turned to go.

"We don't know it's the same doll," Foley said.

Nagler turned back to Foley and glared.

"It's an after-school program for little kids and the handicapped," Nagler snapped back. "Christ. It's not an assembly line. I talked to the director. They had made some dolls as physical therapy for some kids there, not a lot, but stopped years ago. He didn't even know how long ago. Before his time, he said. He wanted to know if he could have it."

Foley again sat quietly.

"I don't get it. It's a god damn clue," Nagler yelled. "Maybe our killer had some emotional connection this doll. Maybe he had even made it. Don't you want to know that? And it was placed in a shed across from my house, with his mark. And that doesn't concern you?"

"We don't know what it means, Detective." Foley rolled down his shirt sleeves, buttoned the cuffs, and sat behind his desk, shifting the chair back and forth a few times before placing his elbows on the desk like a high school principal preparing to scold an errant student. He used a small fist to cover a slight cough. "As Dr. Mulligan says, do not jump to conclusions."

The prissiness finally got to Nagler.

"Is it okay that I might be concerned that my wife who is being tested for a possible return of leukemia is at home while somebody even loosely associated with these murders has been in a shed across the street? Can I be upset about that? Maybe it's that asshole kid you have yet to bring into headquarters. Can I be concerned that you don't seem to give a shit?"

Foley's face flushed and his ears glowed red. His lips formed a hard, firm line. "Of course, I care. I'm sorry about your wife." His voice was soft and flat, a cold threat. "You have no idea what I have done, Detective. We have so many different modes of death, locations. Nothing fits a pattern. I have been speaking with experts and police experienced with serial killings for information and guidance. Applying science and method."

"Yeah, I understand that, Chris," Nagler huffed. "Still…where's the results?"

The edge in Nagler's voice launched Foley from his seat.

"Maybe you'd rather we stumble around until we happened to trip over the killer?" Foley's voice hardened, finally drained of even the slightest bit of emotion. "In fact, Detective, why you don't try that. Let me know it goes."

****

Edie Smith's home had grown dark and dusty, tomblike. Unintentional, Nagler thought, just securing the buildings, but still, the place was a creepy as the Locust Hill Cemetery at midnight.

Her son, Gregory Smith, the banker, had called off the private security patrol, and the city had reduced the drive-bys.

It was time, Nagler thought, as he stood on the porch facing the reconstructed door frame and new locks that had been installed, time to declare Edie Smith and Marion Feldman more than missing and endangered.

Perhaps, Mulligan had said. "But it's been mere weeks, and I don't believe we have exhausted all the possibilities. We need proof."

Instead, the women rested in some in-between status, Nagler thought, as Mulligan droned on about the legalities. Here but not here. A question. A space in each family's life; a shadow.

Mulligan had explained that his declaration that a person was officially dead would trigger a cascade of legal and financial actions that would be difficult to undo if that person was later found to be alive. "It is something I do not do lightly," Mulligan grumbled. "And certainly not without irrefutable evidence, no matter that I actually think. Besides, if I do and the person is in fact alive, the city gets sued, and I spend the rest of my career as a defendant." He glanced over his glasses. "A choice I'd rather not make, Detective."

Nagler at first had shrugged, then he nodded in agreement.

"How do we end it, Doc?" Nagler asked.

"With bodies," Mulligan replied darkly. "Bodies, evidence, and perhaps a killer. In other words, proof."

Nagler's shoulder's sagged. "But…"

"It's out there, Frank. You'll find it."

Nagler drove the neighborhoods again, rolling over in his mind the evidence they had. Each death seemed so different, some with leads, the rest threadbare, which led to guesses.

How do we pull these strings together? He wondered. And how do we connect them to one killer, which was still the operative theory.

For Marion Feldman, with one living relative who was trying to sell her house, it could be a simple affair.

But for Edie Smith, with extensive financial holdings and a widespread family, it would be more difficult, Mulligan had explained. Even for Dr. Nancy Harman, who was confirmed dead, had a medical practice and owned a few pieces of real estate, the case in probate court had dragged on, Nagler knew. No one, the court case confirmed, had killed Nancy Harmon for her money.

But dead she was, Nagler thought. Our victim. His victim.

Gregory Smith had used his banking industry contacts to scour the world for any trace of any financial action tied to his mother's accounts and found no recent entries.

Nagler watched his face as he explained how his mother once was "missing" in Australia for more than four months. She had flown there, withdrew a few thousand in cash and spent the time traveling the desolate parts of the nation by jeep and paying cash for everything. She had eventually surfaced at a hotel in Perth driving a different jeep than the one with which she had started, and with a couple new companions.

"She had become somewhat of a short-term Outback legend, the 'Yank Granny,'" Gregory Smith said. "I'm horrified to think what she had done to deserve that moniker."

He had tried to relate the story with a bemused, disbelieving smile, but his eyes were dark with worry and his voice faltered to a whisper during the telling.

The Smith house felt as cold and stark as one of those old family mausoleums in the cemetery, Nagler thought; air stiff, chilled, scented with a nose-wrinkling dry must. The family had boxed up many of the loose possessions and clothes and stored them in a back room, rolled up the rugs and wrapped them in plastic, and covered the furniture with cloth tarps. Valuables had been removed to a bank safe deposit box.

His every step echoed.

Nagler's question hung in the air: Are you planning for a funeral or for her return? It was odd, he thought, to be between the two, stuck unknowing, emotions both frayed with concern and buoyed with faint hope; odd how much they looked alike, the hollow of emptiness and the fullness of hope.

And here am I, he thought. What do I do?

Martha had entered the hospital for two days. Tests, the doctors said. Recheck her white blood count. Routine. Not to worry. As if that was possible.

Nagler examined the mantle where Gregory Smith had said the doll had rested all those years. Why steal that, a child's toy, and not the jewelry left on the dresser, or the cash on the dining room table? There had to be a connection.

He continued the brooding tour of the house trying to recall if Marion Feldman's granddaughter had said anything was missing after she had examined the boxes left at the home.

CHAPTER SIXTEEN

The hosiery mill

COP CATFIGHT: WOMAN ARE DYING, COPS ARE FIGHTING.
Nagler felt the eyes on him burning as he slipped into the last booth at Barry's. They had followed him as he walked slowly to the booth, peered over coffee cups, leaked out of the corner of faces before they piled back into their bacon and eggs.

Nagler was grateful for the rattle of cook Tony's spatula on the grill as he tonelessly hummed "U Can't Touch This."

"Da, da-da, dum…" His head bopped and his shoulders shrugged in rhythm as he occasionally mumbled, "Can't touch this," and arms outstretched rolled the words across his shoulders and back before returning to the humming and banging.

One regular, leaning over a cup of coffee in the last counter seat, maintained his stare in Nagler's direction; then he shook his head once: No. Nagler returned the look with a hard stare of his own until the man glanced down, drained the coffee cup, stood up and flipped a couple of coins on the counter before leaving; he dragged his stained Ironton High School cap low over his eyes.

Nagler read the first line of Dawson's story again and slapped the paper in a heap onto the wall side chair.

"A dispute between the lead investigators into the deaths of eight women has slowed the probe and possibly allowed the unknown killer to carry on his evil mission unchecked."

Barry arrived with coffee.

"That Dawson, huh? He ain't doin' you no good, Frank. Maybe I throw his ass outta here."

Distracted, Nagler stared then laughed. "Got that right." He nodded thanks for the coffee. "Don't worry about him."

"Eatin'?"

Nagler squinted up at Barry. He hadn't. Laughing: "Yeah." He nodded. "Yeah. Um, an omelet, ham, maybe cheddar and some of that hot sausage. Maybe onions and peppers. Dark toast. You know, the heart-attack special."

Barry laughed. "Ah, Frank. We gotta take care of you." He called out to Tony. "Hey, music man. An omelet, four eggs for Frank. Ham, chorizo, onions, peppers. Cheddar."

"Barry, a question."

"Yeah."

"Your cousin's a florist, right? Could she put together some flowers for Martha? She's not feeling well."

Barry knew the history; a brief, dark sadness settled in his eyes. "I'll take care of it, Frank. Don't you worry."

****

Walking again.

The shaded river alley, potholes, branches broken like bones, gray weeds sprouting from building frames; the river wall, cracked granite blocks four feet wide, tipping at angles.

Wooden doors a hundred years old pried open to dark, endless cellars; a flashlight glare on whiskey and soda bottles, torn blankets, wrappers. But no killer.

Those kids who attacked Leonard could have hidden in that darkness, he thought. We never would have seen them.

Why does this city have so many ghosts?

Then finally down the long, dreary path to Smelly Flats.

The area had been scoured by LaStrada's crew. Bags of stuff, but that's all it was. Debris. Could have blown off the road above, out of the train yard. How is it that this guy is so clean?

In the continued heat of the dry summer, the path had hardened as the river pulled back to a trickling stream.

Tamika Austin had to have been there on her own before she was killed, he decided. She was not a small woman, and on that path even for someone small just walking was tricky, root crossed and in the dark, one step off the line would have put a careless walker in the river, or maybe broken an ankle. Carrying a body? No.

And as he had told LaStrada the night they found her, none of the women and boys working downtown said they would never bring a trick down here. Too remote. "Too damn far, Honey. Ain't worth my time to hike all the way down here. I ain't no lumberjack." That was Jannise, the queen of the streets. Someone said she'd been a teacher, then it went bad.

144

None of them recalled Tamika with a customer that night or for any time before that.

Jannise said, "She was in and out, Frank. Strung out, no good to no one, then straight, as pretty a girl to work down here. Coulda done wonderful things if she had a way out of the life. Maybe she didn't want one."

The last turn. The smell…assaulted. Jesus.

He gagged then covered his nose and mouth with a handkerchief. The silence of the place settled in; a dark, troubled silence, hollow, threatening. Ironton's path to Hell. Not even the Old Iron Bog, with its murky, shifting water, oil-sheened and lightless; mossy coves and barren rocky outcroppings, not even the place they knew bodies had been buried, not even that, matched Smelly Flats; here, he knew was a sinister sense that was unequalled.

This is the last place I want to be, standing in all this gloom. Why doesn't this place ever have any sunlight?

A mirthless, disgusted laugh. Here I am, bitching about the landscape. Man.

He wrapped an elbow around a tree, cocked his feet on the trail for balance and absorbed the darkness. Left to right he scanned the steep, brush covered opposite wall, the curve of the river as it exited the whirlpool, and turning, the rocky cliff behind him.

The silence was broken when a car paused on the bridge above the gorge, and something glass in two paper bags of trash tossed out the window shattered on the rocks, the laughter trailing off.

The sound startled Nagler, who was facing away from the bridge, and he shook his head to recover then took a few steps toward the trash bags.

He glanced up to the bridge and said, "Oh, shit."

Midway across the green metal supporting beam was an upside down red handprint. The accompanying slogan HAND OF DEATH had clearly been painted upside down while the painter lay on the bridge; the slogan was ragged and poorly spaced, because, Nagler concluded, the painter could not see what he was doing. HAND had been painted on one side of the riveted support brace, which had been splashed with a dripping smear of red paint, and OF DEAT unevenly on the other side. The "H" was missing. Did a car come? Could they not reach that far?

"Look at that," he laughed.

Next to the broken bottles and trash was a paint brush with red bristles. Dropped it. That might explain the missing letter "H."

I wonder what else he left up there? Nagler wondered. I'll have to get my car and look.

He surveyed the ground for a route to the paint brush, but the path ended with a slide into the water, and the trees on the bank gave way to a steep, mossy jumble of loose rocks.

His shoes leaked water and mud all the way back to the train station parking lot. His socks rubbed on his heels, slipping forward and back with each step. He thought about stopping at the train station and shedding his shoes to wring out his socks and scrape off the mud, but thought that action might have just seemed odd to anyone watching. Instead, he pulled out a sheet of newspaper wind-jammed into the train yard fence and wiped his shoes and pants.

Let me get this brush to headquarters, and then I'll head home to get dry shoes and socks, he decided.

He wrapped the paint brush in another piece of newsprint and headed back to headquarters.

Idling at the station was a white Coupe de Ville. Mayor Howard Newton.

Waiting, Nagler knew instantly. Waiting for me. He caught his breath and fought off a back-shaking shiver. How did he...doesn't really matter, does it?

Through the tinted window, Nagler could make out the outline of the white Panama, which took full shape as the window slid down and a wave of cigar smoke leaked out.

"Hop in, Detective." Newton looked straight ahead. It was not a friendly invitation.

Nagler leaned to the open window. "It's just two blocks. I'm fine. Thank you, sir."

"Your mayor is offering you a ride. Not everyone gets asked."

It was not a choice; the chill of a command.

Nagler walked around the rear of the Caddy, tapping one finger along the trunk, and slipped into the back seat. The mayor rapped on the glass between seats and the car pulled away from the curb.

The cool of the air conditioning dried the sweat on Nagler's forehead.

Silence, then Nagler nodded, "Thank you, sir. Why were you at the train station, may I ask?"

Newton tipped his head back and then sucked in several long draws on his cigar and the let sweet smoke curl from his mouth, a master of his space. "Cuban," he said with a smile, and inspected the thick rolled tobacco with satisfaction. Silence.

"Illegal," Newton cheerfully sneered then laughed, pleased, secure, untouchable. He pulled down the brim of the Panama so it brushed the frames of the dark sunglasses, eyes and face hidden, the mask complete.

"So, you've been at the Flats." Voice like a dry nail pulled from wood.

Nagler's eyes narrowed. What? One shallow breath.

A short cough.

"Yes, sir. It's a crime scene. Sometimes criminals return."

A soft wheeze. "Ah…true. Heard that. Find anything?"

It would be hard to lie, holding a paint brush wrapped in newspaper.

"A paint brush. I'm sure Detective Foley informed you about the red hands seen around town." Nagler shrugged. "Might be something."

Newton waited for more of an answer. He coughed.

"I heard that you and Detective Foley have had a little pissing match."

Another waft of cigar smoke.

Nagler thought: Yeah…okay, got it now. Lightly: "It was in the paper. A bit of frustration. Not sure how it got there, in the newspaper. Dawson must have a source." Nagler snuck a glance at Newton to see if there was any response to that line.

A smoke-filled smile. "Detective Foley will make a fine police chief. He's diligent, loyal. Understands chain of command."

A glance from Newton, a slight tip of the head.

"Um, I have no opinion on that, sir. I've only worked with him on this case. We are trying, Mr. Mayor. The lack of progress creates stress."

A few deep puffs; smoke hung, filled the space, the air stinging, thicker, warmer, still.

Nagler rolled his eyes to the window and caught a brief glance of an old factory complex in East Ironton. This was not the way to police headquarters, but the opposite direction.

Despite the sour feeling in his gut, Nagler said, his tone less pleasant, "Why were you waiting for me?" He wanted to roll down the window, his head light, the air like ash. He reached a finger toward the electric button; stopped. He coughed, partly fake; a request.

Newton nodded his head slightly three times before smiling through another cloud of smoke; the cigar was a weapon.

His voice was a growl of a grinding, metal shaft, edges rubbing deep. "You and I are a lot alike, Detective. Working families, mill families. Hard working. Seen the ups and downs. Understand how teams work. So, you understand why it's important to find this killer. A stain on our community."

Nagler squinted, blinked away small tears. Firmly: "We need to find him before he kills again." He swallowed a cough. "That's what's important."

Newton abruptly turned his head. "You know where we are, Detective?" The voice more threatening. Inhaled; the cigar a pointer.

"The old hosiery mill."

Eyes and teeth behind smoke. "Correct. Worth nothing empty. Worth millions if occupied. I want you to find the killer before there is no value here whatsoever, just an empty, rotting pile of brick and steel I can't do anything with. The city without a future. I want you and Detective Foley to get along. Be good for both of you. That's what's important."

Both of us? Dawson was right about Foley, the mayor's man. But me? Nagler rubbed his knee so as not to react. He wanted to wave a knowing hand in the air and smile in agreement, happy to share the concerns of his mayor. Can't. He sighed and sank back in seat. It was always about money, isn't it? He bit his lip. A bitter whisper: "Yes, sir."

"Money like that would help this town."

"I'm sure it would. But what's got to do with our killer? Weren't there killers when this mill was running full tilt?"

"That was then. I can't have a crazy killer roaming the streets of Ironton today, Detective." Harshly. Out of patience. "People want action. It is bad for our image."

Nagler let the answer hang in the acid smoke. In deep. Go deeper. He always thought he would know when that imaginary line had been crossed, the one between right and wrong. This was probably it. "You should let me out, Mister Mayor." Flat; a push-back.

A few seconds passed. Newton tapped the window and the car slid to the curb.

"You need to see the bigger picture, Detective Nagler, see what the end to the killings would do for our cause, our image. Clear?"

"The bigger picture, sir?" Nagler said reaching for the door handle; a slight pull. It was still locked. "The picture of the city, needing justice, restoration of calm? Peace to the grieving families?" His voice found an edge. "That is the cause you are speaking about, correct, Mr. Mayor?"

Nagler heard the door lock click.

Newton leaned forward in his seat, and turned his shoulders, head tipped toward Nagler. It was the first time the mayor had moved since Nagler got in the car, other than to shift the cigar to and from his mouth. The Panama shaded the left side of his face and the glasses darkened the rest.

A deep breath and a throaty sigh, his voice a soft growl, the words drawn out. "My...city... My...cause." A threat made worse by the gentle tone.

Nagler shouldered the door open and began to step out. "Yeah, we're doing our best. Like I said." A pause. "Sir." The word spit out; bitter.

Newton leaned back into the seat and stared straight ahead.

"You do know the Trenton Street Club, correct, Detective?" It wasn't a question, but a directive.

Standing in the street, Nagler leaned into the open door, sighed, frowned into the street. "Yeah. Yeah, I do. Pretty exclusive. Invitation only, I heard." I'll pass.

He carefully shut the door, making sure he didn't slam it, masking the trembling in his hand. After a moment the white Caddy jerked from the curb and made a sharp right turn.

In the clean air, Nagler's clothes leaked cigar smoke. The heat drew out sweat.

The Trenton Street Club. Newton's lair, the power base where admission came with a price, names on the guest list like pounds of flesh. You leave there changed. Dawson's voice in his head: Don't get caught.

Nagler leaned against the corner of a brick factory wall and took in a few deep breaths. Eyes closed, he covered his mouth with both shaking hands and exhaled deeply.

Then he walked, head down, short steps, seeking balance; then with longer strides. Then a jog. He turned right into a darkened alley and hands on knees, eyes now wide, shivered. Damn it. Damn it. A breath, two. Damn it.

He crept to the alley opening and glanced in both directions. Quiet streets, pigeons overhead flapping from roof to roof; somewhere water dripping, a grinding of scraping metal from inside the factory walls. Space expanding, sunlight slipping away; darkness rising.

Deep breaths did not displace the shivers.

****

Foley had called them into a squad room. He stood in front of a blackboard with the names of the victims circled in groups: Harmon, Wilson in one, Jones, Chen, and Jackson in a second; and Feldman and Smith in the third.

As he waited for Nagler and LaStrada to sit and examine the board, Foley brushed a dusting of chalk from the sleeve of his brown jacket.

"I think we need to reexamine our theory that there was just one killer," Foley said, tapping the blackboard. "I know Dr. Mulligan insisted that all these deaths are related and the crimes committed by a single person, but since we have had no luck finding that one person, I suggest we take a different look."

Both Nagler and LaStrada started to speak, but Foley raised one hand like a teacher. "Hear me out. If the idea is wrong, it won't take us long to discard it, but if it is right, we might get closer faster to the end of the investigation."

"Okay, lay it out," LaStrada said, while Nagler shrugged.

Foley cleared his throat.

"Our evidence suggests that Harmon, Wilson, and Sanchez were apparently strangled, and we know that Jones, Chen and Jackson were stabbed," he said. "And for Smith and Feldman, we can't say because there is so little evidence. Studies say that serial killers don't change their style, so let's focus on possible suspects who have used these separate methods."

Foley faced LaStrada and Nagler.

"That's it?" Nagler asked. "We sifted through those lists before, Chris. Suspects were either in jail, had moved away or their alibis held up. Remember that one guy, Danny, Rummy…what's his name?"

"Daniel Rumelo," Foley said.

"Yeah, right," Nagler said. "We were hot for him, spent a couple of weeks on him and he was in Miami the whole time."

LaStrada stood up and shook his head.

"No disrespect, Chris, but Ironton hasn't had more than eight murders a year for decades, and the last serial killer was that guy Mulligan named, O'Hanlon, from the old factory days. And now you think there are multiple serial killers operating in the city at the same time? Why?"

Foley glared. "It's just an idea. It is possible. Times have changed." His voice, thin and insubstantial at the best of times, took on a defensive, tinny whine.

After a moment of silence, "I'm open to suggestions, gentlemen. If there aren't any, here's a list of potential suspects, different from the last ones. Divvy them up."

Nagler looked at then back at Foley. "What about the hands? At each crime scene? Did these guys exchange notes?"

"Copycats, Frank. Copycats," Foley sneered. Then he left the room.

CHAPTER SEVENTEEN

The day air burned to the touch

It was the day the temperature cracked one hundred degrees. Desert dry, heat waves distorting distance. The day air burned to the touch; diesel stench thick enough a spark could ignite it.

That was the day Frank Nagler was walking along the narrow trails north of Baker Hills. It was better, he had decided, to sweat in the brambles and swat mosquitos than to kick open the doors to abandoned factories seeking paint cans and listening as the ancient wood creaked in the heat.

"That might be a fingerprint," Mulligan had said while examining the paint brush with gloved hands. "But it just might be a smear."

He placed the brush on the table.

"You said the marking red hand and the lettering were painted on the side of a bridge?"

"Yeah," Nagler said. "The bridge over the Flats. It's about, I don't know, forty feet across. One long steel beam, about fifteen inches wide, tucked underneath the sides of the pavement a bit. You'd have to lean over the side while lying down to reach the beam."

"Which meant they would have held the brush in their fist, correct? Possibly with their palm facing up, and the thumb on the outside, almost painting backward."

Nagler nodded. "That's what I was thinking. Hard place to reach."

Chris Foley growled, "You think it's the killer's brush, without other evidence."

Nagler glanced down at the table and away from Foley. He didn't want to have round three in front of Mulligan, especially after the mayor's tour of the city.

"What are we supposed to think, Chris?" Nagler asked with an edge in his voice. "The handprints have so far only been found at the crime scenes. We need to begin to connect these pieces. And no disrespect to your theory of the other day, these are not copycats. Doesn't make sense. These show up after the bodies have been found. Too planned, especially since the exact locations of the crime scenes have never been released to the public, except for the very public ones." He glanced at Foley and Mulligan. "We never said Tamika Jackson was found in Smelly Flats, so how did a copycat know to place a red hand there?"

Foley had stared at the floor, deflated, like his theory that there were multiple killers in Ironton.

"Alright," he said. "Possible totems, I agree," Foley said with a wisp of dismissal. "Do you agree, Doctor?"

Mulligan shifted his glance between Foley and Nagler. "Without concluding decisively, I concur with Detective Nagler that we must begin to favor the view that these markings belong to our single killer, like a dog scenting his territory, or left as a taunt to us, his pursuers. Remember, we have released publicly little specific information about these deaths, for a reason."

Foley's eyes narrowed. "Fine. Frank, find me the store that sold this brush and a matching gallon of red paint. That would be evidence." Then he left.

Nagler scratched his jaw.

"What if it was not bought at a store?" he asked. "How many leftover cans of paint and brushes could be found in any of the abandoned factories in Ironton, Doctor?"

"If that is the case, Frank, we may never find the source," Mulligan said. "The search would be nearly endless. Instead, I suggest, we presume our killer has his paint and probably more than one brush."

So, jacketless, shirt sleeves rolled to the elbow and tie wrenched one side, Nagler chose the open heat of the woods, rather than the enclosed ovens of stifling, brick factories.

In spots, trees had leafed out, blocking the sun. Dappled stands of maple and oak, ash and poplar, birch and sycamore covered hillsides once barren, the forest ground into charcoal to feed the iron mills.

The paths through the hills were mining trails, or the narrow line of an old railroad.

The trail that ran from the west of Harvard Avenue starting at Marion Feldman's house was such an old route. It followed the cliff at the end of the street for a half mile where it connected with a crossroads of trails and one straight rail path.

Nagler guessed by the apparent clearing that this had been a spot where workers loaded rail cars with the cut trees destined for the mills. The high afternoon sun burned a spot through the open canopy into the stiff, gray underbrush.

It was also as far from the image of old Howie Newton and his white Panama, sunglasses and fat, stupid cigar as Nagler could get and still be in the City of Ironton.

"If Newton shows up here," he laughed to himself.

He had kept the mayor's ride to himself, not sure what to make of it, or how to describe it. More, his silence was a question of whom to tell.

Not Martha. She didn't need to worry. He had tried to say something that night, but she had fallen into a gentle sleep, so he kissed her ear and watched a fleeting smile crossed her lips.

Not Dawson, for sure.

Hanrahan? LaStrada? He knew he could trust Hanrahan but didn't want to spill his troubles onto the sergeant and make others suspicious of him. LaStrada? Good cop, but didn't trust him.

Nagler kicked around the clearing looking for something, what he wasn't sure; asking himself if this remote spot could have been useful to the killer, or even the little sneak thief who kept popping up.

What would you hide up here?

A wheelbarrow, it turned out. Pushed off the path into the bristling underbrush, now blooming with poison ivy.

His stomach dropped. Is that the wheelbarrow from the Feldman's garage?

He wanted to ask, "Why was it here?" but that answer led to the next question: What else from the Feldman's house might be here?

And for the moment, that was too deep a question.

He glanced around for a long stick to lift the poison ivy from the wheelbarrow and pulled out the Polaroid so he could take a few snaps.

Not touching it. He shook his head, smiling. No, no way. I'll blow up like a bad raspberry.

I'll let the crime scene guys in their space suits crawl around in there.

****

On the way back to his car, parked at the Feldman's, Nagler poked at several piles of brush that seemed out of place; they were just sticks and vines, probably there for years. He knelt to examine the ground on the chance that there might be wheelbarrow tracks, but the path was hard and dry, too solid for soft wheels to make an impression.

He leaned on the door of his car. He had called LaStrada and Foley and left the windows open to let the heat seep out.

LaStrada responded. Foley did not.

Just as well, Nagler thought.

The West Harvard neighborhood was silent, almost deserted in its silence.

How could people live here in a dozen homes and make so little noise? The heat, he decided. Drove them indoors behind the buzz of air conditioners. That's one reason they knew so little about Marion Feldman.

We never hid inside in the workers' ghetto. We ran the streets, climbed the rocks, chased the dogs and were chased in return. We had nothing to lose.

He glanced up and down the street, at the neat homes, manicured lawns, pillowed swings on shaded front porches. Too much to lose.

He pushed off from the car and walked toward the Feldman's house.

What happens when all is taken from you?

The house had still not sold; the lawn was a little ragged.

Maybe that wheelbarrow had been missing for months. Marion Feldman surely never used it and might have not known it was missing. But why would someone just take the wheelbarrow, and not the rakes and shovels and the complete sets of hand tools that lined the walls and filled cabinet drawers? They could have been sold and no one would have known.

It's so difficult, he thought. The end of life. Marion Feldman just lived on after her husband died. The house, the car, the garage full of his stuff, left, as if he was coming back from one of his business trips.

And now she is gone. Like the others.

The house had not been touched, as far as Nagler could see. No break-in attempts, doors solidly locked, windows tightly closed.

No newspapers. He chuckled.

He circled the house, for no real reason he could come up with, just to check, maybe to protect something, a silent statement of commitment to Marion Feldman and the other dead and missing women; a way to say we have not found you, or your killer, but we have not forgotten.

Better here than a cemetery.

He released a long, sighing breath. The weight of it all settled, pushed open space for the weight yet to come.

He reached up to the old-fashioned center-poled clothes line and gave it an absent-minded spin.

The flash of color on the garage seen through the spinning lines caught his attention.

He ran to the garage.

"No!" He slapped the wooden siding. "Fuuuck!"

Outlined against the faded blue paint was an oozing red hand and its accompanying phrase: HAND OF DEATH.

****

"Looks fresh," LaStrada said. "Too fresh."

Nagler nodded. "I know."

Chris Foley scratched his head and said, "We can't assume…"

"Yes, we can," LaStrada growled. "This not a copycat or a prank or a joke. It's the killer, Chris. Damn it. Why don't you just say that? Aren't you in charge of this damn investigation?"

He looked over at Nagler. "How many of these have we found, Frank?"

"Seven. The only place we haven't found one is at or near the Edie Smith house. Seven women, seven marks."

LaStrada wiped his hand across his mouth. "Alright, we need to search this whole fucking place again. Where did you find that wheelbarrow, Frank?"

Nagler tipped his head to the left, "Up that trail, half-mile or so. There is a bit of a clearing. I found a piece of old rope and tied it to the tree near the spot. Shit." He looked over at LaStrada. "Rope. What are the odds? Another strangulation?"

"Another search is a good idea," Foley said. "Perhaps our last effort was incomplete."

Nagler began, "Not incomplete…"

"Too focused, too hurried," LaStrada interrupted. "We hit the obvious spots. Need to start over."

Foley said, "Agreed," and began to walk away. "I'll tell the chief and the mayor."

"The mayor don't need to know," LaStrada yelled, and glanced at Nagler. "Tell the chief we need a dozen or so academy recruits." He muttered, "Mister I'm-in-charge gonna file his little report."

Nagler watched LaStrada and thought that maybe he misjudged the lieutenant.

"What's your guess on how long it's been here?" LaStrada asked the officer photographing the painted hand and letters.

"Oh, it's very fresh. Hardly settled. Couple days, at best."

Nagler was staring in the direction of the trail. "It's like he knows something, Sal. What are the odds that a couple days after I said I was going to search along the trail, we found a fresh handprint here? And what are the odds we find one near the Smith house?"

"Thinking the same thing," LaStrada said. "Where's the leak coming from?"

"Not a lot of people in the department know the details," Nagler said.

"A mystery we don't need. Look, Frank, you head up this search, and I'll grab some guys and head over to the Smith house."

"Good. Did we ever check that trail that leads from the back of the Smith property to that homeless camp near the high school?" Nagler asked.

LaStrada spit. "Who the fuck knows. If there was someone in charge of this investigation…" His voice trailed off as he turned away.

As Foley marched away, Nagler wondered aloud, "Why did he come up with that cockamamie multiple killer theory the other day? What's he know that he's not telling us?"

LaStrada looked sharply over at Nagler with a concerned squint. "What are you saying, Frank?"

Nagler shrugged. "Nothing. Just odd."

CHAPTER EIGHTEEN

A test is coming

Once a searcher found the torn and dirty bedsheet, balled and hidden behind a cluster of honeysuckle, it didn't take long to find the skeleton.

When Mulligan arrived, Nagler told him, "It's Marion Feldman."

The medical examiner squinted through the heat and swatted away mosquitoes.

"It's the ring," Nagler explained. "I have a photo. Rocky Calabrese made the ring for their wedding."

"And that bracelet you found the old bog was hers as well," Mulligan said. "Compelling. But we must find more details."

Nagler was staring at the scattered bones, dug up and dragged by some animal. "Yeah...yeah," he finally replied. "Sergeant LaStrada's guys tested the wheelbarrow for prints and found none. Probably wore gloves."

Mulligan sighed. "When did Mrs. Feldman's relative speak with her last?"

"April. But it might have been before that, maybe late March."

"That puts her early in the sequence," Mulligan said. "Possibly a test. An older woman, smaller frame, trouble walking. Perhaps easy to overcome. We have that blood sample from her carpet, and the bloody nail on the Hoosier. Let me examine her skull for a corresponding wound and her hands for any injury. And she broke her hip, correct? All that would help me confirm."

****

Foley's board.

A wall of lists, maps, photos, and a calendar.

A jumble, Nagler thought. Guesses. Wrong guesses.

Reports hanging from clips. A line of photos and mug shots each marked with a black "X," suspects discarded, yet still hanging on the wall.

If stacks of paper solved crimes, we'd be done, Nagler thought.

The list of Ironton's victim's names had been created by separate strips of paper pinned to the wall in the supposed order of their deaths.

It had become gospel: Harmon before Wilson; Wilson before Sanchez. Then the two older women, Smith and Feldman, just because no one really knew. Then the ones with dates certain: Joan Chen, Tamika Austin and Debbie Jones.

Nagler removed Marion Feldman's name and moved it to the top of the list. Then he shifted Edie Smith's below that and above Nancy Harmon. Then he placed the names of the older missing women on the same line.

Somehow, that made sense, he thought.

The sequence fit with the newspapers and cut lawns, and old women living alone suddenly gone. It would have been easy. No one would have noticed, and, he laughed sourly, no one did.

How do we think like a killer?

If the first two were the old women, it might have been easy.

The doctor? Maybe she was ill, preoccupied, so comfortable with her surroundings and routine, she never thought of danger. And maybe as a doctor, she had been called to treat patients in less than perfect circumstances and she thought she could take care of herself.

Nagler glanced at the photo of the warehouse where Nancy Harmon had been found.

You thought we'd find her sooner, didn't you?

And that led to Jamie Wilson, just weeks later it seemed. "No one noticed, so you tried again," Nagler said to the photo of Jamie Wilson. "But you left her at the Old Iron Bog, for crying out loud. No one noticed you. Just her, missing."

Nagler wondered why they had not found Nancy Harmon's car. We must have checked the chop-shops, right? Back then, a disconnected death, I'll bet we didn't. He scratched his head then shook it. What a screw up. But Jaime Wilson's car was in an impound lot. It was still evidence. "I think I'd better check it again," he said.

He scanned the list again.

After Wilson, quicker, Sanchez, and then the latest ones, all more public, all, in their way, more spectacular.

"And that's why we'll find a red hand at the Smith house," Nagler muttered.

Then he understood: The red hand at the Feldman house was not just a claim of ownership, but a warning.

And a taunt: "You ain't got me yet. Just watch."

As the voice echoed in his head, Nagler studied the photos of the red hands. They were taken from different angles, in different lighting.

He called over to Robbie Karpinski, the department photographer.

"Do you think you could shoot these red hands again, straight on, framing them in the same manner as much as possible."

"You mean go back to each site?" Karpinski asked, shoulders slumping.

"Yeah," Nagler said. "Look, I know. These are all shot at different angles, different lighting. I hope you can get a sort of framed, clean head-on shot." He held up his hands and formed sort of a box.

"I get it, like a portrait."

Nagler nodded. "Yeah, exactly.

"Take a day, but I can do that," Karpinski said. "But not the one under the bridge." He nodded. "Know what? with a big lens and a tripod, a possibility. I'll do what I can. Why?"

Nagler tapped the last photo of the red hand, the one from the Feldman house. "I have an idea and need those portraits to prove it."

****

"He's here, Detective Nagler."

Chris Foley had marched to Nagler's desk and stood with a scowl while waiting for Nagler to hang up the phone.

"Who's here?"

Foley turned to walk away before he answered.

"The kid. Downstairs."

Okay, Nagler thought. What's with Foley? Thought he'd be glad to get this off his list. Naw, not him. Needs something to gnaw on.

Sitting at a table in one of the break rooms was a kid drinking a Coke and eating chips from a bag. Seemed about the right size, Nagler thought. Hair color, I guess.

The best memory Nagler had of the kid was that first encounter at the Feldman house, but it was blur, lost in the growing pile of stuff on his mind.

Foley sat at the end of the table.

"Charlie, this is Detective Nagler. He has some questions for you. Detective, this is Charlie Adams."

Nagler extended his hand, which the kid shook with a weak grip. The kid's eyes darted around the room.

"Don't be nervous, Charlie. I'm pleased to meet you," Nagler said in as soft a tone as possible. "I just have a couple questions."

Charlie shrugged. "Yeah, okay. Detective Foley said you wanted to know why I was at the places the old ladies died."

Nagler raised his eyebrows and glanced at Foley. "That's right." Why'd he say that?

"I just like cops and firetrucks, watchin' what they do," Charlie said. "My grandfather was a fireman."

"Good," Nagler said. "You know I used to chase fire trucks, too, when I was your age. Fires can be exciting. How old are you?"

"Twelve."

"Okay, great. Play baseball or anything like that?"

Charlie shoved a few chips in his mouth and stared at the table. "Naw, just hang out," he mumbled, chips dribbling from the corner of his mouth.

"Where?"

"East side. North side." He swigged the Coke.

"Did you ever hang out at the community center, maybe at their workshop?"

The kid grinned.

"Naw, that place is for retards." Charlie Adams laughed.

Nagler nodded, pursed his lips and recorded that answer.

"Didn't know that. Thanks for the information." He glanced up at Foley, perched on the wall like a bird ready to take flight.

"Do you remember seeing me at the old Peterson factory a few weeks ago. I was in there and you started to come in and ran away," Nagler asked, his voice now harsh.

Charlie flicked his eyes at Foley and then placed his head in his hands. "Did I?' he asked. "Wait, I remember. I was just lookin' and got scared."

Nagler closed up his face and thought, something isn't right.

"What were you looking for? Steal stuff?" Nagler smiled. "I used to do that as a kid. Hit the old factories. There was always stuff."

Charlie grinned, relaxed. "Yeah. There's tools and stuff. We sell 'em." He leaned forward, a little panicked. "I won't get in trouble for that, will I? My dad…"

Foley was stone-faced.

Nagler chuckled. "Finders keepers."

Charlie leaned back. "Yeah. I guess."

"We done?" Foley asked.

"One more thing," Nagler said as he pulled out a snapshot of the bracelet he had found at the Old Iron Bog and laid it in front of the boy. "Recognize this?"

The kid's face was not blank, as if he was trying to hide something, but puzzled.

"What is it?" the kid asked, a tremor in his voice. "Never saw it."

Nagler tapped the photo. "You ever been on West Harvard, at that hill that comes down near the hospital?"

The kid glanced at Foley. "No, never. That's west side, right? I live on Mitchell, on the east side near the bus station."

"Some guys who live in the stoveworks said you tried to sell this bracelet to them. Why would they say that?"

The kid's face crumbled in confusion. "I ain't...I never..." the voice of a scared little boy. He breathed hard.

Foley took flight from the wall. "That all, Detective?" He motioned for Charlie to stand.

Nagler eyed the pair. Then, soothing: "Sure. Thanks for coming in, Charlie. Let me know if you find anything valuable in one of those warehouses. We used to look for cash. Had heard there was boxes of money left in the walls and stuff."

The kid's eyes widened, and his breathing slowed. "Really? Man, we just found hammers and drills and stuff. Sell 'em to car shops. Cash, wow."

"Oh, Charlie. One last thing, Nagler said. "You ever hear about a blind kid living on the street? Got beat up a couple week ago?"

Charlie glanced at Foley and then at the floor. "Yeah. I know him," he said in a voice colder than his years. "He was always getting beated up."

"Did you ever beat him up?"

Charlie's face took on a look of disgust. "Why would I? Jeez."

Nagler took a step toward the kid.

"Because you're a punk. Tell your friends who do beat him up that I'm looking for them, and I will find them."

Charlie's face turned white, and he wiped his mouth. "Can I go?"

Foley glared at Nagler and said, "I'll lead you out." Then to Nagler: "Satisfied?"

Nagler just nodded.

It took a couple blocks for Nagler to blow off the steam.

I don't think that was the same kid. What the hell?

He stared into the traffic clogged at Blackwell and Sussex.

The places the old ladies died?

That's what the kid said.

Oh, fuck.

We don't even know that.

That knowledge stewed in Nagler's mind. This is the game, isn't it?

****

This is the last place I want to be, Frank Nagler thought.

Saint Francis Church.

He was sure Sister Katherine would instruct about something; a mother's scolding; she managed to make him feel like he was still seven years old.

He had walked away from police headquarters after the kid's comment about "the places where the old women died" sank in.

There was no way he could have known that, unless he was told to say it, and the only person who could have told him that was Chris Foley.

What is Foley using that kid for?

A horn blast from a hard-braking semi jerked Nagler from absently stepping into the street and chased the thought out of his head. "Damn it. Pay attention." He leaned on a fence post, shaking. He glanced up and down the street before crossing.

He found the old nun in the sheltered flower garden behind the church. He had attended Catholic school for a grade or two until the money ran out and he switched to public school; he smiled — that was when he met Martha Shannon.

Sister Katherine had known his mother well, and in her mystical way, kept her eye on young Frank. It seemed that she knew everything.

"Hello, Sister."

She slowly raised her head from her Bible, placed a red ribbon between the pages, and smiled. He recognized the plain, black dress and the small gold cross, and for a moment, he was sitting again in a sweaty classroom, reciting things multiplied by two.

He hadn't seen her often lately and forgot how she had aged; in her seventies, now, he guessed. Still, she had the most peaceful face, and it calmed him.

"There can only be trouble if you're here, Frank."

"That's not always true," he said, sitting.

"But it's true today, isn't it?"

He, embarrassed, nodded. "Yes, I'm afraid."

"How is Martha?"

He asked himself: How is Martha? How do I describe her condition?

"Sick. Maybe getting sicker." He covered his eyes that had drawn tears. It was the first time he had said that, and he felt his chest hollow out. Whispering, "Maybe for the last time." He leaned back, breathed deeply, and wiped his bruised eyes. Weakly: "What do I do about that?"

She pulled herself to her feet and crossed to the bench where Nagler sat.

"Love her, Frank. Just love her." She touched his face and turned it to hers. "The time will come for more. Trust the Lord, even though that is hard for you."

He smiled softy, nodding. Her lessons never sank in, did they?

Sister Katherine smiled benevolently, standing erect, her face skyward.

"That's not why you are here, is it?"

"No." A sour laugh. "Wondering if you know a street kid named Charlie Adams. He's been hanging around police scenes, and I wonder why. There was something wrong about it."

"I'm sure there was," Sister Katherine said, as she sat again. "Charlie is our little sneak thief. He emptied the poor box from time to time until we added a new lid with a thinner slot, a brace, and an extra lock." She glanced at Nagler and smiled softly. "He's been a troubled kid for as long as I can remember."

"What's he look like?"

"He's about fifteen, short for this age, but strong. Blondish hair. Nothing truly distinguishing." She folded her hands in front of her mouth as if praying. "But there is a presence about him, Frank. Something simmering under the surface that none of the fathers who counseled him could reach. He's a fringe walker. Accepts no rules, follows no guidance. Uses his friends in an instant, because they are not truly friends, but victims." The warning was hard to miss.

"They spoke with him here?" he asked.

"Certainly, we did. After five or six attempts to steal church property, Father Donovan made it a personal mission to set Charlie straight. It is what we do: Offer a path from wickedness." She laughed, then teased, "How easily you forget."

Nagler smiled: He'd heard that before. "I'm guessing it didn't work for him."

She shook her head. "No. I witnessed one or two sessions. Charlie would sit rigidly still, mind elsewhere, eyes half closed, coldly focused on the priest, lips in a sneer. The priest would offer homilies and at times sharp reprimands, with the threat to call in the police should it happen again. At the last one, possibly a year ago, Charlie stood up, spat on the table, and said, 'Look it, you old baby...fudger' — well, you know the word — 'You got nothing to tell me.' And he left, pushing Father Donovan out of the way."

"What's he capable of?"

"Havoc."

Ok-ay. "What happened next? Seen him since?"

Sister Katherine nodded. "I've seen him at night in the alley behind the church, just standing. Sometimes out front across the street when services end. Stalking, Frank." She nodded her head for emphasis. "Stalking. We alerted your department, and Officer Foley said he would look into it."

Shit. Foley. Nagler felt his face flush and wiped his forehead.

"What?" the sister asked. "And don't say it's nothing."

"Foley is the officer in charge of the murder investigation and has been 'handling' Charlie Adams as a street informant, so he said. He brought in a kid he said was Charlie Adams, but he didn't fit your description." He sighed. The kid I interviewed was no menace. "That's, well, a mess." He glanced at Sister Katherine. "But an internal police mess. Not for you to worry about."

Sister Katherine cradled her Bible then, eyes shaded, raised it to her lips and kissed the cracked cover.

"You're troubled, Sister."

"As are you, Frank. And I believe by the same things." She rose and crossed the path to him. He stood. "It is more than these dreadful murders, bless their souls. I see it on the faces of parishioners, the worry, the fear, a great concern they can't explain. They rise from their prayers with deeply worried faces, hearts still heavy. A poisonous air, a darkness settling. They seek answers and even I have to admit that counseling prayer, contemplation and good thoughts is hardly enough to assuage their fears."

Wow, he thought. How bad is it that the most honest soul he had ever known expressed hopelessness?

She patted his shoulder.

"It is time to stand up, Francis. There is a test coming, and more than the test you will face with Martha, because I will help you with that. It will be an undefined challenge, and you will need to face it alone. We speak often about the dark night of the soul. It is coming for this city, and, yes, for you. Are they the same? I cannot say. I will pray for you."

CHAPTER NINETEEN

A claim of ownership

When Nagler heard Ray LaStrada's voice, he didn't need to hear the actual news.

They had found Edie Smith.

The discovery of Marion Feldman's body had kicked off a city-wide search of woods, parks, abandoned canals and factories, homeless camps, the Old Iron Bog, even Smelly Flats.

Searchers found Edie Smith in a shallow grave in deep brush and branches — a manmade cover — a hundred feet off the trail that led from her property past the homeless camps to the high school.

The killer had taken care to place the painted red hand and phrase HAND OF DEATH inside the garage on a wooden panel framed and offset by deep wall beams; in the unlighted garage the marking were hard to detected, even in daylight.

They were found only after the garage was opened and researched. Unlike the markings at the Feldman home, these had been on the wall for some time. There was a light coating of dust and a few dead insects.

"This might have been the first one," LaStrada said.

Nagler nodded. "Maybe this is where he got the idea." He looked around at the benches and cabinets. "And maybe the paint." He nodded to an officer: "Box up all the stuff in the cabinets, especially all that paint and the paint brushes."

LaStrada said, "It seems that her body had been moved, maybe after we had searched the area."

"From where?"

"The house. There was a false wall in the cellar. The son told us about it when we called and asked permission to get back into the house."

Nagler kicked the ground. "Why didn't he tell us that before? Just... shit, ya know?" He stared off into the woods. "Speaking of the son, where is Foley?"

"Heard he was with the mayor."

Howard Newton's smoke-filled voice echoed in Nagler's head. Of

169

course, he is. "Hey, Ray, you think the son told Foley about the false wall?"

LaStrada squinted, and then rolled his eyes at Nagler. "What are you thinking, Frank?"

"That first night, when she was not at home and Foley got into it with the son. What if that was because Foley knew something about what might be in the house? Wanted to throw the son off balance."

"That's nuts, Frank. Need to be careful with that one." LaStrada shook his head. "You serious? I mean, I don't like Foley. He's into something, but I try not to think about it because, you know, we have other things to worry about. And, man, there's been bad cops before." LaStrada took Nagler's elbow. "You sure? You can't be wrong, you know."

"It was something I was told," Nagler said. "And it might not be anything, just chatter, but what I heard, and who told me, it could be something."

"You sound nervous, Frank."

Nagler scratched his jaw. "A little. Foley's been all over me from the start of this thing. And when I first met you, I wasn't sure. I'm trying to make sense of all this."

LaStrada chuckled. "I know you didn't trust me. Don't blame you. This place is a snake pit. But I've watched you and I spoke with Hanrahan. Got your back, Frank." He patted Nagler's shoulder. "When you're ready, I'm with you."

****

The next morning, Nagler, LaStrada, Foley and Chief Mallory met with Mulligan to hear his findings based on the autopsies of Marion Feldman and who they all had presumed was Edie Smith.

Marion Feldman was somewhat easier to identify. The ring that was found was a less expensive duplicate of her wedding ring, the original probably stored at home, her hip showed damage from the fall and a touch of osteoporosis, which he concluded was a factor in the fall her granddaughter had described, and the skull had a crack, consistent with a blow to the head, made either by a fall, or a blow with some object.

Still, he would not commit fully to the identification, but said he was "nearly certain, pending test results."

Identifying Edie Smith required a study of her medical and dental records. Mulligan identified the broken wrist she had suffered at about age thirty, and a broken shin bone that had occurred several years later. The skeleton was approximately the same height; again, pending tests, Mulligan said they had found Edie Smith.

"How did Mrs. Smith die?" LaStrada asked.

"Strangulation," Mulligan said.

Nagler said, "Jamie Wilson was strangled. That would make two, maybe three."

"Indeed. But, gentlemen, there are details to notice," Mulligan said. "Each of these older women before us had their eyes removed," he said.

That was a new detail, and it caused a few deep breaths. "Oh, shit," LaStrada said. Nagler could not force out a word.

"There are gouge marks around the eye sockets of both victims, possibly caused by a sharp knife," Mulligan said.

He held a scalpel balled in his fist and made a circular scraping motion over the eyes of Edie Smith. "Crudely done."

"Why?" Nagler asked.

"A fetish?" Foley asked.

"Except no other victim has exhibited such marks," Mulligan said. "It could have been an experiment, something to test his willingness to abuse. But I think it is more out of cruelty and anger. All the victims have shown some indication of excessive brutality. Excessive stab wounds, repeated blows, even after death, the ambush nature of some of the attacks. Taken together they say this is someone trying to exert power or compensating for a lack of it."

All the officers nodded, absorbing Mulligan's assessment. Nagler thought he could have said his findings proved the killer liked chocolate ice cream and we would have agreed. We are flying blind.

"Before you go, gentlemen, Detective Nagler has an interesting thought on that one part of this case we have not discussed, and I'm glad to say, has not yet leaked into the public realm."

Nagler nodded to the medical examiner. "It's about the red hands," he said.

He had been holding a folder under his arm, and he pulled it out. The other officers gathered, Foley at the outside.

On an empty desk top, Nagler laid out seven centered photographs of the red handprints.

"I asked Robbie, the department photographer, to try to shoot each handprint from the same distance, with the same lighting, and with center framing," Nagler said. "This is the result."

"Jesus," LaStrada said. "Look at that. They are all different sizes."

"Exactly," Nagler said. "I think it's possible he used one hand from each victim to leave the red mark near the spot where they died. Where else would he get something to make the mark? Look at this one, from the Feldman's. We have her wedding ring, so Dr. Mulligan consulted with an expert who based on her ring size, seemed sure that this print was made using her hand. "

He held up another photo.

"This is Joan Chen's hand, we believe. She was a small woman with thin arms, and this hand is small, so it seems to fit. This print was the one found at the old train station, around the corner from the restaurant where she was attacked. Look closely. Each one is different."

The room was silent.

"Why?" the chief asked Mulligan.

"I'm no psychiatrist, but it would seem to be the marker, the claim of ownership we have all speculated about," Mulligan said. "This is an element we have not yet considered. Using the victims' hands. That is perverse."

Nagler noticed that Foley seemed withdrawn.

LaStrada asked the next, obvious, question.

"Where are the hands?"

Mulligan sighed. "That has been the question all along, hasn't it? Did our killer keep them, destroy them, though I think not? They mean something. But he did something different with Edie Smith. He left a right hand behind. I believe it belongs to Jamie Wilson."

"Holy shit," LaStrada blurted out. "So that meant he went back…"

Mulligan glanced at Nagler and nodded.

"It would appear so," Mulligan said.

Mallory stepped to the front of the group. "Thanks, Doc. Okay. Not a word." He tipped his head to Nagler. "Nice work. In my office in thirty minutes. We have to pull this all together."

Before the officer left, Nagler called out to Foley.

"Hey, Chris, a question. The first day I met you at the Feldman's house you said something like we'd find her bones buried in the woods, and that was exactly how we found her. How'd you know that?"

Foley coughed and glared at Nagler.

"What are you saying, Detective?" His voice was hollow.

"Just asking. A pretty good guess. Maybe if we had acted on it we might have found Mrs. Feldman sooner."

Foley smirked and glanced at the other officers who were staring at Nagler.

"It's just an expression, Detective," Foley said. "Nothing more. I didn't know anything. It was just an expression." He left the room first.

"What did you mean by that, Frank?" the chief asked.

"Nothing," Nagler said flatly. "It was just something I recalled when we found Mrs. Feldman. Just seemed odd, that's all."

LaStrada waited until Foley and the chief departed.

"You think that will tip his hand?"

Nagler nodded. "I think he's been busting, holding stuff in. He wants to spread something around."

"You're right. Let me know. Hey, Frank, if we're wrong, we're screwed."

Nagler smiled. "If we're wrong, Sal, we're dead."

****

Nagler had just extended the tape measure to reach the mark he had placed on the old train station wall when he heard the call: "Hey, cop. Over here."

He glanced in the direction of the voice, but at first saw no one.

He retracted the tape, placed it in his pocket and stared again across the street. Then in the shadowed alley between the Greek restaurant and a small insurance office — squat, stone buildings left from the canal days — he saw a hand wave to him, and then the face of a kid slip momentarily from the darkness into the light and then retreat.

Nagler waited for two cars to pass by and then crossed the empty Sussex Street to the alley.

At the alley opening, he asked. "You alone?"

"Yeah,"

"Step out a bit so I can see you."

Feet shuffled, but the kid did not move forward. Then he shifted into the half light of the opening.

It was the kid who had pretended to be Charlie Adams. He had been beaten.

"Who did that?" Nagler said, reached out to lift the kid's bruised chin.

The kid flinched then stepped closer. He had a bruised eye that was partly closed, his chin had been cut and his right hand was wrapped in a dirty, bloody t-shirt. The kid winced, grabbed his right elbow and then leaned against the wall, dropped his head and began to cry.

"You're hurt pretty bad, kid. Let me help you. What's your name?"

The kid just sagged at the wall and breathed with difficulty. He huffed out a few breaths. Slowly: "George Santorini." A cough. "Sorry I…"

Nagler knelt and pulled out a handkerchief. "Don't worry about it. We've gotta get you some medical help."

"No." the kid cried. "He'll… He'll know?"

"Who? The real Charlie Adams?" Nagler asked.

George, in pain, tipped his head sideways. "Yeah," he croaked.

"When I was talking to you at the station, you said something odd," Nagler said. "Remember what it was?"

George stared the ground.

"It was about being at the scenes where the old ladies had died," Nagler said. "How did you know that? We never told anyone."

George coughed several times and spit out a gob of blood. "Help me, man." He took a deep breath. "It was just a guess?"

"Bullshit, kid. Who told you that?"

George wrapped his good arm around his chest and slumped to the ground, knees up. He buried his face in his arm.

Nagler glanced back to the train station and stared at the red hand.

"You know something about those red hands, don't you?" Nagler leaned in. "Don't you?"

The kid looked up at the cop. The pain in his face could not hide the terror in his eyes.

****

Sister Katherine closed to door to the room where George was being treated by a nurse.

"Nothing broken," the sister said. "Sister Margaret is our school nurse. She said it was just a few cuts and some deep bruises. We'll keep him here at the residence for a day."

Nagler scratched his left ear and asked, "Do you know him?"

Sister Katherine smiled and nodded her head, as if to say, "Of course."

She moved behind her desk. "He is one of eight or ten foster children who slip in and out of the system regularly. Some run away, some are abused and then run away. We track them as best we can."

"But…" Skeptically.

"Yes, but. They are all headed down the wrong path, and I don't think we can head them off." She pursed her lips and gazed out the window. "They know the system too well."

"Including Charlie Adams."

Scoffing, "Certainly."

"Why would George impersonate Charlie Adams, knowing it wouldn't work?"

She leaned forward.

"Someone paid him, Frank. It's the same reason they have sex in dark alleys. For money. To survive."

Nagler considered the answer and dipped his head.

"How long before Adams knows George has been here?"

"He may know now," Sister Katherine said. "He's like a collector, a street boss. His gang is supposed to check in regularly."

"Okay. And the beating is just a message."

"For certain. Don't worry, Frank. I'll make a few calls. I'll keep George here for a day or two and then find a safe place out of Ironton for him. That would give him a modicum of protection."

Distracted, Nagler nodded. "Don't hide him too well, Sister. I need to talk to him again."

****

After he left George Santorini with the nuns, Nagler returned to the old train station to continue measuring the red hands. There was something about the height from the ground that had bothered him from the beginning. They were too low.

We thought our killer was a full-grown adult male because of the ambush nature of the attacks, the power needed to overcome the victims, and the literature on serial killers, he had thought. We're all about the same height, except Foley. So, we thought the killer would be our size. What if we're wrong?

The train station was the last one. All the others, except the one on the bridge at Smelly Flats, had been measured. At each place, standing on flat ground, he had reached out his own left hand to mark the top of his fingers, and measured the distance, about nine feet. Then he measured the height of the red hands and the slogans from the ground and found them on average about two feet below the top of his fingers.

He had also brought out the portraits of each hand marking. There was no indication that any effort had been made to jump to place the mark. They were square on. Direct.

Whoever placed the mark wanted them to be as accurate a measure of…something; Nagler didn't know what.

But it changed their suspect profile.

Our old drunk guy was right after all, Nagler admitted. He saw a short person.

Sal LaStrada thought the notion was intriguing and said he would search the files again for suspects of smaller stature. "Could it be a woman?" he asked. "That would be different."

Chris Foley narrowed his eyes and seemed to turn pale when Nagler told him the concept.

Nagler asked him if he was alright.

"Rather late in the game for a new plan, isn't it?" Foley asked.

"Late?" Nagler asked. "We don't have a suspect, Chris. How would it be late?"

"Done a lot of work up to now, could have worked smarter," Foley said.

"But you don't think it's wrong, do you?"

Foley closed his face. "It's very ingenious, Detective. We'll see."

Nagler thought Mulligan's response was more telling.

"Let me re-examine our evidence," he said. "We have slashes and stab wounds. Angles can be tricky."

CHAPTER TWENTY

It's just about power, isn't it, Jimmy?

Jimmy Dawson dodged the falling water in the dripping, shadowed alley between buildings at the former hosiery mill. He'd look up at the roof as the fading light bejeweled the thin stream of water, only to lose sight of it as it slivered into a dozen drops during its four-story fall through darkness.

Once it was the largest maker of women's hosiery in the world and brought hundreds of German workers to Ironton. Now, its glory past, the mill was a sprawling wreck, six square blocks of rusted metal, broken-windowed brick walls, alleys for grunting sex and whispered drug deals.

But if Harrington was right, the place was worth millions.

The darkness settled, the fading sunlight slipping up the walls, red brick turning black then crowning the arches at the top of the old mill in a golden flash before fading to a pale dusk. Sound sharpened, distant noises enlarged in echo.

Dawson peered anxiously around the corner of the alley. Nagler was supposed to meet him; Dawson wanted to give him a heads-up about the story about the alleged shifty finances that was going to be in the next day's newspaper.

"Dawson."

Nagler's voice bounced down the narrow stone alley like water over broken stones.

Dawson jumped. He saw no one in the dark. The voice echoed then faded.

"Nagler?"

Nothing.

Then the voice closer. "Where are you?"

Dawson jumped as Nagler stepped from the dark street into the even darker alley. "What the hell are you doing here? Barry's is a lot more pleasant."

"Jesus, Frank." Dawson felt the sweat collect on his forehead. He closed his fist to quell the shaking.

"What's going on Jimmy?" Nagler asked with questioning concern.
Dawson took two deep breaths to calm himself.

"Barry's is too public. Got a story in tomorrow's paper saying that some company bought this place from the city for peanuts. We have a paper trail, but not much else."

"You're sure of it?" Nagler asked.

Dawson smiled weakly. "Yeah." Then with force. "Yeah. We have to have it, or I'm screwed. The unnamed cronies have bought this complex with city funds and sold it to themselves. They hid the purchase in a number of city accounts, shifting the cash from account to account in small amounts so it would not be noticed." Dawson exhaled. "I threw it past the paper's lawyer and accountants and after they looked at the paperwork I gave them, they practically wrote the story. It's not all we know, just what we can say at this time."

"The mayor's gonna be pissed, you know," Nagler laughed. "He has everyone believing he's a straight up guy. Why are you telling me?"

"Because it might be tied to the murder investigation," Dawson said, glancing sideways at Nagler.

That's a reach, Nagler thought, but then thought, No.

"That's why Newton brought me down here," he said, finally understanding.

"What?" Dawson waved his hands in the air, disbelieving. "When?"

Nagler nodded. "A couple of weeks ago. I was coming out of the train station after I had found what might be evidence at Smelly Flats. He was just there, him and his limo and those damn cigars. Thought I was gonna choke on the smoke. How'd he know?"

Dawson smiled at Nagler's apparent naiveté, even after all these months. "One of his stooges. Take a guess?"

Nagler laughed. "I'm not really that slow, Jimmy. Had to be Foley. Newman said I had to work better with Foley and that he would make a fine police chief because he was loyal."

"That's what's important to Newton. Loyalty. And the ability to forget how the law works," Dawson said. "Why'd he bring you here?"

"He made some big spiel about how I needed to solve the murders so the value of this place would rise." Nagler laughed bitterly. "He was telegraphing this deal, thinking I'd never understand it. Bragging." Nagler shook his head at the plan, now made obvious. He said it was his 'cause,' and he wasn't talking about making Ironton safer for the city's women." He exhaled through fat cheeks. "It's just about power, isn't it, Jimmy? The power to do what you want, to whom you want, for only selfish reasons."

Dawson shook his head and raised his eyebrows as he stared at the ground. "And you're surprised? That was a warning from the boss, there, Frank. That and a recruitment pitch."

"I know. Scared the crap out of me, so much so I haven't told anyone about this, not even Martha."

"What are you gonna do?"

Nagler smiled oddly. "Attack. Been waiting for the moment, and this seems to be it. He handed Dawson a manila envelope.

"What's this?"

Nagler just smiled.

PART THREE

Fire

Cicadas rubbed the air into a grating cascade of pain, grinding the last softness from the skin of the city; scratching away the last layer of protection that separates the paper from the match.

— *Jimmy Dawson* —

CHAPTER TWENTY-ONE

I want to remember taste and touch

"Look at this!" Mayor Howard Newton yelled from the City Hall steps.

He waved a copy of that day's Register with Dawson's story splashed across Page One with an all-caps headline: "CITY FUNDS DELIVER HOSIERY MILL TO UNKNOWN COMPANY."

"Who are these criminals?" Newton sneered. "The reporter, little Jimmy Dawson, is trying to make a name for himself. You remember him? He covered middle school basketball. Not even varsity. Middle school. What a joke."

A voice from the murmuring crowd. "You tell him, Mayor."

Newton waved and smiled. "Okay, okay," He motioned for the crowd to calm down. "You know me. I'm a humble man from modest beginnings. I sell fruits and vegetables. As a kid, I lived around the corner from the hosiery mill. Watched hundreds of workers arrive daily. And now it's empty. I want it to be filled with jobs. Owned by a real company. If someone in City Hall is behind this, we will expose them."

A mangled roar rose from the crowd, then "You're one of us, Mayor Newton. Save our city."

Newton waved a fist in the air. "City of Ironton. I've got your back!"

The crowd roared its approval.

Frank Nagler watched the scene from half a block away. The chief assigned him to crowd duty, just in case. It seemed that nearly every recent gathering had produced trouble. Ballgames, picnics, even church services as priests and ministers tried to offer celestial guidance in the troubled times, fights broke out in the congregations. Angry echoed shouts cracked the silent nights; gunshots followed.

Nagler heard someone approach from the alley and he turned quickly to the sound.

"Hello, Detective Nagler. Bartholomew Harrington."

Nagler looked up into Harrington's face; he had heard the lawyer was a drunk.

"I don't drink, Detective," Harrington noticed Nagler's quick examination. Then he pointed toward the crowd cheering Newton. "You notice he did not deny any of the allegations in Dawson's story. Classic."

"I've heard of you," Nagler said. "You tipped off Dawson, right?"

A tiny smile crossed Harrington mouth. "If that was an official question, I shall decline to answer."

Nagler smiled. "You didn't deny it."

"Touché."

"Why? What do you know about Newton?"

Harrington stepped into the shadow of the alley and motioned for Nagler to follow him. He peered back into the street and cleared his throat.

"One of the very first cases I handled as an attorney was that of a young family who had bought a home from Newton, or thought they did. He manipulated the sale, inflated the interest rate on the loan he had originated for them and then foreclosed when they could not pay. I've been watching him ever since. He's a serial thief, Detective. A master."

"Why isn't he in jail?"

"Very good question." Harrington raised his eyebrows and smiled. "Because real estate crime is easy. Lots of paperwork — it's easy to lose paperwork — no one quite remembers, contracts longer than your arm, filled with clauses and obtuse language, stuff no one reads because the agent directs the buyer to the lines that must be initialed, the places that must be signed, and whisks the papers away like a magician." He slipped a quick glance at Nagler. "It seems simple to prove, but the masters have layers of paper that is sometimes nearly impossible to decipher, even for a lawyer like myself. I've been trying to decipher our vegetable seller for years."

"What happened to that family?"

"We won the case, and they kept their home but were ruined by the financial burden and sold out." Harrington saw Nagler's frown. "I took the case pro bono." He slowly shook his head with appreciation. "Newton bought the house back from a shell buyer. I thought later he had deliberately lost that case. He made thousands when he resold the house."

Nagler pursed his lips and nodded. Impressive. "Sounds like that's what he's doing this time."

"Indeed, Detective. Just on a larger scale."

Nagler glanced back at the crowd and the mayor, who was still speaking.

Harrington peeked around the corner towards the mayor and the crowd.

"Look at them all, Detective. Eager, yearning, seeking leadership, salvation, and praise. But all is lost. Buying the image not the reality of the man they worship, for that is the word. Look at their faces, the peaceful innocence, wanting to believe." He paused and smiled. "Do you recognize yourself in that crowd, Detective?"

"What?" Nagler scoffed. "Hardly. I'm no fan of Mayor Newton, and I'm hardly a fawning follower. I trust very little."

Harrington stepped deeper into the alley.

"That's not what I meant. You're certainly not a follower, but you, like your city, carry a hurt in your heart, a pain that is seeking relief. Look at them. They want someone to tell them that things will be better, that their pain, however defined, will be relieved. Your good mayor exploits that pain, and you try to ease it. Those two ideas are doomed to clash."

Nagler's eyes narrowed as he pondered Harrington's assessment. "What's going to come of all this, Mr. Harrington?"

Harrington folded his hands in front of his still face and sighed.

"There have been political crooks forever, Detective. Ward healers, mayors, machine politicians whose systematic tentacles wrap themselves around a city and strangle it. They surround themselves with fawning lackeys, plant spies and cronies in key positions and pull their chains, sometimes just for amusement. Newton's tentacles reach deep and wide. Too deep, I'm afraid."

Nagler frowned. "You're sneaking information to the papers. Isn't that a start?"

Harrington shook his head. "No. It calls for someone braver than I. Someone willing to swallow their fear and step to the front of the charging army. That is not me. I am the spy, and when I am suspected of anything, I can fall back on my reputation as a drunk as a defense. I prod, but I prefer the background. Suits me better."

A cowardly answer, Nagler thought.

"Be ready, just in case, Mr. Harrington," Nagler warned the lawyer.

"The game is about to change."

Harrington smiled. "Well!"

Before Harrington could make another comment, cries and shouts rolled from the direction of City Hall. Nagler saw the mayor duck, losing his white Panama as some object was thrown at him. He stepped from the alley to the street in time to see a rushing mob of men smashing into the mayor's speech crowd swinging sticks, fists and signs.

"Perhaps this is your chance, Detective," Harrington said as he slipped away down the alley.

Nagler looked back to see him disappear, and then called dispatch. "Back-up City Hall, fight. Big fight."

Then he charged into the melee, looking for the mayor.

Nagler pushed his way through the fight, breaking up a pair of combatants. Sirens sounded from all directions. At the City Hall steps, he found Mayor Newton crouched alone behind a city trash can and pillar.

"Are you hurt?" Nagler asked, as he pulled the mayor to his feet.

Newton unwadded the Panama and brushed it off. "No."

"Good, come with me," Nagler ordered.

At the end of the steps, he grabbed a patrolman's elbow and nodded to the mayor. "Get him inside."

The fight had spread out to cover a block. Pairs and threesomes of fighters slammed one another with their hands, feet, and the sticks that were lying on the ground. Nagler could see eight or ten men on the ground bleeding.

He motioned to three officers who had just arrived, and said, "Follow me."

They broke up fights, took weapons, sat the wounded against walls and handcuffed a few of the most belligerent fighters.

The crowd on the fringe broke and ran as more police arrived. Nagler ordered officers to block off Sussex and herd the fleeing fighters into the police department parking lot.

When he stepped back into the thinning crowd, Nagler was hit from behind at the shoulders with board or a stick of some sort. He turned and fell to the ground. Head spinning, he pushed himself to his knees and shook out the dizziness and pain. He was struck again across his shoulders. He looked to both sides to see who might have struck him.

He tried to stand but lost his balance. Then he sat and shook his head. In a disoriented haze, he saw someone a few feet away drop a stick. Then the assailant smiled.

With sweat in his eyes, and a growing pain that distorted his vision, Nagler swore it was the kid, Charlie Adams.

Nagler shook his head and tried again to stand. He felt a hand on his arm. It was LaStrada.

"Come on, Frank. I'll get you out of here," LaStrada yelled.

Nagler tried to pull away. "It's that kid, Sal. The kid…we… Looking for…"

"Fuck the kid, Frank. We'll find him. You're bleeding."

****

Nagler closed his eyes to stop the hospital hallway from spinning and to dull the iridescent glow at the edge of his vision.

But when he closed his eyes, he saw that grinning, stupid kid, Charlie Adams. What the hell was he doing there?

He heard a voice say, "He should stay overnight, you know, Martha. I wonder if you are up to caring… In your condition."

"My condition, Doc? I'm dying. Why is everyone afraid to say that? But I ain't dead. Yet. Don't push it. I'll be back here soon enough. In the meantime, there's him."

Nagler felt a small smile cross his lips. Fight on, Martha. Still, he knew that edge in her voice had become more common of late.

Then her voice, the hall chatter and his sense of balance faded as his body sagged in weariness and pain against the wall. The blows had separated his shoulder, and the doctor said most likely he was concussed; the pain killers had kicked in, and his head swirled in more ways than he thought possible.

"Come on, hero," Martha's soft voice cut through the fog. She slipped her arm under his good shoulder and helped him stand. "The department sent a ride."

"Got you, Detective."

It was Chris Foley.

What? Somewhere in the back of his brain Nagler asked, What the hell is he doing here? But then the thought rolled down some open channel and was flushed away.

"We have car outside, Mrs. Nagler," Foley said. "You're not to report for work for a few days, Detective. Chief's and the doctor's orders."

Nagler slipped in and out of a bad sleep as the police car rolled toward their house.

"In here, Officer... I'm sorry..." he heard Martha say as he fell back on the bed in her grandmother's old room.

"Foley, Ma'am. Chief Detective Chris Foley."

"Well, thank you." Martha replied.

"The Detective saved the mayor today. The mayor is grateful," Foley said.

The ceiling swirled. The disembodied voices seemed to be leaking from an unseen source, wispy and insubstantial.

Well, fuck the mayor, Nagler thought.

Martha chuckled. "He always wants to be the hero."

Nagler felt a hand on his shoulder. "Stay out for a few days until the doctor clears you, Detective," Foley said. "Wonderful to meet you, Mrs. Nagler."

"Oh, please, Martha."

"Yes, Martha. You have a lovely home. I'll let myself out. Remember, Detective. Stay home."

The front door closed.

"What an odd man," she said. "Does he always call you Detective?"

****

Martha's warm kiss on his forehead woke him. She brushed his forehead and cheek. "What am I going to do with you?"

Martha compressed her body to his side.

For several minutes, Nagler absorbed the warmth from Martha's body, and the room stopped spinning. Her black bandanna slipped up from her forehead and a few strands of her hair, now graying, emerged.

"What...?" The word stuck in his closed, dry throat, and he coughed and swallowed whatever saliva he could raise. Martha was still, maybe asleep, he thought, and he didn't want to rouse her; the glass of water was out of reach. Then she lifted her head. "What did the doctor mean about 'your condition?'" he finally asked. "What changed?"

Martha pushed herself up and leaned on the pillows at the side of the bed.

She straightened the bandanna then brushed his hair from his eyes "It's worse."

He reached for her and his shoulder screamed in pain and he could not extend his arm to her. He leaned back.

Her face was placid and pale. She closed her eyes and expelled a brief, soft breath. "We knew it would be. The last test came back... my white blood cells..." The tiniest smile, then lightly: "Another box checked." She stared into his half-closed eyes. "One last fight, my love."

Nagler's head swirled, his eyes closed then opened. Stay awake.

A radio played softly in the dark house.

Something by Bette Midler. She had left it on when they came to take her to the hospital, he guessed. Unless he was imagining the music.

He pushed through the pain in his head and shoulder and turned to her. He shook his head. It seemed darker, past sunset. Martha hugged his side.

"What can I do?" he rasped. He brushed her cheek, and the touch pulled her from sleep. He kissed her hair, then again, buried his face in her hair at her neck, and pulled at her shoulder wincing as if he could cover her, create a shield, absorb her silent pain. His damaged shoulder shrieked in pain and he loosened his grip. "Damn it," he muttered harshly.

Her face closed darkly. "Fight for me, Frank. Fight for yourself. "Don't give..." then she smiled and shook her head. "Look at you." A laugh. "What a mess. You can barely lay on a bed, you hurt so much."

"But I have..." he protested. "Something..."

She pushed a finger to his lips. "Shush."

She leaned back, squeezed her face shut for a second, and then took three short huffing breaths, squinting. Then her face relaxed, and she opened it with a shy, toothy grin.

"Tell me about the park," she said as if it was a question, her voice cracking. "About the wet cool grass on your back when I sat on your hips. Tell me about the sweet aroma of wild roses and the soft pink petals you'd pick off my tits with your tongue." A soft laugh.

Martha rolled to her side and held his face in her hands, her eyes fierce, seeking calm.

Then firmer: "Tell me about walking home when we were seven and you had this confused look on your face when I took your hand, and I laughed and said 'Oh, Frank, it will always be yours to hold.'"

She kissed him and pulled his arms around her back, as he winced.

"Sorry," she said as she kissed his shoulder. "I want to remember touch and taste, your tongue in my mouth, fingers dripping chocolate ice cream on my chin, what it felt like that first time you took off my blouse in the old bog as we wondered standing naked if anyone could see us. That sly, knowing look on my mother's face when I brought you home after our first time, you in ripped at the knees jeans and an old sweatshirt, the shadow of the workers ghetto in your eyes, and then her smile, and mine."

Martha sat up and pulled her knees to her chest and rested her head there, staring at Frank, who laid back stunned to silence, clenching as he breathed trying to ease the tightness in his neck. He tried to keep his face calm. It was that day, the one he had avoided thinking about, the one they both knew lurked in the darkness, to which they had been blinded by the light of her recovery years before; the one they feared on that day they celebrated with laughter and silent hope her remission, wrapped and lost in the soft bedding of her grandmother's room, in that very bed.

"I thought…" he said as the ache escaped and crawled across his face.

"It's easy to think that," she said. "A luxury, but not a guarantee." She smiled softly into his torn face. "This is the guarantee," and touched her black scarf. She brushed his eyes with a finger and pressed it into his lips. "Everything else is a gamble, Frank, dear Frank. We gambled with time and for a while came out ahead."

He tried to speak.

"Hush, my love. I want to remember how it feels to be with you, how alive. The salty taste of you on my fingers, on my lips, the things we laughed about, the tears of stupid teenage fights."

She rolled over to him again and pressed her forehead to his mouth.

"To remember this, just this, you and me and that great big world out there and how we ran into it yelling, telling it to catch up, thinking it never would." She closed her eyes tightly leaking tears. "I want to hear the morning lark, the robin sing, and sparrows twitter in the bushes. I want to see the sun and you squinting hopelessly toward the horizon. But that night is coming and the only bird I will hear will be the nightingale, announcing darkness. Not yet, but it will come, one last darkness." A dark growl in her voice. "We're in the last act. But I don't want to be Juliet lying cold and dead in that crypt. I don't want to end at all. I want to be her on the day before, laughing. I want a new ending. Hey, Shakespeare. A rewrite, now." Then softly. "Please?"

She settled, crying softly into his shoulder and slowly drifted to a quiet repose; a sigh, then shallowing breath, leaving him to stare at the dark ceiling, the hum of night leaking through open windows.

He brushed her forehead and pushed back the scarf. He tearfully gasped when he saw the bald patch.

He rolled in and out of sleep, the body pain pulling him one way, stabbing at his arm when he turned awkwardly, and the drugs dragging him into a soft stupor.

The sad face of Delvin Williams filled his vision, the dark, smoky stoveworks, the smell that assaulted his nose. If Del is on that cliff one step from falling, what am I?

He slept and dreamed. A small high school gym, the crowd cheering, sound bouncing off hard walls, a concussive wave that at times felt like it pushed the players across the floor. The slap of the ball on the floor, the squeak of cheap sneakers on the hard wood; then a glance, a movement like the wind and the ball out of his hand into Del's and the sound of rope twine being rippled by a heavy ball; then the cheer. A smile; Del's wink.

And that kid sneaking through the dark back alleys. Breaking into homes, but more, homes we are watching, knowing something.

Did he sleep?

Dawson, Nagler thought, as sunlight shimmered on the closed window shade.

And Martha. Sleeping at his side. He closed his eyes and wept, trying not to move as the pain grabbed his shoulder and neck. And Martha.

CHAPTER TWENTY-TWO

The fall guy

"Hey, Frank, you're not gonna believe this."

It was LaStrada, and he tossed a copy of the Register on the porch where Nagler had fallen asleep crosswise in an Adirondack chair. His eyes popped wide open, not from the intrusion but from the stabbing pain that had pinned his shoulder to the chair as he tried to rise.

"What's going on?" Nagler asked, shaking off the drowsiness.

LaStrada picked up the paper, unfolded it and displayed the front page. "SUSPECT IN CUSTODY," the headline blared.

Amazing, Nagler thought. Two days at home, and they catch someone. He shook his head. "Who is it, Sal? Did we really?" He pulled himself to sit sideways at the foot of the chair.

LaStrada sat on the top step.

"I guess so, but it's news to me. Guy named Bill Wallinski," LaStrada said. "Patrol found him asleep in his truck across the street from the Smith house. He's a house painter, he said. Had a contract to paint the Smith house, or so he said. But the son, Gregory Smith, is out of the country and Wallinski didn't have a copy of a contract. He had a couple empty bottles of cheap gin in the truck and patrol nabbed him when he stepped out of the van to take a leak on the Smith house lawn."

Nagler squeezed his face together to push back the pain.

"Do you believe it, Sal? Sounds almost silly. A drunk housepainter? And he had red paint in his truck, didn't he? Where was this guy before?"

LaStrada put down the paper. "While I found it odd that he went from watering the lawn to being a suspect in the city's most notorious killing spree in maybe a century, he does fit your theory of a shorter killer, Frank. He's five-six, but fat, maybe close to three hundred, possibly strong enough to knock over our victims in an ambush attack and carry Joan Chen to the railroad station. Had a truck filled with ladders and paint and brushes...and in a way he fits the profile that Mulligan floated — a common working man. We all bought that, especially with the newspapers on the lawns, and all."

Nagler shifted to lean against the chair back. He stared at the mug shot on page one. A balding, squinty eyed, sleepy guy with a fat face, a short flat nose and who looked more bewildered than dangerous.

He leaned back and closed his eyes. "Anything is possible. Let's hope this is the guy," then solemnly, "It would be good for the city." He grinned, "Foley must be beside himself."

LaStrada laughed. "Yeah, he was a little more peacock-ish than usual. Press conference with the mayor tomorrow morning. Wants to wait for the New York media. Make a big splash."

"Maybe I'll go," Nagler said, his voice fading into the drug induced hollow. "Hey, Sal, anything on that scuffle outside City Hall?"

"Someone paid those kids to break up the mayor's press conference, just for the sake of creating chaos," LaStrada said. "A night in jail had a few of those kids talking. They couldn't ID the guy. Never saw him before, dark alleys and all that shit."

"Any of them say anything about that kid we've been looking for?"

"That Charlie Adams kid? The kid you think whacked you? No. Not a word." LaStrada leaned toward Nagler's chair. "That's the name you posted on the killing spree wall, wasn't it?"

"Yeah, it was a call-in on the hot line. The only name we got. And it wasn't the stevedore." He wanted to shake his head, but it wouldn't move. "We've hauled in three guys on this case and two of them were wrong. Let's hope we're right this time."

After LaStrada left, Nagler settled stiffly back into the chair and let the silence settle.

As he rested, he scanned the street and the messy lot across from his house, seeking hiding places, closing off the light and darkening the neighborhood as he imagined it on those nights noises from the lot were heard, and those nights that the doll was placed, and the red hand was painted.

He scooched to the end of the chair, then reaching for porch railing, he stood up and pushed back at the dizziness that wanted to spin him back to the chair. As he scanned the street, he felt the change as his mind sharpened, asked the questions it needed to ask, felt that investigative skepticism again take its place; felt the injured softness fade and the hardness return.

Then he stared at the shed and the red hand. It shouldn't be there, just shouldn't be there, and yet it was. He leaned on the railing and stepped off the porch. He forgot his shoes.

He looked at the sloping rocky, branch strewn ground. Did a fat guy like Bill Wallinski really slip from the street to that shed without falling or making a sound?

Across the street, he maneuvered around broken glass, sharp stones, and fallen tree limbs to run his fingers around the ends of the hand.

He placed his own hand over it. It was too small to be an adult's hand, too short, fingers too thin.

If they were right and the red handprints were made by dipping the victims' own hands in red paint, then whose handprint was this?

****

"You're not supposed to be back at work yet, Detective," Chris Foley told Nagler, his voice disapproving. "Why are you here?"

"You seem disappointed," Nagler said. "Called the doctor and the chief. They said okay." I'm not here to steal your glory. "Figured you needed help putting the evidence in order for this guy's eventual court hearing, what's his name, Wallinski? How'd you find him?"

Foley pursed his lips and half closed his eyes but said nothing.

"Yes. Glad you're back." Foley began to walk away.

"Wait. How did you find him? At least tell me that. We've been working on this stuff for months, and you just found him outside the Smith house in a truck with paint. When did you get on to him?"

Foley sighed. "You remember we had rolling patrols outside the Smith home, and the son poised private investigators there. I compared their reports and there were several references to a painting contractor's truck. We followed it up."

"Why didn't you share this with LaStrada and me?"

"It just came together, Detective. I wanted to secure the suspect before anything else happened or he left the area. His work records show he had business in three states. I'm sorry if you're offended."

Nagler closed his eyes and shook away a wave of dizziness.

"Not offended. Relieved." Something here… "We can wrap this up and people in Ironton can sleep at night." He offered Foley his hand. "Good work. Now no one will be creeping around that old shed across from my house."

After a second, Foley shook Nagler's hand. "Thank you, Detective." Then he walked away.

"Hey, Chris. When can I talk to him?"

Foley didn't stop walking, just replied over his shoulder. "Don't know. He's lawyered up. Arraignment's tomorrow. Then he'll be sent up to the county jail till trial."

Nagler stared at Foley's back as the officer walked away, a little jump in his step.

"This will give me time to find that kid who whacked me in the head," Nagler said, hoping Foley heard the sarcasm.

Foley stopped and turned, his cheery face now serious. "You do that, Detective. That would surely make the city safer." Then he turned again and walked away, without the jump.

"Make me feel better," Nagler muttered, as the pain rose in his shoulder. Then he thought that maybe the kid had seen Wallinski at a crime scene.

****

The growl crawled its way out of the crowd sardined inside the rope barrier around the courthouse, crept up the walls of the opposite buildings and slammed into the burning granite face of the ancient building, then bounced back to the crowd in an endless circle of sound; the air vibrated. Bodies pressed together, a hypnotic, undulating wave of kaleidoscopic humanity, a single mass, then split, divided, then crashing together. A dance, a constant movement generating friction and heat. Sunlight simmered in the window glass.

Nagler wondered when it would spontaneously combust. Or would someone light a match?

He and LaStrada were among the rows of police that lined the front of the building. The heat tugged at their faces, as they sweated under the weight of vests.

They had both questioned why they were not in the courtroom where Bill Wallinski was going to have an initial hearing, but Foley dismissed their concerns.

"It's a reading of the charges and a plea declaration. Nothing more," Foley had said. "We'll need you when the trial actually begins. Meantime, we expect a hostile crowd."

196

The department had received hundreds of telephoned threats overnight. A dozen red hands had been painted on the side of City Hall.

The city rose up to confront the killer.

"KILL HIM!!!"

"Death to the killer."

"Give him to us. We'll show him justice."

A chant of "Kill him, kill him" swept through the masses.

Nagler nodded to LaStrada, who slowly shook his head. Each officer scanned a portion of the crowd, trying into detect hidden weapons. Scuffles and loud shouts erupted when officers in riot gear mixed in the crowd grabbed signs and long sticks from some participants. A loud, "Hey, you!" or a "Get outta my face!" drew the focus of the police. Rolling flashes of protest echoed, but quickly died when a couple of the more rowdy crowd members were manhandled away. A cry rose: "Fascists! Fascists!"

"Reminds me of one of those old movies about England in the Middle Ages," LaStrada said, trying to lighten the mood. "The peasants drooling and cheering as the poor slob who was about to lose his head was hauled on a cart to the platform."

"Or a movie about the Romans," Nagler added. "Thumps up, thumbs down. What will the emperor do?" He shook his head, and then nodded when he spotted Jimmy Dawson at the fringe of the crowd. "We're really not much better, are we?"

LaStrada huffed. "Not really."

Nagler and LaStrada were not at the courthouse to actually protect Bill Wallinski as he was transferred to the county jail. There would be no perp walk.

Wallinski would be taken from the courtroom to the cellar and then unseen by the crowd loaded into an armored van for the ride to Morristown.

The police were in fact a decoy; they had been warned to expect a violent reaction from the crowd when they discovered they had been duped and their bloodlust unrewarded.

Nagler shifted his shoulder in and out of position in an effort to keep the pain at bay. Crap, I don't want a fight, he thought. It had just started feeling better.

The air was stiff, a breath held too long. The heat from the sun beating down, and then reflected up from the sidewalks and streets, sucked the frenzy out of the baking crowd trapped in a burning vice.

A cry went up from the right side and rippled along the top of the gathering as Nagler watched three or four cops push through the people to break up a fight between two sign-wielding combatants. Nagler tensed as one of the cops disappeared, but then relaxed when he saw the officer rise holding one of the fighters in a headlock and pushed him out of the street. He flinched and imagined being struck again, and the nasty, smiling face of Charlie Adams.

He was there, somewhere, Nagler knew. Charlie Adams and his gang of hustlers. I'll bet they are making a killing from the wallets and pockets of the protesters, he thought.

"He's probably gone now, isn't he, Wallinski?" Nagler asked.

LaStrada glanced at his watch. "Yeah, about now."

"Did..." Nagler paused as he spotted a group of protestors walking along the left fringe of the crowd. They stopped and a couple of them yelled something unintelligible toward the cops before they took a right turn away from City Hall and left.

"Sorry. Did you see any of the evidence?"

LaStrada said, "No. A summary. Coincidental dates and times to his painting jobs near the killing sites. Circumstantial. But he has a little history. A few early break-ins, a couple drunk drivings. Foley's keeping it close to his vest."

"Think he did it? Can we prove it?"

LaStrada turned to face him. "I don't know, Frank. There seems to be opportunity, but thinking about it, it was hard to assign a motive. Saw him in the holding cell. He's a short, fat, slobby guy. Had sad, empty eyes. He looked around wondering what the hell he was there for. Kept asking if his lawyer had shown up." He paused. "But Gacy was a fat slob, too. So, I guess ya never know."

LaStrada scanned the crowd again. They were leaving. The steam of their purpose cooled and deflated. No hanging today. "Where's Wallinski's anger, Frank? Where's the drive that would lead to eight deaths, especially with the slashings and brutality we've seen? Anything is possible and maybe we could build a case, but do I really think old fat fuck Bill Wallinski is our guy? Did he show up at Smelly Flats and drag Tamika Austin around? He glanced at Nagler and shrugged once.

"That's what we need to prove."

"So, if not Wallinski, who?"

"Dunno," LaStrada laughed.

"Then why was Bill Wallinski in our lock-up?" Nagler asked.

The weight of the question landed in LaStrada's face, which sank into a gray, resigned mess.

You could think about it, but you were never supposed to ask that question out loud. The question was a hole, a cavern from which rose a stinking, putrefied cloud of suspicion, doubt, and accusation. The question that should not be asked, but once it was, could never be un-asked. Sal LaStrada danced with the question, rolled it around his tongue; he wanted to spit it out, but it would not be dislodged.

He glanced over at Frank Nagler and knew in that instant that Nagler understood how deep a hole that question was, but had asked it anyway, breathed it in into the air.

"You ask anyone else that question?" LaStrada asked.

Nagler shook his head once. "There's no one who could give me an answer," he said. "Or an answer I'd believe."

"Why'd you ask me?"

"Because you asked it yourself the other day when you came to my house with the newspaper," Nagler said. "That was why you came to my house."

LaStrada just smiled.

****

"So?"

Jimmy Dawson flopped into the seat across from Nagler, dropped a copy of that day's Register on the table, and threw the question at him. Barry's was busy, but the usual hum was subdued.

Nagler recognized some of the faces he had seen in the crowd outside City Hall. Their white-circled, squinting eyes seemed astonished, their red cheeks and foreheads blushing with a disappointed embarrassment. All that yelling for nothing. Yelling for harm for a man they didn't know. But it made them feel better, maybe dampened the rage, Nagler thought; better than the worry that had carved lines into their faces.

Better than sitting in the hallway at home with a shot gun, Nagler decided.

"Is that really your killer?" Dawson asked. "He was quite meek and lost in the court hearing?"

Nagler grinned slightly. "What did you expect? That he'd be a snarling, drooling monster? He's a man. Maybe a man with dark secrets, but a man none the less."

Dawson leaned back. "Sounds like you're trying to talk yourself into it."

Nagler smiled into the table.

"He looked like he was going to cry," Dawson said. "You know they didn't send him to the county. They sent him to the state prison with a psych unit."

"Maybe that's safer," Nagler said. "If they put him in general population, he wouldn't last. Imagine that jail crown. I'm the killer of the Ironton Slasher."

Nagler flinched away one more pain in his shoulder. "Who was his lawyer? Some kid from the public defender's office?"

Dawson chuckled. "No. You'll like this. Bart Harrington."

Nagler shook his head and rolled his eyes. "Harrington will get him off, for Chrissakes."

"Should have seen Foley's face. Why weren't you and LaStrada in the courtroom?"

Nagler scratched his cheek. "Banished by Foley. He said it was just to enter a plea."

Dawson leaned in and shook his head. "No. More than that. They had to present a version of the case, to ensure there would be no bail. Harrington wasted no time in ripping it apart, and the judge sat him down about five times." He smiled. "Have to admire that skill. There was no jury to influence, and he was already preparing that part of Act One."

"What if our fat painter ain't the guy, Jimmy? Then what?" Nagler asked.

"What?"

"This city will go nuts," Nagler said as he rose and started to walk away with a look on his face. "Gotta go."

Dawson turned in his seat. "What do you know?"

Nagler shrugged.

"Just so you know. I still have that envelope you gave me. Started to look, but got delayed when Wallinski was arrested," Dawson said. "Does it still matter?"

"If you don't think it matters, why are you checking it out?" Nagler asked. Then he left.

Dawson caught Nagler's smirk, turned back to the table, glanced at the newspaper headline and stared at Wallinski's photo. Harrington was right. There's their fall guy.

CHAPTER TWENTY-THREE

George Santorini

"What are you doing, Detective?"

Nagler glanced up from the table he had covered with a couple hundred photos, saw it was Foley, and returned his attention to the pictures.

"Crowd shots from several of the crime scenes. Since the Smith house, I had asked Robbie Karpinski to shoot the crowds," Nagler said. "That was how we identified that Adams kid. We've guessed the killer has been watching us, so there's a good chance Wallinski could be in these photos."

"But..." Foley began.

Nagler stood and faced Foley. "It's the same reason he puts red handprints on buildings near the crime scenes, Chris. The reason he put one on a shed across the street from my house. He's watching, claiming. With these pictures, we're watching back. Besides, if we put Wallinski at a crime scene, everything becomes a little less circumstantial, right?"

"We have evidence, Detective," an irritated Foley said as he shuffled the folders in his hands.

"Did we match paint in Wallinski's truck to the red hands?" Nagler asked, pushing back.

"Are you challenging, me again, Detective?"

Nagler looked at the photos, shook his head, and scratched his right ear.

"Not everything is a challenge, Chris. Just thought we'd need the best evidence we could gather to nail the city's first serial killer in a century, don't you think?"

"Yes, well. Let me know what you find," Foley said, marching stiffly off.

Nagler palmed the photos around the table. He had examined more than a hundred but had not detected Wallinski or the Adams kid. As he pushed them into a pile, he recognized a familiar face and put that photo aside.

****

Leonard had insisted on walking.

"I was on the streets a long time, Frank. I know the intersections by sound," he said.

"But what about…"

"We're at Bergen and Blackwell," Leonard interrupted. "The train station is behind us to the right and the traffic light at the park is to the left." He breathed deeply. "And if I'm right, Marcella's Bakery has cinnamon rolls in the oven."

Nagler laughed, mostly at his own embarrassment. "How…"

Leonard pointed to the left. "They have an exhaust fan from the kitchen." He dipped his head. "I could never stand at this corner long because of that smell, especially on the days that I had not eaten." He tapped the curb. "Let's move on."

Leonard led Nagler nimbly down Blackwell and through several narrow alleys, stopping at broken doors that opened on musty, dark cellars, or at the back opening to empty mills. All places he had lived.

After the fourth or fifth stop, Nagler leaned on a doorframe and weakly asked, "How did you survive?"

Leonard tapped the stone steps with his cane. "We took care of each other, Frank. I've heard you speak of your friend Delvin and your concern for him." He glanced up. "There's a network, as in all societies, an underground pipeline for information. We needed to stick together for safety and survival. But we mostly needed to protect ourselves from the gang Charlie Adams runs. Thieves and thugs." He tapped the path and walked on. "Why do you need to find him?"

The question pulled Nagler from the sadness he felt.

"He may know something about our murder suspect," Nagler said. "Maybe had seen him somewhere."

Leonard stopped, reached out to a broken wall to his right, nodded as he felt the landmark, and pointed toward a small brick shed thirty yards away.

"That was their meeting point," he said. "We're behind that old car repair shop. They used to break in there."

Nagler just shook his head and smiled. "How do you know this?"

Leonard smiled back. "I'd follow them, follow the sounds of their bragging laughs and crude jokes. They had taken so many belongings of mine, I felt I had to get them back. They often failed to lock up the shed."

"Alone?"

"No one expects much from a blind boy, Frank. Worked to my advantage." Leonard smiled.

"Did you get your stuff back?"

"Much of it," Leonard replied, a hint of pride in his voice. "What are you going to do now?"

Nagler scratched his arm. "Wait and watch, Leonard. Wait and watch."

Back on Blackwell, Leonard stopped walking and turned to face Nagler.

"Martha's dying, isn't she, Frank?" It was a soft question, delivered with reluctance.

Nagler felt the street spin and he leaned on a window frame for support.

The question. That question. Right in front of him. Surely, Leonard was just concerned. Nagler felt his chest tighten.

Leonard listened a moment. "I'm sorry, Frank. I can tell I upset you. I...I just see her at the house. I know she is in the bathroom staring at her face and pulling at her hair because she talks to it, like a friend who has betrayed her. It must have been so beautiful. Probably still is." Then, with sorrow: "I wouldn't know. I hear her crying, and I think she gasps in pain at times. And she asks, 'How will I tell Frank? A few more days, please.'"

Leonard heard Nagler's coughing cry.

"Frank..."

Nagler touched Leonard's arm. "Don't apologize. You've been more comfort to Martha than I can be. I am grateful. Yes, she's dying. I just tell myself that it's not true, not yet even though I know it is. She deserves a long and wonderful life. She would open the world." He bowed his head and wiped his eyes.

"I'm trained as a cop to find answers. But for this, I have no answer. I don't want it to be about me, my loss. I thought that after she got sick at nineteen and then got better, I knew how to handle it. But you don't learn from it, Leonard. It's a sneak attack every time. I try to imagine how the families of our murder victims handle the pain and loss, and I can't. I can't reach down that far." He released Leonard's arm. "I don't know what to do."

****

205

"Heard your suspect got beat up in jail," Dawson said to Nagler at Barry's.

The meeting over coffee had become a stare-down: Dawson asking questions he knew Nagler could not answer, and Nagler rolling his eyes, and with a shrug, refusing to answer them.

"Um, yeah, Harrington asked the court to move him out of there," Nagler said. "Jail's a dangerous place."

"Where would you put him?"

"Isolation at the county lock-up. Some hard-core cases there, but mostly short-timers for burglary, drugs. The killers end up in Trenton." He signed and shook his head. "Our Mr. Wallinski would not survive that state prison."

Dawson slugged back some coffee. "Why do you care, if he's guilty?"

Nagler signaled to Barry for a refill, and finished off his doughnut, using the pastry as an excuse not to answer Dawson's question.

Dawson just smiled and nodded to Barry for a refill when he poised the coffee pot over his cup. "What aren't you telling me?" Then Dawson nodded, "Okay," when Nagler raised one quick eyebrow.

****

Wallinski lived two towns over in a rundown building that had once been a railroad hotel; his neighbors scratched their heads when presented a photo of him.

Police had found boxes of receipts, half-used phone log books, a couple sets of paint-stained coveralls, work clothes and boots, brushes, and a few unopened cans of paint.

"I'd hate to be his accountant," LaStrada joked, as he pulled from the truck a third box of receipts. Some of the receipts were three years old. Some had checks paper clipped to the top.

It took Nagler half a day to sort through all the paper to develop a list of painting jobs Wallinski had done in Ironton, finally settling for twenty-five done in the past eighteen months.

There were a lot of small jobs: Porches, single rooms, a couple of offices, one or two complete house jobs.

How'd he do a house job, Nagler wondered, since they found no records of employees or part-time helpers.

And how did a buttoned-down, organized banker like Gregory Smith find someone as disorganized as Bill Wallinski, who didn't even have a Yellow Pages listing, just a line in the white pages: "Wallinski, William, painter."

The piles of paper, the mess in the truck and home, the inconsistencies all gave Nagler a headache.

Because the one thing they had not found was a random collection of newspapers, like had been found near the Smith and Feldman homes. But maybe that was just the kid, that Charlie Adams, his game. That scheme would work better for a kid than a fat guy like Wallinski.

More concerning, Nagler thought, was that they had not found in Wallinski's truck or home a knife of any type, or a cloth or rope that might have been used to strangle at least two of the victims, blood on clothes or truck seats or flooring, or anything that could directly link Wallinski to the eight murders.

But maybe that was Wallinski's game. Nagler thought. The apparent chaos somehow a cover for a man who prowled neighborhoods for work, maybe searched homes he painted for information and studied the habits of his customers.

"Think this guy was into drugs, using the painting business as a cover?" Nagler had asked LaStrada as they pawed through the paper records.

LaStrada pondered the question then said, "No. I worked in narcotics for years. Never heard of this guy." He had scanned the six boxes of paper on the table in front of them. "Something in here has to make sense."

Nagler pocketed the list of Wallinski's Ironton paint jobs. "I'm gonna check these out."

There's not much there, Nagler had said to himself as he left the police station. "We're gonna have to work hard to make this stick," he muttered.

And the person who knows that is Bart Harrington.

Two of the first stops on Wallinski's job list said he performed the work at night. One, a beauty salon, was being remodeled and the owner said she wanted the walls and ceiling painted before the new seats and fixtures arrived. The other, a law office, said the same thing.

Neither owner noticed any unusual behavior, and other than Wallinski's size and body odor, he was unremarkable. The beauty salon owner paid in cash, five-hundred, and the lawyer wrote a check.

Nagler compared the work list to the home and business address, and the locations of the death of all the known victims.

One matched: He had painted the office of Dr. Nancy Harmon, the first victim.

"You're kidding," LaStrada said when Nagler showed him the work order. "The doctor. Damn it. But there's no date. Could have been two years ago." He covered his mouth and breathed into his hands. "Maybe I was wrong about this guy. Think he did any work for that bank where Jamie Wilson worked? And that cab driver, Sanchez? His time sheets showed he worked at night a lot. Saw her maybe?"

Nagler scratched his neck. "Maybe. But what about the attacks we know where the victim was ambushed? Joan Chen? The dishwasher and the drunk at the train station said it was smaller person. Wallinski ain't exactly small, and I doubt he's that damn nimble that he could rush Debbie Jones in the parking lot."

"Yeah, but with his size he could have just overpowered them," LaStrada said. "Witnesses have been wrong, you know." He stared at Nagler's puzzled face. "Just follow the evidence, Frank. Don't guess."

****

Nagler kicked open the broken door to the brick shed that Leonard had pointed out the other day. It smelled like piss. Over-heated, closed-in, eye-watering, nose wrinkling, skin crawling piss.

Gagging at the stench, Nagler quickly stepped back outside to let some air circulate in the shed and spit to expel the bitter taste. Mouth open, he breathed deeply.

How the hell…kids!

He had returned to the search for Charlie Adams after a week of sifting through all the junk that Bill Wallinski had in his company truck and scattered through his apartment. A trial was weeks off.

Holding his breath, Nagler stepped back into the shed and waited while his eyes adjusted to the darkness. He wasn't sure what he would find. More to the point, he wasn't sure what he wanted to find; it was more like what he needed to find.

The bracelet that was stolen was the Feldman's home could not have been the only thing taken.

He kicked at some empty boxes on the floor, and opened a couple wooden casks, but they were empty, too.

Then he wrenched open an old built-in cabinet and out fell flyers like the ones that had been posted around town, the missing persons' posters, and even a couple of the posters identifying a suspect that the crowd chasing that guy down Blackwell Street had in their possession. Those little bastards, he thought. More chaos, more opportunity to break into houses. They were just lucky that none of them got shot.

"Looks like this place was cleaned out," he said, and stepped to the door.

In the alley, someone yelled, "Crap. Someone's in there. Run!"

Nagler recognized George Santorini's voice.

Two kids ran off in opposite directions, with George left behind, dragging an injured leg. Nagler quickly caught him and roughly pinned him against a wall.

"What the fuck are you doing, kid?" Nagler demanded.

"Let me go!" George tried to twist out of Nagler's grasp. "You're hurtin' my leg."

"Sit down!"

George slipped to the ground, grabbed his leg, and grimaced.

"Why'd you leave the home where Sister Katherine sent you?" Nagler asked.

"'Cause he found me, sent one of his guys to threaten me." George rubbed his eyes with his fists and let out a long sigh. "He knows I talked to you. He just knows."

"How'd you hurt your leg?"

George spit. "It was hurt for me. Couple of guys with a pipe."

Nagler considered the answer. I need to find some place for this kid, he thought.

"Okay, look," Nagler said. "Even though you screwed me once, I'll help you. Don't want to find you dead somewhere. But you're going to help me find Charlie Adams. And you'll start by telling me what you came back here for."

"Ain't no place safe," George whispered.

Nagler smiled. "Oh, there's a place. You're not going to like it, but there's a place."

"He'll find me in lock-up," George said.

"I'm not sending you to jail, George. You're right. Jail's not safe. But I have friends and they'll take care of you. Okay? You have to trust me and do what I say."

George stared at the ground as he wiped his eyes. "Okay."

"We'll get your leg taken care of," Nagler replied softly. "Think it's broken?"

"Could be. Just hurts."

"I'll bet. Why are you here?" Nagler asked as he helped the kid to stand.

"We were going to dig up the cash," George said.

"Buried cash? Here?"

A missing-tooth grin split the kid's face. "Yeah. That's why we pissed all over the floor. To keep people out. Worked, didn't it?"

Nagler shook his head and laughed, recalling the thick sour air. "Yeah, it did. How much cash?"

"Couple years' worth."

"Christ. Show me."

George limped into the shed and from the right, rear corner took a hoe and scraped away a couple inches of dirt until he struck a metal box. Inside was a loose pile of bills, mostly tens and twenties; a grand or more, Nagler guessed.

He took about half. "Put the rest back, George."

"Hey, cop, that's mine."

"It sure is, and it's gonna buy you some medical attention, and then protection. And if you take it all, Charlie Adams is really going to come after you."

After they reburied the box, Nagler took the kid to Sister Katherine, who cleaned up his leg.

"Where are you taking him?" she asked Nagler.

He smiled. "To see Del Williams."

Sister Katherine just smiled.

At the homeless camp at the stoveworks, Nagler called out, "Hey, Del, need a favor."

"I ain't staying here with the creeps," George said, as he tried to shake out of Nagler's grasp of his collar.

Nagler pulled up on the shirt and George winced as he had to lean on his bad leg.

s are going to keep you safe, George. They've had
h Charlie Adams, and he's not welcome here." Nagler
. "Del's my friend. Just do what he says, and you'll be
be here forever, but I need to keep you out of sight for

l smoldering face, George nodded, yes.
ler. What's up?" Del shuffled over to Nagler and the

l. Even after all the trouble in his life, he knew he could

keep an eye on this kid for a while. His name is George.
.... kid I told you about? Stole that jewelry?"

Del's face closed up while the pondered the question. Then it brightened. "Oh, that kid. Tried to sell us that piece."

"Well, that kid is Charlie Adams, and if he had a chance I believe he'd try to kill George here. That right, George?"

The kids scanned the camp, and then nodded. "About right."

"Maybe a week, Del." Nagler pulled out a wad of bills. "He's gonna need food, some clothes and medicine."

Del slipped the cash inside his coat. "Okay."

"Don't let your pals mess with him. If they do, I mess with them."

Del smiled at the kid and nodded at Nagler. "This man is my best friend. Stands by me when I screw up. I'd do anything for him." He reached for Nagler's hand. "We'll take care of him, Frank."

"You do what he says, George. Understand?"

The kid was crying, his face collapsing and shoulders shaking. He nodded.

Nagler squeezed his shoulder. "A week, George."

"We've chased him outta here before," Del said. "Ain't that something. The safest place for you is in our little campground. Yessah!"

CHAPTER TWENTY-FOUR

Maybe a little civil unrest lowers the price

Barry stood in the doorway to his diner with a long kitchen knife in one hand and a meat cleaver in the other and watched the looters run from door to door, pulling at the handles and then kicking at the glass when the door did not open.

A block away, an overturned car was on fire.

Three men in masks stopped in front of Barry's and took a step or two toward the front door, backing away when Barry unwrapped his arms and flashed his weapons.

Mournful sirens echoed through the canyon of brick buildings, eerie cries of order collapsing, the whine of the rebellion rising, the crackle of flames licking ancient wood.

Nagler had been pulled off the street by the chief.

"One hospital visit is enough this month," Chief Madden said. "With help from other towns, we have enough forces on the street."

So Nagler monitored the spreading chaos on a scanner and police radio. There seemed to be four or five groups of ten to fifteen members scattered around downtown. The train station had been splattered with paint and a few cars in the commuter parking lot overturned. Store front windows had been smashed, and a dozen residents fended off a masked mob at the library.

An hour went by, two. The scanner traffic filtered to a few bursts of shouted news. The police radio went silent.

Barry watched as Warren Street in front of his restaurant emptied as emergency vehicles blocked off the ends of the street and five or six helmeted police officers took up their posts. Smoke flowed, the air acrid and dark.

"Damn it," Barry muttered. "Damn it to hell."

He bent over and picked up a muddy, trampled copy of that day's Register with a three-inch headline: KILLER USED VICTIM'S HANDS FOR IMPRINTS.

"Damn, you, Dawson. I'll kick you out."

He threw the paper back into the street.

213

****

Sal LaStrada sat on the edge of Nagler's desk and unfolded a copy of the paper with the flagrant headline.

"You?"

Nagler leaned back in his chair and shook his head.

"No. My guess he got it through his usual leak," Nagler said with a slight grin. "What I can't figure is why. In a way, this information weakens the case against Wallinski. Harrington can prove through work records where Wallinski was on every occasion that a handprint appeared.

"Someone is just stirring up trouble," LaStrada said.

"But why?" Nagler asked. "And why out of the PD? If Harrington is right, and someone in City Hall is scamming the city, wouldn't all these riots scare away buyers?"

LaStrada considered the answer. "Maybe they ain't bought them yet because the price is too high. Maybe a little civil unrest lowers the price." He started to walk away. "It's shit, Frank. All shit."

****

The heat had killed off all the insects, Nagler thought. For the first time in weeks, the still, oppressive air was quiet; a moody train whistle moaned softly in the distance.

He sat shirtless on the edge of the bed. He dipped a cloth into a bowl of cold water with a few ice cubes and gently wiped Martha's forehead, cheeks, arms and neck.

Her face was pale, made even seeming paler by the black scarf that wrapped her head; yet, eyes closed, she smiled.

"Here," she whispered, as she unbuttoned her nightshirt and pulled it off her shoulders, exposing her breasts.

Nagler touched her chest and shoulders with the cool cloth, wincing at the weight she had lost as he saw how prominent her collar bones had become. He rinsed the cloth again.

"That's better, sweetie," she said. "It's been so hot."

He had stopped asking the doctor about her prognosis.

"More?" he asked.

She shifted. "No, just hold me."

He smiled and dropped the cloth into the bowl and settled on the pillows and pulled her close. He kissed her forehead, and then her eyes.

"What's on your mind, Frank, that is, on the part of it that's not worried about me?"

"All of it is worried about you." He kissed her.

"You lie, boy," she said and softly punched his jaw. "Most of it is worried about that damn city."

He squinted at the ceiling and sighed.

"It's burning, Martha," his voice a question. "The whole damn place. Fights and marches that lead to more fights. Corruption and murder, just all one big flaming pit. There's not enough water to put out the fire, I'm afraid. Everything that my parents killed themselves for, and your parents and grandparents, crumbling right before our eyes. How do we fight it? Why do we fight it?" His voice was weak in soft confusion. "And then you…"

Martha leaned up on one elbow and closed her eyes to settle the brief dizziness.

"I'm fighting, Frank." Her voice was dry and guttural, but hard. "I'm fighting for me and you. So you have to fight, too. They're gonna have to drag me out of here. I know what you are doing out there, and I know it's hard. I can fight. You have to. That's who you are. If you don't, who will? I'm going to lose this battle one day, but not yet. But you're gonna win yours." She stopped and took deep breaths. "They want you to lose, Frank. They come here to see how you are losing."

"Who?"

"That creep Foley," she said, lying back. "He brought me flowers. Leonard lied and said I was asleep."

"What the hell!"

Martha smiled. "I threw them out, Frank. Chucked them out the back door. They were the cheapest damn things."

He pushed out of the bed and stalked the bedroom.

"That little asshole, that punky little asshole."

"Come back, Frank," Martha said, her voice suddenly strong. "Come back here. The hell with them. I need you more.

He stood in the window fuming. All that noise in that empty lot, the handprints, the doll, the shuffling. Not an accident. Just a way to create doubt and fear. "Fuck them," he muttered.

"Yes, fuck 'em, Frank." She laughed weakly. "But not now, not tonight." She flipped open the bed sheets. "Tonight, it's just us."

He glanced at her and then at the floor before reentering the bed.

"I'm sorry, Martha." He bit his lip. "All this is swirling around. If we don't nail that killer the city will explode. And then you…"

"That fight can wait, dear Frank. And fight you will. But now, "And she took his hand and placed it between her legs, "Touch me. Kiss my neck and ears and eyes and bite my breasts. I can't roll and wiggle and sigh as I used to, can't swallow you, but I can feel. I want to feel, Frank. Want to feel you for as long as I can." Her voice trembled; her eyes closed, and she drifted into a smile.

CHAPTER TWENTY-FIVE

Walter's Waltham watch

"You planning on killing someone, Frank?"

Jimmy Dawson leaned back in his chair at Barry's. Nagler's face was a dark as any he had seen lately.

Nagler had been staring absently out the window into the street. He pulled back his gaze, glanced at Dawson, and firmly said, "No."

Martha had been so still when he awoke; cold skin when he touched her face sent a shock through his fingers. Then she rolled and breathed.

"Still here." She winked.

But the usual tease in her voice when she made remarks about dying was missing, replaced by a hollow whisper.

It was morning, Nagler told himself. Dry throat.

His kiss to her forehead and the squeeze of her hand lingered.

The drive to downtown had seemed surreal, the landscape of homes, trees and roads, like cardboard, like a fake TV set. He drew into a shell as each block passed by, pulled behind a screen as the colors were drained away, the sounds faded and there was a wall of silence between him and the world.

Dawson slurped up some coffee for a distraction.

"If this about your wife, I'm sorry," he said. "I know she's sick. I can't imagine…"

"I'm gonna lose her, Jimmy." Nagler stared at the table in silence.

The front door rattled open and the street, alive with noise, announced itself.

"Harrington's scheduled for court in a couple of days to get the charges dismissed," Dawson said. "You heard?"

"Yeah. Foley's handling it." Nagler rolled his eyes. "As the chief investigator."

"You sound doubtful."

Nagler whistled out a breath. "He's not ready, and he doesn't listen to anyone. He can't handle Harrington. Foley will put up Mulligan for the medical evidence, and I think Sal LaStrada will go up for the physical evidence, and he'll be good, but it's all so circumstantial."

"Sounds tough. What about you…?"

Before Nagler could answer, an officer opened the door and said with a wave, "Frank, they need you."

"What?" Dawson asked.

"Dunno."

Barry looked up from the counter he was wiping with a "what-the-hell?" look; Nagler replied with a "damned-if-I-know" shrug.

In the street, Nagler thought: I hope it's not Martha.

Inside Barry's, Dawson pulled out of a pocket the photo that Nagler had given him. An old beat-up door on a wooden garage on a forgotten alley in East Ironton. Dawson had planned to ask about it.

"Guess I'll just go look," he muttered.

****

Headquarters was jammed with state police and Ironton cops in riot gear.

Nagler saw the chief and pushed his way over. "What?"

"LaStrada's been stabbed," the chief said. "He's at Ironton General in critical condition. Two or three stab wounds."

"How…?"

Madden pulled Nagler into his office. "Sal was taking his usual morning run. He was near the old silk mill when it seems someone maybe jumped out of unmowed field there. Just tall grass, couple junk cars. The EMT said one wound was a sort of slash, a passing wound then two more stabs."

"Shit, an ambush," Nagler said.

"Yeah," the chief replied softly. "Some neighbor driving to work found him. Lost a lot of blood. Seems no witnesses."

Nagler scanned the overheated room, growling with anger. "Why Sal? An old case or something like that?" He rubbed his face with his hands and ran his fingers roughly through his hair. "Damn it! Where do you want me?"

"Check the scene again. We were there to get Sal off the street. But, no one's done a close look." Madden turned away then back. "Take someone with you. No one's alone anymore. And Frank. This one's yours, wherever it goes." He nodded.

Nagler stared at the chief's back as he stepped into a mass of officers at the end of the hall. What does he know?

218

****

The silk mill was a blackened, sunken evil looking mess. A decades-old fire had scorched the red brick and left a black scar, now half covered by vines. Broken windows and stone sills covered with bird shit lined the upper floors and the wrinkled tin screens were all that was left of the first-floor windows. A broken chain-link fence stood in some places, but in most had been hammered to the ground. Not even the homeless occupied the wreck.

The scrap of an old poster clung to a wall: A red fist and the letters "RIKE!" was all that remained of an ancient labor dispute.

A red fist, Nagler thought. Fitting.

We can at least be sure that our murder suspect Wallinski didn't do this. So who did?

"Why here, Sal?" Nagler asked aloud.

LaStrada lived about a mile east of the mill that sat in a bowl of a neighborhood carved from Ironton's hills. A stream, now a dry path, had provided power years ago. The streets ran east to west, down one side of the bowl and up the other.

Maybe it was the challenge of the hills, Nagler thought. The mill site was two square blocks. Behind the main building, a long wooden shipping building had collapsed when the pillars rotted, and a couple smaller outbuildings leaned over busted walls. There was no sign that anyone had been in that section of the site for a long time.

But why now? He knew that LaStrada and been running those hills for years.

He sent the patrol officer with him into the weed infested yard to examine the rusted cars while he kicked along the broken sidewalk.

The stain on the sidewalk showed where LaStrada had fallen at a telephone pole, and a trail of small drops from there traced back toward the lot with the cars.

"Anything?" Nagler asked as the officer emerged from the grass. "A weapon?"

"Someone's been in the cars," he said, brushing off the beads of the tall, dry grass. "You can see a path was pushed through weeds, and there's burger joint bags and some soda cans. But there's a lot of junk hidden under the grass. Not sure it would be easy to get a clean running start. There's also a small shed."

"Good, thanks," Nagler said, scanning the street for some point of attack. "We'll have to collect all that trash." But the grass near the building had not been disturbed, so it seemed unlikely that someone was lying in wait. So maybe they approached LaStrada from the opposite direction, like someone running or walking. Nagler imagined the scene: two people passing, then the weapon emerges from a long sleeve, LaStrada staggers, holds himself up at the pole, then is stabbed twice more.

"There was this," the officer said, displaying a gold pocket watch. "Probably stolen."

Nagler pulled out his handkerchief to cradle the watch. Nice, he thought. Stem wound, Waltham. His grandfather had one, from about 1910 or so, the old man had said.

Nagler brushed dirt off the intricate design of the cover, and then opened the watch to find an engraving: "Thanks, Walt. 1949."

Walt.

Walter Feldman.

"Jesus Christ. Those damn kids."

Didn't mean they attacked LaStrada. But why here?

After he left the silk mill, Nagler drove go the old stoveworks looking for George Santorini.

The camp was mostly empty, but Nagler found Del Williams and George playing cards.

"Hello, Frank, my friend," Del yelled out. "Your boy George here is quite the card player. Cleaned me out of pennies again." Del grinned at the kid. "But I think he cheats."

George smiled and playful punched at Del's arm. "Naw. Just luck."

Nagler was actually glad to see the kid was still there; he had expected that he would sneak out, trying to outrun Charlie Adams.

"What do you know about the silk mill, George?"

The kid's face flushed.

"Slept there once in a while."

Nagler shook his head. "Why there? That's more than a mile from your usual stomping grounds. Branching out?"

Nagler watched as George shifted his shoulder, and his face became hard with narrow eyes, watched as the kid slipped back into his street punk mode.

"Don't know nothing about that, cop," George muttered in his best tough guy voice.

"Oh, bullshit. Hey, Del, kick him out of here. Let's put him back on the street with a sign on his back. Helping the cops. Charlie would like that."

Del just smiled into his hand.

"You can't do that," George said his voice weak and wavering. "You promised."

"Sure as hell can. Changed my mind." Nagler replied as he turned away. "See ya, Del. Thanks."

"Anytime my friend," Del Williams said. "Come on kid, get your shit."

It only took a second. Too easy, Nagler thought.

"What do ya want to know?"

George nodded thanks to Del and turned to Nagler.

"As much as you can tell me."

****

"Why are you afraid of Charlie Adams?" Nagler asked George as they sat in a back office in the county building. They were waiting for the social worker who was going process him into the system. A Morristown agency had a spot in a shelter in another part of the county.

"He's mean," George said. "Hates everything. Angry all the time. Beats kids up. Had kids beat me up."

"Why do you hang with him?"

George pulled himself smaller. "My old man is in jail, and my mom left. No one else. I knew some other kids, so I joined 'em."

"Stealing?"

"Yeah. Little shit. But then he beat up some Chinese store owner and the whole game changed. A little guy, had a general store. Charlie picked up a piece of wood or something and whacked the shit outta him. Then took his money. Charlie said he was illegal, didn't deserve to be here." George placed his face in his hands. "Crap, half the kids I hang out with are illegal, so what the hell?"

"Why'd Charlie do stuff like that?"

"To get back at people. Says he gonna make 'em pay."

"Who's 'them'?"

George shrugged. "Anybody" He grinned softly. "Everybody."

"Pay for what?"

"Don't you get it? It don't matter. One minute he's as nice as can be, the next he's yelling at everybody? It's like, dunno, like some switch. Try to stay out of the way when it comes."

"Why'd Charlie have you beat up. Didn't you pretend to be him at the police station when you talked to me?"

"He said it was a joke."

"Did that cop, Foley, who brought you in, know about the joke?"

"What do you think?"

Nagler tipped his head to the floor and closed his. He didn't want George to see the anger rise to his face. Foley, Damn it. In time.

"So why did he beat you up?"

George's breathing got deeper and his hands jittered all over the table, fingers tapping, one at a time, then all at once.

"Because what he did to that old lady?"

"What old lady?" This time Nagler could not hide the alarm.

"Old lady in the fancy house in the west end. We were stealing stuff, a lot of stuff, it was all piled up in boxes, so we took it. Watches, rings, necklaces, a little cash." He looked up. "It was more stuff than we had ever see'd, ya know?"

"How did you find her, this old lady?"

"We stole newspapers from street boxes and tried to sell 'em. Whole bunch of us. Said we were doing a sales drive, or some shit. We were just scouting, you know, places to rob. It's easy, man. People believe anything. We'd read the list of dead people, and hit those places, too."

"What happened to the old lady in the west end?"

"She was asleep on the couch when we walked in. At first, Charlie was nice to her, talking low, telling her we were just gonna take stuff, she didn't need to worry. She was just old, and crying, saying 'don't hurt me.' We kinda laughed at her. We were leaving, and she stood up from the couch, standin' there, wringing her hands, and crying. Then she yelled at us, told us to get out. Called us little hoodlums, little shit hoodlums. I remember the look on Charlie's face, so dark and evil. I pulled on his arm said, 'Come on, leave her alone, she's just scared.' He pushed me against the wall with his arm on my throat and told me never to tell him what to do. And then he took a couple of steps toward the old lady and hit her in the head. She fell into a small table. Then he spit on her."

"Did she move after she hit her head?"

"Yeah. She was moaning and holding her head." Voice in a panic. "She was alive when we left there, man. She was, really." A sigh and a whimper. "Gotta believe me."

Nagler's face was placid in disgust, a bitter taste in his throat. Marion Feldman.

"Think Charlie could kill someone?"

George Santorini sat straight in the chair, his face taking on age, but his eyes pulled back in fear.

"In a minute. He'd kill me." He stared at the table. Softly: "He don't care."

CHAPTER TWENTY-SIX

Romeo's a-traveling to Mantua

The dirt on the wooden garage door window would not even come off with a napkin soaked in coffee. His wiping with the wet napkins produced a brown, gritty circular smear.

The dirt had been on that glass for years, Jimmy Dawson guessed. Coated with dust blown up from the street, wet down, coated again, layer after layer.

He glanced at the photograph that Nagler had given him, and at the one-story, two-door garage before him.

He leaned toward the filthy glass, shielded his eyes, and tried to peer though the smeary spot he had created, but the window was like a mirror so thick was the dirt; he saw an incomplete copy of his eyeball; his eyebrow felt greasy.

This was a deep back alley in one of the forgotten industrial zones in Ironton. Squat wooden buildings, years and years old, weeds yellow from lack of sunlight half-a-story high, narrow, winding alleys more like foot paths or horse cart trails.

But someone had come here, Dawson knew. Footprints scattered the dust; smudged handprints grabbed the splintered corners of the empty wooden shells.

And if Nagler was right, inside the building before him, was Dr. Nancy Harmon's 1987 Ford Bronco.

Dawson scratched his neck, flicking away dust. Why did Nagler give this to me instead of investigating it himself? What's he trying to prove?

The garage door was canted to the left, as if it stuck closed, and then forced open, sliding up unevenly. Dawson kicked the bottom of the door, but it was solidly jammed.

A side door seemed more promising because there was no lock and it hung loosely in the doorframe. With an old rag he had brought, Dawson turned the knob and the door popped open. Dawson smiled, pleased with himself. He had even brought a flashlight.

Old stuff hanging on the walls flashed in the dark as the light beam passed: Chains, leather straps, some rope, tools, an odd shirt or two — geez, who wore those?

In the middle of the garage was a squarish vehicle draped by a dust covered canvas tarp. Dawson lifted one edge of the front of the tarp and nodded: It was a Ford.

The right headlight and the grill had been smashed. He lifted more of the tarp then stopped.

I should call Nagler, he thought.

He exposed the entire front of the Ford.

What if there's a body in there?

He gingerly rolled back more tarp and enticed more dust into the heavy air.

Come on, Dawson. Suck it up. This could be the scoop of the year.

"Yup."

He grabbed the tarp with both hands and pulled it off the car in a storm of gray dust that covered his hair and clothing; he coughed out a mouthful and then stared through the windshield.

No one was sitting there. Nothing.

Dawson shook the dust from his hair and brushed off his clothes. "What'd you expect? Christ."

He slid down the side of the car to the passenger door and with his sleeve wiped the dirt from the window. What's that? He yanked at the unlocked door and it creaked open. He passed the flashlight beam over the seats and the floor. The keys were in the starter.

"Oh, man."

On the floor of the passenger's side was a stethoscope and a torn doctor's gown and one shoe, a woman's flat. In the back, Dawson saw a bag and what looked like a wad of clothes stuffed under the bench seat.

Dawson wrote down what he saw, the description of the Bronco, the license plate and vehicle numbers, notes on the condition of the garage, the car and the alley, and the dates on some papers muddied on the floor of the front seat and left.

At the diner Barry hadn't seen Frank Nagler yet that day, so Dawson found a white envelope, and put a three-word note inside and sealed it. He dropped it off at the front police desk, handing it to an officer he trusted.

"You were right."

Then he walked over to the city's central park, found a bench and grabbed his head with his shaking hands, both rattled and frightened by what the Bronco contained and the thrill of understanding what it all meant: What was in that car would either prove that Wallinski was the killer, or blow the whole theory apart.

"Holy shit. What if the cops were wrong?"

****

"Dawson!"

Chris Foley yelled at the reporter over the grinding whine of the tow truck winch hauling the Bronco out of the garage.

Dawson was at the side of the garage talking to the property owner, both surprised the reporter had found him.

"I dunno anything," Jake Garoppolo said through clenched teeth. "I ain't been here for years. Tried to sell these pieces of junk forever. Had a buyer. This will scare him off."

Dawson asked, "So how did they get in?"

"Busted in. You stupid or what?"

Dawson wiped his chin. "Busted what? The doors? The windows? They're all in one piece?"

Jake Garoppolo spit on the ground and said nothing.

"Someone pay you to park that vehicle there?" Dawson asked.

Garoppolo turned away then turned back and took a swing a Dawson, who ducked, but fell to the ground.

"Hey, fuck you, mister." Garoppolo yelled. "Paid me? You a wise guy?" He leaned over Dawson and was preparing another swing when a patrolman grabbed his arm. "Hey, knock it off,"

Garoppolo stumbled away and gave Dawson the finger. "Fuckin' wise guy."

By the time Dawson stood and brushed himself off, Foley was waving a copy of that day's paper in his face.

"How'd you know about this place?" Foley demanded, and slapped the paper against his leg.

Dawson drew his face tight. "Got a tip, Officer Foley." He knew the slight would set Foley off.

"It's Detective Foley. Chief Detective Foley."

Dawson put his tongue in his cheek. "Sorry, Chief Detective Foley, I left my score card at home." He started to move away, but Foley grabbed his arm.

"Who tipped you off? A cop?"

Dawson shook away Foley's hand. He knew he didn't have to answer Foley's question about a source, but he did want to protect Nagler, so he said, "Someone dropped off a picture of this place in an envelope with my name on it. That's all. Never saw them. After I saw what was here, I called you guys."

Foley's face was gray and sullen. "After you wrote a story for the newspaper."

Dawson shook his head and chuckled, "That's my job, Chief Detective Foley."

"I want that photo."

"I know you do. But you can't have it." Dawson rolled his right hand over a couple of times. "That's how this works. Now, if you'll excuse me." He took a couple steps then stopped and turned back. "Kinda blows a hole in your theory of the crimes, doesn't it?"

"What do you mean?"

"You've said you believe the Dr. Harmon had been killed in maybe February, right?" He grinned. "Wallinski was in Florida in February. So why is he in the county jail charged with her murder?"

Dawson left Foley stammering and red-faced and caught up to Garoppolo. "So, who wanted to buy this place?"

****

Dawson was a jittering mess. He glanced furtively at the empty counter seats at Barry's and the quickly back at his table. He ta-ta-ta-tapped a chaotic rhythm with a spoon on the table and stirred his half-empty cup of cold coffee, ringing the sides, placed the spoon on the table, picked it up again.

Across from him, Frank Nagler sat stone like, eyes withdrawn and face dark with worry. Martha had had a bad night. Whispering to her pillow, crying, moaning in pain. He had tried to calm her, to hold her tightly, but she seemed to be somewhere else. In the morning she laid motionless, nearly breathless; when he jerked awake to the silence, he could barely catch his breath.

At Barry's, he shoved inside the worry and withdrew.

Dawson, looking elsewhere, reached for his cup and spilled the coffee on the table.

"Jesus. Sorry, Frank. Hey, Barry…"

"I'd be nervous, too, Dawson, after that story in the paper," Barry said as he wiped up the spilled coffee. "Want fresh?"

Dawson nodded. "Sorry again. Yeah."

"What story?" Nagler asked, then he shrugged. "Haven't seen the paper."

"I said that Wallinski can't be the killer." Dawson hunched in his shoulders and winced. "Can't be. The timing, the bloody clothes in the Bronco couldn't have fit him, and he wouldn't have known about as secret a place as that old garage. I spoke with some of his customers. He was also always late because he'd get lost. He doesn't know Ironton at all."

Nagler just raised his eyebrows.

"So how did he find it?"

"Not sure Wallinski did. Someone paid the owner of the place to let them park the Bronco there."

"Did you tell anyone else beside me?"

"Yeah, Foley overheard my conversation with Garoppolo, the owner. Hustled the guy off."

"What's the connection?"

"Not sure. Interesting though."

Nagler stared absently out the window into the street, letting the traffic blur by.

"You've got something on your mind that ain't Wallinski, is it?" Dawson asked.

"Yeah," Nagler replied in almost a whisper. He shook his head, not wanting to talk about Martha.

"Why are you sitting here with me?" Dawson asked. "The world will wait, Frank."

A slight smile, a push of the chair scraping on the floor, a silent exit.

****

He walked. Past the old mills, past the stoops, past the troubles that weren't his own; out of the light of downtown into the darkness of the worker's ghetto, along the paths he had played on, had run along trailing

Del Williams, shouting. Across the dividing line from the dingy ghetto to the newer, brighter, nicer neighborhoods, the divide between torn pants and broken shoes, leaking roofs and dirt lawns and pale blue seersucker Sunday suits, iced tea on the patio and green trimmed lawns lined with perfect flowers … from childhood to manhood; across that divide that had defined his entire life, each step shedding the Chris Foleys, Charlie Adams, Bill Wallinskis of the world, the present woes cast upon Ironton like a curse. Losing the heat, the noise until there was only his shuffling steps along the broken sidewalks; walking till there was only Martha… turning, blindly taking a block at a time, surprised to find himself at their old school, then turning again past the bus stop, each house a marker deeper into his past, deeper into the days when he and Martha walked hand-in-hand, she shouting out hellos to all, he stumbling in an amazed and embarrassed joy that she was with him. Stopping at corners, smiling into his astonished face, he wordless in crazy happiness, thrilled as she wrinkled her freckled nose and brushed that red, red hair from her face; stunned at the lightness he felt, a lightness that even the cold shadow of the ghetto could not dampen…walked along the familiar route from the school to her house, which then seemed to shine, but now resting before the rising ridge behind, was dark and hollow, especially the shaded windows of the second floor where they lived. Walked now out of the light into a shade, feet leaden, a sensation that confused him because he wanted to hurry, to run to her side, but instead walked as if he was leaning into a head wind.

Finally, home, the street silent and blinking with the fractured light of a broken street lamp, the ancient, damaged shed and red hand mark flashing in and out of sight; even here the writhing troubles of Ironton seethed.

His damaged shoulder sagged as he leaned to open the heat-swollen front door, snapping off a creak that pried open the silence of the hallway.

The last few days had been bad for Martha, pain rising then ebbing, the heat drawing life from her body leaving it in soaking sheets.

Yet, she smiled. Each morning. Each afternoon when he came home. And at night when the weight of him slipping into the bed woke her briefly, her eyes unfocused then closing in pain.

"How's my girl?" he asked softly as he kissed her; he dried her face with the clean cloth nearby.

He didn't expect an answer. Sometimes her sleep was so deep and her breathing so shallow he leaned back startled, and expecting the worst, laid his head on her chest, only to breathe again when he detected her beating heart.

Her eyes popped open, then the right one closed.

"Catch the bastard yet?" A dry creaky voice.

The question drew a laugh from him. He kissed her. "No. Not yet." Tears formed at the corners of his eyes. "We will."

"Hurry up, damn it. I want to be around to read about it in the paper."

"Oh, Martha…"

"Frank, I dreamed of you. Of you and me. Us playing, teasing, standing naked in the dark, your shining skin against mine, the salt of your sweat on my tongue…" She stopped, motionless. "I loved your hands on me, fingers probing, you inside, me licking you, all those dirty little things the priests told us not to do, the things that would condemn our souls…" Three or four short, ragged breaths. "It's a wide world, Frank. And I followed you…"

He pulled himself in, chest collapsing, shoulders sagging, voice a hollow breath. "No, sweetie, Martha. No. I'm here."

"I saw you clapping the day I graduated. Standing alone for so long, clapping and cheering, I could feel you." A pause, she brushed her fingers across her lips. "We went to the park and you sprinkled rose petals on my belly. And they stuck to everything…" A coughing laugh. "And when you were done my tits were so hard and I was so wet. No one can use that park anymore, Frank. No more. Never."

"Hey…"

"You chased him away. My dark companion. But he comes back and I push him off. You gave me that strength, to push him away. I have to."

This time when she fell silent, her head rolled to one side and she seemed empty.

"Don't go," he whimpered, broken.

He wiped her face with the cloth again and she turned her head to him. "Don't be scared. Look at me. Let me see your eyes. That's my strength, Frank. Your eyes. Always." Silence. Then a whisper. "Romeo's a-traveling to Mantua. Fetch him."

Frank and her parents huddled in the front room as the emergency crew slid the gurney awkwardly down the narrow, platformed staircase.

They paused at the bottom of the stairs and popped out the wheels before rolling the mobile bed with Martha to the awaiting ambulance.

He could only watch; the confusion of the end.

One of the crew took his elbow and said, "You need to come, Frank."

The ambulance rattled through Ironton's rough streets. He knelt beside her, holding her hand and kissing her forehead.

He wanted to speak softly to her, whisper assurances in her ear. What was the word beyond love? His throat was dry, closed. He could only stare at her.

Her eyes flickered open, then closed, then opened for several minutes. Together they gazed at each other, and she managed a tiny smile. "My Frank," she said. "My Frank."

He reached to take off his tie, that damn tie, suddenly feeling choked by the garment. He yanked it from the shirt collar and jammed it into his pockets, the tie the victim of his pain.

He extracted the hard object he discovered in his pocket, puzzled it was there; he bit his lower lip and cried and laughed together.

It was a seam ripper. Martha had used it on his first day as a detective to open the sewn-closed pockets of his new jacket, which he was wearing.

He leaned over and kissed her cheek, and then stared into the darkness sliding by.

****

She had spent a couple of hours choosing his new wardrobe at Benny's Menswear, dragging him chuckling from rack to rack. He recalled how he and she cheerfully fought and argued and he denied he needed new clothes, but she won that battle, smiling all the way.

And then on the first day, he conceded; he had gazed at himself in the bedroom mirror again. Okay, not bad.

When he had tried to put his hands in the side pockets, he had laughed.

"Martha," he had called out over the clock-radio blaring Top 40 hits. "Do you have a small scissors or something I could use to open these pockets?"

He sidestepped into the family room from the bedroom, looking for his wife of two years. This house had too many doors, he thought.

"I have a seam ripper," she said seductively, stepping from behind the kitchen door leading to the living room while slipping her shoulder out of the over-sized t-shirt neck and winking. She spun out of the kitchen into the pantry, opened a cabinet drawer and removed a sewing box.

"That's not all you have," Nagler said, as he reached around her waist when she returned and kissed her neck.

"Oh, how true," she said as she kissed him, while displaying a small instrument with a plastic handle and a short, curved metal blade. "Watch it," she had laughed, leaning in. "I could swoon and accidentally trim your nose hair." She comically rolled her eyes as her red hair glistened with scarlet highlights in the morning sunlight.

"With luck it would be the only violent thing that happens to you today, Mister Detective," Martha whispered, before biting his ear. "I like saying that. Mister Detective. My Mister Detective."

She had pulled off his jacket, laid it on the kitchen table, cut way the stitches and opened the pockets. She had smoothed the fabric.

"There." She watched as her husband again donned the jacket. Then she had leaned into his chest and hugged him.

In the ambulance, he stared at the seam ripper. When had he put it in his pocket? Why would I? He thought of her hair.

It was her singular vanity. Long and thick, it cascaded off her shoulders to her waist. She wore it loose, and teasingly buried her face in it when they loved; let him part it and discover her bare shoulders and breasts; he would bury his face in it to draw in the scent of her.

He winced at the memory. In the days of despair and loathing, nearly bald, she wrapped her head in a black scarf while she had tried to hide from the world what her pale, thin face announced.

His face collapsed, eyes closed, asking the question for which there was no answer. He blocked out the road rumbles, the reflections of the flashing lights.

He fingered the seam ripper and brushed her thinned, grayed hair.

Then he knew: He hadn't put it in his jacket pocket. It wasn't there the last time he had worn that jacket a week ago.

One last gift. He turned to Martha, but she seemed so still, knowing her dark companion was close by. He watched.

"Rest, my sweet."

CHAPTER TWENTY-SEVEN

Today, he sank

The cemetery hollowed out, the wind and echo of scratching road sounds faded, footsteps on stone paths, the voices, whispers, "be well... So sorry... Praying for you," even the silent random pat on the back, all gone, drifted away.

Frank Nagler had nodded, eyes wrinkled in a sadness, his face a clay mask, forehead creased, trying to cast a smile back to the well wishes, a face seeking a permanent expression between the joy of Martha's life and the depthless pain of loneliness.

Only Sister Katherine knew.

The good Catholic sister in her wanted to hold Nagler's hands, kiss the bruised knuckles and draw him toward the peace and forgiveness of God's love. But as his friend and observer of his life, she knew that Nagler would nod in an empty gesture, accept the words, but reject the message; knew that he would battle against the dreads of his world in his own way; knew that only Martha had been able to penetrate his protective shell.

"Her love will be with you always. Francis," she had whispered. "Always."

Nagler had nodded, but as she walked away, Sister Katherine knew the withdrawal had begun. "I will watch out for you, Frank."

In the cemetery's silence, he tried to rise from the grave.

He had smoothed the rough, pebbly soil, breaking up small clumps between his thumb and fingers then brushing again the surface.

He tried to rise, but felt anchored, compelled to stay.

His hand would not pull away from the grave, suddenly weak, his knees and legs had no strength to push him upright.

"Why did you choose me?" his cracked voice said, kneeling still. "You could have done so much better than me. But there you were, beautiful girl, and I could not turn away, could not say no. So, we ran, and laughed and loved and told the world to get out of the way. And all that was you." He closed his eyes while tears gathered and dropped to the dark soil. "It was all you. I could barely keep up."

With his free hand, he brushed a finger along the letters of her name carved into the red headstone; then his hand trembled. His face closed, then opened, contorted through anger and pain and sorrow, and settled on the question.

"Why?" he pleaded. Then silently, a voiceless word, drenched in pain as the weight of the day settled, said to closed fists curled at his mouth. Why?

Finally, a strong push; he rose, and the coldness coalesced, the pain sealed.

"I will protect you by being hard," he whispered. "The world hurt you enough."

****

Walked again.

Through the clanking, riotous rush hour streets. Walked through train whistles and shouts for cabs, walked past squealing trucks forcing left turns, past cackling crowds at street corners; stalked along Ironton's cluttered sidewalks as if he was alone.

Walked as if the motion would grind away the pain; walked as if the pushed-aside shoulders would buff his grief to a hardened sheen.

Walked past the little troubles. Don't care that you hurt. I won't listen. Don't care what you want. I can't fix it for you. Fix it yourself. We all have our problems, and I don't want yours.

Stumbled through the dark broken streets of the worker's ghetto; walked past the misery that still hung on porches of sad houses, past his own life's sad beginning, looking for that turn to sunlight and Martha.

Walked through the city's pain of death and senseless killing, past wailing voices of families, the hollow eyes of victims, the hate filled darkness of a murderer, past the senselessness, past the killer's mirthless laugh; walked to that point when they would meet.

Walked finally to the Old Iron Bog and breathed in the stinking hollowness of it all.

Nagler stumbled off Mount Pleasant to the narrow path that led to the flat, tree shaded landing where he and Martha first had come alone. Oh, those little tenuous kisses, dry, then longer, lingering. The moment with a wicked grin she leaned against the car and pulled off her t-shirt, said "yes" and he touched her; then her mouth so soft, and the lavender scent of her hair; her hands reaching into his pants, the relief.

His shriek rippled over the dark water. Loud and long, it cast nearby birds from hiding. He turned and slammed his open hand against a small tree. Then again. He leaned his forehead against the tree and pulled out the unwilling tears.

"I'll not cry for myself," he whispered harshly. "There are only tears for Martha."

"Don't cry for me," she had said on one of the last days. "Rejoice for me. I'll love in your happiness, Frank. Not your grief."

Oh, he wanted to believe that.

But not today.

Today, he sank.

Shadows slipped across the moody black bog, hollow in its depth, a place for his trembling soul.

As he returned to Mount Pleasant, his police radio chirped to life.

"Yeah, Nagler."

It was dispatcher Mattie Washington.

"Sorry to bother you, Frank. We have another body."

A cold smile. The target for his rage announced.

CHAPTER TWENTY-EIGHT

Got a story for you

Jimmy Dawson leaned over to the open window of Mayor Howard Newton's Cadillac. It was parked at the far edge of the City Hall lot, distant enough to be out of the way, and thus not seen, but close enough so Newton could monitor the recovery of the latest murder victim.

There were now nine.

But this one was more public than the rest. Michelle Hanson's body was found in the river next to City Hall in the shallow, muddy millrace that once served the Union Iron Mill. She was naked. The surrounding public nervously had a firsthand view of that detail that up to now they had only read about in the paper: Her hands had been removed. If there had been any rain in recent months, her body would most likely have floated along the open concrete-lined channel to a point below, where she might have been snagged on some fallen tree.

Instead, she was face down in the hard, gray mud. The murmuring crowds gathered and pointed, covered their mouths and gasped, all the horrors of their imaginations made real.

"Pretty symbolic, don't you think, Mayor?" Dawson asked.

"You got a tone, Dawson. I'm not talking to you." Newton scowled. Go talk to Foley."

Dawson leaned on the door. "Already did. He's scared shitless. He's got a guy in the state psych ward charged with these killings, and guess what, we have another one, just like the rest. Little embarrassing."

"Bah." Newton blew a mouthful of cigar smoke out of the window, inhaled once more, then tossed the half-smoked Cuban into the parking lot. "Copycat."

Dawson smiled. "Naw. Got a story for you."

"I don't need stories. I make stories."

Dawson sank his chin to his chest and smiled. He leaned to the window, hands on the car's roof. "I know."

Newton scowled, then with a brief nod, unlocked the car doors.

Dawson settled into the back seat; Nagler was right: The car reeked of cigar smoke. Newton stared straight ahead. And unlit cigar bounced in his fingers.

"There's this guy," Dawson began. "And there's this city, hard luck town, stumbling through bad times again. So, the guy sees an opportunity, not for the town, but for himself to make money. It's an easy scheme to set up. A couple of dummy companies, friends on the inside shuffling cash around, taking care of the paperwork. But it's not going well. He can't raise cash fast enough and the price of the land he wants won't drop fast enough. He's stuck…"

"Damn it, Dawson, get to the point."

Dawson hid a little smile. "To help matters along, the guy and a friend latch on to a petty criminal to raise a little havoc, drive up the crime rate, so the guy can ask for lower prices. Then he promises to take care of the little hoodlum, but little do they know that he's been killing people, women, all along. Instead of putting an end to it, they let him run with it, you know, just to see."

Dawson turned to Newton. "This is where it gets interesting, because it gets complicated. The guy's friend loses control of the hoodlum. He tried to direct the cops in another direction, and then what do you know, another woman turns up dead, and right at City Hall."

"Get out of the car," Newton growled. "You're full of shit."

Dawson pushed open the door. "Umm. That's what the guy said."

Newton lit the Cuban, drew in a mouthful of smoke and blew it toward Dawson. "Nobody could prove that. Nobody."

"Not in a day, but over time," Dawson said. "And you'll never get away with it."

The cigar quivered. "Fuck you, Dawson."

****

"What's going to happen with Wallinski?"

Jimmy Dawson leaned over the table at Barry's, watching as Frank Nagler's dark eyes sheltered his pain. Dawson told himself he would have collapsed under that weight; he recalled watching Nagler as Michelle Hanson was removed from the river, face filled with disgust and loathing, but distracted eyes.

"I mean, you don't have…"

"It's okay, Jimmy." Nagler nodded. "Thanks." He wiped his mouth with a napkin and pushed his half-filled plate away. "Bart Harrington has asked for a hearing to have the charges dismissed, in light of the recent new activity." His weary voice was light and mocking. "Couple of days," he offered, and then withdrew.

"I don't mean…"

"I've got a job to do, Jimmy. Everything…" He waved away the comment. "She was just a kid. Eighteen. Lived up in the hills in one of the newer subdivisions. Parents were out of town. Mulligan says she was drowned, probably in the family pool. Then her hands were cut off and she was thrown in the river."

"How'd he get her to the river?"

"Car?" Nagler shrugged. "We haven't found it." He ran both hands through his hair. That was when Dawson noticed Nagler hadn't shaved.

"I'm sick of it, Jimmy. Sick of all this murder and mayhem and anger. All the pain in this city, all the cheap tricks and cheap tricksters… Just tired of it all." He covered his face with his hands and let out a deep breath. "But the fucker's still out there." He stood up to leave. "Heard you had a meeting with the mayor."

"Dawson chuckled, "Sort of."

Nagler nodded. "Watch your back."

****

The neighborhood was wrong. Too quiet, too sheltered and too far from the center of Ironton.

Nagler walked the tree-lined streets questioning Michelle Hanson's neighbors. Nice girl, good student. Babysat for my kids. Parents traveled, and she held parties. Wore skimpy bikinis. Sunbathed in the nude. How did you know that? Saw her from my second story window. Aren't you special.

Nagler wearied of the answers. Blamed her parents: Too permissive. Blamed Michelle for being a pretty teenager, having friends, being promiscuous, as if lying naked on a towel in one's own fenced backyard was somehow wrong.

But that's where we were, he thought. Blame everyone but the killer.

As he stalked the perimeter of the Hanson's yard again, one question remained: Where was the red hand and the HAND OF DEATH slogan?

It had been three days.

It had also been three days since Nagler had seen Chris Foley. That didn't seem like a coincidence.

****

From his hospital bed, Sal LaStrada had a theory that the killer was just expanding his territory since the downtown and east side, his old killing grounds, were now heavily patrolled day and night. The silk mill, where he had been attacked was a half-mile from the Hanson's neighborhood.

He recalled more details of his attack.

"The sun had just popped over the hill, the light coming down just between the roof of that tenement at the corner and a line of trees. Pretty sharp," he told Nagler. "I had my head down to avoid looking directly into the light and was sort of squinting. He was on me before I looked up. I could hear the rush of him running, but he was on me. Once across the chest, just missed any organs, then two stabs. Knocked me back."

He shifted in the bed slightly, absorbing the pain from the stitched-up wound.

"I'm not supposed to move, but damn it, it's hard to keep still."

LaStrada dipped his head and nodded for Nagler to come closer.

"It's the same guy, Frank. This is the Joan Chen attack and the Debbie Jones attack in the parking lot. A rush, a slash, a couple stabs. Then gone." He winced. "The only thing that saved me was my size and probably the thick sweatshirt I was wearing. So, a short-bladed knife, six inches or less. No one found anything, huh?"

Nagler shook his head.

"This is not Wallinski, Frank. That fat man could not have moved with the speed needed to complete the ambush attacks. Go back and talk to that dishwasher at the China Song again. I'll bet he remembers something."

In the hospital hallway, waiting for the elevator, Nagler stared into waving and washed-out version of his face in the square dirty, wire-crossed window in the heavy metal elevator door. If the killer is attacking cops, who's next? His face slid away as the doors opened, splitting in the center.

****

Standing on the top step of the courthouse entrance Bartholomew Harrington towered over the gaggle of reporters before him. He had won a reduction of bail for Bill Wallinski, which would get him released from the state psychiatric detention center.

"The judge seemed to agree with you that your client might be innocent," a reporter shouted.

Harrington waved his hand. "No, not at all, sir. What the judge said was that there was enough doubt that Mr. Wallinski committed eight murders, and thus did not require such a high amount of bail. That's all. We still have to prove that he is not the mass murderer threatening this city."

The reporter persisted. "Doesn't a new murder, done in the same way, mean your client is innocent?"

"Of one murder, committed while my client was in jail. That's all it means. We have the evidence that will show he did not commit any of these killings, but that must wait for court."

"But what else did you say? That these killings are part of a larger, organized crime pattern? What's that mean?"

Harrington smiled, one of his famously arrogant smiles. "I'm not going to give away my case before I can present it in court, but ask yourself, who might benefit from the chaos that has filled these streets over the past months? Who might be in a position to take advantage of the circumstances, and who might be willing to create the chaos for their benefit?" He turned away.

"Are you saying that someone in an official capacity might be using these murders as a cover-up?"

Harrington turned back and smiled. The question had come from Jimmy Dawson.

"Ah, Mr. Dawson. You are right. There is more here than meets the eye."

At the edge of the crowd, Harrington approached Frank Nagler.

"Detective, I've heard you are interested in a certain person in this city. Consider this my contribution to that search." He handed Nagler a manila envelope and walked away.

Nagler opened the envelope and slipped out the three pages and stared at the name on the top sheet.

What the hell?

George Santorini had quite a record as a juvenile, starting when he was nine. Thefts, fights, assaults, delinquencies, school suspensions. Three pages of a troubled kid's resume. What had the kid said? Father in jail, mother gone. A street kid. How did they survive and escape the system? Nagler wondered. Leonard, George Santorini, Charlie Adams — all dumped on the street like an old dog. Martha had asked that question. Who are the feral kids? Who are the throwaways?

What happened when their need to survive turned to anger?

He flipped the three pages of dates and incidents. You strike out in little ways and then in larger ways.

But George Santorini was not some leader of a street gang. He was a follower who got beaten for his loyalty. Charlie Adams is the leader.

Nagler recalled kneeling in the street after Charlie Adams had clubbed him during that rally. The cold eyes and the sneer. Was that the look of a kid laying out revenge for the bad hand he had been dealt, or something else?

Either way, Nagler thought, it's time to get him off the street.

****

The first shed Nagler had torn down was the one behind the auto parts store that Leonard had pointed out and where George Santorini dug up the tin filled with cash. Five police cadets armed with saws, sledges and shovels leveled the soft brick and dug up the ground.

The second was next to the silk mill where LaStrada had been attacked. For good measure, the city mowed the field. Two others were detailed in the juvenile court papers Harrington had provided Nagler. The first of those was in the woods near the high school and reminded Nagler of a latrine, and the second was behind an empty home on lower Blackwell.

Stash houses, organized, secret, and now, empty.

Nagler was amazed at the number of items they had recovered: Fourteen plastic bags of stuff they had yet to sort; twelve tins of cash, and an assortment of individually wrapped items including a couple of rusty pistols.

Sergeant Hanrahan, who had supervised one group of cadets, whistled when he saw the five tables covered with loot.

"Made a lot of noise, Frank," he said. "Think it got their attention?"

Nagler smiled. "Oh, yeah. And there's more to come."

"What's up?"

"There's about ten kids in this gang. We identified a few of them after that rally when I got clubbed on the head. "This" —he waved at the tables— "Will get the rest. Tell your patrols to be aware of the possibility that there could be a spike in burglaries and store robberies. They're gonna need the income."

Two voices filled Nagler's head as he left City Hall: Martha's, telling him to fight on, and Del Williams reminding him to take the game to them. He smiled into the dark street.

****

This was the part of Nagler's plan the chief was not thrilled with: Nagler alone patrolling the east side streets.

"You'll be a target, Frank."

"That's the plan. We gotta smoke this kid out."

Chief Mallory held Nagler's stare with a disapproving gaze then said, "Yeah, okay. Got a portable?"

Nagler reached under his jacket and pulled out the radio.

"You're not doing this because your wife died, are you Frank?"

Nagler squinted at the floor. Am I? "No, sir. I might be doing it because this kid hit me over the head, and maybe stabbed Sergeant LaStrada. Mostly, Chief, it's because with questions about Wallinski, this kid might know something. And if he doesn't, he's one more dangerous punk we get off the street."

As the chief walked away, Nagler thought that maybe Martha's death had everything to do with the latest activity. There was a hollow in his heart that needed to be filled and a simmering anger ready to fill it.

CHAPTER TWENTY-NINE

I'm the future. The future is a mess

The lower east side was the section of Ironton where the industries that later boomed began. Small shops, fragile wooden walls, single forges and foundries, two-man metal works, now all black with age, leaning on rat-chewed bases.

Nagler's grandfather had told him that as the operations grew, they took what they needed and built larger shops, again and again until Ironton could boast fifteen industrial metal works and canal boats flowing east and west to the braying of mules, then rail cars hauling coal and iron ore daily, then finished goods.

All that was left on the old streets now was the whistle of wind though gaps in walls, the echoed drip of water like a bad dream, and the heaviness of time past.

The first two nights generated no contacts. Nagler was actually relieved, because walking those streets gave him the opportunity to know the alleys, the unlocked doors, and the places he could potentially run, or his suspect could hide.

On the third night, a fog settled it. It hadn't rained, but air was cooling with the arrival of fall.

"This is like Frankensteinville," Nagler muttered to himself tip-toeing through the fog. The buildings were softer-edged, the stunted trees more witchly, and the night noises dribbled along the alleys with a ringing tone, the only sounds.

Nagler heard the voice before he spotted the blurred figure.

"You lookin' for me."

Nagler pointed his flashlight toward the figure, but the light was diffused by the fog; he thought he detected the flash of metal at the side of the body.

"Come closer," he said.

"Not stupid, cop."

"Probably not. But not smart enough to hide your loot from us. I think we got it all, right?"

247

Nagler scanned the alley with his light, seeking a better angle that might provide a glimpse of the kid. "So, what are you going to do? We're picking up your little gang, one by one. They'll talk, and we'll have you."

Something was kicked down the alley toward Nagler.

"You don't get it, cop," the kid said in a cold, hollow voice. "I don't care. Don't care about my little gang, or the people I've robbed, the kids I've beaten up. I don't care about anything. It's all shit, something to break, something to kick around."

"You care about something or you wouldn't be here," Nagler replied, recalling the kid's hard face above him as he laid in the street after that blow. "You care about something or you wouldn't have hit me over the head."

"You ain't important. You were just there."

"Not important? Then why did you spy on my house from that old shed? Paint a red hand there? Put Edie Smith's old doll there as a warning? Trying to scare me away?" Nagler raised his voice to a threatening level. "I'm here. I don't scare. And I'm sure as hell not scared of little teenage punks."

"You oughtta be," the kid sneered. "You're the past. I'm the future. The future is a mess."

Nagler laughed. "What the hell is that supposed to mean?"

No reply. Nagler walked forward and scanned the deepening fog with his light. The kid had slipped away.

"Round one," he said.

****

LaStrada had been released from the hospital and allowed to return to desk duty, and he spent the time plowing through three boxes of juvenile court records that Harrington's manila envelope had opened up.

Dozens of kids, hundreds of incidents. Divorces, drunken parents, rapes, physical assaults, robberies, school suspensions, list after list, year after year, from all parts of the city, kids of all ages.

"What'd we do wrong?" Nagler asked as he examined the piles of reports.

"I recognized some of these names from narcotics," LaStrada said. "Some of it is generational, some just because there's no jobs. A few of these people were in organized, small time drug gangs, some were knee breakers for actual mobsters. But most were just down on their luck schmucks." He leaned back slowly, letting the abdomen pain diffuse. "Why are we looking at all this?"

Nagler shrugged. "Because we haven't got anything else?" he asked. "We don't have Wallinski. He'll be out today, and Harrington will get the rest of the charges dismissed. No one we've looked at had profiled as our killer." He nodded to the papers. "So we have this."

"Why did Harrington give us this tip?"

"Why does Harrington do anything?" Nagler smiled. "Because he's after the mayor and his cronies. That's what it is. That's gotta be in there." He pulled out a chair and grabbed a pile of files.

****

Nagler prowled the room filled with five tables of loot collected from the sheds. It had all finally been tagged and photographed. Sergeant Hanrahan was supervising five officers and cadets shifting through five years of unsolved burglaries to match the descriptions of the stolen items with what the tables held.

Nagler was looking for something more specific: Any item that matched the description or the photos of items from Marion Feldman's house. Her granddaughter had placed the boxes left in the house in storage and had allowed police to examine them again. Made sense, he thought. They had found Marion's bracelet at the Old Iron Bog, and Walter's watch in the shed at the silk mill. Another item or two would give him leverage when he interviewed the gang members. George Santorini already had placed Charlie Adams and the rest of the gang inside the Feldman's house for a robbery. A couple more items and another statement or two, and they would be able to detain the gang leader.

****

If there had been any remaining speculation about Bill Wallinski's guilt, Dr. Mulligan ended it. The blood infused into clothes found in Dr. Harmon's Bronco matched only Joan Chen. Besides, Nagler thought, the clothes were mismatched. A pair of small, ragged jeans and an old-style and somewhat larger cheap hooded pullover, as described by the

China Song dishwasher, both too small to fit Wallinski, who weighed over three-hundred pounds. The only clothes found in Wallinski's apartment and truck were green industrial style work clothes. His entire wardrobe, it seemed, consisted of uniforms, some with paint splatters and oil stains, some clean, but all with a white name patch that said "Bill" in red script.

More interesting, Nagler thought, was the stethoscope and doctor office jacket found in the car. The earpieces of the stethoscope had been twisted and the rubber of the device showed evidence of being stretched. The jacket had three buttons missing and the stain on the right bottom side was her own blood.

Possibly, she too had been stabbed, Mulligan had said. Since they had found only a partial skeleton, it was impossible to prove. Tests on the car's vinyl seats were less conclusive.

"So, she was apparently killed in her car?" Nagler asked the medical examiner. Mulligan said it seemed so, since her office showed no signs of a struggle and no blood was found there.

"Where did she park her car?" Nagler wondered aloud. Certainly not in the old industrial district where it had been found. That section of East Ironton was more than a mile from her office. More neighborhood walking, he thought.

It was an odd place for an office. In the middle of a block of single, one-story buildings, most of which were not occupied, and no parking lot, just on-street parking. The "For Rent" signs seemed weathered.

One shop was open, a locksmith. Nagler smiled as he approached the door: It had six locks.

He rattled the door and stepped into a room lined with key blanks, local samples and window bars.

"Be right with ya," a voice from the back yelled over the grinding whine of a key making machine. "Hello, officer," the man said, as he stepped to the front. "I'd like to thank ya for all the extra business I got lately," he said extending a thin, grease stained hand. "Them killings. I'm Bob Lockett. Ain't that something, Bob Lockett owning a lock store. Hee, hee."

Nagler grinned; had to.

"I'm Detective Frank Nagler. Got a question about the doctor's office down the street."

"Yeah, Doctor Nancy. She's dead."

"That's why I'm here. Where'd she park her car when she was working? Not…"

"Here and there. We all do." Bob Lockett said. "Within a block." He shrugged. "No meters."

Ah, Nagler thought. "Customers…?

"Park here and there."

"You here at night?"

"No. I close about three. Installations. I'm one guy. Doing a lot lately. And I'm gonna do a lot more after what's in today's paper?"

Nagler hadn't seen the paper. "What's that?"

"Aw, you ain't seen it," Bob Lockett said. He reached behind him to a small desk and returned with a folded copy of the paper and handed it to Nagler. "Keep it. Wouldn't want to be you guys."

Nagler unfolded the paper, puzzled. "Shit. Damn it."

WALLINSKI KILLED IN PRISON.

Bob Lockett just shrugged.

CHAPTER THIRTY

Bones

A crowd had already gathered at City Hall by the time Nagler returned, a murmuring, slithering gathering responding to the bellowed jeremiad of Bart Harrington.

"Mayor Newton killed my client," Harrington yelled. "William Wallinski is much a victim of this criminal regime as any of the nine women who have died during his time in office. Come brothers and sisters. We will stand for it no longer!"

The crowd roared approval and waved their signs and pumped their fists.

"Who do you believe?" Harrington shouted. "Are you so enthralled you cannot see the truth? The mayor does not dance with the truth, he stomps on it. There is more than his reality. Challenge it, my brothers and sisters. Demand that he show you his dirty hands. Do not let his darkness overtake you. It is too long a road to find again the light."

Nagler skirted the edges. Oh, boy. Harrington in full bloom.

The kid would be here, he told himself; there is loot to be made.

And there he was. Blue jacket and red cap. Why so obvious? Nagler asked as he watched Charlie Adams slide behind someone, look left, then right, shift his shoulders and step away. A few feet away, he turned and bumped face to face into a young woman, paused and stepped aside. Nagler watched Adams shift through the protestors for a few more minutes and then with a furtive look over his shoulder, drift away down Sussex.

Nagler followed. The sidewalks were jammed with commuters and shoppers and those drawn to Harrington's siren call. They pushed through traffic, closed intersections with bodies that froze cars in the street, honking, shouting, swearing; then it all stalled, sidewalks and streets a swirling mob.

And through it all, Charlie Adams moved down Blackwell, sliding in gaps, pace slow and calm, his red cap an easy mark for Nagler half a block behind.

He took a left at Bergen, and crossed into the yards of three abandoned houses, dipping out of sight behind fallen trees and swing sets left to rot, only to emerge half a block away, walking with a quickened pace. Nagler stopped to pick up two wallets Adams had dropped. He jammed them in an inside jacket pocket. There had to be more than this, he thought.

Nagler trailed cautiously. The only cover was a series of broad maples and oaks that lined the street. Adams turned right down an alley then right again along Franklin. Nagler waited. Franklin reached a dead-end when it met another alley behind a row of businesses and the river. The alley there was cluttered, and stump filled, debris from old storms and dying trees the city had never removed.

Adams headed back toward the center of downtown at that alley, a shift that shoved Nagler into the shadow of a staircase at the rear of one of the shops.

Where the hell is he going? he wondered. Maybe he knows he's being followed, and this is a wild goose chase.

"Let's end it, then," Nagler said to himself and quickstepped to the end of the alley where it seemed Adams had to emerge.

The alley was empty, so Nagler began a slow patrol, shifting behind the cover of a wall every few feet. The echo of Harrington's rally, like the cheers after a touchdown at a football game, filtered along the river bed.

He recognized the building as one Leonard had pointed out; the oval doors and shallow ceilings were a quick hidey-hole for the street gang. Nagler cursed. They had not examined these doorways and cellars. What could be there?

A new, indistinct sound emerged. A little digging? The fall of a table or shelf? Something metal. Nagler tucked in deeper below a staircase.

Adams emerged with a black satchel and ran to the end of the alley and turned right toward Blackwell and back into the raucous crowd.

Nagler a block away but parallel to Adams' path, reversed his direction and moved through the crowd toward the train station. He's heading to Smelly Flats, has to be.

Adams emerged from the crowd near the Methodist Church, his red cap bright against the church's dull stone face. He entered the train station platform at the rear gate, but Nagler knew there was only one place to cross the double tracks and enter the railroad maintenance yard that led to Smelly Flats. He would have to walk along the track-level sidewalk and cross at Morris street's signal and crossing gate.

Nagler paused at the entry to the station watching the red cap shuffle through the commuter crowd to Morris. Adams had darted across the tracks just before the crossing gate dropped and a locomotive hauling five cars pulled into the station. Then he crossed and turned left, into the train maintenance lot.

Nagler pushed his way to the platform and through the train windows saw the red cap quickly move east, away from the station.

He realized he left his portable radio in his car, and he pushed over to the pay phone to call for back-up. The phone had been removed. "Of course, it's busted," he muttered, shaking his head. "Everything here is broken."

He jogged over to Morris and ducked under the crossing gate and began to walk to Smelly Flats, using the train passenger cars in the maintenance yard as cover.

The red cap bobbed ahead, more slowly.

Maybe he thinks no one saw him, Nagler thought. But then why all the changes of direction?

Nagler held back until he was sure Adams entered the path to Smelly Flats; he knew there was no way out of that path once he walked about a hundred feet because the sloping sides grew steeper and the trail narrower. Nagler thought that he could even reveal himself to Adams, but then decided he needed to see what the kid was going to do with the satchel.

The path had become rock hard as the summer heat and lack of rain dried up the river, but the whirlpool that formed when the river hit the channel's granite walls would still be there, swirling more slowly, but still wet and dangerous enough to prevent Adams's escape.

Nagler quickened his pace as he approached the last turn in the path.

He heard Adams say, "Shit," and then a splash.

Nagler quickened his pace, reaching out to trees and stumps, jumping over exposed roots as he tried not to slide into the muddy river bank.

"Stop!" he yelled when Adams came into view.

The kid in wet pants held the satchel in one hand, reached in and pulled out an object and threw it into the whirlpool. Nagler ran toward him, slipping and tripping to his hands, but rising in time to grab Adam's arm and take the satchel.

"I said stop." He pushed the kid to a sitting position.

Adams's eyes burned with hate, his lips in a sneer. "You followed me here to stop me from littering?" He spit out a harsh laugh. "How stupid are you?"

Nagler set the satchel on the ground and pulled out the two wallets he had picked up.

"Littering is not issue, kid, but being a pickpocket and petty thief is. I found these after you dropped them on the street, and if I made you empty your pockets we'd find the cash."

"That's nothing." But the sneer was gone, and Adams's eyes went dark with worry.

"Stand up," Nagler ordered.

"Fuck you. Make me."

Nagler grabbed the kid by the arm pit and stood him up; he held Adams in place while he handcuffed him to a tree.

Adams rattled the cuffs against the tree and yelled, "You can't..."

Nagler leaned in. "I can. I did. Shut up. You're a dangerous suspect with a violent past. I have the marks to prove it. I've been chasing you for months. And I'm gonna find out who your cop friends are, and why you were watching my house..." His voice faltered, and he stared at the ground.

Adams tried to head-butt Nagler but missed.

Nagler reached into a side pocket and pulled out a laminated card. "I'm going to read you your rights now, so you understand how important all this is." He waved the card in front to Adams face for emphasis. "Do you understand what I just read?"

The kid didn't answer.

"Okay, look, screw you. I'm going to leave you hooked to this tree and head back to headquarters for some more cops so we can search this area. Could take an hour, maybe. You'd be here alone. Yelling won't help. Just you as night falls. But you're a tough kid, street tough, beats people up, robs stores and houses. Up to you. Did you understand what I just read to you?"

Silence, again.

"Okay..." and he turned away.

"I get it," Adams growled.

"Good." Nagler's tone was softer. "What's in the satchel?"

Adams spit. "Stuff."

****

Stuff: Earrings, bracelets, gold necklaces, some with diamonds, emeralds, tie pins, broaches, artsy music boxes, wrist watches and pocket watches.

High-end stuff. Way beyond this punk's range, Nagler thought.

And then this: He didn't find those houses by himself.

Then, among the jewelry in the satchel and fished out of Smelly Flats' whirlpool: Marion Feldman's wedding ring, the one crafted for her by Rocky Calabrese.

"That'll help place him in the Feldman house," Nagler said to Dr. Mulligan, "While we sort out the rest."

"The rest, Detective?" Mulligan's tone was dismissive. "All these human hands are 'the rest?'"

"That's not what I meant," Nagler replied. "I'm sorry. I feel stupid."

Mulligan shook his head. "That's not what you feel, Frank. What you are feeling is the intellectual reluctance to make the next statement, the unwillingness to make that next, long step — that our kid here, Charlie Adams, is our serial killer."

"Is that it?"

"Your deepening involvement with this boy began right from the start," Mulligan said. "He was photographed at crimes scenes, you suspected him of being a housebreaker and thief, and then he assaulted you. Why not take the next step? Why not ask how someone so violent and anti-social could be a killer?"

"Seems like a big leap, Doctor, from petty thief to serial killer. Didn't you say that the serial killer was a term devised for intellectual discussions?"

"It is both, Frank. They exist. Remember I also called this spree 'an experiment in death.' The different means, the different types of victims suggest that there was a thrill in killing in different ways, just to see what he could get away with." He paused. "Like a kid breaking into nice houses to steal from the more well-to-do. In a city like Ironton, with its checkered history of economic progress, such resentment is as much a part of life as bad air and dirty streets."

Nagler's face wrinkled. "I grew up in that same city, and I'm not a serial killer. I had the same chances as he did, until…" Tears formed.

"Until…"

"Until Martha," Nagler choked out her name. "Until Martha."

Mulligan touched Nagler's shoulder. "Yes. Exactly. Love matters. That seems to have been lacking in the lives of Charlie Adams and his gang."

"So …?"

"So leave the psychology to the professors, Frank. Let's focus on the evidence. If he is our killer, let's get him off the street."

"Yeah," Nagler nodded. "What have you made of this so far?"

"That I have a collection of human hand bones, that if assembled, would produce complete hands. I have carpels, from one's wrist, phalanges, lower finger bones, to distal phalanges, the tips of one's fingers. But I am uncertain that I could accurately reconstruct the hands of our eight victims from these."

"You mean nine victims."

Mulligan shook his head. "No, eight. Michelle Hanson was killed so recently that the flesh on her hands would not have decomposed completely. The rest of these hands have been exposed to air for months. We don't have Michelle's hands."

"Maybe that's how we get him," Nagler said.

Mulligan nodded, and a slight smile crossed his lips. "And this." He picked up one hand. "This is a carpel bone. Notice the ragged cut. It had been crudely removed, perhaps an axe or hatchet, or dull knife. Have we found such a weapon?"

****

Michelle Hanson's parents had put their home up for sale. It stood, hooded and silent, surrounded by trees bare of their leaves, a cold sun sliding through the gaps.

Nagler prowled the neighborhood hungry for answers. Any strangers here? Any disturbances, stolen cars, trash cans knocked over, rowdy kids, loud parties?

All the neighbors said no. And they all lied, Nagler knew. No one's neighborhood was that quiet. The answers were the same in the Baker Hills: No one saw anything; no one wanted to see anything. That's was why Marion Feldman could be murdered right under their noses, and why Michelle Hanson could be taken at the same time. We turned up the TV when the shouting gets too loud, draw the blinds, lock the doors, sell the house because what could we possibly do?

Looking is my job, Nagler thought.

So, he looked.

Why was there no painted red hand and threating scrawl at Michelle Hanson's home? But the worst question of all was this: Where were her hands?

A daytime search of Smelly Flats had produced a few more pieces of jewelry, but nothing else. Searches of the cellars visited by Charlie Adams had also produced nothing new; a small victory, Nagler thought.

Adams was being held at the county's juvenile jail charged with theft and assault on a police officer. That was something.

But something was missing.

Including Chris Foley.

Chief Mallory said he had seen in at City Hall, but Foley had not returned phone calls. "If I find him, I'll suspend him," Mallory said.

"The mayor won't like that," Nagler replied.

"Well, the mayor won't like this either," Mallory said. "Look at the headline."

"CITY'S ECONOMIC PLAN CRUMBLES. LOCAL LAWYER SUES FOR RECORDS."

Nagler shook his head. "Harrington." Then asked the chief: "Will this help us or hurt us?"

****

Gregory Smith seemed smaller, hollowed out. The angry, vigorous defender of his mother's raucous life seemed shrunken by her death. He greeted Nagler at her home that he was selling, the finality of the act a burden that sagged his shoulders and softened his once brash voice.

"This was really never my home," Gregory Smith said, "I lived here as a youth, but went to private schools then college and into business. But it was hers, so in that sense it was our homestead. I wish I had appreciated that now. In a way I envy you, Detective Nagler, Ironton is your home, something to defend. I gave my life to business and making money, developing things and places, but I never knew them." He patted a pillar on the front porch. "And now I never will."

Smith's face wrinkled into a sad mask. "I understand that we share a similar sorrow, Detective. I was told about your wife. I'm sorry for your loss."

Nagler rubbed his forehead and said thanks. "I think my Martha and your mother would have been great friends," he said. "There was something about their spirits that ran roughshod over the daily troubles and worries."

"Indeed," Smith replied.

The son had agreed to meet with Nagler to examine photos of some of the jewelry police had gathered. Nagler also brought on a chance, photos of Michelle Hanson, Bill Wallinski, Charlie Adams and George Santorini.

Smith grabbed his forehead and wiped his eyes as he recognized his mother's rings and broaches. "I gave her this piece," he said with a sigh, "And this was for her sixtieth birthday." His face grew dark. "So, her killer took these?"

"We think so."

"Do you know who it is?"

Nagler glanced into the street. "We believe we have narrowed it down."

Smith took the answer in stride. "I understand. You can't say much."

"That's about right. Let me ask you, though, do you recognize any of these people."

Smith flipped through the photos.

"That's Wallinski, a commercial painter. Never showed up. Good thing I never paid his deposit. These kids, no." He flipped back to the photo of Michelle Hanson. "Maybe, this girl." He closed his eyes as he thought. "You know, maybe from the community center, where Mother dropped off the soup, and where they made that doll that was stolen. She had them to the house once or twice. Maybe her, maybe there. Who is she?"

Nagler collected the photos. He didn't tell Smith she was dead. "Just a kid we came across. Thanks."

****

Nico Gonzalez, the soup kitchen manager, tapped the photos of Charlie Adams and George Santorini, and spat on the ground. "Troublemakers. Punks. Gave our guests nothing but trouble. Threw them out finally. I didn't think they came back."

"They were together, these two?"

"Yeah, all the time."

"When was the last time you saw them?"

"Weeks ago, after Miss Edie was missing."

Damn it, Nagler thought. Both those punks are playing us, playing me.

"Last thing," he asked. "This girl…"

"Yeah, Michelle. She volunteered. Quit when those punks bothered her."

****

All these pieces. And none of them fit.

Frank Nagler watched the gray water of the Old Iron Bog glow red then purple as the last sunlight faded. The keeper of secrets had lived up to its name this time. The swamp had been searched by boat and on foot, the paths had been raked and the dirt sifted again and no more of Jamie Wilson had been found.

Old warehouses had been swept, walls opened, piles of wrecked cars dismantled and nothing more of Dr. Nancy Harmon or Felice Sanchez was discovered.

All the wreckage had been probed, all the debris examined, all the city's souls purged, prayers raised, cries unchained and still there was no learning, no light. Families stood over the cold graves, watched the rough wind sweep away the petals of the soft flowers left in memory; embraced, cursed, wailed, but nothing pushed back the darkness, which grabbed the horizon and nailed it shut in pain.

It was as if Michelle Hanson's death, so brutal and public, had squashed the hopes of the city. Her death, so careless and unnecessary, somehow meant more than all the others, as if her youth and the loss of it made more heartless the collective shame and guilt the city carried in its aching heart.

Even Barry's was muted. The eatery, so loud and alive even in the worst of times, was deeply quiet most days, just the soft rattle of dishes and silverware filling the edges. Tony in the back played the radio a little bit louder to fill the place with sound; but even Tony, usually off-key and exuberant, did not sing along.

Mayor Howard Newton had gone underground, following Dawson's story about Harrington's lawsuit. A subsequent story that detailed the moving parts brought the squirming financial mess to Newton's door at the Trenton Street Club, but no further.

The photo on the front page of the Register that featured a grinning Bart Harrington seemed both self-congratulatory and evil.

"When's it end?" Dawson asked Nagler the day the story appeared.

CHAPTER THIRTY-ONE

Charlie Adams

"What do you mean you don't care?" Frank Nagler's voice ripped the air.

He laid another photo of stolen jewelry in front of Charlie Adams. Then he shifted to the side of the table and leaned in close, breathing-in-your-face-close.

"We found your fingerprints on these rings and bracelets. That doesn't concern you?" He tapped the photo.

The kid frowned, and then smiled a distracted smile. "I don't care."

Nagler glanced at Adam's representative, a legal aid from children's services. "That's fourteen times, your client has said he doesn't care."

The representative shrugged. "He's not…"

"I know. He's not your client. But you have some responsibility to make sure this young man treats these allegations seriously. And he is not." The rep stared at the wall, paying scant attention to the photos or Adams. "Am I boring you?"

"Yeah, okay," the man said, shook his head, and sat up a little straighter.

Nagler had chosen the dark, cell-like room at the youth lock-up deliberately. One small table, three chairs, a few boxes in the corner, a single light and a small window. Three people crammed into the dry, warm space; Charlie Adams was at home on the street, freewheeling through empty buildings, and not accustomed to such tight quarters, Nagler had figured.

"So," Nagler began, "Tell me again why you hit me with a piece of wood?" He had spun in a half circle to plant his face a few inches away from the kid's. "Who told you to do it?"

"That was you?" A smirk and rolling, disinterested eyes.

"You know it was me. You stood over me and smiled."

"I don't care."

"Who paid you?"

Adams paused. "Maybe I just wanted to hit you."

"Was it a cop?"

Adams chuckled. "Naw. Someone from City Hall."

Nagler leaned in close. "We didn't know that. Thanks."

Adams nailed his eyes to the table, shook his head, and shrugged. Then: "I don't care."

A crack in the façade? Nagler wondered. He circled the table again.

"Of course you don't." Nagler stepped behind Adams. "Because that would make you a human being. You know, caring. Would make you worth caring about."

The representative said, "Hey, ease up."

Nagler silenced him with a hard glance.

The sting of Nagler's last remark drove Adams' eyes deep into their sockets. Too far? Nagler asked himself. No. There is no "too far" anymore. That's it, isn't it. Charlie Adams didn't care, because no one cared about him. That's what he said in the alley, replaced family with street mayhem. Push the edge. Wipe the smirk off his face.

Nagler placed both hands in the table next to Adams and smiled at the representative. "Don't think so. Know why? Because Charlie here is a punk, a user. His friends say so. He steals. He beats his friends up when they don't do what he says. We have their statements. And we're going to have those statements admitted to get this case kicked up to superior court, not juvenile court. Because, Charlie. You're a bad guy. Gotta keep you off the streets."

Nagler left the room, slamming the door. Outside, LaStrada and Chief Mallory waited.

"Anything?" The Chief asked.

"He doesn't care," Nagler replied with a smile. "He probably doesn't. He's cold."

"He has to know we have him on the robberies," LaStrada said. "He knows he led us to the loot."

Nagler pondered the next moves.

"Okay, um, but somehow that doesn't seem to matter. I'll go after his attack on me then, the one on you, Sal, then go to the stolen doll from the Smith house and then to the assault of Marion Feldman. His partners in crime gave that up."

Nagler stared through the small window at the cold, gray mask that was Adams' face. It had come down to this. I need to get behind that mask.

"Do you think that he thinks he's still being protected?" LaStrada asked. "Weren't you trying to tie him to Foley? Try him on that. Push him."

Back in the room, Nagler leaned against the door in silence, arms folded. He waited. The representative from children's services began to speak but Nagler shook his head, No.

Nagler waited; he loudly scraped one leg up the wall so his knee jutted out.

Adams stared at the table, eyes half-closed, but his hands, locked together, pulsed with nervous movement.

Without moving his head, Adams glanced sideways at Nagler.

Nagler dropped his foot with a slam and in one step was at the table across from Adams.

"How fast to you have to be running to knock over a big cop? I mean, you're a little guy, wiry and tough, but you weigh, what maybe one-ten?"

"I didn't run into no cop."

"I got a cop who says otherwise. Ran into him and slashed him with a knife."

Nagler pulled out a box that had been sitting on the empty chair. "This knife."

He slammed it on the table with an echoing bang.

"We found it in the shed by the silk mill with these."

Nagler pulled out photos of Marion Feldman's wedding ring and Walter Feldman's Waltham pocket watch. "You took these from their house on West Harvard. We know that. Your friends told us."

Adams pushed the photos to the floor but didn't touch the knife. "Don't care. Don't mean nothing." His face was flushed and his voice weaker, but the mask remained.

"Why?" Nagler asked. "Because the cop who protected you after you beat up that Chinese store owner told you he'd take care of it? He didn't, did he? He let you run your little gang causing havoc and misery because he told you something good would come to you in the end, right?"

Nagler leaned on the inside wall. He added a hard, sarcastic edge to his voice. "Well, Charlie, he's gone. Vanished. When the heat got too high, he took off. We don't even know where he is. Some friend and protector, huh?"

Adams leaned back and kicked the chair to the floor. He tried to reach for Nagler, but the representative grabbed him and said, "No, Charlie."

Again sitting, Adams spit out a reply, "I still know people. You got nothing."

But his hands were shaking.

Now? Nagler asked himself? Why am I hesitating? This is the guy. Why am holding back? All the pain he's caused, all the misery and hate let loose.

Nagler pulled out a handkerchief and wiped his forehead as his own hands shook. He glanced at LaStrada's blurred face in the small window; LaStrada nodded, and mouthed, "Now."

"What's it like to run up a woman, knock her over, and stab her, Charlie?"

Adam's face changed, became lighter and with distant eyes, he smiled.

"That's nothing." His face filled with a peaceful, self-satisfied glow.

Nagler, surprised, cast a quizzical look at LaStrada.

"So, you've done that? Ran up and stabbed a woman?"

"Just thinkin' about how easy it would be, man." Adams' voice took a cheerful tone. "They don't think. They're just out there doing their stuff, not payin' attention." He smiled at Nagler. "Easy pickings."

"So, you haven't done it, but thought about it? Come naturally, do they, these thoughts of violence?"

Adams, smirked at first, then Nagler saw it emerge: That cold, dark, and distant stare, the haughty curl of his lips, the feeling draining from his face as his soul retreated. That was the visage Nagler saw while prone in the street after being clubbed on the back. The empty face of a killer.

"Thought about a lot of things I ain't ever done. Like finishing off that blind kid. Wanted to, but never did. I mean I know where he is."

Nagler felt his face flush, shocked and then angered by Adams's declaration. He thought he had made Leonard safe. He stared at the floor and then recovered.

"Why didn't you?"

"Checked it out a couple of times. Decided it wasn't worth it, with your wife and all, you woulda figured out it was me."

"If…" Nagler clenched a fist behind his leg to stop the question. That was bait. Don't take it. He dragged the third chair loudly on the floor and sat.

He pulled out an envelope and began to spread eight photos across the table.

"How easy was it to cut off their hands, Charlie?" His voice found its own coldness.

Nagler pulled out the photos, one by one. Nancy Harmon, Jamie Wilson, Felice Sanchez, Joan Chen, Tamika Austin, Debbie Jones, Michelle Hanson.

Adams smiled when Michelle Hanson's photos was laid on the table.

"Sweet little cunt," he whispered, and bit his lower lip.

"How long did you watch her, Charlie? Naked, ankles crossed, sleeping alongside the pool? Got you excited?"

Adams' head rolled to one side, eyes half-closed. "Man…" He shook his head a couple of times. Dreamily: "Sweet."

Nagler reached slowly into the box and produced a short-handled hatchet.

"Was this sweet, too? We found her blood."

Adams issued a bored sigh.

Then last, photos of Marion Feldman and Edie Smith.

Then he laid out photos of reassembled human hands.

"Why, Charlie?"

Adams face was calm and relaxed, as if facing the photos of the dead woman soothed him.

He looked at Nagler and smiled. "They touched me." A soft, chilling voice. He placed a finger on one of the photos of a hand and ran it up and down the digits. "They touched me."

He began a pantomime of reaching out to hold an unseen object, then twisted it and bit his lower lip and, his eyes blazing, snapped his hands apart. "They couldn't touch me no more."

Nagler sat in silence and nodded to the child services rep. "You heard that? You…"

"These two," Adams said as he touched the photos of Edie Smith and Marion Feldman. He ran a finger across their mouths, along their jawline and then jabbed at their eyes, first Marion Feldman, then Edie Smith. "Their eyes. So soft and afraid." He looked up at Nagler. "I used a spoon on this one," touching Marion Feldman's face. "That's all I could grab. She was dead. I don't think she got over that whack on the head I gave her. "This one," and he tapped the photo of Edie Smith,

"She just kept smiling, saying she was rich and wanted to help me. I pushed her and grabbed a fork." He raised his eyebrows. "She might have been alive." He was pleased.

"You don't even know who they are, do you?" Nagler asked, his voice shaking.

Adams shrugged. "Why should I? I don't care."

CHAPTER THIRTY-TWO

There would never be enough rain

The fall brought rain.

The closed, burning cauldron that had for months been Ironton cracked; a communal sigh like steam escaping, rose.

The Charlie Adams killing spree had ended. He sat snarling and smirking in a jail cell.

As he walked the streets again filled with shoppers and citizens, Detective Frank Nagler saw a few more smiles, a few more friendly greetings, clusters of people on sidewalks talking, testing the air for the acid that for months had been present.

They nodded to him, reached to shake his hand, to thank him for his role in ending the madness.

He would smile back then dip his head and walk on.

Not all had been cleansed.

The mayor's financial schemes lurked, hidden under layers of paper that Nagler suspected would take years to unraveled and expose, and whatever hidden actions taken by officials including cops to perpetuate the killings and the financings were being buried even while the public celebrations were ongoing. New narratives were being crafted, polish applied to lies.

Foley had been brought before a review board, but escaped with a mild reprimand, the mayor's work

Nagler sought solitude.

The dark back alleys provided cover for his grief, the light leaking from behind curtained windows signals to the paths to avoid as he sought silence and darkness.

The homeless had again been moved from the old stoveworks; he prowled the empty spaces, kicked over piles of junk, stared sorrowfully at the torn pants and shirts, broken whiskey bottles, needles and burned tin foil, as if the sad detritus of that life would offer him a place to bury his pain.

Not even the Locust Street Cemetery, where he ended many of his walks, offered peace. He spoke kind words to Martha, and brushed away stray leaves, pulled weeds and left fresh flowers each time.

What can I give you now? he would ask her. How did my love fail you?

Then returning home, he would draw from her pillow the faint scent of lavender. He had sat on the end of their bed for several nights after she had died, wrapped the pillow to his chest and absorbing what life of her it contained.

He would sleep on the couch; the emptiness of their bed more than he could bear.

Finally, Leonard would stumble across the room and take Nagler's hand.

"Walk with me, Frank. I once sat as you do now, wallowing in self-pity because I had lost my sight."

"No, Leonard," Nagler said. "It's not the same."

"Oh, my friend, it is," Leonard said. "I lost the only thing that mattered to me, my ability to see. You lost Martha, her companionship, but you did not lose her love. Did you not understand what she was telling you at the end: Love is not something you keep, but something to give away. You gave it to her, and she gave hers to you. She would want you to share that."

Nagler would smile at his friend's entreaties, smile and walk; he wanted to feel weightless.

After Adams' arrest and the flurry of police activity needed to secure the evidence and present the case, Nagler brought several boxes to the office to store the piles of reports, the photographs, the maps, the drawings and all the wall decorations the case had generated.

He slipped each victim's photo into a glassine envelope. It was a bitter act.

We couldn't save any of you, he thought; we could only catch Adams and that seemed inadequate.

The hands remained. Red, perfectly framed in Robbie Karpinski's photos. Nagler pulled them off the wall and slapped them into a manila folder, face down.

"I don't want to look at you again," he said aloud. "Not now."

Following Adam's confession, they found Michelle Hanson's severed hands in the shed across from Nagler's house, along with a new red hand and HAND OF DEATH slogan painted on the inside of the door.

In the office, Nagler paused before he pulled off the last picture, a photo of the original red hand left on that shed. He held his own hand to the photo; his adult hand dwarfing Adam's smaller, teenage fingers. Nagler wanted to crumple that photo, wad it into a ball and toss it away.

He recalled the fear in Martha's eyes when from their bedroom she spied that red hand, so bright and obvious on the shed wall, felt again the tremble in her shoulder as he embraced her, heard the wrinkle in her voice as he told her it would be alright.

The shock of that moment returned, and as it did, Nagler knew that he had sidestepped the rage that red hand so close to his wife and their life had generated. He had swallowed it for the good of the investigation. Pondered its meaning calmly with LaStrada, professionally directed Karpinski's photo efforts, checked a list of things that needed more information before they could draw conclusions.

"I put them first," Nagler said to the vacant wall. "I put Martha second." No sigh would ever be deep enough.

He turned his back to the wall and dropped his chin to his chest; breath by breath, he felt the anger rise. He balled his fists and slammed them on the wall; Never again. Never again.

****

It only took a few sledge hammer blows to loosen the panel with the red hand from the shed.

Nagler picked it up and propped it against a rock and smashed the hammer into the dry brittle wood. He swung again, and again, breaking the panel into smaller and smaller bits until the red hand was indistinguishable from dirt.

Nagler wanted that to be satisfying.

Instead, he felt hollow.

"Damn, you, damn you, damn…you." He swung the sledge and broke the shed window, swung again and crashed the door frame, then the wall, then the corner framing and the stone pilings beneath. A running start, and a wild swing or two. A kick at a loose panels, dropping the hammer and tearing the boards with his bare hands. Three blows later, the underpinning collapsed and the shed leaned. He smashed the bracing again and the corner collapsed, the slamming of the hammer and his grunts filling the air.

Blow after blow and the shed leaned, then fell; blow after blow, his hands raw, his voice grabbing in his throat, eyes wet with tears.

He wanted to tap a rage and power as if that would purge his pain, as if everything in the end would be equal and that Martha's death was not just some sad eventuality.

Instead, he ached. She was gone.

The shed settled into a dusty pile, and he stared the mess.

He laughed. That's my life, now, he thought, and my city, all piled into a wreck, smashed beyond hope.

The sun dipped behind Baker Hill. A gray mist settled over the neighborhood, sucking light and sound from the air.

He dropped the sledge and held out his arms and leaned his head back, eyes closed. My Martha. Take me in, he thought. He wanted to feel whole.

He wanted rain.

He wanted tears.

Wash me clean.

His scream echoed through the empty streets, the scream he had been unable to release until that moment.

He kicked a stray piece of board toward the wreckage of the shed.

There would never be enough rain.

*****

Continue reading for a free preview of the book that started the *Frank Nagler Mystery Series*, *The Swamps of Jersey*.

The
SWAMPS OF JERSEY

A Frank Nagler Mystery

MICHAEL STEPHEN DAIGLE

CHAPTER 1

The ringing phone grabbed Detective Frank Nagler from the fitful sleep he had found crammed into an office chair like a discarded suit jacket. It was three a.m.

The phone rang again, buzzing like a swarm of flies. He rolled dizzily sideways, slammed his feet to the floor and sat in the chair, feeling his back clench. *Crap, that hurt.* The phone rang again. And again. He rubbed his eyes with the palms of his hands and waited for one more ring, then picked up the receiver. "You're kidding," he replied wearily to the dispatcher's request. "What's next, locusts? Yeah, never mind. Thanks. Just what we need after all this. Be there soon."

He wrapped himself in his long black raincoat that had become his shield against the wet and raging world, and leaned into the outer door as the hurricane winds slapped him awake.

He had not seen the sky for days, felt the heat of the sun, wore dry shoes or walked outside without that raincoat since the storm blew in and sealed the hills above the city with a dense smothering grayness, a swirling menace of thunder clouds and shrieking winds that pounded the city with an apocalyptic rain that sent the Baptist preachers howling to the hills about sin and damnation. It emptied the grocery store shelves of everything but a few cans of cream of mushroom soup, and locked the residents in the top floors of their homes as the river crashed its banks, flooded streets and rearranged the city landscape like a madman with an earth mover.

The placid, blue August sky had been replaced by rain that came and stayed. Rain with menace, rain that pulsed around corners dark with dislodged pieces of the earth as it ripped away every weak thing it could; rain that claimed, rain soulless and dark as evil; that challenged knowledge; rain that took possession.

The ancients knew what to do with rain like this, he thought wickedly, squinting into the horizontal blast of water.

Conjure an honest man with a ship and spin a parable about the wages of sin. Nagler laughed sourly. *And then get out of town.*

Nagler plowed his car through the treacherous bumper-deep water that filled the downtown streets. Random spotlights, swinging loosely from dangling wires on damaged poles or hanging off ripped roof tops banged with the hollow, doomed echo of cathedral bells at the end of times and flashed a shifting and sinister light on flooded parking lots or intersections rippling with dark water. Store after store was dark, some with boards covering glass windows; others had jagged shards of glass that gleamed menacingly in the fractured light, hanging in dented window frames.

****

The storm had knocked out power to the city, and as the streets void of humans filled with the rising river, the mayor declared an emergency. The usual drive from downtown Ironton to the Old Iron Bog took ten minutes, a straight shot up Rockaway Avenue. But at turn after turn, Nagler found new roadblocks, orange-and-white barriers with flashing yellow lights manned by some poor cop in a gleaming, black slicker with orange stripes and water streaming off his wide-brimmed hat, waving a flash light.

Nagler rolled down the car's window and flinched as he caught a face full of rain.

"What's open? Gotta get to the north side. Got an emergency call from dispatch." He blinked to keep the water out of his eyes.

"The only bridge open is Sussex, but Rockaway's flooded, so you'll have to head up

Washington to the high school and circle around," the cop yelled back. "Caught some of the radio chatter. What's up?"

"Got it," Nagler yelled back as he rolled up the window and wiped the water off his face, failing to answer the cop's question.

****

Half an hour later Nagler edged his old Ford down Mount Pleasant, squinting through the wet, smeary windshield into the flashing safety lights as he looked for a place to park. He found one that was too narrow but jammed the car in edgewise anyway, braking hard when at the fringe of his headlights he saw a jagged black space where the embankment had washed away.

"Oh, damn." *Great, all I need now is to drive off the road.*

He shouldered the car door open and the scene exploded into sound: Yakking radios, a dozen vehicles left running, grinding fire trucks, winches, distant shouting voices. But the sound that mattered most to Nagler was that of his right shoe being sucked into the liquid soil. "Aw, shit. Damn it." *Dress shoes. What was I thinking? This is the fine quality of decisions we make when we don't sleep.*

Ironton was sprawled at the bottom of a narrow bowl-like valley, with streets climbing the hills like fingers hanging on for dear life. For the better part of a week as the last waves of an August tropical storm stalled over the state, the bowl filled and overflowed.

Nagler, like the rest of the police department, had been on extra duty to deal with the storm emergency. The weariness of sleepless nights, more than the dampness, dripped through his skin to his bones and joints and he walked with a heaviness that made him think that if he stopped moving he would end up standing in one place for hours, unable to lift a foot or bend a knee.

He tugged his foot from its watery hole, almost losing his shoe, and winced at the discomfort of wet socks and wet shoes and general unpleasantness of what he was about to examine.

Floods and disaster. And now this. He looked back at his car, the tires inches from the torn edge of the roadway. He pulled his long coat tighter, his dry foot slapping at the wet pavement and his wet foot clumping along like an oversized clown shoe -- Slap, clump. Slap, clump. Slap, clump -- until he reached the soft opposite path, where both shoes sank in.

The days of rain left city families with waterlogged mattresses floating in their living rooms, powerless refrigerators filled with rotting, soggy food, natural gas bubbling through black water from a broken main and the family photos on the hallway walls bled white, the faces, the scenery, the goofy hats washed away. City officials had debris-filled streets caked with mud and blocks of holy wreckage, rivers where streets used to be, holes where there used to be walls and a city that looked like someone had tossed it in the air and let it fall again in a creative chaos that only disaster brings.

And Detective Frank Nagler had the headless, handless body of a young woman in the Old Iron Bog.

He paused at the edge of the road that led into the bog just as a bank of lights hoisted above a fire truck blasted to life. Before him was a shadowy scene of twisted trees and shrubs, dark paths to nowhere and ghostly forms shifting in and out of the dim lights.

277

Nagler took a deep breath and plunged in. "Where's the victim?" he asked a crime scene tech, who nodded in a general direction of a small clearing off the single-lane road that was the main entrance into the bog.

"It'd be easier if she had a head, huh, detective?"

Nagler squinted down at the rescue squad kid waiting as a medical technician zipped up a black body bag that contained the torso of a young woman.

"And maybe hands," the kid added brightly. "Man, I don't envy you," he said as he turned to carry the bag toward the ambulance. Nagler just nodded. *Why are you so excited? It's the middle of the night in a raging storm and you're hauling a corpse. And that's good for you? You're lucky I'm exhausted.*

"Open the bag," Nagler grumbled. "Unzip it."

The kid fumbled at the zipper but finally opened the side of the bag halfway. "All the way." And the kid complied.

She was young, Nagler thought, too young to be here. Why did that surprise him? *What were you expecting?* Someone had hacked off her head and hands, just like the kid said. She was thin and looking at her hips, underdeveloped and still growing. Maybe late teens, early twenties. There were no needle tracks he could see. "Thanks," Nagler said, and stepped aside as the kid re-zipped the bag, and the kid and another fire fighter lifted it and walked up the muddy slope in the rain. "Jesus," he said. "Just a kid."

He pulled his collar tighter, shoved his hands into the coat's deep pockets and scanned the old bog, cast gray, dark and suspicious in the heavy rain. Tall reeds and cattails, grabbed by the swirling, growling wind, dipped and rose, twisted and flattened and filled the area with soft missiles as the plants were shredded. The air slammed him like a wet fist. *The world's in a rage. And it all landed on your pretty head.* He shrugged. *Wherever it might be.*

****

Police Supervisor Chris Foley reached Nagler's side and shoved a cup of coffee into his hand. Nagler nodded, but wondered what Foley was doing there. He let the silent query pass. The man had coffee.

"What do we know?" Nagler asked.

Foley was a straight shooter, a razor cut, white shirt kind of cop.

He examined crime scenes as if they were math problems and left no remainders. But he never saw the magic the math produced, Nagler knew, never imaged that in a crime sometimes one and one equaled three. Crimes for Chris Foley were a formula, a step-one, step-two affair. Sometimes the formula worked; sometimes it didn't.

Foley read from his notes, which were wrapped inside a plastic bag. *The man is prepared, I'll give him that.*

"The body was found by a couple of high school kids out here drinking beer and fornicating. They were underage. We will speak with their parents. I mean, in the middle of this storm, they come out here, and? Anyway… About one hundred hours. Let's see. They said they fell asleep, woke up when they heard a vehicle drive in, started throwing on their clothes since they said they assumed it was the authorities … Hum … vehicle stopped in the distance … heard some voices, at least two."

He turned a page. "Door slammed, vehicle drove away." He stopped reading. "The kids said they sat in their vehicle for a while. They figured it was no big deal. Someone dumping trash, happens out here all the time, they said. But they decided they had better leave. They said they saw the body as they drove out, stopped their vehicle, walked around a little bit and then left when they discovered it had no head. The boy said he slipped as he scrambled back to his vehicle and planted his hands in the mud, but in this rain, it's not going to matter."

"Speak to their parents, Chris?" Nagler said. "Jesus, they're just kids out here screwing. This ain't Sunday school." Nagler scanned the damp, muddy scene, and for the first time became aware of the sharp aroma of oily rot that boiled out of the soft, churned up soil and stuck to his clothes like bad dreams. Then he smiled. *Not all the dreams were bad.* "I suppose you would have turned me in, too."

Foley paused a moment, looked at Nagler, and then again at his notes. "What?"

Nagler turned away so Foley would not see his grin.

It's early in the morning. Cut him some slack. Car drove in? In this mess? The road was fairly solid, despite the rain, so maybe it was possible.

"Where'd you park, Chris?" Nagler wondered why he had not been told Foley would be there.

"Off Mount Pleasant to the right. There's a little wide spot, like a turnaround," Foley said. "Why?"

"Just wondering how a car got in here in with all this muck. Maybe four-wheel-drive, a small truck or something with high clearance."

"The kid was driving a big, high-wheeled pick-up with wide off-road tires, probably his dad's," Foley said. "I mean I'm driving my city emergency management SUV. High clearance, all-wheel-drive. Something like that would get in here." Foley laughed. "I wish it was painted a different color. It's bright yellow, for crying out loud."

"A little too conspicuous, Chris?"

Nagler had always known Foley was a good investigator. Started at the local department and worked his way through the ranks and was appointed to a regional task force a couple of years ago. They had worked cases together in the past. But he was as stiff as a two-by-four and as narrow minded as a telescope viewed through the wrong end. Didn't make him a bad guy, just a pain in the ass, especially at three in the morning standing in the rain in a damn swamp.

The coffee landed in Nagler's stomach with a crash and was jamming its way to his brain, pushing back the sleepless, dull ache. Nagler shook his head to force himself to stay awake and felt a surge of alertness as a couple of cylinders began to fire.

Foley gave Nagler the once over. "Little casual this morning, aren't we, detective?"

Was that a joke? I'm wearing pants, right? Never could tell with Foley. Nagler ran a hand through his hair and scratched the stubble on his chin.

"Dressed in the dark, maybe two days ago. Little hard to match my socks and tie when I can't see them. Been out in the streets for the better part of the last week. Besides, I wanted to look my best for you. You have power?"

Foley shrugged. "No. I just have my week's wardrobe set up in the closet.... Never mind, Frank."

"Yeah, sure." Nagler pursed his lips and shrugged. Then he asked, "What are you doing here, Chris? Aren't you in charge of the city's emergency response to the storm?"

Foley turned slowly. "Yes, I am, but we haven't had a decapitated body in some time. Thought you might need the help. I am, after all, a police supervisor. I'm headed to the emergency office after I leave here."

Can't be soon enough. Nagler slugged back some coffee rather than say anything. "So where'd they find her?" *Guess I better find out what he knows.*

"Over here."

Foley led Nagler along a narrow sandy road overgrown with small trees, cattails and waist-high grass to reach a clearing. Nagler noticed there was a sustained groove in the road, possibly a sideways tire track and a truck wide path where the grass had been knocked over, possibly by the kid's truck.

Foley stepped carefully around the mud and debris so his tasseled loafers would not get ruined, but caught his jacket sleeve on a small tree branch and spent more than a minute examining the cloth. "Sorry, Frank. I just got it back from the dry cleaners."

Whatever. Nagler pushed through the dripping overgrowth. *Rain, mud, no sleep, no coffee and now Foley. No more slack. That was quick. Jesus.*

This was The Old Iron Bog, an old swamp that for generations going back to the iron mining days three hundred years ago had been a dumping ground for waste rock, slag, bad iron parts, bent rails, then in modern times, trash, cars, and everything society needed to hide. The roads had been cut by the miners to gain access to the swamp, and improved, if that was the word, by the towns that dumped garbage here for years before it was outlawed.

The place seemed undisturbed by a week's rain, as if the hole at the bottom of the bog was deeper than anyone could guess. Nagler recalled a story about the construction of the interstate highway. Engineers were battering a steel piling into a hole on the edge of the bog when the piling broke through the roof of an old mine shaft and disappeared into the void. The engineers stared at one another, pushed back their yellow hard hats, scratched their heads, consulted their maps, and stared into the hole.

In the heavy rain, with muddy filth coating everything he touched and the dank, smell of pollution and rot thick enough to taste, Nagler decided the old bog had no romance or redeeming quality; it was just a big hole in the ground. *This swamp will swallow us all.* They were going to build a shopping mall there, Nagler thought. A peeling, battered billboard hung for a year or so along Mount Pleasant. Wonder what happened to it.

Yellow tape marked off several hundred feet of road and swamp. Foley's voice brought Nagler back from the fatigue-driven dreamy state. "The car stopped about here" – Foley walked about ten feet away. "They took the body out of the car, and dropped it. Seems they might have tried to wipe out their footprints because there appeared to be some drag marks in the mud."

"How many people do you guess?"

Foley shrugged. "At least two. The kids said they heard voices, more than one. One thing I don't like?" Foley said with a question in his voice. "They could have pushed her into the water. Why not? Look at this place. There's five feet of thick weeds and brush on either side of the road here. She would have sunk out of sight -- the water is absolutely pitch black -- maybe got hooked on some roots and never came back up. Even if she did, you'd never see her."

"You're saying they were just sloppy?" Nagler asked. "Or they wanted us to find her?"

Foley just waved his hand in the air as he turned to walk away.

"What about tire tracks?" Nagler asked. "Still looking for good ones. Rain's making it harder," Foley said before walking away.

Then Foley stopped, turned and looked at Nagler with hard eyes and a crystal stare. Nagler wanted to be impressed with the determination, but with water dripping off Foley's hair and down his nose, all Nagler wanted to do was laugh; he stared down at the muddy ground so he wouldn't smile. "What, Chris?" Crap, I'm tired.

"We've been here before, you know, Frank. Charlie Adams."

That name. Nagler placed a hand over his face and wiped away the water while he closed his eyes and felt the darkness return. *That's when you learned to be cold. We're not going there. Not now. Not again.* "This isn't Charlie Adams, Chris," Nagler said harshly. "He's still in jail and not getting out anytime soon. I was at his last parole hearing about three months ago. It was denied, again. Why did you think of Adams?"

"But he loved dumping bodies here," Foley said.

"He loved dumping bodies all over. That was twenty years ago, Chris. He had no copycats and the killing stopped when we caught him. A lot has changed in this city in that time. Let's not head in that direction unless the evidence leads us that way."

"You're right, Frank."

Charlie Adams, the city's last serial killer. There had been a feel to that case from the beginning and this one with one butchered girl doesn't yet feel like that. "But if we find another body, I'll reconsider."

****

About a dozen police, rescue and fire vehicles lined Mount Pleasant with one set of wheels in the road and the other in the muddy ditch. Cops in hip waders crashed in and out of the brush and weeds, and a fire boat was being backed into the swamp. They had not yet found any clothes, or her head and hands, and the body had no jewelry. It was just the body. Naked. Butchered. Forgotten. *That's why it's not Charlie Adams.* Nagler slowly felt his way through the slippery paths of the dark bog, heading back to Mount Pleasant. *Adams brought bodies here, sure, but made finding them easy. He liked the fame, the publicity, liked knowing we knew it was him and thinking that he was one step ahead of us. This is not the same. But for the life of me, at three a.m. and on one cup of coffee, I don't know what the hell this is.* "Damn it," Nagler muttered as his foot slipped off the path into a watery hole.

Nagler stopped to regain his balance, lifted his head and gazed over the old bog. The rain had let up, and in the earliest light of dawn, the black canopy began to shift to a lighter gray. Maybe, finally, it would stop raining. The muted rumble of rush hour traffic on the interstate about a half-mile away started to filter into the swamp to fill in what until that moment had been an oddly quiet place. The sounds, even the chatter of the police radios, had been sucked into the deep endlessness of the swamp. The overgrowth absorbed all the noise just like it sucked nourishment from the water. But the roar of daily life on the highway would soon overpower the dense swamp. By mid-morning once the trucks started rolling down from the quarry, ten at once, each carrying forty tons of rock, the water would begin a tremble that would shimmer on the surface until well after dark.

It's a hell of a place to die. He felt his weight slide into his tired legs and he turned around and grabbed a small tree for balance.

Nagler slowly walked the site for a few more minutes, talking off and on to a fire captain, one of the county investigators, or just observing, trying to imprint the scene on his very tired brain.

The sand coated his already soaked shoes and had squeezed inside his socks so it felt he was walking on wet sandpaper; he knew he'd find a ragged blister on his heel.

The rubberneckers lined Mount Pleasant, crawling by in dark vehicles, faces white in the glare of passing headlights, watching the lights flash on the police cars. With the power out, and most streets blocked by fallen trees and floods, there weren't many other routes out of town. A local cop with a flashlight waved them on and they passed, one by one, a solemn parade as they took in what they could see and imagined the rest.

Nagler rubbed his forehead, stopped and looked up and down the street into the confusion of cars and lights. Where the hell did I park? He wondered. He squeezed his eyes shut and let the kaleidoscope of swirls and circles fade to black. Then he turned to face the swamp and remembered he had come in from the left, then walked that way.

Add another thing to the list. He began to mentally schedule who he had to see and how quickly they might have any information: the crime scene techs, the medical examiner, re-interview the kids who called it in. Another session with Foley. It was odd he came to the scene. He was the leader of the city's emergency response office and had a whole city trying to get its head above water. Nagler laughed. *I must be really tired if that line is funny.*

Not like I don't have anything else to do.

For the last three weeks he had been receiving packages with invoices and letters on City of Ironton letterhead. The letters said the material was a link to a big cover-up of theft in city hall. But what he had received so far was so disjointed it was hard to see that. After the first few letters he wondered who was trying to pull a fast one -- he asked himself more than once, *who did I piss off* -- or use all that paper to make a little, tiny point about government waste. There were two or three media-savvy gadflies who had filed several complaints to state agencies about access to public records and other things, and maybe these records were from one of them. But why send it to him, Nagler had asked himself. The invoices had information that had been blacked out, none of the dates were in any sequence, and even if one or two of the invoices seemed to be leading from one account to another, the last pieces were missing. *God, it's like some stupid Russian novel.* Sometimes he wanted to dump it on someone else, let them wade through the pile of paper, but then he would flip through a couple more pages and think: What if it was real? Nagler had asked the chief about it and was told to just keep collecting the letters, just in case it began to make more sense.

He sighed and turned to walk back to his car; fine mist began to fall again. "Just send the last chapter."

"To what?"

"Shit, did I say that out loud?" Nagler asked.

"Yeah, you did. Said 'just send the last chapter,' out loud. Didn't think anyone was listening, did ya?"

It was Jimmy Dawson. "And now you're gonna have to tell me the rest."

"Don't you ever sleep?" Nagler shook Dawson's hand and actually wondered what had taken him so long to get there.

"I'm Ichabod Crane. I hear the headless horseman is out tonight."

Dawson was a reporter for the local paper. He was cynical, hard-nosed, fairly nasty at times, but always got it right. He knew the rules of the game and Nagler knew he could lay out a story on background and no one would ever know the source.

"Yeah," Nagler said. "Some young woman. Headless, handless. Good chance she was dumped here after being killed elsewhere. A car, no description, was seen in the neighborhood. No clothes, no ID." He shrugged. "Right now, no clue."

Dawson finished writing and waited for more description.

"How do you do that?" Nagler asked.

"What?" Dawson asked.

"Read your hand writing. Especially while taking notes in the dark."

"Write extra big. Trick I learn when I was a movie reviewer."

Nagler and Dawson had been meeting like that for years. There was a respect between them, a knowledge that comes from being in the same places under the same circumstances too many times.

"You have power?" Nagler asked. It was the question of the day.

Dawson laughed. "Been almost living at the office. My road was flooded and half the trees are down. Office complex has a generator. There's a couple of us there."

"Sounds chummy."

"You in later?" Dawson asked.

"After ten."

"I'll call you," Dawson said as he walked away.

Then he stopped.

"Hear from Lauren Fox?"

Are you kidding? Nagler stared at the reporter as he walked away.

"Hey, Dawson. Don't you want an answer?" Dawson stopped walking and half-turned back toward Nagler, spreading his hands and bowing, as if to say, "Well…"

Nagler stared a moment. Too much to say about it. "No," he finally said.

After he watched Dawson walk down Mount Pleasant, Nagler wandered back to his car, stopping every few steps to shake mud off his shoes and to imagine the street several hours earlier without the police vehicles, fire trucks and a slow parade of cars, when an unknown vehicle drove slowly and carefully through the darkness, the driver probably stopping more than once looking for a dumping spot, then moving on until the side road was found. Did someone get out and shine a flashlight down that road into the darkness? Did the driver have companions with whom they discussed their options? How many people were in that car?

He knew this street well as a dark, slightly spooky section of Ironton. Little had been built along the road, mostly because of the bog which spread for acres in each direction. Even if the electric power had been on, there were only a couple street lights and those were hundreds of feet apart. Everything here moved in shadows.

Nagler looked up and down the street again. A gray dawn was rising, and Nagler shut his eyes against the light to hold the image of the blackness and a single vehicle slowly moving through a murky night. With the power on there might have been enough light to make this little side road visible, but in the blackness of a heavily clouded sky, air still damp with mist or slight rain, it seemed a long shot. The kids who reported the body to the police said they had been here dozens of times – man that kid was getting a lot of action – so for them finding the top of that side road in the dark was easy. But a stranger?

That knowledge made the case more local, more personal.

When he got to his car Nagler was surprised to see how close he had come to driving into the gully. "Damn," he said, "That was lucky."

What wasn't lucky was how close his car was to the vehicles on either side. While he was at the crime scene, the compact sedan that had been parked to his left had been replaced by an extended body pick-up with an emergency light rack on its cab, whose owner it seemed took delight in parking as close as he could to Nagler's car. *One of us,* Nagler thought wickedly as he started his car and slipped the transmission into reverse, *ain't going to like this.* The car rolled for second or two and he felt the satisfying thump as the bumpers touched. He rolled forward, then back, and again felt the slight collision. Three or four such efforts allowed him to get the front wheels correctly angled and pull the Ford into street while the alarm in the truck sounded, a whoop-whoop echoing off the dark silence of the Old Iron Bog.

The effort to extract his car from the tight space allowed Nagler to avoid the name that was trying to edge its way into his head.

Lauren Fox. Damn you, Dawson.

He turned up the volume on his police radio and let the irritating squawking overwhelm the silence in the car. He slammed the car door as he stopped by his home to get dry socks and shoes.

Not now.

****

The Swamps of Jersey is available at the following retailers:

Amazon
Barnes & Noble
Kobo
Walmart

Buy your copy today!

ABOUT THE AUTHOR

Michael Stephen Daigle is a writer who lives in New Jersey with his family. He was born in Philadelphia, one of five "Navy brats" who lived in several Northeast U.S. states and is an award-winning journalist.

Other books in his Frank Nagler Mystery series are, "The Swamps of Jersey", "A Game Called Dead" and "The Weight of Living; with a fifth book already in progress.

Aside from this series he has also published an electronic collection of short stories, "The Resurrection of Leo," and a story about teen-ager Smitty, baseball and growing up, "The Summer of the Homerun."

Smitty is the hero of a work-in-progress, entitled, since these things must have titles, "Three Rivers."

Another work in progress is a generational novel called "That Time the World Visited Mount Jensen, Maine."

Samples of his work are available at
www.michaelstephendaigle.com

OTHER TITLES FROM IMZADI PUBLISHING

Gabriel's Wing

The Rain Song

Going to California

I Found My Heart in Prague

The Hedgerows of June

The Other Vietnam War

Vietnam Again

Dragon Bone

Staring Into the Blizzard

Who Shot the Smart Guy at the Blackboard?

Frank Nagler Mystery Series

(Reading Order)

The Red Hand

The Swamps of Jersey

A Game Called Dead

The Weight of Living

www.imzadipublishing.com

A NOTE FROM IMZADI PUBLISHING

We hope you have enjoyed *The Red Hand* and the preview of *The Swamps of Jersey* by Michael Stephen Daigle, Imzadi Publishing's own award-winning author.

You, the reader, are the backbone of the publishing industry; without you our industry simply would not exist. As such we depend upon you and your feedback.

Please take a few moments to leave a book rating and review. The review does not need to be long, just a few words will do. Reviews are remarkably difficult to obtain and we are incredibly grateful for every single one. They make all the difference.

Happy reading!

Made in the USA
Middletown, DE
24 July 2019